One N

Lucy Diamond lives in Bath with her husband and their three children. When she isn't slaving away on a new book (ahem) you can find her on Twitter @LDiamondAuthor or Facebook at www.facebook.com/LucyDiamondAuthor.

What Lucy's fans say . . .

'Wonderful characters and the stories are always great, with twists and turns'
Gemma

'Lucy's books are as snuggly as a blanket, as warm as a cup of tea and as welcoming as family'
Cheryl

'Full of friendship, family and how when life throws something at you, you have to fight back!'
Emily

'A skilful writer with the ability to place herself in anyone's shoes'
Sue

'Lucy's books make me smile, cry and give me happiness, a little bit of escapism from everyday life. Page-turners I just can't put down!'
Mandy

BY THE SAME AUTHOR

Novels

Any Way You Want Me

Over You

Hens Reunited

Sweet Temptation

The Beach Café

Summer with My Sister

Me and Mr Jones

One Night in Italy

The Year of Taking Chances

Summer at Shell Cottage

The Secrets of Happiness

The House of New Beginnings

On a Beautiful Day

Something to Tell You

An Almost Perfect Holiday

The Promise

Novellas

A Baby at the Beach Café

Ebook novellas

Christmas at the Beach Café

Christmas Gifts at the Beach Café

Lucy Diamond

One Night in Italy

PAN BOOKS

First published 2014 by Macmillan

First published in paperback 2016 by Pan Books

This edition first published 2022 by Pan Books
an imprint of Pan Macmillan
The Smithson, 6 Briset Street, London EC1M 5NR
EU representative: Macmillan Publishers Ireland Ltd, 1st Floor,
The Liffey Trust Centre, 117–126 Sheriff Street Upper,
Dublin 1, D01 YC43
Associated companies throughout the world
www.panmacmillan.com

ISBN 978-1-5290-8824-3

1 3 5 7 9 8 6 4 2

A CIP catalogue record for this book is available from the British Library.

Typeset in Dante MT Std
Printed and bound by CPI Group (UK) Ltd, Croydon, CR0 4YY

Acknowledgements

You can't write a book about an Italian class without trying one for yourself. Massive thanks therefore to Cinzia Azzali and a big *buongiorno* to Lindsey, Dina, Annabel and Maria. And see – I told you this book wasn't about you, you can relax now.

Thanks as ever to Lizzy Kremer, agent extraordinaire, for feedback, guidance and laughs. It's great being on Team Kremer! *Grazie* to the wonderful people at Pan Macmillan: Caroline, Natasha, Jeremy, Wayne, Anna, Jodie, Becky . . . I feel so lucky to work with you. Aperol Spritzes all round!

Love and thanks to Fran Punnett, as well as Dave, Ella, Darcey and Marnie who told me about the coolest places in Sheffield and took me to some of them. You are all so much fun to hang out with. When can I come back?

A glass of prosecco to my writing buddies in Bath – Jo Nadin, Anna Wilson, Catherine Bruton and the entire Monday night collective. I love our authorly chats . . . and lunches . . . and drinks . . .

Thanks to everyone who has left me nice messages on Facebook and Twitter, or has emailed to say they enjoyed one of my books. It makes all the difference! I hope you like this one as much. Finally, thanks to my family – Martin, Hannah, Tom and Holly – for too many reasons to list. You're the best.

Prologue

Io ricordo – I remember

For years afterwards, whenever she thought about that summer in Italy, she remembered the scent first: the fragrant pink bougainvilleas around Lucca's poolside bar mingling intoxicatingly with the tang of coconut sun oil and cigarette smoke. Back then, she was young and carefree, with a red dress, a devil-may-care attitude and the best tan of her life. The air had shimmered with heat and a million possibilities. Anything might happen.

On the day that everything changed, she had spread her towel on a sunlounger, peeled off her dress and sat down, adjusting the straps of her bikini. Then, just as she was about to lean back and relax, her skin prickled: a sixth sense, maybe. Peering through her sunglasses, she noticed a man in the deep end of the pool, leaning against the side, his broad tanned arms gleaming with tiny water droplets. He seemed to be looking right at her.

Was she imagining it or was he giving her the eye? She propped up her sunglasses to check, the world swinging into sudden brightness. He totally *was* giving her the eye. What was more, he was bloody gorgeous.

Heat flooded her body as they exchanged a long, loaded look. The clamour of the poolside seemed to vanish as if the world had been muted. All she could hear was the thud of her heart.

Oh, what the hell, she thought recklessly; she was single and on holiday and up for some fun. He might be all of those things too. Without a second thought, she winked at him. Her heart galloped as he grinned back, revealing perfect white teeth. And then he was pulling himself out of the pool, water streaming down his muscular arms: he was tall and athletic, early-twenties at a guess; golden skin and a crooked smile. As he straightened up, she couldn't help noticing the way his swimming shorts just revealed the tops of his hip bones, and she shivered with sudden desire.

He walked over to her, beads of water still clinging to his body, his eyes never leaving hers. '*Ciao, bella,*' he said, his voice low and husky.

Her blood drummed through her. Her breath caught in her throat. It felt as if this was the moment she'd been waiting for all summer. She raised an eyebrow flirtatiously and smiled back. '*Ciao,*' she said.

Chapter One

Mio padre – My father

As a journalist, Anna Morley was used to thinking in headlines; it was second nature to her. Without consciously doing it, even the most ordinary event in her life was transformed into a punchy soundbite etched in large black capitals in her mind.

HACKED OFF! Female journalist, 32, misses bus home.

DANGER ON OUR STREETS! Loose paving slab 'an accident waiting to happen', says local resident, 32.

LET THERE BE LIGHT Council slammed over patchy streetlighting. The Herald *campaign starts today!*

THE HUNGER GAME Starving writer, 32, curses self for not stopping at the corner shop for a tin of beans.

Admittedly, none of the headlines were particularly scintillating. But then neither was her life, to be frank. If she died right now, and needed an epitaph for her grave, the words 'Same old, same old' would sum things up perfectly.

But then came the most shocking news story of all, right when she was least expecting it, and afterwards nothing felt 'same old, same old' again. It was astonishing how one conversation could change everything.

Clemency House was the care home eight miles out of Sheffield where Anna's grandmother, Nora, lived. With its strong smell of wee, disinfectant and overcooked cabbage, it was home to an assortment of pensioners in varying states of confusion and decrepitude. It was certainly the last place on earth you would expect to experience an epiphany.

Anna visited her nan on the last Sunday of the month and knew almost all the residents by now. An excited twittering would greet her arrival in the lounge – 'Ooh, it's Anna'; 'Wake up, duck, Anna's here, look, come to see Nora'; 'Anna! Cooee!' – which always made her feel like a minor celebrity as she worked her way through the sea of white hair and support stockings.

'Hello, Mrs Ransome, that's a lovely dress you've got on today.'

'Hello, Violet, how's your great-grandson doing?'

'Hello, Elsie, I've brought you today's crossword if you want it?'

Nora would rise up from her favourite toffee-coloured wingback chair and offer her soft, powdery cheek for a kiss, then they'd drink stewed tea and chat together for an hour or so, before taking a slow turn around the garden so that Nora could moan in private about whichever resident was getting on her nerves that week. And that was usually that.

This time, however, the pattern changed. It was a windy autumn day with dark clouds shouldering each other across the sky, while inside, the central heating was cranked up to soporific levels. Anna was just about to suggest going out for some fresh air when a storm suddenly broke and rain began sheeting down dramatically, spattering great heavy drops against the windows.

'Goodness!' Nora quavered, blinking in alarm, one hand up at her crepey throat. She was dressed as ever in a strange combination of garments, today's outfit a cream blouse and bobbly green fleece cardigan, her favourite tweed skirt and thick brown tights that pooled in wrinkles around her swollen ankles.

'Maybe we'll stay indoors after all,' Anna said, discreetly checking her watch. Three o'clock. Pete was meant to be coming round for dinner later – 'a roast', she'd promised him ambitiously, and she knew for a fact that there wasn't a single vegetable to be found in her house, let alone anything she could conceivably baste in oil and bung in the oven.

Nora turned and stared at Anna as if seeing her for the first time. Her dementia was an unpredictable beast; some days she seemed perfectly lucid and managed to keep up with a conversation, but other times, a veil of bewilderment would slide over her face and she would spout gibberish. 'You do look like him, you know,' she said from out of nowhere.

'Gino, wasn't it?' Her false teeth were slipping, making her words indistinct.

'Gino?' Anna echoed. 'What are you talking about, Nan?'

'The Italian. You know.' Her eyes were cloudy and faraway, her gaze wandering from Anna's face. 'Your father.'

Anna's stomach lurched. She must have misheard, surely. 'My *father*?'

Nora frowned. 'Didn't I just say that? Your poor mum.' She shook her head, gnarled fingers clenched around the arms of her chair. 'Nothing but trouble!'

Anna had difficulty breathing for a moment. She opened and shut her mouth, her brain fusing red hot with shocked, urgent questions. 'Was that his name?' she asked dazedly. At last, she thought. At last! 'Gino? Was that his name?'

'It's a long way to Tipperary,' Mrs Ransome started singing in the background, her voice high and reedy. 'It's a long way to go.' Several others joined in, and Anna had to raise her voice.

'Nan?' she urged when no answer came. 'Was my father called Gino?'

Nora blinked. 'Look at that rain!' she marvelled. 'I'd better get my washing in, hadn't I?'

'Nan, you don't have any washing here. We're in Clemency House, remember?'

'It's a long way to Tipperary, to the sweetest girl I knooooow . . .'

'I did my whites this morning,' Nora said dreamily. 'Albert's shirts and the bed sheets. Meredith's Sunday school dress with pink ribbons.'

And she was gone, swallowed up by the confusing mists of the past once more. Albert was her husband, long since buried. Anna had no idea who Meredith might be.

'Nan, listen to me. Do you remember Gino? What did he look like?'

Somebody was clapping out of time, Anna registered dimly. 'Goodbye, Piccadilly – join in, Nora! – Farewell, Leicester Square . . .'

Nora wasn't listening; she was in her own parallel version of the world, her head cocked as if hearing distant voices. 'And the tablecloth! That gravy took some scrubbing to wash out, didn't it, Susan?'

Anna sagged with dismay. Susan was her grandmother's long-dead sister with whom she sometimes confused Anna. The subject of Gino was already as distant as Tipperary.

'And now it's getting soaked. Come on! Where's the basket?'

She rose from her seat but Anna caught her thin arm. 'Sit down,' she said gently. 'Mrs Eccles will get the washing in.'

Mrs Eccles often got a mention when her nan went off at a tangent; Anna still wasn't entirely sure who she was, but chucking her name into the mix now, while Nora was off on one, was worth a try.

'It's a long, long way to Tipperary, but my heart's still theeeeeere!'

Nora stared at her. 'Ivy Eccles? Are you sure?'

'Oh yes,' Anna said reassuringly. 'But about Gino . . .'

'Give over! Ivy Eccles has been stone dead for thirty years. What *are* you talking about, dear?'

'Cup of tea anyone?' One of the careworkers wheeled in a trolley, smiling brightly. 'Chocolate Bourbon?'

The singing stopped abruptly, replaced by pleased murmurs of anticipation.

'Lovely,' Nora said. 'Yes, please, over here, pet!' She turned back to Anna, eyes twinkling. 'Are you going to have one, Susan?'

Later that afternoon, as Anna drove home, her mind was a whirl of blaring new headlines.

WHO'S THE DADDY? A clue at last.

DO YOU KNOW GINO? Hunt begins for mystery Italian.

DADDY'S GIRL Long-lost daughter reunited with father.

Gino. Her father was called Gino. He was Italian. It felt as if a door had been opened and light was flooding into a dark, closed room after years of nothing.

Her mother had always steadfastly refused to speak a word about Anna's father. His name wasn't even on her birth certificate. 'You don't have a daddy,' she'd said kindly when Anna was a little girl and becoming aware that most of the other children in her class had two parents, not just one. 'You've got me, and I'm enough.'

Later, as Anna grew older and discovered that, actually, technically there must have been a daddy involved at some stage in the process, her mother dug her heels in. 'Don't talk to me about that waste of space,' she hissed when Anna plucked up the courage to enquire again. 'Believe me, love, you're better off not knowing.'

Growing up in Chesterfield, just the two of them in a poky council house, Anna never felt better off not knowing, not for a minute. She hated not knowing. Was her dad some kind of psychopath? Was he a dangerous criminal? Had he hurt her mother in some way? He must have done something absolutely dreadful if nobody would even speak his name aloud. (She was pretty sure he wasn't Voldemort, but this last fact did make her wonder.)

Her mum was a midwife and it had occurred fleetingly to Anna that she might have snatched Anna as a baby from a maternity ward somewhere, hence the impenetrable secrecy. Maybe this stuff about her dad being a waste of space was all a smokescreen, because her mum wasn't even her real mum. But no, she must be, because they both had the same curvy bum and big boobs, and the same laughably small feet. Different colouring, though – her mum had blonde wavy hair and blue eyes with porcelain-pale skin, whereas Anna was dark-haired with brown eyes and an olive complexion.

'Gino,' she murmured under her breath as she navigated the roundabout to leave the ring road. An image appeared in her mind of a swarthy man with eyes like glossy brown dates. *The Italian,* Nan had said, and new questions formed like scrolling tickertape. Did Mum meet him on holiday in Italy, maybe? Had it been a summer fling that ended acrimoniously? Where was her father now?

She flipped open the mirror in her sun visor and peered at her reflection as she waited in a queue of traffic, the cars stop-starting their way towards the city centre. She looked Mediterranean herself, didn't she? She'd always been the fastest to pick up a tan on girls' holidays, much to her friends' envy, and had wondered previously if some small slice of her genetic make-up was Greek or Persian or even Indian.

Now she had an answer, a fact for the very first time. An Italian father, adding an exotic dash to her mother's solidly Yorkshire stock. It made her feel different: more interesting, more attractive. '*Mamma mia!*' she said aloud, turning into her road and backing inelegantly into a parking space.

Excitement and intrigue coursing through her, she ran up the stairs to her flat. Anna had come to Sheffield as a student fourteen years ago, and never left. She'd graduated from uni accommodation through to shared houses in Broomhill and Crookesmoor to her own small first-floor flat near Ecclesall Road. She hadn't intended to stay long in the flat; just a few months while she saved up enough to do something exciting like live in London or go travelling. But then she landed a job at the local paper, and somehow, six years later, hadn't moved either job or home. Her dreams of working in the newsroom of one of the nationals, or backpacking to far-flung beaches, remained mere dreams, less likely with every passing year.

Returning to the flat now, she found herself eyeing it anew. It was cramped and cluttered, with persistent damp in one corner of the ceiling where the roof leaked. A plant was in its death throes on top of the TV and a grey sprinkling of dust lined the skirting boards. It definitely looked like a 'Before' picture in the 'Clear Out Your Clutter' features the newspaper ran every spring. She was totally going to make it amazing and chic one day, though. Definitely. It just hadn't quite happened yet.

Impulsively she dialled a number on her phone and sank into the ageing red sofa. Her mum picked up after three rings. 'Hello?'

'Mum, it's me. Listen, I saw Nan today and . . .' The words suddenly tangled together in her mouth and she hesitated, unsure how to go on.

'Is everything all right? Is she okay?'

'She's fine.' Anna swallowed. 'The thing is, she said . . .' Again, her voice faltered at the crucial moment. *Ask her! Just ask her!*

'This is a terrible line. You keep breaking up. What did

she say? Is she having one of her turns? Only nobody's told me anything about it.'

'No, she's fine, it's just . . .' She ran a hand through her long hair helplessly, then her eye was caught by a photo on the dusty mantelpiece. Her and her mum on holiday in Rhyl one summer, back when she was about nine, both of them tanned and wearing sunglasses, smiling into the camera. It was one of her favourite photos, conjuring up memories of sandcastles, ice cream, and a ride on a sandy, hairy donkey. They'd gone through a lot together, she and her mum. Could she really do this, now, over the phone?

'It's nothing,' she mumbled. 'I just thought I'd let you know that she's fine. Everything's fine.'

'Oh good,' Tracey replied, sounding slightly confused. 'Great. And you're all right, are you? Has that cough gone yet?'

'I'm fine, Mum, yeah. I'd better go. Love to Graham. Bye.'

She ended the call, feeling like a coward. Talk about bottling it. Now she was none the wiser, no further along at all.

Abandoning her phone, Anna hunted through the books and folders heaped randomly on her shelves until she found her old school atlas, then leafed through the pages. Italy, Italy, Italy, Italy . . . there it was.

She stared at the outline of the country as if it could reveal secrets to her, running a finger down the Alps, tracing a path along the wild eastern coastline. There was a pull in her stomach as she whispered the names of towns and cities to herself. *Naples. Florence. Siena.* 'Where are you, Gino?' she murmured under her breath.

She knew virtually nothing about the place, she realized in shame, other than pizza and Chianti and the Romans. Pathetic. And to think this was the land of her father!

Well, then. High time she started swotting up, wasn't it?

In all the drama, Anna had completely forgotten about Pete and the roast she was meant to be cooking until the doorbell rang at six o'clock and she jumped, startled out of her day-dreams. Oh shit. *Dinner.*

Pete was not exactly the hunk of burning love Anna had always imagined herself with – it was more of a 'he'll do' arrangement if she was brutally honest, a Cornish pasty of a man rather than pure beef steak. That said, he was a decent bloke who had never cheated on her, ripped her off for thousands of pounds, or turned out to be gay – all of which had happened to her friends. Okay, so he might not be the most dynamic or passionate man in the world – she had wondered in the past if he even knew the word 'romance' existed – but he was good enough. They had a laugh together. Not that he was laughing now, mind.

'What do you mean, you forgot?' he moaned plaintively as she let him in. 'All the trimmings, you said. I've been looking forward to it since breakfast!' His whole face drooped with dismay, like a bloodhound having a bad day.

'Sorry, Pete, I lost track of time. Something really amazing happened, you see,' she began, then blurted out what her grandmother had let slip, the tiny shining fragment of truth. 'I've not been able to think about anything else all afternoon.'

He gazed around the grubby, food-free kitchen area where no bronzed roast chicken sat waiting to be carved, no thick bread sauce bubbled volcanically on the hob, and no roast potatoes sizzled golden and crunchy in the oven. 'Shall we go to the pub, then?' he sighed, one hand on his belly. 'My stomach thinks my throat's been cut.'

It was all right for him, Anna thought sourly. Pete knew exactly where he was from, with his china-cat-collecting mum and dad in their spotless semi (aptly named Wits' End), and his two sisters, married with kids elsewhere in Sheffield, both of whom had lives as thrilling as a pair of socks. He had a family, roots, he was certain of his place in his world. He had no idea how lucky that made him.

'Pete – here's me telling you I'm on the verge of tracking down my dad, and all you can talk about is your stomach? Can you not show a *bit* more interest?'

Her voice came out sharper than she'd intended and a look of bafflement crossed his face. 'Love, with the greatest respect, you've hardly "tracked him down", finding out his name and nationality,' he pointed out with his usual annoying pedantry. 'There's probably quite a few blokes called Gino from Italy, don't forget.'

She gritted her teeth. 'Yeah, you're dead right there, Pete,' she replied sarcastically. 'Might as well give up already.'

He nodded as if that was the end of it. 'Shall we go, then?'

Oh, what was the point? He didn't have a clue. 'I suppose so,' she muttered, rolling her eyes.

She wondered where her father would be having his Sunday dinner. You could bet your last penny it wouldn't be in some noisy dive where the toilets didn't flush properly and the landlord was always trying to look down your top. No way. He – Gino – would be holding court at a large outdoor table on a sunny Tuscan hillside, with olive trees shimmering in the fields below. There would be fat scarlet tomatoes, creamy mozzarella drizzled with olive oil, rustic red wine in a carafe. Bambinos scampering barefoot on the hot dusty ground, a dog lifting its head drowsily and barking at them from time to time . . .

Did he know he had a daughter here in drizzly Sheffield? Had he ever even *seen* her before?

'You're not listening, are you?' Pete said, sounding exasperated as she locked the flat and they traipsed downstairs. 'You've not heard a single thing I've just said.'

She was still in Italy. It was so much nicer there. 'Sorry, no,' she confessed. 'What did you say?'

'I was asking if you saw the United result. I watched the match at my dad's, you know he's just got Sky Sports? Bloody amazing. That new striker is gold, I'm telling you . . .'

'Great,' she said, but she was already slipping away, flying back to her father and his sun-drenched life. She had to find him. She simply had to.

Guilt for the roast dinner debacle along with most of a bottle of red wine meant that Anna didn't protest when Pete pawed at her later that night back at her flat, despite feeling about as amorous as an oven glove. It was an in-out, in-out, breast squeeze, grunt and collapse sort of event, and she felt unsexy and distracted for the entire three minutes.

'Cor,' he said afterwards, rolling off her. 'Reckon that was a seven and a half.'

Anna had thought he was joking the first time he gave their sex sessions marks out of ten, but he was apparently deadly serious. Much to her horror she had then discovered that he actually charted the scores on a spreadsheet on his laptop. Seriously. She hadn't been snooping but he'd left the page open accidentally one day and the title 'Sex With Anna' had leapt out at her. And there it was in black and white: the date, score and a brief description of each act.

A on top, baby oil, light on – that had scored a ten. But *A in strop, too pissed, bit of rush* merited a measly six.

'Oh my God,' she'd said, aghast, eyes boggling. 'Pete – what the hell is this?'

'You don't mind, do you?' he'd replied, looking shifty. 'I thought it was kind of sexy.'

Kind of sexy? A bit nerdy, more like. It was hardly love letters on scented notepaper, or a passion-filled journal. She wished she'd never seen it, that she could erase it from her brain. 'You're not going to . . . show it to anyone else, are you?'

'Course not, babe. This is private. Password protected. For our eyes only.' He scrolled up the page. 'Look, you got a ten here. Remember that night? Hell-o, Nurse.'

And hell-o, Doctor Perv, Anna thought with a queasy lurch, but he seemed so boyishly pleased with himself that she didn't have the heart to argue. From then on though, she couldn't help wondering – often during the act itself – how he'd describe each sexual encounter. Talk about killing the moment.

'Pete,' she said to him now, 'maybe keep the scoring thing in your head? Like, just in your head? It makes me feel under pressure, like I'm a performing seal or something.'

He reached out and twiddled one of her nipples. It was extremely irritating. 'I don't want to have sex with a seal though, babe,' he said, snuggling up to her. She could feel his warm alcoholic breath on her neck.

'I know, but . . .' *And don't call me babe,* she wanted to say.

That just made her feel like a pig. A bad-tempered pig who didn't want to be marked out of ten each time she spread her trotters. 'I just don't like it, all right?' she said after a few moments. 'Pete?'

But his hand had fallen slack on her chest, and a guttural snoring started up in his throat. Now who was the pig? she thought, turning away from him crossly and putting the pillow over her head.

WOMAN SUFFOCATES CRAP BOYFRIEND spooled a new headline in her brain. But just then he rolled over and flung an arm across her. 'Night, gorgeous,' he murmured in his sleep, and she felt herself softening. He loved her really. She knew that. And being with him was a damn sight better than being on her own, surely?

She shut her eyes, hoping she'd dream of Italy. Her quest would continue in the morning, she vowed. Whatever Pete said.

Chapter Two

Arrivederci – Goodbye

Catherine Evans gazed out of the window as rain speckled the glass, and knew that a chapter was closing.

Matthew and Emily were down in the driveway with Mike, who was helping them load the car, cramming in all those student essentials like hair straighteners and iPod speakers. She'd come up here on the pretence of a last check around their bedrooms, but really so that she could gulp back her tears in private and delay the inevitable moment of parting. What would she do without them?

Last night they'd had a takeaway from Hong Kong Garden and popped open a bottle of frothing cava. Like spokes in a wheel, they'd each stretched an arm in to clink glasses across the table, all giddy with excitement. Well, except for her. She'd barely tasted a mouthful of the food, the noodles slithering like cold worms down her throat, the smell of alcohol and soy sauce turning her stomach. *I don't want them to go.* Mike had made a toast ('To Matthew and Emily: happy times ahead. Thank goodness you inherited your father's brains, eh?') and it was all she could do to stop herself from bolting the doors and refusing to let them leave.

Her heart was being ripped out. Her lungs felt as if they were contracting. *I don't want them to go.*

'Oi, sod off, that's my charger,' came an indignant voice from below just then. It was Emily, hands on hips, the fur-edged hood on her gilet pulled up to protect her long hair from frizzing in the rain. 'I *knew* you'd try to sneak it in with your stuff, just because your one's crap.'

'Yeah, right,' retorted Matthew. He'd always been stubborn and steady in comparison with Emily's more mercurial, volatile nature; the rock and the firework, the tortoise and the hare. '*Yours* is the crap charger. You were the one who spilled Coke on it, which means that—'

'Let's not have an argument, guys.' There was Mike, doing his 'Whoa' hands at them. 'What's happened to your mum, anyway? Got herself lost upstairs or what?'

'I think she went to sniff Matthew's pillow for the last time,' said Emily, trying to snatch the charger from her brother.

'Don't be unkind, Em. This is a big deal for her.'

'I'm not being unkind! You're the one who said—'

'There she is, look, up in the window. Mum! We're ready to go!'

Misty-eyed, Catherine did her best to smile back at the three faces gazing up questioningly. 'Just coming,' she called.

Sniffing Matthew's pillow indeed. Honestly! As if she'd ever do such a thing.

She straightened the bed covers before going out of the room; they'd never know.

They were off to university – 'We're so *proud,*' she'd been telling everyone, beaming fakely whenever the subject came up – Matthew to Manchester, Emily to Liverpool. Okay, so geographically speaking, neither was very far from Sheffield, but no map on earth could measure a mother's missing-you feelings. They might as well be going to Venus.

She'd been dreading this day. For the last eighteen years, they had been the epicentre of her world. They *were* her world. Both sandy-blonde like Mike, with laughing blue eyes and upturned noses, rather than red-haired and freckly like she was; they were taller than her now, and radiant with youth and beauty, spending hours in the bathroom and even longer on the phone, filling the house with music, hair styling products and friends with trousers hanging round their bums. But now they were leaving her and she could hardly bear it.

'Let's get this show on the road then,' she said, emerging from the house with her best and bravest smile. 'Everyone ready? Anyone need the loo before we go?'

'Oh, Mum,' Emily groaned, eyes to heaven.

'Sorry,' Catherine said, feeling like an idiot. She'd be trying to blow their noses for them in a minute.

'Bye then, Dad,' Matthew said.

Mike gave him a matey slap on the back. 'Bye, son,' he said. 'Go and show 'em what you're made of.' Mike wasn't coming with them today, unfortunately. As the most senior GP in his practice, he had been on a number of conferences lately, and now had a ton of paperwork to tackle.

'Come here, Em,' he said next, grabbing her and kissing the top of her head. 'Work hard, play hard, yeah?'

'Yeah, yeah,' Emily said good-naturedly, wriggling away. 'Course I will.'

Catherine dabbed her eyes. Daddy's girl, that was Emily. She wouldn't spoil it for either of them by telling Mike about the contraceptive pills she'd found in their daughter's underwear drawer, or the small bag of grass she'd come across in her jeans' pocket, and definitely not the times Emily had smuggled Rhys Blackwood up to her bedroom for who knows what. Catherine had dealt with these trespasses in her own quiet way each time; all hell would break loose if Mike discovered just how casually his countless lectures about drugs, alcohol and sexual health had been ignored.

'See you later,' he said to Catherine as she got into the driver's seat. 'Drive carefully, won't you? Don't dab your brakes on every ten seconds, you know it winds other people up.' He pulled a long-suffering face at Matthew and Emily who both laughed.

Catherine said nothing, but started the engine and reversed carefully out of the drive. She could see him waving in the rear-view mirror the whole way down the road. Then they turned right, heading for the motorway, and he was gone.

Matthew's new halls of residence was their first port of call an hour later. 'This is it then,' Catherine said faintly as she cut the engine and gazed up at the looming block of flats.

'Awesome,' said Matthew, first out of the car. He was six foot two now, her little boy, and his hair was shaggy and shoulder-length, much to Mike's disapproval. He wore a snowboarding hoodie, battered jeans and his beloved Vans, as he stood gazing around at his new turf. Then he put his hands in the air and bellowed, 'Hello, Manchester!' as if he were on stage at his own stadium gig.

Heads turned. A couple of girls with long hair and skinny jeans standing nearby grinned at him then giggled together conspiratorially. A dad unloading a clapped-out old Volvo in the next row of cars gave Catherine a wry smile of recognition. *Teenagers,* his eyes seemed to say. *On another planet, aren't they?*

In the short space of time it took to unload Matthew's boxes from the Toyota and lug them up to his plain, rather utilitarian room, he'd already struck up an animated conversation with a Londoner in a BABE MAGNET T-shirt and a guy with dreadlocks and a pierced nose. The three of them were now arranging an imminent trip to the union bar. 'I think I'm in with these girls I saw downstairs,' Catherine heard Matthew tell them in a lofty, unrecognizable manner.

Catherine cleared her throat in the background. 'Well,' she said, 'I'll leave you to it then.'

She had imagined this moment endlessly over the last few weeks, dreamed about it even. Tears, hugs, a moment of recognition and gratitude for everything she'd done for him. Matthew's lower lip might even tremble . . .

'See you then, Mum,' he said coolly.

Wait . . . was that it? He was fobbing her off with a paltry 'See you'? He could think again. She threw her arms around him and held him, but he felt wooden in her embrace. He was already looking over his shoulder, ready to move on as they pulled apart.

Oh. That *was* it. Catherine felt as if she'd been stabbed as she shakily made it back to the car. Her heart ached and she put a hand to her chest, trying to breathe deeply.

'Next stop, Liverpool!' Emily cried, clambering into the front seat as her phone beeped with the hundredth text of the morning. She glanced at the screen and laughed.

'Is it from Matthew?' Catherine asked hopefully.

'What? No. Just Flo mucking about. Are we off, then?'

'We're off,' Catherine replied.

Her daughter would be different, she consoled herself as they drove the extra thirty or so miles west to Liverpool. Girls were better at these situations, weren't they? Emily would want her to linger for coffee and a chat; maybe they could find somewhere special for a goodbye lunch, just the two of them. Perhaps there'd be a repeat of the shyness she'd suffered from at infant school, where she'd clung to Catherine's legs, one thumb jammed in her mouth, not daring to speak to another person. Well, okay, she probably wouldn't go that far, but all the same. Em needed her more than Matthew, always had, always would.

Emily's new home was a bleach-smelling flat with heavy fire doors that slammed shut behind you. It was cold and bare, a far cry from her comfortable bedroom back home with its soft carpet and thick curtains, its ceiling still sporting the glow-in-the-dark stars and moons they'd stuck there for her as a little girl.

Catherine was seized by the impulse to grab her by the shoulders and bundle her back into the car, but Emily was already bonding with a girl wearing a blue Hollister sweatshirt and red jeans. 'I love your boots,' she said with a winning smile, ignoring Catherine hovering behind her.

Catherine fetched and carried her daughter's belongings, huffing and puffing up the stairs with boxes of shoes and bin-bags filled with clothes. When the car boot was finally empty save for a single forlorn pair of orange flip-flops (discarded at the last minute as being uncool), she lingered in the flat's kitchen while Emily and her new flatmates discussed festivals and awful summer jobs, waiting to be offered a drink or even an introduction. 'Anyone want a brew?' she asked finally when neither seemed forthcoming.

Emily's head spun round, eyes accusing. *Are you still here?* they seemed to say as she hurried over. 'Mum, you're like totally cramping my style,' she hissed, shooing her out. 'I'll ring you in a few days, all right?'

'Oh,' Catherine replied. 'Sure, darling. Should I just help you unpack a bit, make your room more homely? We could put up some of your p—'

'No, honest, Mum, it's fine. I'll do it later.'

'Make sure you wear your thermals if it's cold, won't you? You know how chesty you get in winter. And keep up with your homework. Remember—'

'Muuum!' Emily glanced over her shoulder in fear of anyone eavesdropping. 'I can look after myself now!'

Catherine opened her mouth then shut it again. It seemed only yesterday that Emily would cry out in the night for her, scared of monsters lurking in dark corners of her bedroom. *Mummy! Mumm-ee!* Mummy wasn't needed now, though, that much was clear. 'Okay, then,' she said at last, chastened. 'Well . . . Bye then. I love you. Take care.'

'Bye, Mum.'

Catherine trudged back to the car and sat in the driver's seat, feeling bruised and rejected, a visceral pain in her chest. Her children couldn't wait to get away from her. They had cast her off like last season's fashions, as unwanted as the orange flip-flops.

Tears brimmed in her eyes and she sat immobile for a few moments, waves of self-pity washing over her. How ironic that she'd worried about *them* feeling abandoned in their new homes, when in actual fact she was the one pushed out in the cold, the door shut in her face. Meanwhile, her little chicks had flown the nest for new horizons and hadn't looked back. Oh, why hadn't she talked them into taking a gap year and staying at home for a bit longer?

Two cars away in the student parking area she could see another set of parents sitting just like her, staring gormlessly through their windscreen, no doubt equally shellshocked by a recent separation. They too would have to pick up the pieces and begin a new, strange life without their boisterous, shower-hogging, fridge-pillaging children. A quieter, emptier life.

She blew her nose and pulled herself up straighter in the driver's seat. She might as well go home then. There was no reason to hang around here all afternoon.

As she reversed slowly out of the parking space, with one last look up at the block of flats where Emily now lived (*Goodbye, love*), it crossed her mind that she should text Mike, let him know she'd be home sooner than expected. Early evening, she'd told him, imagining a much more drawn-out day than this.

But a car was already behind her, the other desolate parents putting a brave face on and tearing themselves away too. She wouldn't stop now that she'd started, she decided; she'd give Mike a nice surprise by turning up early.

If only she'd known what a surprise they'd both get by her early return, she would have sat in the Liverpool Uni car park a good while longer. In fact, she might not have driven home at all.

Traffic was gratifyingly light and it seemed no time before Catherine was turning into the quiet cul-de-sac where they'd lived for the last ten years. Wetherstone was a pretty South Yorkshire village with picture-postcard stone cottages, a tree-edged village green and a close-knit friendly community. It was convenient for Sheffield, where the twins had gone to school, and a short commute to the Health Centre for Mike.

Catherine got out of the car and gazed up at her daughter's bedroom, wishing Emily was still there, sprawled on the faded pink duvet texting her mates and listening to music. Sadness cut her like a knife and she swayed against the car for a moment.

Come on, Catherine. Be positive. New chapter and all that. Besides, this could be a new start for her and Mike, too.

They could take holidays in term-time now, try to reconnect a little (he had been so distant lately). They could even be romantic again without hearing an 'Ugh, gross, get a room' comment in the background. Why not? They weren't past it yet, were they?

Feeling a flare of optimism, she unlocked the front door and stepped inside. 'I'm back!' she called, chucking her handbag onto the bench in the hall and kicking off her shoes.

He must be in the garden, she thought idly when no answer came. She went upstairs, meaning to have a quick wash before she made herself a cup of tea and started thinking about dinner. Goodness, she'd be cooking for just the two of them now, that would be a novelty. The shopping list would shrink unrecognizably without marauding teenagers wolfing their way through the fridge. They could treat themselves to steak without Emily tutting about vegetarianism, and have a few glasses of wine together without feeling they should be setting a good example.

Music was playing from their bedroom. Ooh, excellent. It sounded like he'd finished his work already.

'Mike, are you – ' she began, pushing open the door.

Then she stopped dead. And screamed.

There was a blonde woman in her bed wearing nothing but red lipstick and a surprised expression. And Mike, also stark bollock naked, between the woman's thighs, his bum muscles clenched, eyes widening in horror. No, thought Catherine, stumbling back, stricken. No.

The woman tittered. 'Oops,' she said in a lazy drawl. She seemed amused, of all things. Amused!

'Shit,' Mike cried, wrenching himself off her. He grabbed a pair of discarded boxers and covered his privates, strangely coy. 'Cath – I wasn't expecting you. I . . .'

Catherine's brain still couldn't process what was in front of her. No way. This could not be happening.

'Catherine . . .' Mike said, advancing towards her.

A sob escaped her throat and she backed away. Then adrenalin ricocheted through her as she ran downstairs, her heart banging in her ribcage. No. No way. Not Mike.

'Wait!' she heard Mike yelling frantically. 'Catherine!'

For the first time in years, she didn't obey him. She went straight back through the front door and scrambled into the car, her fingers shaking so violently on the seatbelt it took her three attempts to clip it in. Then she started the engine, reversed wildly out of the drive and drove away.

Chapter Three

Una telefonata – A phone call

'*Buongiorno. Due cappuccini, una coca* and . . . Did you say you wanted ice cream, Lily? . . . Um . . . *Gelato? Per favore?*'

Sophie Frost took pity on the woman with the pink nose and halterneck top who was floundering for the right words. 'Don't worry, I'm English too,' she said. 'And we've got chocolate or vanilla ice cream.'

The woman smiled gratefully. 'Oh good! Thank you. My Italian is limited to say the least.' She bent down to the little girl beside her who whispered into her ear. 'And she'd love a chocolate ice cream, please.'

'Coming right up,' Sophie replied. 'If you take a seat, I'll bring those over in a few minutes.'

She turned to the cappuccino machine, humming along with the radio as she set about the order. Other people might moan about bar and café work, but it reminded Sophie of being on a stage, performing to a crowd, particularly when the place was full and buzzing. If only you got a round of applause and a curtain call now and then, rather than measly single-euro tips, she'd like it even more . . .

Still, working here had its compensations, not least being in sunny Sorrento, her own corner of paradise. Above the clatter and music of the café, you could just make out the high-pitched shrieks of seagulls down in the bay below, and she knew without looking that the usual collection of impossibly wrinkled *nonnas* would be sitting across the cobbled square doing their endless crochet together, their potbellied husbands animatedly setting the world to rights over tiny cups of espresso or a grappa at a table outside the bar. She knew the trattoria next door would soon be firing up its ovens and the warm air would be filled with the tantalizing scents of pizza and oregano, while the yachties paraded past, heading for Corso Italia and the designer shops. Girls with bare legs buzzed by on Vespas and car horns honked. Up above, the sun languorously traced an arc across the sky, casting golden light on the glorious old stone buildings.

It was all so perfect. And she lived here! There wasn't a single place in the world she'd rather be. Uncapping the Coke bottle, she found herself wondering what the weather was like back in Sheffield, and shivered as images of wet leaves, frosty mornings and chilblains sprang to mind. It was mid-autumn now, but still a balmy twenty-three degrees in Sorrento.

'There we are,' she said, as she took the tray over to the

English customers. 'Two cappuccinos, a Coke – is this for you? And one yummy chocolate ice cream.'

'Thank you,' the woman said, pouring Coke into the glass for her son. 'What do you say, kids?'

'Fank you,' the boy mumbled.

'*Grazie*,' the girl lisped winningly.

'Clever girl,' her father said, ruffling her hair. 'Thanks,' he added to Sophie, ripping open a sachet of sugar and tipping it into his coffee.

Sophie left them to it, but found she was clutching the empty tray to herself like a shield as she walked back behind the counter. She always felt extra judgemental about the British families when they came in – couldn't help herself. This lot seemed okay, but you got some real horrors in affluent tourist areas like Sorrento: braying moneyed types who badgered their blushing, stammering children to order in Italian whether they wanted to or not; the ones you heard pushing, pushing, pushing all the time, never able to let their kids just chill out and enjoy their holiday.

Parents like hers, in other words, who seemed to think that success was measured by the size of your bank account. It left you unable to ever quite shake off the feeling of being a disappointment, however far you travelled.

'Waitressing in a café?' she imagined her mother shrieking if she had the slightest inkling that Sophie was here. 'What a waste of your education! All those years of private school – for nothing!'

'Waste of your brain, more like,' her father would thunder. 'When you could turn your hand to anything you choose. Is this *really* what you want to do with your life?'

Whatever! Was it any wonder she'd cut herself free, deliberately stayed away like a sparkle on the breeze, unable to be pinned down by them or anyone else?

Okay, so she was not the good little daughter they'd hoped for, even after all the riding lessons and dance tuition and piano recitals they'd bombarded her with, not to mention the awful girls' school she'd suffered, packed wall-to-wall with snobby princess-types who'd looked down their noses at her for being 'new money'. Being an only child sucked, she had often thought, wishing for a sibling so that the weight of her parents' expectations could have been borne equally. As it was, she'd thrown their expectations right back in their faces. *Get over it.*

She had been away eight years now: eight years of extraordinary adventures, of bustling foreign cities and white sand beaches, finding jobs, homes and friends in umpteen different countries. She had even been sent spinning by the love affair to end all love affairs, not that it had lasted, unfortunately.

And here she was now, with bright Mediterranean sunshine streaming through the window, with beach life and *bella Italia* and her beloved passport. Not tied down to any person or any place. Not working in a dreary grey office saving a pension as her parents would no doubt have liked. I win, she thought.

'*Signorina. Signorina!*'

Oh Christ, someone was clicking his fingers at her. Actually clicking his fingers. Rude bastard. She raised an eyebrow and sauntered over with pointed slowness to the man in question, who seemed to have lost his manners on the way in. He rattled off a lunch order without a single please or thank you, addressing her breasts throughout the entire list of dishes. Then, as she turned in the direction of the kitchen, he grabbed her bottom and gave it a hard squeeze.

'*Mi scusi!*' she cried, yanking herself away as he and his friends sniggered behind her. It was all she could do not to brain the lot of them with the nearest menu.

Trembling with rage, she went into the kitchen to pass the order on to Vito, the chef. 'Feel free to spit in any of it,' she added in Italian afterwards.

Well, okay, so perhaps not absolutely everything was perfect, she thought, taking a few deep breaths before returning to the café area. Still, it was a small price to pay for freedom. And that, at the end of the day, was what she valued above anything else.

Home these days was a small flat in an apartment block overlooking the bustling Piazza Torquato Tasso. Her budget hadn't stretched to a sea view, but from her window you could see the *passeggiata* every evening, the leisurely stroll enjoyed by locals and tourists alike as the sun sank in the sky. She had her own titchy bathroom with a dribbling shower, a single bed, a few changes of clothes, her laptop and a temperamental fan to stir up the soupy air. She didn't need much else.

When she'd arrived in Sorrento eight months ago, she'd envisaged herself settling down here, making the city her home. Her Italian was pretty good, and she thought it would be an easy matter of blending in with the community, making friends, getting to know her neighbours. Who needed family anyway?

Unfortunately, it hadn't really worked out like that. She knew Vito from the café, sure, and the manager, Federica, and both had always been friendly enough, but there wasn't the same camaraderie there as other places she'd worked in. No shared drinks after work, no out-of-hours socializing. The one time Federica had taken pity on her and invited her along to a family party, Sophie had felt completely out of place, her choppy blonde bob and green eyes immediately marking her as an outsider.

Oh well. Being alone every night wasn't the end of the world; she liked her own company, had always been an independent sort. She checked in with Facebook now and then if she felt lonely. She had books. She had the blogging community too, a whole host of virtual friends around the world who followed her adventures on the travel blog she'd written for years. It was enough. Of course it was enough!

Anyway, she would probably move on soon now that the season here was winding down. She'd worked in a ski lodge in Val Thorens a couple of winters ago, and it had been a right laugh, just what she needed to recover from her broken heart. The staff had all celebrated Christmas and New Year together, and it had been one long, glorious party, way better than strained silence around the turkey back in Sheffield. There was always plenty of work up in the north-west, near the Swiss border, over the winter. Maybe it was time to leave the sea and head for the mountains . . .

Perched in her usual spot on the balcony, with a book, a glass of red wine and a ripe juicy nectarine, Sophie was surprised by a knock at her apartment door that evening. Knocks at the door were extremely rare – unheard of, really. It was probably a mistake, somebody with the wrong apartment number, looking for the surly Polish guys upstairs.

She opened the door. '*Si?* Oh. *Buonasera, Signor Russo.*' It was her landlord. Help. Was he about to give her notice, turf her out? Maybe someone had complained about her drying her knickers and vest tops on the small balcony railing. There had been that embarrassing occasion when her pink bra had actually fallen off in a gust of wind and landed on an old man's shoulder in the street below, but he'd seen the funny side, thankfully – or so she'd thought at the time.

'*Telefonata*,' he said, thrusting a piece of paper at her. 'For you.'

'Somebody called me?' she blurted out in surprise, then saw the scribbled name – Samantha, one of her cousins – and a British phone number. Her stomach clenched. '*Grazie*,' she said, her fingers folding around the paper. '*Grazie, signor*.'

Oh shit. She shut the door blindly, her heart pounding. This was a million times worse than a free-falling bra. Samantha was married to Julian, a nice vicar, and busy with a toddler and a new baby according to Facebook. She would not have gone to the bother of tracking down her cousin all the way to the Amalfi coast for a pleasant chit-chat. Something must have happened. Something serious.

'Oh, thank goodness, Sophie! I thought you'd fallen off the planet. I've been emailing you and messaging you, but was running out of ideas how to— Julian, could you take Henry for me, please? It's Sophie. No, my cousin Sophie. There you go, my good little sausage . . .'

'Hello? Sam? Are you still there?' Sophie was in the echoing hall of the apartment block, cramming euros into the payphone. She didn't have time to waste.

'Sorry, yes I am. Listen, I hate to say this but it's bad news. It's your dad. He's had a massive heart attack. He's . . . well, he's out of intensive care, but he's pretty ill. Will you come home and see him?'

Each sentence was like a hammer blow. *Dad. Heart attack. Intensive care.* 'Oh God,' she said hoarsely. 'Yes. Yes, I'll come.'

'If it was my dad, I'd want to see him, so I just thought . . .'

'Yeah. Sure. Thanks, Sam. Tell him . . . Tell him I'm on my way.'

She sagged against the cool wall of the lobby once she'd hung up, the shock leaving her lightheaded, as if she was drunk or ill, not really there at all. Shit. A massive heart attack. Oh, Dad . . .

Jim, her dad, had always been such a bon viveur – he liked wine and good food, and hogged the conversation at get-togethers with his anecdotes. A tall, robust man, he was never happier than when striding around the Peak District with muddy hiking boots and a compass. It was horrible to imagine him collapsing in pain, falling to the floor perhaps, one hand clutching uselessly at his chest.

She had to go back, it was as simple as that. Contact with her parents had been limited since she'd left home so dramatically – a cursory postcard now and then, a brief, awkward phone call at Christmas – but this was her *dad*, a cornerstone of her life, desperately ill in hospital. She'd never really given any thought to the idea of her dad or mum not being around any more. The prospect made her feel as if she was sobering up very fast from a wild party.

Up in her flat again, she gazed around at the drab, small space as if seeing it for the first time: the brown curtains that didn't block out the sun properly, the film of dirt over the window caused by the never-ending traffic jams below, the tiny rubbish kitchen with only a hob and fridge . . . It made her want to cry all of a sudden. She had been playing at living here, she realized with a sinking feeling. Camping out in a den, just as she'd done as a child, taking doll's tea cups and her teddies under the table and playing house.

Never look back, she'd always said to herself. But this time there was no avoiding it.

Two days later, she was boarding the plane. It had all been worryingly easy, leaving her Italian job and home. Federica had hugged her and said she understood. *Your papa? But of course you must go!*

She'd packed her scant possessions, then put the keys to her flat in an envelope and left it downstairs for Signor Russo. That had been that. The merest snipping of ties, and she was cut loose once more.

Stepping foot on a plane usually filled Sophie with joy, yet today's journey felt more like a backwards move, laced with dread. But she was not a coward – far from it. And this wasn't going to be for ever. She would visit her father and make sure he was okay, she vowed. She'd keep her cool, be polite, refuse to let her parents get to her. And then she'd be off again, to enjoy a schnapps-fuelled winter somewhere snowy. Simple as that.

'And we're ready for take-off,' the pilot said over the loudspeakers as the engines roared. 'Cabin crew to positions, please.'

Goodbye Italy, Sophie thought to herself, sucking on her boiled sweet and staring out of the window as the land tilted and swung away beneath her. *Arrivederci.* I hope it's not too long before I'm back . . .

'Here he is,' the nurse said, opening the curtains around the bed. 'Okay?'

'Thanks,' Sophie stammered, not feeling remotely okay. There was her father, lying in a hospital bed, eyes shut, grey hair at his temples. When had he got those wrinkles? she wondered in shock. When had he got so *old*?

Monitors attached to him narrated the passage of time with regular bleeping and whirring. Through the narrow window, Sophie could see heavy rain falling, as it had done constantly since the plane had landed in Manchester. Sorrento seemed a million miles away already, a colourful dream from which she'd just woken. I don't want to be here, she thought unhappily.

She hesitated, her backpack sodden on her shoulders, wet

jeans sticking to her legs. It was so strange being back here. All those Yorkshire accents. The flat grey look of the place. And the assault of memories that had battered her as the coach navigated the Sheffield streets: rehearsals in a dusty school hall, drinking cider underage in the Gladstone, the satisfying slam of the front door the day she left home . . .

'Hi, Dad,' she whispered, still not moving any closer. There was an empty chair beside the bed, pulled up companionably as if awaiting her presence. A short film played in her head, of her slinging down the heavy backpack, walking the few steps to the chair, lowering herself into it and taking her father's hand in hers. *Do it,* she urged herself. *Do it!* But she couldn't.

She watched his face as he slept, noted every new line around his eyes, the silvering of his hair. His jutting eyebrows and proud nose still gave him the air of a statesman, but he looked old and weary, a different man from the one who'd taught her to play chess and hardly ever let her win; who'd taught her to ride her bike, one big hand holding the back of her T-shirt as she pedalled; who'd given her her love of Elvis and loud guitar.

'Dad?' she said, a little louder. 'It's me, Soph. It's . . .' She blinked, stopping herself at the last moment from saying *It's Sophie-pops,* his old nickname for her. She wondered if she'd ever hear him say it again, and her throat tightened. Just how ill *was* he, anyway? Were they talking not-gonna-pull-through ill, or two-weeks-off-work ill? Samantha had only given her the basics on the phone, and when Sophie had plucked up the nerve to ring her mum to ask for details later that evening, there had been no answer. She'd imagined the ringtone echoing through the empty house while her mum sat keeping vigil at her dad's bedside and felt very far away.

Her heart sped up. She wasn't sure she wanted to know details any more. What if the truth was too painful to swallow? Maybe she should just go; retreat to blissful ignorance. She could turn around, head back to the airport, jump on a plane to somewhere new, drown her sorrows in cheap foreign whisky and—

'Oh! Sophie. Goodness.'

Too late. There was her mother, almost cannoning into her as she appeared. Three words spoken and already it felt like the start of a row. Sophie braced herself for the ruck.

'Hi, Mum,' she said. Those words hadn't passed her lips since Christmas Day last year, when she'd been in a phone booth in Rome, incoherently drunk. Eight years since they'd been in the same room together, and just look at them now: one bedraggled and soggy, the other groomed to within an inch of her life with perfect make-up, a smart blouse, not a single hair daring to fly out of place. It was important to maintain one's standards, Sophie imagined her saying to herself as she dusted on her face powder that morning. 'How is he?' she asked.

'He's stable,' her mum replied crisply. She walked over to the bed and put her hand on her husband's. 'Jim, love, it's me.'

And there it was, the old power-dynamic reasserting itself: Mum siding physically with Dad, ganging up and leaving her out in the cold. Well, in the warm, she should say. It was stifling in there. She let her backpack slip off her shoulders and dumped it by the wall. 'What happened?' she asked. 'With the heart attack, I mean.'

'We were in Meadowhall,' her mum replied. 'Looking at luggage in Hanleys. We're meant to be going to the Canaries in February, thought we'd splash out on some new cases for the occasion. Your dad found one he liked, this smart, brown . . . Well, anyway. All of a sudden, he couldn't breathe, he just keeled over, collapsed in agony right there on the shop floor.' Her lips tightened, reliving the moment. 'The girl behind the till had to call an ambulance because I'd forgotten to charge my phone.' She breathed in sharply, her knuckles blanching as she clutched her handbag. 'We were rushed here, sirens blaring. He's been in ever since.'

'Oh, Mum.' Sophie could feel her pain, how awful it must have been, but still couldn't bring herself to move a step closer. Her mum would probably only shove her away if she attempted a hug. 'Samantha said it was quite a big heart attack,' she ventured wretchedly after a moment.

'Yes. Cardiac arrest.' There was a pause. 'Samantha's been very good to us. Visiting all the time, even though she's so busy with the little ones. Tracking you down to the depths of . . . wherever you were.'

Sophie's skin prickled with the implicit criticism. Samantha the golden girl, Sophie the drop-out; she'd heard it a million times before. She kept her eyes on the motionless figure in the bed. 'He has come round, since, hasn't he?' she asked.

'Yes. He was unconscious for a few hours, and they had to put a vent in his heart – a sort of balloon thing to help it work properly,' her mum said. 'His coronary artery was completely blocked, so he needed stents in that and two others. He's . . .' A tear trembled on her lower lashes. 'He's doing okay, though. Better.'

'It must have been terrifying,' Sophie said.

Down rattled the shutters on her mum's face, as if the flicker of emotion had been a momentary error. 'We'll be fine,' she said briskly.

Ahh, the royal we, that tiny little word that said so much. Sophie stiffened as the atmosphere changed. 'So . . . what happens now? How long will he have to . . . ?'

She broke off as her dad moved under the covers, frowning in his sleep. 'How long will he have to stay here?' she whispered, not wanting to wake him. She was scared she wouldn't know how to respond to him when his eyes opened.

'Hopefully not much longer,' her mum replied. 'They're pleased with his progress, but it all depends.'

Jim moved again, and this time his eyes did open and he blinked. Then he saw Sophie and his face changed from discomfort to surprise. 'Soph! Hello, love. I was just dreaming about you.'

She went over to him – the other side of the bed from where her mum was standing – and tentatively took his hand. His fingers looked pale and crumpled like those of an old man. 'Dad. How are you?'

'Oh, you know,' he said. 'On the mend now. Soon be up and about, back to normal.'

'Not quite, Jim,' muttered his wife, lips pinched.

'Were the prices in Hanleys really *that* bad?' Sophie asked, trying to make light of the situation. Pathetic coping strategy or what. 'I know they say Yorkshiremen are tight, but really, Dad . . .'

'There are probably better ways of getting a discount,' he admitted with a laugh, then squeezed her hand. 'It's good to see you, Soph. Really good. Almost worth having a heart attack to see you again.'

'Oh, Dad. Don't say that.'

'Seriously, though. You look well. How's life?'

She hesitated. Somehow they seemed to have leapfrogged all the big stuff into an ordinary conversation. 'Um . . . great,' she said cagily. 'I've been living in Sorrento – met some lovely people, really got into the Italian lifestyle, you know . . .'

'Good for you, love. That's a cracking tan you've got there.'

'Yeah. Sunshine every day.' She raised an eyebrow in the direction of the rain-spattered window and he smiled.

'Jim, I've just spoken to the doctor who has given me an update,' her mum announced then, and Sophie tried to listen as she talked about medication and test results. The world seemed to be tilting dizzily though; she felt giddy and off-balance all of a sudden.

'Are you okay?' her dad asked, noticing. 'You've gone a bit green beneath that tan.'

'I'm fine. Honestly.' She hadn't had any breakfast in the rush to catch the airport bus, and then the prices on board the plane had been so extortionate (four quid for a sandwich – as if!) she hadn't been able to bring herself to shell out for anything. Then, once she'd landed, her mind had been taken up with catching a coach here, and Dad, and . . .

'I'll just nip out and get a coffee,' she decided. 'Anyone want anything?'

Her dad eyed her. 'Only for you to come back again,' he replied. 'You are going to stay a while now you're here, aren't you?'

'Um,' she said, caught off-guard. She had nowhere to stay, she realized, hadn't even thought about what she'd do once here.

'You can have your old room. Can't she, Trish? Be like old times.'

Old times? Not likely. She didn't want to go back to 'old

times'. And there was Trish, mouth already pursing up like a cat's bum; it was clear that the words 'Over my dead body' were just lining up to be spoken. She didn't want to revisit old times either.

'I'll stay with a mate,' Sophie said quickly, to let them both off the hook. 'Back in a minute.'

She left the room, her legs trembly, her heart seeming to buck and stutter just like her dad's had done. Stay with her parents? Never again. She would rather sleep on the streets.

She walked down the corridor, trying to think who to phone first. Er . . . nobody. She'd lost touch with all her school friends years ago. Sod it, she'd stay in a hostel if she had to. The airfare had eaten up most of her savings, but she could scrape enough cash for a night or two somewhere cheap. *Keep your distance,* she reminded herself. That way she'd avoid getting hurt again.

Chapter Four

Il segreto – The secret

Catherine didn't have a clue where she was going as she accelerated away from the house, tears pouring down her cheeks. She just had to get away, far from her husband, and . . . *her*. That woman. How could Mike have done such a thing? In *their bed!*

She couldn't concentrate on the road, barely saw the junctions and bends as she hurtled along, adrenalin roaring. The woman's face kept slamming into her mind, the casual way she'd said 'Oops,' like she thought the situation was funny. To think she'd had the nerve to look Catherine in the eye and smirk, actually smirk, while she was lying on Catherine's Marks and Spencer sheets with Catherine's husband sticking his traitorous cock in her.

How had it happened? She didn't understand. What about the paperwork Mike was meant to be doing? Had it all been a lie? Had he thought, *Great, the wife and kids are out of the house all day, I'll shag someone else?*

No. Not Mike. No way.

She was already starting to doubt her own eyes, her own brain. She must have made a mistake somewhere during that bizarre two minutes up in their bedroom. Mike always did say she was about as observant as Stevie Wonder. He was right. What was more, he was not the sort of man who had sex with strange women in broad daylight on a Sunday afternoon. He just wasn't. 'You muppet,' she imagined him saying when she came back. 'Did you seriously think I'd do the dirty on you? Even for you, that's ridiculous.'

Maybe it was some weird hallucination. Some terrible feverish brain strain, brought on by the stress of the children going. But . . .

She gulped loudly and snottily. Wise up, Catherine. Deep down, she knew there had been no hallucination, no mistake. She had seen them, however much she wanted to pretend otherwise. Mike and the blonde woman. The blonde, nubile, pert-boobed, definitely younger, definitely sexier woman. Naked. On their marital bed, the goose-feather duvet kicked off onto the carpet. She had seen them.

Overcome with shock and grief, she pulled into a layby and sat with her head on the steering wheel, hazard lights flashing, and burst into tears.

Nearly nineteen years earlier, Catherine had marched into hospital fully braced to say, 'I don't want it.' She planned to book herself in for an abortion as soon as possible to get rid of the interloper in her womb – the mistake – and that would be the end of it. Well, she was only twenty, wasn't she? Two years into her degree and accidentally pregnant from a holiday fling – it wasn't like she could possibly go *through* with it.

She lay there on the hard paper-towel-covered bed, waiting as the sonographer rubbed the cold blue jelly on her tummy then started moving the transducer around. 'Don't even look,' her friend Zoe had advised. 'It's only a blob, not a baby.' But then the sonographer announced 'Twins!' in an excited sort of way, and Catherine found herself unexpectedly transfixed by the monitor, showing the two bulbous heads and bodies. Twins! Not blobs of cells but two actual babies growing inside her. Tiny little people. Whoa.

Their heads were close together as if they were having a private conversation in the shared dark intimacy. In fact ... 'They're holding hands,' she whispered, eyes wide in shocked delight.

'It does look like it, doesn't it,' the sonographer said. 'Sweet.'

It *was* sweet. It was the sweetest thing Catherine had ever seen. And in the next moment, a force had taken over her, something primitive and rushing and fierce, and she knew, just like that, that an abortion was out of the question. 'Thank you,' she said faintly as the sonographer wiped the goo off her belly with professional briskness.

After a sleepless night, she got on a train to Sheffield the next day, carrying herself with a new sense of wonder, still shocked by her own momentous decision. The evening before, she'd sat in the science section of the university library, poring over everything she could find on the subject of babies and childbirth. Her body felt like a ticking clock, a precious vessel, rich with mystery.

Clutching the bit of paper with Mike's address, she knocked tremulously on his door and waited there in her parka and fingerless gloves, the grainy scan photos tucked carefully in her pocket.

Mike's mum Shirley answered, a pewter-haired woman in a grey wool dress, a small silver cross around her neck. 'Yes, dear?' she asked.

'Is Mike there? Mike Evans?'

The woman looked at her with curiosity. 'No, dear, he's at university down in Nottingham. Won't be back for another few weeks.' She hesitated. Clearly something in Catherine's face signified that this wasn't a casual popping-round visit. 'Can I give him a message?'

Catherine's hands stole instinctively to her belly. She had recently felt the babies moving inside her for the first time and the strange fluttering sensation had returned. 'I . . .'

Shirley noted the positioning of the girl's hands, the pinched look on her face, the urgency with which she'd asked after Mike. She was a practical woman who could recognize disaster when it appeared on her doorstep. 'You'd better come in,' she said.

It was nearly six o'clock in the evening now and Catherine had been sitting in the layby for hours. The sun had slipped behind the hills without her even noticing; the other cars had their headlights on as they zoomed through the thickening darkness. She didn't know what to do. Her brain wouldn't function properly. What if she went home and that woman was still there? What if she walked in and Mike and that woman were still having sex, both laughing at her?

Oops, the woman might say again cattily. *She's back, Mike. Take a hint, can't you, love?*

Feeling cold, she put her arms around herself, tucking her hands in her armpits for warmth. She still couldn't believe it. The whole thing felt like a bad dream, a joke. If only she hadn't hurried home so quickly! If the twins hadn't been so keen to see the back of her and the motorway traffic hadn't been so light, she might never have interrupted Mike and *her.* Who was she, anyway? And how long had she been stripping off and having sex with Catherine's husband?

Oh God. It was so awful, like something from a soap opera. The mistress in the bedroom while the wife was out of the house. Talk about tacky. And talk about out of character. Was Mike ill? Having a breakdown? Maybe he was in some kind of fugue state where you didn't know what you were doing. She'd seen it once on TV. There must be some explanation because he loved her, didn't he? She was his *wife!*

Unless . . . A cold fear pierced her. Unless he wasn't ill. Unless he knew exactly what he was doing. Unless he didn't love her at all.

Her phone was ringing, she realized after a while. It was past seven o'clock now and becoming darker by the minute. Another whole hour had slid silently by without her even noticing. Maybe *she* was having a breakdown?

Her fingers were numb with cold as she reached into her handbag to retrieve the phone. 'Hello?' she said hoarsely, her throat aching from crying.

'Catherine,' said Mike. 'Where are you?'

'I'm . . .' She blinked and stared out of the window. She could see nothing. 'I don't know,' she admitted.

Pathetic. She knew that was what he was thinking. Pathetic. How could anyone drive somewhere and not know where they were? Sometimes he spoke to her with such scorn it made her want to shrink out of sight.

'Don't make a scene, Catherine,' he said eventually. 'Just come home and we'll talk.'

Then her phone must have lost connection because all of a sudden the dial tone buzzed in her ear.

She leaned back against the moulded head rest and heaved a long, juddering sigh. He wanted to talk. He'd said, 'Come home.' Those were good things, weren't they? Practically an apology. He must be feeling terrible about this.

Yes. She would go home and he would explain that it had been a stupid mistake, never to happen again. A moment of madness, he would tell her. Then she would forgive him, cry a bit probably, and pop one of her sleeping pills to blot the whole thing out. Tomorrow, they would carry on as before. They never need mention it again.

Other couples managed to survive infidelity, didn't they? She and Mike could too. They had to. Because without him, she was nothing.

When she walked into the house, the first thing she saw was his suitcase in the hall, black and ominous. A suit-carrier hung from the coatrack and she looked at it, then back at the bulging suitcase. No, she thought, panicking. No.

She went through to the living room as if in a dream. Mike was sitting on the sofa, his knee joggling impatiently. He stood up when he saw her.

'I'm sorry you had to find out this way,' he said. The line sounded well rehearsed. 'I've been meaning to tell you for some time.'

Wait a minute. The moment of madness had been going on for 'some time'?

'We both know we shouldn't have married each other in

the first place,' he went on. 'I've made it work for the sake of the kids, but now they're no longer here I . . .'

Whoa. Shouldn't have married each other in the first place?

'I want to move out. I've met someone else.'

'The blonde woman,' she said stupidly. Derrr. Ten out of ten, Catherine. Well spotted.

'Yes. Rebecca.'

There was a deafening silence. Blood pounded in her ears. She thought for a moment she might faint. 'Is this really . . .' She swallowed. 'Are you serious?'

'Well, I'm hardly going to joke about it, am I?' The sharpness of his tone cut her to the quick.

'I . . .' She was gaping like a halfwit. 'I don't understand.'

He got to his feet. 'I don't love you,' he said, slowly and deliberately. 'Do you understand that? You trapped me, getting pregnant. I never wanted any of this.'

Tears dribbled from her eyes. She sank into the armchair, her legs suddenly weak. 'But . . .'

'Look,' he said, exasperated. 'We reached the end of the road years ago. We both know it. This is the best thing for both of us – there's no point struggling on, being unhappy together for the rest of our lives.'

Unhappy? Did he really think that? Every marriage had its ups and downs. That was life. Wasn't it?

'I'll be back in a few days to get some more of my stuff,' he said. 'Bye, Catherine.'

Chapter Five

L'investigatrice – The detective

Anna hadn't got very far in her quest to track down her mysterious Italian father. Annoyingly, it turned out that Pete was right, and Gino was an extremely popular first name in Italy; there were tens of thousands of them. She would need a lot more information if she was ever going to narrow the field.

Her grandmother hadn't been much help, other than the initial slip of the tongue that had started all of this. Anna had returned to the care home several times since, hoping to jog her memory with different techniques, but nothing had come of the venture other than to thoroughly confuse her. Despite the dementia, there was clearly some lockdown in Nora's head which meant that she would go on loyally protecting her secrets the best she could till the end.

Anna had spoken twice more to her mum on the phone, but each time she had bottled out of asking her outright for information. Still, Anna was a journalist, wasn't she? She could uncover a story better than most people. There had to be a way around it.

'Colin,' she said to the most senior writer on the paper one November morning. 'If you were looking for a person and only had a first name to go on, what would you do about it?'

'Give up,' he replied, deadpan. Colin, who'd had a long career as an investigative journalist for the BBC up in Edinburgh, as well as a stint as a crime correspondent for the *Telegraph*, was one for telling it straight.

'Oh. Right. But if you did decide to pursue it, I mean, what would you do to track them down? Where would you start?'

'If all I had to go on was a first name? I wouldn't bother starting at all. It would be impossible.' His white, bushy eyebrows twitched with the beginnings of a frown. He could be something of a curmudgeon, Colin, especially if you bothered him before his lunchtime pint.

'Who are you looking for, Anna?' asked Joe, one of the sports writers, ambling through the office with a coffee just then. 'Don't tell me someone's done the dirty on you.'

Anna, who had returned dispiritedly to writing copy on the big Christmas light switch-on due next week, looked up and gave a wan smile. 'Not exactly,' she said. 'It's my dad.'

She hadn't meant to be so transparent but there was something about amiable, friendly Joe that always disarmed her. He was all long limbs and cheekbones, and half the girls in the office fancied him with his chiselled face and black hair cut in a cool mod crop. 'Oh,' he said, halting and looking awkward. 'Sorry – I didn't mean to pry.'

'It's all right,' she said. She was aware that several other pairs of ears had pricked up around the office; there was suddenly an intense, alert silence. Every journalist was a nosey parker, it was part of the job description. 'I've never known him – I don't know anything about him. But I've recently discovered he's called Gino, and he's Italian. Well, he was, anyway. He might have snuffed it by now, of course.'

'Wow,' said Joe. He perched on the edge of her desk. 'That must be weird.'

'Yeah,' Anna replied. 'You could say that.'

'So you're half-Italian? Cool.'

'I know. That's the good bit. The bad bit is . . . well, not knowing anything else.'

Colin raised an eyebrow. Even the grumpiest hack couldn't resist a tantalizing story. 'If you ask me, there's only one thing for it.'

'What's that? And don't say "give up" again because I don't think I can.'

'You have to return to the source,' Colin told her. 'In other words, ask your mother to tell you the truth.'

Anna pulled a face. 'If only it was so easy, Col. Believe me, I've tried before.'

'Worth trying again though, surely,' Colin said mildly. 'All the best stories take a bit of digging to unearth. Ask the right questions, you never know what you might find out.'

'I suppose, but . . .' An image of Anna's mother, tight-lipped, shaking her head crossly, appeared in her mind. It was not going to be an easy conversation. She might even end up losing the one parent she did have if her mum got the hump.

'Good luck,' Joe said, getting up and wandering away. 'Or rather, *buona fortuna.*'

'What's that when it's at home?'

'Good luck in Italian, isn't it?' Joe replied. He tutted at her in mock-disapproval. 'Thought you'd know that, with your Italian heritage and all. Keep up, Morley.'

Anna went back to her work, but Joe's words had struck a chord. *Your Italian heritage.* It sounded great. What was more, he was right. She owed it to herself to find out more about her father's country.

Abandoning the Christmas lights again, she opened up a search engine and typed 'Learn Italian'. She might not have got very far with finding her father yet, but she could at least make sure she was ready to speak to him when she did.

It seemed she had missed the boat with an Italian language course – all the colleges had started new ones in September, most of which ran through until summer. Ahh – not quite all. Hurst College, an adult education centre, offered a three-month 'Beginners' Italian: Conversation' course starting in January.

'That'll do,' she murmured, whipping out her Visa card

and signing up there and then. Afterwards she hesitated, reluctant to put her credit card back in her wallet just yet. January was ages away. She needed something to chew on in the meantime.

Back she went to her list of search results. You could study great Italian architecture at the university – hmm, that was a module in a degree, maybe not. There was a course in Italian history too, but that was less her thing. Then she saw it. Giovanni's, a lovely deli on Sharrowvale Road, ran Italian cookery courses in their kitchens above the premises. *Rustic Italian Suppers. Fresh Pasta. Classic Italian Desserts.*

Her stomach rumbled. This was more like it. She loved Italian food! With a few quick clicks, she signed up for an 'Introduction to Italian Cooking' course the Saturday after next. Then, hearing the brisk clip-clopping of high heels in the vicinity, she hastily closed the browser. That sound meant only one thing: Imogen, her editor, on the prowl, and those laser eyes of hers never missed a skiving worker.

Anna returned to her boring article about the mysterious special guest who was switching on this year's Christmas lights, looking every inch the diligent hack as her fingers ran across the keyboard. Her mind, though, was a feast of home-made pesto and chocolate truffles and an Italian chef kissing his fingertips and exclaiming over her culinary skills. Maybe she'd turn out to be a natural. Maybe there was this hidden depth to her, previously unseen. 'Well, my father's Italian,' she imagined telling the others in the class airily. 'I must get it from him.'

Then she remembered that she was never actually going to meet this father of hers unless she took action. 'Return to the source,' Colin had advised. Like it or not, that seemed her only option. She was going to have to bite the bullet and approach her mum.

Tracey Morley was now Tracey Waldon, having married Graham Waldon five years ago. The two of them lived in a quiet suburb of Leeds with their sulky ginger cat Lambert (Butler, Lambert's brother, had gone to meet his maker the year before) and Graham's extensive cacti collection.

Although it had always been just the two of them during Anna's childhood, mother and daughter were not bonded at the hip as you might expect. Theirs was not a cosy relationship of daily chats on the phone and long gossipy lunches or spa days in white waffle robes like some of her friends and their mums. This was fine. Anna knew that her mum loved the very bones of her and would leap in front of a speeding bus to push her to safety if need be, but Tracey was tough too, suspicious of any touchy-feely stuff. She held her cards close to her chest, always had done.

'Christmas shopping?' Tracey repeated doubtfully when Anna rang to suggest meeting up. 'What, us two?'

'I thought it would be nice to do something together,'

Anna said, slightly wounded that her idea hadn't been welcomed with open arms. 'We don't have to actually *buy* Christmas presents or anything,' she went on, when her mum didn't reply immediately. 'We can just have lunch and a chat, you know.'

There was a suspicious silence. 'Oh God,' her mum said suddenly. 'Are you pregnant, Anna? Is that what this is all about?'

'No!'

'Because I did think you were looking a bit chubby about the face last time we saw each other, and I said to Graham, you wait, I think our Anna's going to have some news for us soon. And—'

'Mum! MUM! I am not pregnant!' She hunched over the phone, wishing she hadn't made this call in the office. Her colleagues must be having a field day with so much personal information flying around. 'For heaven's sake! Can I not suggest a coffee or lunch without you jumping to ridiculous conclusions?' She rolled her eyes at Marla whose desk was opposite, and Marla grinned back, clearly enjoying the show.

'All right, calm down, I was only wondering,' Tracey replied. 'Thank Christ for that, though. No offence, but I'm not ready to be a grandma just yet, thank you very much.'

'Don't worry, there's no chance of it happening any time soon,' Anna said dryly. However disloyal this made her, she actually felt faintly nauseous at the thought of carrying Pete's baby. A mini-Pete, who would draw up a spreadsheet and score her on her inept mothering attempts, no doubt. 'So anyway. Meeting up. Why don't we go to the Living Room for lunch?'

'Blimey, that's a bit posh, isn't it?' her mum said. 'Are you *sure* there's nothing going on? You're not trying to sweeten me up before confessing some terrible crime you've committed, are you?'

'All right, we'll go to Maccy D's if you'd rather,' Anna snapped. 'Or we can bring our own flipping packed lunches! It was only an idea.' She was on the verge of lapsing into teenage petulance – *I won't bother next time!* – but managed to bite it back. This was supposed to be a charm offensive after all; she didn't want to blow it before they'd even been given the menus.

'Keep your hair on! I can do posh. I was only saying.'

'Brilliant,' Anna said through gritted teeth. 'So I'll book a table for one-ish and text you to confirm, okay? Look forward to seeing you then.'

'Me too. I think.'

Anna arrived in Leeds half an hour early on Saturday so popped into the big Waterstones on Albion Street to while away some time. She walked straight past all the tables of new fiction and headed for the travel section. Maybe it wasn't just about asking the right questions, she thought, searching the shelves for what she needed. Maybe it was about coming prepared with a few props as well.

The next twenty minutes vanished as she lost herself leafing through travel guides and maps. She gazed at the colour photos, drinking in the sights: the splendour of Rome, the glorious scarlet poppy fields of Tuscany, beautiful unique Venice, the wild coastline and magnificent beaches . . . Oh, she loved it all. The best thing was, this was her country too now. She felt such a strong pull to the place, it almost came as a surprise to look up from the pages and find herself still in Yorkshire. Glancing at her watch she realized she would be late if she didn't hurry, so she paid quickly for her purchases and left.

The Living Room was a smart, classy restaurant. Anna had been once before during a friend's hen weekend, and it wasn't the sort of place her mum would be able to storm out of mid-hissy-fit. She hoped.

Tracey was already there when Anna arrived, sipping a cappuccino at a corner table while filling in a Sudoku game on her phone. 'Hi, love,' she said, rising to kiss Anna's cheek.

'Sorry I'm late,' Anna said, shaking off her damp coat and hanging it on the back of her chair. 'I got distracted buying books. Planning a holiday.'

'You and Pete? Where are you thinking of going?'

'Italy,' Anna replied. There. She'd said it already, before she'd even sat down. Her heart raced as she checked her mum's face and body language for any kind of reaction. 'Have you ever been?'

'Me? Yeah. Years back, before you were born. Girls' holiday, me and your Aunty Marie. Two weeks in Rimini, it was bloody magic.' She looked wistful, and Anna's fingers felt clammy as she pulled her new guidebooks from the bag.

'Rimini. Where's that then?' she asked, oh-so-casual, swallowing back the other, more obvious questions bubbling up inside. Caution – that was what this was all about. Stealth. No sudden moves. No blurting out 'Where did you meet my dad then?', much as she was dying to. To her surprise, the approach actually seemed to be working.

'It's in the north, I think. Give that here, I'll find it on a map. Smashing beaches.' She flicked through the pages then stopped and looked at Anna quizzically. 'Hang on, I thought Pete wasn't keen on "abroad". How did you manage to talk him into it?'

'Oh . . .' Damn. She hadn't thought this through very well. And she definitely didn't want to go off on a tangent about Pete, she wanted to get back to Rimini and her mum's memories. 'I haven't told him yet, to be honest. Working up to that bit. I thought I'd suss it all out first and then present him with this dream holiday. So if you reckon Rimini's a good bet . . .' Had she got away with that?

'It's lovely. Probably changed a bit since I was there – God, over thirty years ago, that's a scary thought.'

Over thirty years ago. Yes, that fitted. 'And you never went back?'

Tracey narrowed her eyes. 'Well, no, because then you came along, didn't you? I didn't have the money to go jetting abroad after that.'

'Sorry,' Anna said automatically, but her skin was prickling. *No, because then you came along, didn't you?* Oh. Em. Gee. Her mother had practically admitted it: an Italian holiday romance ending in an unexpected pregnancy. No wonder she'd never wanted to talk about Anna's father. She'd have had to admit she didn't even know where he lived!

'No need to apologize, you daft thing,' her mum said, interrupting Anna's train of thought. 'It wasn't your fault.'

'No.' Anna took a deep breath. 'The thing is, Mum—'

'I could do with a holiday myself, to be honest. Get away from it all. Bit of winter sunshine would be lovely right now.'

'Yes.' Anna clutched her knees under the table and braced herself. *Just ask her.* 'Mum . . . I was wondering . . .'

'It's been so cold lately, hasn't it? Two duvets on the bed, we've got at the moment, *and* one of them is a super-tog-doodah or whatever they're called.' Tracey broke off and fixed her with an intense gaze. 'Are you okay? You look a bit odd. Peaky. Are you coming down with something?'

'I'm fine, Mum. Listen, I wanted to ask you—'

'Maybe you and Pete should bring your holiday forward, that's all. Go sooner rather than later. Although I'm not sure how warm it'll be in Italy right now, mind.' She traced the cover of the guidebook, a dreamy expression on her face.

Anna lost her nerve. Maybe this was too public a place to start asking blunt questions after all. A new approach was called for. 'I hadn't thought about what time of year would be best to go,' she said, her mind working quickly. 'I've heard July and August are roasting. Maybe going earlier would be better, say, June?' She crossed her fingers under the table, hoping her mum would take the bait. Ka-ching! Jackpot.

'When were *we* there? Let me think. I've got a feeling it was June for us too. That's right, because Marie had just finished her A-levels, and . . .' A strange look passed across her face. 'Anyway. Check in your book, that's the best idea. But not now, yeah? Let's decide what we're going to eat, I'm starving.'

They both studied the menu but Anna could hardly read the words. Oh my goodness. This was totally stacking up. If Mum and Marie went in June, it tallied completely with her mum getting pregnant there. Her birthday was in March, exactly nine months later. And there was no denying that weird look on her mum's face just then. In a split-second she had turned all shifty and secretive, clearly doing what Anna had just done, counting nine months back from her date of birth. The jigsaw was coming together so much easier than Anna had ever anticipated. Although . . . Wait. She still needed to check out the exact year, just to be sure.

'Still,' she said breezily, as if it had just occurred to her. 'If you're going to take a last fabulous holiday before you have a baby, it sounds like that's a good place to do it.'

There was silence from Tracey, and Anna hid her smile behind the open menu. Mum certainly wasn't denying the fact that it had been her last holiday before motherhood. Proof. More proof!

She began reading through the list of anti-pasti, trying to concentrate on the food options. 'Are you having a starter?' she asked.

Silence. Lowering the menu, she saw her mother's aghast expression. 'What?'

'So you *are* going to have a baby,' Tracey replied. She was not radiating grandmotherly joy, it had to be said. More like pity.

'Eh?'

'Last fabulous holiday before you have a baby – you just said it. Oh, Anna. Have you thought this through?'

'No, I meant—'

'Don't make the mistake I did. Ach, that sounds terrible. You were not a *mistake* as such . . .'

'Mum, no, you've got it wrong.'

'Well, okay, yes, you were an accident – a surprise! – but I've never not wanted you. Being a parent is hard work though, and you and Pete . . . Are you really cut out to do this? I mean, you're not even living together.'

'Mum! I—'

'Is he going to move in with you? Only, with the best will in the world, there's not a lot of room in that flat, is there? Certainly not enough for three of you.'

'MUM! Stop. You've got the wrong end of the stick. We . . .' Anna sighed. 'Do you know what? I give up. Whatever. I'm having the chicken skewers to start, then the monkfish. How about you?'

Chapter Six

A casa – At home

Sophie had been back in the UK for a whole fortnight, to her and everyone else's surprise. It was the longest she'd spent in Sheffield for years. She'd only planned to spend a day or two there, to see her dad, but almost as soon as she'd arrived he'd come down with a chest infection and become quite ill. Even the hardest-hearted person couldn't have walked away.

At first she'd checked herself into a backpacker hostel, much to the palpable relief of her mum. But the place was full of exuberant Aussies and Kiwis, living it up away from home, getting loudly hammered every night. Fair enough; she'd done exactly the same when she'd worked her way round Australia and New Zealand, partying every step of the way. She didn't have the slightest inclination to join them on the lash now, though, not when she was freaking out that her dad was going to die.

Aware that she was killing the mood in the shared dorm with her fuming and dagger-eyes, she paid extra to move into a single room, but that wasn't much better. Now she was right at the front of the building, overlooking a noisy road. If it wasn't the raucous party animals waking her at two in the morning, it was the buses and lorries trundling by outside.

'You look done in, love,' her dad commented when she visited him after yet another sleepless night. She popped in every day; there wasn't much else for her to do. She'd lost touch with all her old school friends and there were only so many times you could wander round a city when it was raining and you were skint.

'Says you with a drip and a heart monitor,' Sophie replied. 'Thanks a bunch.'

'No, really. Where are you staying? Are you actually staying anywhere? Tell me it's not a park bench or something.'

'Dad! Give me some credit. I'm not sleeping on a park bench. I don't look that rough, do I?' God! She'd managed to look after herself for the last eight years all around the world, for heaven's sake.

He took her hand affectionately, and his fingers felt as warm and strong as ever, belying his current frailty. He'd always been the soppiest of her parents, the one she turned to for advice – until she'd discovered he'd betrayed her every bit as much as her mum, that was. Her hand stiffened in his grasp as she remembered how hurt she'd been, how shocked that he'd colluded against her. 'C'mon, Soph,' he said now. 'Why don't you just stay with your mum? I know the three of us have—'

'No way.'

'. . . have had our disagreements in the past, but—'

'Yeah, and the rest, Dad.' Disagreements indeed. That was one way of putting it.

'But you're our *daughter*. We want to look after you.'

Sophie looked away. She could almost believe him when he said things like this, but her mum still acted cold and distant whenever they were in the same room. Whatever he might say, there was no way Trish wanted her home, end of story. Besides, Sophie was too proud to go back there anyway, even if the red carpet was rolled out for her. Even if her mum got down on her knees and begged.

'What about money? Have you got enough to live on?'

'Of course I have!' She crossed her fingers behind her back.

'Let me give you a sub,' he said, the persistent old bugger. Even in the throes of severe ill-health he wouldn't let it go. He reached out for the bedside cupboard. 'My wallet's in there somewhere.'

'Dad, honestly, I don't want your money.' No way would she take it. She hadn't had a penny off them for years, and wasn't about to change that now, even though, in all honesty, she was almost broke. She had to start making decisions, and fast. If she stayed in Sheffield too much longer, her cash would all be blown on the crappy hostel. Then what would she do?

'You've got savings, then? Some rainy day money?'

'Yes, I've got a bit. Enough. Don't worry, I'm fine. Really.'

'Sorry. Humour me though, eh? It's been a while since I got to fuss over you in person.'

She said nothing. *And why was that then, Dad?*

Trish, Sophie's mum, came in just then. 'Oh,' she said, as she always did when she saw Sophie. It was the same tone you might use when noticing bird poo on the car – one of displeasure and mild annoyance. 'Good morning. How did you sleep, Jim? Nurse said she thought you had a better night.'

'I slept like a log,' he replied cheerfully. 'I was just telling our Soph that she's the one who looks like she needs a proper kip.'

Her mum's face was impassive. Probably thought Sophie's dark circles were caused by her being up all night at some wild party or other. *You've only got yourself to blame.* 'Mmm,' she said, as if the subject didn't particularly interest her.

'I was saying, I think she should stay with you for a bit,' Jim added, the bloody great stirrer. Sophie glared at him but he seemed impervious. 'You know, it would make a dying man very happy, seeing you two sort out your differences.'

Neither of them was about to put up with this sort of talk. 'Jim! You're not dying!'

'Don't *say* things like that!' Their voices tumbled together, equally horrified.

'Please,' Trish begged. 'Don't even joke about it.'

'You can lay off the guilt-tripping and all,' Sophie told him.

His eyes twinkled. 'So you agree about something, at least,' he said craftily.

Sophie and her mum looked at one another, a strained, uneasy atmosphere between them. Then Trish pursed her lips. 'Look, if you do need somewhere to stay,' she said unexpectedly, 'well . . . it's daft to pay out good money when you could be home, isn't it? It's just plain silly.'

The room seemed to be holding its breath, waiting for Sophie's response. *Home*, her mum had said. Not any more it wasn't.

'That's very kind,' she began stiffly, 'but—'

'Oh for crying out loud,' said Jim, just as she was about to invent an imaginary friend she could stay with. 'Do I have to drop dead before you two start speaking to each other like human beings again? Please! Can you not do this one thing for me?'

'Don't get overexcited, Jim,' Trish warned.

'All right,' Sophie mumbled.

'I'm just saying—'

'I said, all right!' Sophie's voice came out louder than she'd intended. 'Fine,' she added in a quieter tone. 'Obviously I'll pay you board and lodging,' she said, as a last stab at independence.

'You'll do no such thing,' her mum told her. Stubbornness was rather a theme in the Frost family.

'Good,' Jim said, looking exhausted all of a sudden. He shut his eyes and Sophie noticed how pale his face was against the pillow. 'I'm going to have a kip now,' he murmured, as if his work here was done. 'See you later.'

Sophie and her mum looked at one another. 'Well,' said Trish uncertainly.

'Well,' echoed Sophie.

'I'll leave him to it for a bit,' Trish said. 'I need to pop into town anyway. I'll pick up a few things.' She hesitated. 'Fancy a chop for tea?'

'I'm vegetarian,' Sophie said, then felt bad for the injured expression that appeared on her mum's face. *Try harder, Sophie.* 'Maybe I could cook us something instead. Save you the hassle.'

Trish looked as if she was about to argue, but then glanced back down at Jim who was frowning slightly, eyes still shut. 'That would be . . . nice,' she said weakly. 'Thank you.'

Sophie went to pick up her stuff from the hostel then got the bus up the Fulwood Road to her parents' house in Ranmoor later that afternoon. There were the houses and shops she'd walked past a million times looking both familiar yet different at the same time. She could almost hear the sound of rollerskates whizzing as she remembered how she and Kirsty, the girl next door, had zoomed around together on these streets, hand in hand, squealing as they careered along. She'd had her first cigarette skulking in that bus shelter (coughing and spluttering, green in the face) and drank her first underage half-pint of lager in the Gladstone Arms up the road. And now here she was again, getting nearer her parents' house with every step.

Oh God. It had seemed the right thing to do back at the hospital – the *only* thing to do, when her dad had fixed her with that imploring expression – but now she was bitterly regretting caving in to his whim. She hesitated outside the pub, suddenly longing for a vodka tonic to take the edge off things. Then she opened her purse and gazed at the meagre contents. Three tenners, a crumpled fiver, some pound coins and a handful of silver. Thirty-nine pounds. That was it.

'There you are!' called a voice from behind her just then, as a young, good-looking mixed-race guy with a buzz cut came out of the pub.

Sophie thought he was talking to her for a minute, but then saw a woman approaching, wearing a black bomber jacket with skinny jeans and thigh boots, her long, dark hair pulled up in a messy bun. 'Freddie!' she called, hurrying over to him. The two of them kissed passionately right there in the doorway of the pub, hands sliding all over each other. Sophie turned her gaze away. It had been a long time since anyone had held her like that. Three years and two months, in fact: Dan, in Sydney. But she didn't think about him any more, she reminded herself.

She shoved her purse back in her bag and walked reluctantly past the pub. 'Here goes nothing,' she muttered under her breath as she went on up the road.

Trisha Frost obviously didn't trust her daughter's ability in the kitchen because the fridge was full of Waitrose vegetarian ready meals. Sophie, who was used to existing on the tightest of tight budgets, even if that meant eating noodles seven days a week, wasn't sure whether to be thrilled (massive treat) or scandalized (massive waste of money). Hunger won out though. Everything looked bloody delicious.

'Thanks, Mum,' she said as Trish showed her where the biscuits were kept (like she would have forgotten *that!*) and the new extension which housed the utility room and a downstairs loo.

'Just leave any washing in the basket here,' Trish told her. 'I do the ironing on Sundays, so if there's anything you want doing . . .'

'It's fine, Mum, honestly.'

'Dinner will be at six,' Trish went on, 'and I'd appreciate it if you didn't smoke in the house. That includes leaning out your bedroom window to do it. It makes the curtains stink.'

'I don't smoke,' Sophie said, taken aback. 'Haven't done for years.' God, they really didn't know each other at all. This woman might have the same green eyes and small nose as her, but she felt like a total stranger. 'And I meant it, about cooking,' she added. 'Why don't we take turns? I promise I've moved on from when I used to set off the fire alarm every time I fried an egg.'

Trish didn't reply. 'I've put the portable television in your room,' she went on, 'and by the way, the shower is a bit temperamental. The hot water cycles around, so don't panic if it suddenly goes cold when you're in there. It won't be for long.'

'Okay.'

'I thought I'd pop back to see your dad after dinner. I could give you a lift if you want to come along too.'

'Great. Thanks.'

'Right then. I'll let you unpack.'

Sophie's breath caught in her throat as she walked into her old bedroom. There was the same red and black zigzag-patterned duvet on the bed, the same matching curtains, the same soft blue carpet, but everything else had changed. The smell of Impulse and patchouli had been replaced by one of laundry powder, the walls were now clear of posters, the chest of drawers empty of the tangle of jewellery and make-up that had littered its surface. It was quiet, too; she'd had music booming out at all times, prompting regular screams of 'Turn that racket DOWN please, Sophie!'

She gave herself a shake, surprised by the sudden rush of emotion she felt. Don't be daft, Sophie. It's only a room.

Unpacking didn't take long – it never did – but her few clothes looked shabby and past-it here in the relatively luxurious setting of her parents' home. She wasn't sure whether to bundle everything straight into the washing machine or torch the lot. The former, she decided, remembering that she had no money to buy replacements. Still, it would be a huge treat to have a washing machine at her disposal again, rather than having to handwash everything and hang it out in the sun to dry. Not to mention the combined delights of soaking in a hot bath, a fridge full of food, British TV . . .

She glanced over at the portable television her mum had left on the chest of drawers. Did that mean she was not allowed to watch the big flatscreen she'd glimpsed downstairs, then? Was the plan that they'd be sitting in separate rooms every evening?

Oh Lord. For all the creature comforts, it was going to be very *un*comfortable living under the same roof as her mum for any amount of time. The sooner they were out of each other's lives again, the better. But to do that, she needed some money . . .

She took her laptop downstairs. 'Do you have wifi here?' she asked, opening it up on the kitchen table.

Trish hesitated. 'Yes,' she said guardedly.

'Can I have the password, please? I'm going to start looking for a job.'

Trish's mouth fell open. 'You're looking for a job? Here in Sheffield?'

Sophie shrugged. 'I can't exactly go abroad again while Dad's still ill, can I?'

Trish muttered something which might have been 'Never stopped you before.'

'Pardon?'

'Nothing.'

Sophie gritted her teeth. 'Don't worry, I'll be out of here as soon as I can. I don't like this any more than you do.'

'I never said—'

'Yeah, well, you didn't have to. Look, I need to earn some money so I can go travelling again. Hopefully there'll be a bit of Christmas work going at one of the shops or cafés in town.'

'Oh. Do you think you'll be here that long?'

Sophie bristled. 'Why? Is that a problem?' Just give me the frigging password, she thought impatiently. Was everything going to be such a power struggle?

'No, of course it's not a problem,' said Trish, although her voice conveyed the exact opposite. 'Here.' She unpinned a small card from the kitchen noticeboard with the wifi log-in details and put it next to Sophie.

'Thank you.' Just like the old days, it seemed impossible

to have an ordinary conversation with her mum without some petty sniping in the mix. Staying here was going to be more exhausting than the hostel, she could tell already.

'Sophie's looking for a job,' Trish said to Jim that evening when they went back to visit him.

'Oh aye? Where are you off to this time? And can I come with you? I could do with some sunshine to shake off this cough.'

Sophie scowled at her mum. It wasn't that her job quest was a state secret or anything, but she didn't like the way Trish had announced it, with a hint of mockery as if it was all a big joke. 'I'm not off anywhere yet. That's why I need a job.'

'Ahh.' He thought about this for a moment. 'Where do you think you'll go next time, then? Any ideas?'

'Maybe a ski resort over the winter,' she replied. 'Or I might save a bit more and travel around south-east Asia for a few months. Wherever the wind takes me.'

He nodded, his eyes on her keenly. 'And then what? Are you just planning to keep on moving, year after year, until you're my age? Do you never think about putting down roots, making a go of anything properly?'

The questions felt like an attack. *Making a go of anything properly?* That was a bit harsh.

'Dad, you have no idea what I've been doing for the last few years,' she said, hackles rising.

'I do, actually. I know quite a lot. What's it called again, that blog of yours? "Independent Traveller", is it?'

'You . . . You've been reading my blog?'

'Well, of course we have. It's up there for the world to see, isn't it? How glad you are to be shot of your interfering parents, how delighted you are to be free of the shackles of home life . . .' His eyes narrowed. 'How lonely you've been at times. How you hate having to pretend that you're having a wonderful adventure when occasionally you're downright miserable.'

'How . . . ? But . . .' She couldn't actually speak for a moment, just gaped. Oh shit. They'd *read* it?

'What are you running away from, Soph?' he asked, gentler now. 'Surely not us any more. Yourself?'

'I'm not running away from anything!' she cried, feeling as if she was a teenager all over again. Why couldn't they just get off her back? 'What's it to do with you anyway?' Then she whirled around and rushed out of the room.

She ran blindly down the corridor, her heart pounding, her breath tight and short in her lungs. The thought of her parents spying on her like that, reading about her intimate experiences – and some had been *really* intimate – was mortifying. How could they? How *dare* they?

Leaning against a wall, she shut her eyes, feeling sick as detail after detail flashed up in her mind. So they'd have read about her being hospitalized in Wellington when she came off her bike and was knocked unconscious. They'd have read about her tempestuous affair with Dan, and how broken she'd been left afterwards. And they'd have read all the nasty stuff about *them,* too; she'd savagely ripped them apart in print, blaming them for her hang-ups, mocking them for their dull suburban lives.

Shit. She thought she might throw up. No wonder her mum had been so off with her. No wonder she'd freaked out when Sophie had asked about the wifi code – she probably thought a new blog entry was in the making, all about how dreadful it was to be back *chez* Mum and Dad!

The impulse to run beat loudly through her. She'd known all along she wasn't welcome back in Ranmoor. She'd collect her stuff then get a train somewhere and start afresh. Her dad was on the mend, wasn't he? Anywhere was better than here.

Then she hesitated. It was already eight in the evening and dark outside. A horrible sleety rain had pelted them as they'd dashed from the car park to the hospital; her coat was still wet. Besides, she only had thirty or so quid left. She was trapped.

She pushed a hand through her short blonde hair, trying to make a decision, her dad's words still echoing in her head. *What are you running away from, Soph? Surely not us any more. Yourself?*

Chapter Seven

Una amica – A friend (female)

After Mike left, Catherine did nothing but lie unmoving in bed, tears leaking into the pillow. The world seemed to have shrunk around her to the lavender-painted walls of her bedroom, a telescope closing up as she lay there, willing Mike to come back. He didn't.

Any minute now, she kept thinking, I'll wake up from this terrible dream and it'll be Sunday morning again, with the twins still here, ready to go to uni. Because this can't have happened in real life. It just can't.

But the clock went on ticking, quiet and insistent. The room became darker as night fell, then suffused with pinky-gold light when the sun rose. Cars growled outside as people went to work. Footsteps clicked down the street.

Any minute now, she thought, I'll hear his key in the door. He'll bring flowers, apologies, explanations. He'll tell me how sorry he is, how wrong he was.

He didn't.

On Monday, she peeled herself out of bed and made a

few phone calls. The care home, to say that she wouldn't be in to do her voluntary shift. The primary school, to say she couldn't read with the Year 3s that afternoon. The charity shop, to say she'd fallen ill and wouldn't be able to help out for a few days. Flu. Really bad flu.

Exhausted by all the lies and at a loss for what to do next, she turned to the computer and opened up a search engine.

I feel s— she typed and a whole list of options appeared.

I feel sick

I feel suicidal

I feel so lonely

I feel sad

God, there was so much pain on the internet. So many unhappy souls calling out for comfort.

I feel scared she typed, and again more options popped up.

I feel scared all the time

I feel scared

I feel scared for no reason

I feel scared and alone

Tears pricked her eyes. All of the above, she thought, as a list of mental health websites appeared below the prompt box, along with the Samaritans helpline number and various anxiety forums. The letters blurred and swam, her brain too fogged to make any sense of them.

She backspaced through her words and took a deep breath.

My husband left me she typed, her fingers shaking, and a new string of results appeared instantly.

My husband left me for another woman

My husband left me for a man

My husband left me after I cheated

All those leaving husbands, all those front doors slammed, all those wives left behind, weeping and lonely. It would have been enough to break your heart if Catherine's wasn't already pulverized.

She switched off the computer, unable to cope with anybody else's misery, then went back to bed and pulled the covers over her head.

Mike had been living in a grungey student house in Nottingham when Catherine eventually tracked him down and broke the news that she was pregnant. His eyes had bulged in horror. 'You're fucking kidding me,' he said.

'I'm not,' Catherine replied.

Left to his own devices, Catherine suspected Mike would have washed his hands of her and the babies, but Shirley wasn't about to let him – or Catherine – off the hook. They were married just two months later. 'God has willed it,' she said simply, drawing up the invitation list and unearthing her best hat. 'As ye sow, so shall ye reap.'

All Catherine's friends thought she had lost the plot. 'Are you sure you want to do this?' they kept asking fearfully, eyes darting to her swollen belly. 'You really want to give up uni and be a *wife*?'

Her mum thought she was nuts, too. She had split up with Catherine's dad many years earlier and since then had made no bones about the fact that she preferred cats to men. 'You're only twenty, darling. Don't write yourself off with a bloke and kiddies yet, whatever you do.'

Buffeted by the rollercoaster she seemed to be on – the exhausting pregnancy, the wedding, the plans to live with Mike's parents while he continued his degree in Nottingham ('I think it'll be for the best,' Shirley said in the no-arguments voice Catherine had already come to dread) – Catherine felt powerless to make any decisions, as if she'd had her chance at a life and blown it. 'I'll finish my degree another year,' she promised her friends vaguely, but she already knew she wouldn't.

It had not been an easy time. Shirley was firmly in the 'You've made your bed now lie on it' camp and, when the babies arrived, she left Catherine to cope with them alone, all day every day, while she busied herself organizing prayer sessions for starving children in Uganda in the nearby church hall. The first few months were a blur of snatched naps, feeding, nappies and long, limb-aching walks around the local park in an attempt to soothe the babies to sleep. Her student life of essays and lectures and parties seemed very far away, on another galaxy, impossibly out of reach.

Once Mike graduated, he came to join her in Sheffield and she thought the balance might even out between them, especially when they moved into their own little house – but no. He was working insane hours trying to prove himself in his first job at the hospital. She, on the other hand, felt like a milch-cow put out to pasture. Although for a while she clung to the faint hope of returning to university, she never did. After a few years, she stopped mentioning it altogether.

'What do you need a degree for anyway?' Mike once asked. 'It's not like you were ever going to be an academic. Besides, who would look after the kids?'

It wasn't until Tuesday, when the doorbell rang insistently, followed by some energetic knocking, that the real world intruded. 'Cath? Are you in there? Catherine!'

Catherine jerked at the noise. The voice was strident and loud. It was Penny, she realized, Penny from down the road, with whom she played tennis every Tuesday. Was it Tuesday already? It must be.

She staggered out of bed and pushed open the bedroom window. Her hair was lank and straggling, her body unwashed; her tears had probably worn grooves into her face. 'Oh, Pen,' she began. 'I . . .' She meant to say she was unwell again – flu, really bad flu – but she was caught off guard and the lie refused to trip off her tongue.

Penny tipped her head back and stared up at Catherine in

alarm. She was used to seeing Catherine clean and wholesome, with lipstick and a sensible coat, not like something recently exhumed. 'Bloody Nora, you look terrible, girl,' she said, as tactful and sensitive as ever. 'What the frig is up with you?'

'I'm . . .' To Catherine's horror, tears plopped from her eyes and onto the roof of her car below. Drip drop drip drop, little puddles on the Toyota. 'I'm . . .'

'Let me in,' Penny ordered. 'Let me in this minute. You need sorting out.'

Catherine had never been very good at covering up. Her resistance was at an all-time low, too. It was only a matter of seconds, therefore, before Penny was in her kitchen, making them both strong coffee and hunting out the last few chocolate digestives with the air of a woman well used to crisis management.

'Go on then, tell me,' Penny said, plonking down their steaming mugs and sitting opposite her at the old scrubbed pine table. Tall and rangy, she had a glossy black bob with an electric-blue streak in the fringe, and sharp brown eyes that didn't miss a thing. 'What in chuff's name has happened?'

Catherine obediently told her. It took two whole biscuits to get the story out, with a brief pause for nose-blowing, eye-dabbing and a hug from Penny that was so tight and strong she could have had King Kong in a headlock.

'Flaming hell,' said Penny. 'And here's me thinking you had a dodgy tummy or were missing the children. I wasn't expecting any of *that.*'

'Nor was I,' said Catherine, her voice wobbling.

'Oh, love,' said Penny, putting a hand on hers. 'He must be having one of those mid-life crises. He'll be back by the end of the week, I bet you, tail between his legs, begging your forgiveness.'

'He said he'd never loved me, Penny, that I'd trapped him by getting pregnant. He said we should never have got married.'

Penny sucked in a breath. 'That's just nasty. Bloody men, they've got no idea, have they?'

'It was probably my fault,' Catherine ventured in a small voice.

'Bollocks, was it,' Penny told her. 'Your fault that he's been such a bastard? Don't give me that shite.'

Nobody had ever called Mike a bastard in Catherine's presence before. He was a doctor, a pillar of the community, her *husband.* 'He's not a . . .' she began, automatically leaping to his defence.

Penny raised an eyebrow. 'He shags another woman and tells you he's never loved you? He totally is a bastard, love. I'm sorry, I don't want to hurt your feelings, but that's pretty much as bastard as bastard gets.'

Catherine's head was ringing with all this bastardliness. She opened her mouth to speak but nothing came out.

Penny squeezed her hand. 'Don't worry, you'll get over him,' she said. 'Good riddance. And you've got me to look after you in the meantime.'

'I don't think I need . . .'

'You do. Trust me, you do. Now, I'm your friend, Cath, so I'm allowed to ask: when was the last time you ate a proper meal?'

It was hard to remember when she'd last done anything that felt ordinary. 'Saturday?' she guessed.

'And no offence, love, but you don't half pong. Have you actually washed recently? Be honest now.'

'Not really.'

'Yeah. As I thought. Go and have a shower while I make you something to eat. Go on!'

'Penny, you don't have to. I . . .'

'And wash that hair, for crying out loud. It looks like there's been a natural oil disaster on your head. Really, Cath. Now. Do it.'

Catherine opened her mouth to protest but Penny had her hands on her hips and a certain look in her eye. Penny had brought up three children and six bloody-minded dogs in her time and was definitely not a person to start arguing with unless you had the stamina of an Olympian. She was already rummaging through the larder in search of ingredients. As

Catherine trudged upstairs, she heard the radio go on, then *Woman's Hour* being retuned to a channel playing pop music. Seconds later there came the sound of singing and clattering pots.

Catherine stood in the shower and let the water cascade over her, feeling nothing but terror and dread about what lay in the future. Surely not even Penny could rescue her from this nightmare?

'You know, you could see this as an opportunity,' Penny told her twenty minutes later, running hot water into the bowl at the sink and adding a squirt of washing-up liquid.

Catherine was now fully dressed with clean, dry hair, and tucking hungrily into the cheese and ham omelette her friend had rustled up. God, she was famished. 'An opportunity?' she echoed, her mouth full of hot gooey cheddar.

'Yes, an opportunity. A new start. A chance to do all those things you always wanted to but never had the nerve.' Penny swished the foamy water around while she thought. 'You could go and live abroad for a while. You could—'

'I don't want to live abroad.'

'You could have a holiday, then. Escape Britain and catch some rays. Play your cards right and you might even catch something else, if you know what I mean.'

Catherine tucked a stray red tendril behind her ear and gave her friend a withering look. 'Gonorrhea?'

'No! Killjoy. I meant a holiday fling, a handsome Pedro or Jean-Paul. Just what you need to forget your cheating bastard husband.'

'Penny!'

'Just saying!'

'Well, don't. Anyway, I did that once before – the holiday fling, I mean – and look where it got me.'

'Yeah, eighteen happy years and two lovely kids. My point exactly.'

Catherine forked another mouthful of omelette in, not bothering to argue. Penny had been divorced twice and was now having a fling with a thirty-year-old toyboy. She didn't have a clue.

'Or,' Penny went on, sensing they'd hit a brick wall, 'you could go back to college. You could go back to uni!'

'To finish the twenty-one-year degree course? Surely that'd be a record.'

'Get a job, then. A proper job. Never too late to have a career change, and you're still young. Younger than me, you cow.'

'How can I have a career change when I've never even had a career?' Catherine pointed out. 'Anyway, I'm too busy with all my other things.'

'What, making tea for old ladies and selling musty clothes in the charity shop?'

'There's the dog rescue centre, too. And all that ironing I said I'd do for Mrs Archbold.'

'Sounds to me like you need a break, Cath. Hey, best idea yet. How about a girls' holiday, just us two? Get some winter sun . . . what do you say?'

Catherine sighed. She couldn't decide anything. She'd had enough trouble deciding whether or not she wanted salad with her omelette. 'I don't know,' she said faintly. 'I've got to talk to Mike first.'

'Sod Mike. You don't have to talk to him if you don't want to. And you certainly don't need his permission for—'

'No, I mean money-wise. If we split up . . .' She broke off, suddenly losing her appetite again. 'If we split up, I'm not going to have any money, am I? I can't start flouncing off abroad on his savings.'

'Sure you bloody can. It's the least he can do, after the psychological scarring he's inflicted on you, the unfaithful shitbag.'

The fight had gone out of Catherine as well as her appetite. She pushed the plate away feeling tired of this conversation. 'I can't think straight,' she mumbled.

'No worries. Sorry to go on at you. That's all you need, right?'

Catherine's bottom lip was wobbling again. She blew her nose quickly, not meeting Penny's eye.

Penny finished washing up and dried her hands on the

nearest tea towel before sitting down at the table. 'Do you want to come and stay with us for a while? Just until you've got your head around this? I promise I won't nag on at you all the time.'

Catherine managed a weak smile. Penny's house was noisy and chaotic, with teenagers and dogs spilling out of every nook and cranny. Last time she'd popped round there had also been Toyboy Darren hunking about the place, with his buff bare chest and a towel round his waist. She wasn't sure she had the energy to cope with that lot right now. 'That's really kind, but I just need to hibernate for a bit, if you know what I mean. Pull the duvet over my head and shut out the world.'

Penny wouldn't know what she meant; Penny's idea of getting over a man was to doll up in a short dress and heels, get lairy on tequila and go clubbing with anyone game enough to accompany her.

But she nodded and clasped Catherine's hand all the same. 'Whatever you want, Cath. Whatever it takes. But you know I'm here, right? And I'll help you get through this, I swear I will.'

Chapter Eight

La Cucina – Cooking

It was a cold, frost-glittering Saturday morning in December and Anna was on her way to Giovanni's deli for her day-long Italian cookery course. She hoped she wasn't about to disgrace her father's people. Knowing her, she'd hack off a thumb amidst some ambitiously fast garlic chopping, or worse. Maybe that was why her father had abandoned her, she thought wildly, clutching the banister as she climbed the stairs to the class. Maybe he had seen in her eyes, even as a mewling baby, that she was not cut out to be a proper Italian daughter. Maybe he—

'*Buongiorno*,' Giovanni said, smiling warmly.

Anna blushed to the roots of her hair. '*Buongiorno*,' she replied.

'You are Anna, I am thinking? Welcome. Now everybody is here and we can begin.'

There were twelve of them in the class: a broad assortment of people, old and young, none of whom seemed particularly cheffy, much to Anna's relief. After coffee and a round of introductions, they washed their hands, put on aprons and got stuck in. First they made their own egg-yellow pasta sheets (surprisingly simple), and used them for spinach and ricotta ravioli (amazing). Then they learned how to make focaccia (yum) and an authentic Italian minestrone (the key was a great chicken stock) before finishing with a creamy pannacotta served with berries. Best of all, when they had finished cooking, they sat down together and devoured the lot. Every single mouthful was scrumptious.

'You like?' Giovanni said, seeing Anna's blissed-out expression as she scraped the last streaks of pannacotta from her bowl. He was tall and weather-beaten, threads of grey through his hair and dark, sparkly eyes.

'I like,' she replied with a grin. 'Actually my Dad's Italian, so . . .'

She broke off, cringing at how lame she sounded, but Giovanni seemed delighted. 'Your papa? Ahh! Now you can cook some Italian treats for him, eh?'

His enthusiasm was infectious. 'I'd love to,' she replied truthfully.

The class was so interesting and fun that she spent the following afternoon baking another focaccia at home, this time with rosemary and garlic. Okay, so it wasn't quite as perfect as the one kneaded and baked under Giovanni's watchful eye, but it made her whole flat smell amazing, and she was so pleased with herself, she took half of it into work for her colleagues to sample on Monday.

'This is bloody epic,' Joe said, cramming two pieces in at once. He licked his fingers and grinned at her. 'You seem more Italian already, you know.'

'Oh, you *are* lucky,' sighed Marla, who wrote restaurant reviews and occasional features. She was the office bombshell – all hair extensions and polished nails – and today was wearing a short candy-floss pink dress, sheer tights and vertiginous heels, despite it being minus two and snowy outside. 'Being able to eat carbs, I mean. You can get away with it when you've got curves, but people with a slimmer build like me . . .' She pouted down at her non-existent stomach. 'I'd better say no.'

Anna flinched at the not-so-subtle insult, but Joe was already speaking. 'Calling me fat? Cheeky cow,' he said in mock-indignation, stuffing more bread into his mouth.

'No, I . . .' Marla said, flustered. *No, I didn't mean you, I was having a dig at Anna,* she didn't quite say.

'Only I'm happy with my curves, thank you very much,' he went on, putting a hand on his hip and batting his eyelashes.

Anna snorted as discreetly as she could. Joe didn't have a spare ounce of fat on him; he was lean and wiry and knew damn well what Marla had been insinuating. The whole office knew what Marla had been insinuating.

Marla pressed her lips together and typed very fast, and Joe grinned at Anna. 'Like I said, bloody delicious,' he said loudly.

Even grouchy Colin pronounced her efforts a triumph. 'Excellent work,' he said. 'Can we look forward to more of the same?'

'Yeah, when's the next cookery course?' Joe asked. 'Have you booked it yet? Maybe you could make us all dinner next time. Marla will be having a plate of raw vegetables, mind . . .'

'I can *hear*, you know,' Marla snapped.

'. . . But we'd rather have plates of pasta. Or risotto. Do you like risotto, Col? Not vegetarian, are you, or denying yourself any major food groups?'

'Love risotto,' Colin replied. 'Although I prefer a steak pie, to be honest.'

'So that's one risotto, one steak pie, a carrot for Marla and whatever you're having.'

'Don't hold your breath,' Anna laughed, but she glowed with the praise nonetheless. She didn't tell them that she'd already gone hunting online for another challenge and discovered a fantastic-sounding cookery school in Tuscany which offered week-long courses. Maybe when she could actually speak the language, she promised herself.

'What's all this? Somebody been baking?'

Anna's expression froze as Imogen came click-clacking

towards them. She was wearing a boxy lilac jacket and matching heels, which made her resemble a purposeful Parma Violet.

'Just a bit of bread,' Anna said lamely as Joe melted away. 'Help yourself.'

'Oh God, focaccia, my *bête noire,*' Imogen exclaimed, reaching out for the smallest square. She was tall and elegant with coiffed silvery hair, and had a sixth sense when it came to a) journalists behaving badly and b) free food in the office. 'Hell, it doesn't count when you're standing up, does it?' she said.

'Said the actress to the bishop,' muttered Colin.

'A moment on the lips and . . . Mmmm.' Imogen's eyes widened as she bit into the bread. 'Ooh, I say. That's excellent, Anna. Super. I didn't have you down as the domestic type, if you don't mind me saying.'

Anna shrugged off the slur. 'I didn't have myself down as the domestic type either, to be honest,' she said. 'This baking business is kind of a voyage of discovery.'

'Mmmm,' Imogen said again, frowning slightly as she considered Anna. Then she nodded to herself and walked away. 'Interesting,' she said aloud.

Anna flushed, not quite sure how to take that. Marla looked up from her work and rolled her eyes. 'Interesting,' she mouthed sarcastically behind their boss's lilac back.

✲

Anna soon found out what had made Imogen so thoughtful. The very next day, she was called in to her boss's office for 'a little chat' – three words that strike fear into the soul of any employee.

Entering Imogen's office was rather like walking into a junk shop. Life-size cardboard cut-outs of Jess Ennis and Sean Bean leaned matily against the filing cabinet, and the shelves were lined with signed photos of every local hero from David Blunkett to Jarvis Cocker.

'You wanted to see me?' Anna asked politely, edging around a pile of next year's Sheffield Wednesday calendars which had been dumped on the floor.

'Yes, I'd like you to take over the cookery column in the newspaper,' Imogen replied without preamble, steepling her fingers together and regarding Anna over the top of her Armani glasses.

'You want me to . . . *what*?' To say Anna was surprised was an understatement. For the last twelve years, the column had been written by Jean Partington, a former chef who'd once had her own restaurant in town. Admittedly, it was common knowledge that Jean, now in her sixties, was keen to hang up her apron and take life a bit easier, but Anna had assumed, like everyone else, that Imogen would either cull the column or shell out for a syndicated recipe as lots of other local newspapers did.

'I want you to write it,' Imogen repeated, her smile becoming slightly more fixed.

'But . . . Well, I don't really know anything about cookery,' Anna said as politely as she could manage. 'I mean, the focaccia was a bit of a one-off for me. I don't usually . . .'

Her voice trailed off at the disapproval on her boss's face. Imogen was wearing a beige suit today and now looked very much like an irritated Werther's Original. 'It'll take you ten minutes,' she said. 'Just Google some recipes. Any idiot could do it. You said yourself that baking was a voyage of self-discovery, didn't you? I like that. Share it with the readers. Take them along with you, mistakes and all. You're the obvious choice.'

Right. The obvious sucker, more like. 'It was an Italian cookery course,' she found herself mumbling. 'At Giovanni's.'

'Even better! You could write a little feature about your experience there, get permission to use one of the recipes. Maybe wangle some kind of giveaway from Giovanni while you're at it. Come *on,* Anna! You don't need me to spoonfeed you like this.'

'Fine,' Anna said, heading for the door. There was obviously no point arguing any longer. 'Leave it to me.'

She walked back to her desk, reeling. Had that actually just happened?

'Everything all right?' Marla asked nosily as Anna sat down again.

'Yeah, actually,' Anna replied. 'She wants me to take over Jean's cookery column.'

Marla's perfectly plucked eyebrows shot up. 'Whoa! Your own column? How come?' She forced her thin, red lips into some semblance of a smile. 'I mean . . . Great.'

Anna ignored the insincerity in her voice. She was feeling chirpier by the second as the news sank in. *Her own column.* Yes! She'd have a proper byline for the first time ever. Okay, so it was only a crummy cookery column, a tiny bit of space midway through the newspaper, but even so . . . Her own column! About food! Wait till she told Giovanni. Wait till she told her father!

'Does that mean you'll be bringing in more bread and stuff for us to try?' asked Charlotte, one of the secretaries. 'Only, you know, if you ever need any testers . . .'

Anna grinned. 'You'll be first on my list,' she promised. Then, feeling slightly giddy, she looked up Giovanni's number and gave him a call.

The first column ran the following week. She and Geoff, one of the staff photographers, had gone along to the deli and mocked up a scene in Giovanni's kitchen: Anna in a chef's hat and apron, beaming, as she stood with an array of food in front of her. Giovanni told her he was happy for her to use his focaccia recipe provided she credited him for it, and offered to give the newspaper an exclusive £5-off deal if they spent £25 in the deli. So with the recipe, the voucher, the photo and a short piece about the day's course, Anna's column took up a good third of a page, much more than Jean's had ever done.

I'll be honest with you, she began, *I'm nowhere near as competent a chef as Jean. But I intend to learn something new every week, and I hope you'll come along for the ride with me and try out my recipes as I go. If I can do it, anyone can!*

Imogen pronounced herself 'thrilled' with the results. 'Splendid,' she said. 'Very nice. Just what I was looking for, Anna.'

Encouraged by this response, Anna went on to explore further recipes for her next column. Writing about food, she soon decided, was way more interesting than writing about the council's recycling targets.

I recently became aware of some Italian ancestry in my family, she wrote, safe in the knowledge that her mum would never read it, *so what better reason to try my hand at that Italian classic, tiramisu. In my quest to discover the perfect recipe, I've whipped up a couple of variations, but this one is definitely the tastiest, in my opinion. I hope you like it – let me know what you think!*

'This is good,' Imogen said when she read it, nodding so vigorously with approval that her hair actually moved. 'Nice and friendly. I like that you're telling us a story with the column as you go. Keep it up!'

As the newspaper threw itself into all things Christmassy,

Anna dutifully provided a recipe for mince pies, suggesting ways to give them a new twist. *I tried adding cranberries to the mincemeat in my mince pies,* she told her readers. *It gave them that extra little zing. Plus, the added fruit content made me feel better about using real butter and lots of sugar in the recipe. I'm sure one of my mince pies counts towards your five a day . . . In fact, they're so delicious, you'll have trouble restraining yourself from eating five at once!*

It wasn't long before she began to get letters and emails from readers – a slow trickle at first, but more every day. Usually it was just people letting her know how they'd got on with her recipes, but sometimes the readers would offer suggestions of their own.

I make my mince pies with flaky puff pastry for their lids, one lady wrote in. *Somehow it makes them seem a bit more special.*

Try adding a little grated lemon or orange zest to the mincemeat, another suggested. *You can really taste the difference.*

My mum always puts a dollop of custard beneath the mincemeat, a third emailed in. *It's amazing – a complete pudding!*

'This is awesome,' Anna murmured to herself, loving how keen everyone was to share their baking expertise. The only feedback from readers she'd had before now was the occasional nasty comment on the paper's website telling her that her face looked fat in photos, or complaining that she'd spelled somebody's name wrong. She made a point of listing the best mince pie tips she'd received in the following week's column, and thanked all the senders. *Please let me know how you find this week's recipe,* she finished, *as I really enjoy hearing from you. Do look online to read a selection of comments and tips. Everyone has been so helpful!*

Buoyed by her initial success, Anna found herself planning hearty Italian stews and sticky cakes for the winter months ahead, and perhaps even a Valentine's special – the food of love, and all that. For the first time in months – years! – she discovered a new degree of enthusiasm for her job. No longer was she racing out of the door with relief when five-thirty struck. Nowadays she wandered dreamily homewards, barely noticing the icy pavements because her mind was full of dainty tartlets and steaming soups.

'Your fan-mail's arrived,' Joe said on Christmas Eve, dragging a huge mail sack behind him through the office.

'No way,' Anna breathed, staring in wonder. 'Are you serious?'

He laughed. 'Course I'm not, you div,' he said, his dark eyes twinkling. 'Just winding you up. These are the entry slips for our FA Cup tickets competition.'

She wrinkled her nose. 'Very funny.'

'*This* lot's yours,' he added, dumping a parcel and some letters on her desk.

'Are you moonlighting as one of the postroom boys now or something?' she teased. 'Don't tell me you've finally had enough of rainy Saturday afternoons at the football?'

'Never,' he said. 'Just helping out. I saw you had a few

things, thought I'd bring them up for you.' He grinned. 'I was dying to know what this is anyway,' he admitted, holding up a strange-shaped package. 'Early Christmas present?'

Anna took it from him and ripped it open. A selection of kitchen utensils clattered on to her desk: a bright green spatula, a turquoise whisk, a nifty microplane grater and . . .

'What the hell is this? Some kind of sex toy?' Joe spluttered, picking up the last one.

Anna gave him a look. 'I think it's a lemon reamer – you know, for squeezing the juice out.'

'Is that what you call it?' He twirled it between his fingers, a suggestive look on his face.

Anna laughed and picked up the accompanying note. 'They're from the Kitchen Shop in Meadowhall,' she read. 'They love the column and wondered if I'd like to try their new range. Oh my God. Freebies, Joe. I'm getting freebies!'

'All right for some,' he said. 'No one's ever sent *me* a free spatula.'

'You should try being a professional reviewer like me,' Marla said airily from her desk. 'I'm bombarded with freebies all the time. To be honest, the novelty wears off after a while. I mean, free theatre tickets and meals every night . . . bor-ing.'

Joe and Anna exchanged a look, then Joe hoisted the mail sack over his shoulder like a young, good-looking Santa. 'My mum's made your panettone by the way,' he added, turning to go. 'She won't let anyone try it before Christmas Day, but it looks amazing. Nice one.'

'Oh, that's strange,' Marla put in innocently, and Anna braced herself. Marla was about as innocent as Bill Sikes. 'I wasn't going to say anything, but my mum told me she'd tried that recipe too. She actually wondered if you'd printed the wrong measurements? Hers turned out very strange, like totally gross. Ended up in the dog's bowl and even he wouldn't touch it.'

'It's best not to give dogs sugary things,' Anna said, refusing to take the bait. 'Anyway, cheers Joe. Glad the measurements were printed correctly in *your* mum's newspaper,' she couldn't resist adding. 'And happy Christmas if I don't see you later.'

'You too, Anna. Hope it's a tasty one.'

She smiled as he walked away, then stacked her new utensils at the side of her desk. Freebies from the Kitchen Shop! That was praise indeed. Maybe she could suggest a kitchen gadgets review section to Imogen next, where she tried out different pieces of equipment . . .

She began typing again with a new burst of energy. Thank you, Jean Partington, for your timely retirement decision, she thought. This is the best thing that ever happened to my career. And thank you, Joe's mum, for trying my recipe too. How many other people, she wondered, had read her words and made their own panettone for the festive period? She loved imagining full cake tins around the county, safely stored in cupboards, as everyone waited for the big day to arrive. Her father would surely be proud of her if he knew she was bringing a little slice of Italy to Yorkshire.

Chapter Nine

Il diario – The diary

April 19, 1993

So I know it was v bad but I couldn't help myself – I picked up his Newky Brown and tipped it all over Jamie's head. He was like, What the hell . . . ? – but the girls all gave me this massive cheer as I walked away. It was SO FUNNY!

June 2, 1993

Alex Zetland can KISS MY ARSE if he thinks he's got a chance with me now. I'm fuming! Stupid lairy bastard. I elbowed him right in the nuts when he tried to grope me. To think I used to fancy him!

July 11, 1993

Me and Zoe are OFF tomorrow! Soooooo hysterically excited I might wee myself. Gary was all like, Are we still an item or what, but I was just like, Sorry, Gazza, I'm off inter-railing, let's not tie ourselves down, yeah?

He looked a bit excited at the 'tying ourselves down' bit until he clocked what I meant. Was that harsh of me? I don't actually care.

I'm off for some European fun and adventures and copious amounts of la-la-la-la-lager!

During a massive, cathartic clear-out, Catherine had come across some of her old diaries. God, she'd been a feisty thing in her student years. Ballsy and bolshy, not putting up with any shite. Admittedly, Catherine wasn't exactly *proud* of this behaviour now: throwing alcohol over men, assaulting their privates, dumping them heartlessly as she left the country . . . She hoped Emily wasn't behaving like this at university – or Matthew, come to that. Mind you, the nothing's-gonna-stop-me attitude that shone from the pages of her diary was one she kind of admired.

She'd been so sure of herself back then, so confident. But then she'd met Mike and everything had changed. *She* had changed. It was only now he had gone that she was starting to question herself, to re-evaluate their relationship. Had it really been as solid as she'd always assumed? Had she and Mike truly completed one another?

A few weeks earlier, she'd been working at the care home and overheard Nora and Violet, two of her favourite old ladies, reminiscing about their passionate romances in times gone by and giggling naughtily together. Their tales made Catherine feel empty – then envious. How they'd adored their beaus and flings! Could she honestly say she had ever felt that way about Mike?

Then, a week or so ago, when she was doing a shift in the charity shop, a tanned young blonde woman had come in, looking for cheap black trousers and white shirts she could wear for a waitressing job 'because I've been travelling for eight years and all my other clothes are fit for the bin'. Again, it brought Catherine up short, and she couldn't help feeling a wrench inside for that younger Catherine, who'd travelled around Europe with her friend Zoe, working here and there, then hopping on another train when they felt like it. When was the last time she had done anything adventurous?

The last straw had come a few days ago when one of the pipes had burst at home and flooded the kitchen. Panicking, she'd tried to get hold of Mike at work, only to be told he was on holiday in the Seychelles. 'Oh,' said Lindsay the receptionist in confusion, 'that's weird. I assumed you were with him, Mrs E?'

'No,' she had replied heavily. She was not with him. She was still here in Wetherstone, ankle-deep in dirty water, worrying about her plumbing. How the hell could Mike afford a holiday in the Seychelles anyway?

It occurred to her that maybe, just maybe, she had been getting her priorities wrong all this time. And maybe, just maybe, she should do something about that.

Penny, of course, thoroughly approved of this positive new outlook when Catherine told her about it on the way back from tennis one morning. 'Yes. Absolutely. Seize the day!' she said, banging on the steering wheel for emphasis. They were in Penny's ancient Beamer, which smelled of dogs and was littered with crisp packets and old cigarette boxes. 'So what are you going to do? What's the plan of action?'

'Well . . .' Catherine quailed at her friend's bossy tone. 'I suppose I just want some fun. I don't want to end up an old lady in a retirement home with nothing to say for myself.'

'Fun,' Penny echoed thoughtfully and her eyes gleamed. 'Darren's got this lovely friend I could—'

'Not that kind of fun,' Catherine said firmly. The idea of dipping a toe back in the dating pool made her feel like throwing up. Or maybe that was just Penny's driving, she thought, as her friend swerved wildly to overtake a dawdling white Fiesta. 'I need to get some kind of job,' she said after a moment.

Penny made a scornful noise. 'I thought you said fun? Look, why don't you come along to my line dancing class on Thursday? That's a total laugh. And there are some real hotties there.'

Line dancing did not appeal, nor did the thought of 'hotties' in cowboy boots. 'Um . . .' Catherine said politely, 'I was thinking some other kind of class actually. Maybe.'

'Brilliant idea, Cath. Agony aunts are always saying that, aren't they? Take an evening class, cop off with the sexy woodwork tutor, blah blah.'

'I don't want to learn woodwork,' Catherine told her.

'Derrr,' Penny said. 'Woodwork and car maintenance and . . . I don't know, building – those courses are going to be full of men. FULL.'

'Woodwork and building do not sound like fun to me,' Catherine said. 'I was thinking more along the lines of pottery, or—'

'Nah.'

'Jewellery-making.'

'Too many women.'

'A language, then. Italian, maybe.'

'Ooh, now you're talking. The language of love and all that. I like it, Cath. Do it!' She braked hard at a roundabout, sending Catherine flying forward in her seat. Being Penny's passenger was like playing whiplash roulette. 'By the way, I meant to say, what are you doing for Christmas? Do you and the kids want to come to mine? We've got my parents this year, but we can squeeze in a few more. I need to order my turkey soon so just let me know, yeah?'

'Thanks, but . . .' Catherine was glad Penny was navigating the roundabout and couldn't see her expression. 'We're actually going to have Christmas at home,' she said hesitantly. 'The four of us, and Mike's parents.'

'*What?*' Penny yelped. 'What are you saying? Are you back together with him? I thought he was in the frigging Seychelles?'

'No. It's just . . .'

'But he's coming to you for *Christmas*? How's that going to work? I'm confused. Do the twins know? I feel like I've missed a crucial event here.'

'No, they don't know. And you mustn't say anything. It was Mike's idea. We're going to . . .' She coughed, dreading her friend's reaction. 'We're going to kind of pretend everything's okay.'

Penny almost crashed into the back of a van. 'You're going to *what*?' She veered out of the way and overtook badly, earning herself a beeped horn and a rude hand gesture. 'You're going to *pretend* everything's *okay*?'

Her tone of voice made it blindingly obvious that she thought this was nothing short of madness. She was probably right. 'I just can't bring myself to tell them,' Catherine admitted. 'And Mike doesn't want to either.'

'Jesus, Cath. That's crazy! That's totally fucking nuts, pardon my French. So, what, you're going to be back in the double bed with him, acting like happy old mum and dad? And you think they won't even *notice*?'

Catherine folded her arms across herself defensively. It hadn't sounded *that* crazy when Mike had proposed it the other week. In fact, it had seemed like quite good sense, the easiest way all round. She had even wondered, in a moment of weakness, if he was hoping to move back in permanently; if there might yet be a change of heart, kisses under the mistletoe, a Santa-size apology. That was before she knew he'd jetted off abroad on holiday with somebody else, mind.

Penny was like a Jack Russell with a rodent. She would not give it up. 'What about when other people say stuff?' she asked. 'You know that *I'd* take a secret to the grave, but don't you think gossips like Mrs Archbold will stir things up? *Haven't seen your dad around here lately. Has he moved back in?* That's all it'll take – one little comment and the whole thing will fall apart.'

Penny parked in their street, pulling on the handbrake with unnecessary force, and Catherine glanced at Mrs Archbold's neat house two doors down from hers with a miserable shrug. Those net curtains of hers had been twitched so often lately, Catherine was surprised the rail hadn't fallen down. 'Well . . . we're going to give it a try,' she said. 'If they find out, they find out. But for me, I think it's worth it. I'd give anything for one last Christmas together, even if it *is* as fake as spray-on snow.'

Penny patted her hand. 'Sorry. Didn't mean to upset you. And I do totally get the family Christmas thing, but . . .' She unclipped her seatbelt. 'Well, good luck to you, that's all. Just remember, there's a tin of Quality Street and a party hat with your name on it over at my place if it all goes tits-up.'

✲

Catherine tried to ignore Penny's doom-laden words as she dumped her tennis stuff in the hall, grabbed the pile of post on the mat and wandered through to the kitchen.

She flicked through the letters – all for Mike, as usual – but the last envelope caught her eye as it had a Barclays Bank logo on the front. Her brow furrowed. That was weird. They'd always done their banking through the Co-op. Why were Barclays writing to him?

It was probably junk mail, she thought, putting it with the other letters that had arrived for him. Mike had asked her to drop his post off at the surgery every now and then, but she'd been posting it all in a big envelope rather than go along in person and undergo the humiliation of the receptionists' sympathetic looks and hushed silence. Just imagining it made her cringe. *Here she is. You know he's left her, don't you? Poor cow, look at the state of her. Not sure what he saw in her anyway, to be honest. And you know that holiday he went on recently? He only went and took someone else. I know!*

Catherine sighed for a moment, imagining him and Rebecca hand in hand on a white sandy beach together, frolicking in the crystal blue waters. Cocktails. Sun cream. Laughter. It was unbearable.

Oh, sod it. And sod him. He hadn't wasted any time crying over their broken marriage, had he? It was high time she got on with her own life without him. Time she started channelling the Catherine she'd been all those years ago, who was ballsy and brave, and who grabbed life by the throat.

Without another minute's hesitation, she switched on the computer and booked herself onto an Italian evening class, beginning in January. There. It was a start. The start of the new go-getting Catherine. She could almost hear her younger self cheering her on.

Chapter Ten

Buon Natale! – Merry Christmas!

Somehow or other, it was already December and Sophie was still at her parents' house in Sheffield. This was almost as surprising as the fact that she and her mother hadn't actually killed each other yet.

Her dad was home now, rattling around with various pills from the GP and convalescing, which so far had meant a lot of moaning at the television and half-hearted jigsaw puzzles, while her mum slaved over vats of home-made soup in her attempt to build him back up. He was a terrible invalid, bored and impatient about staying at home, desperate to get back to work, and insisting on phoning the office every morning for updates. Prior to this he had only ever had two days off sick in his life.

Anything strenuous was strictly forbidden, according to Trish, though. 'You're not out of the woods yet, Jim,' she kept reminding him. 'You're meant to be taking it easy, not haring around like you used to. Stay indoors and finish that jigsaw, for heaven's sake.'

Christmas had evolved since Sophie last spent it with her parents. Back when she was growing up, it had always been just the three of them for the first part of the day, followed by an afternoon visit to her grandma for a slice of Christmas cake and more presents, with a trip to the panto the following week. Now it seemed as if her parents ran the whole show, with her aunt and uncle and grandma over for Christmas dinner, and her cousins Sam and Richard arriving later, children and partners in tow. 'Whoa,' she said to her mum when she got wind of the busy schedule ahead. 'When did Christmas get so hectic around here?'

Her mum was pressing pastry circles into the tray for mince pie bases and didn't meet her eye. 'We didn't want to be alone, just me and Jim, once you went away,' she confessed. 'So we invited everyone to us – and they keep coming back every year.'

Sophie didn't know how to respond. All the far-flung Christmases she'd enjoyed, and she'd never really given a thought to her parents left behind, waking up in a quiet house together and yearning for company. 'Must be your amazing cooking, Mum,' she said eventually.

Trish raised an eyebrow. 'Either that, or they felt sorry for us.'

Ouch. There was an awkward silence. 'Can I help you with those mince pies?' Sophie ventured after a moment.

'Thank you,' her mum replied. 'Although they're not exactly Italian delicacies, like you're used to, of course.'

'Oh, Mum, would you give over? I love mince pies, all right? And I haven't had a decent one in years.' Her words came out sharper than she intended and Trish flinched.

'There's no need to shout,' she said, looking wounded.

'I'm not, it's just . . .' Sophie gritted her teeth. 'I feel like you're angry with me all the time.'

Her mum put down her pastry cutter. 'I'm not angry,' she said after a moment. She passed a hand across her face, leaving a streak of flour there. 'I . . . Oh, it doesn't matter.'

'It does matter, clearly. What is it? Let's just talk about it. Do you want me to go?'

'No. Of course I don't. You're our daughter. ' She sighed. 'You just make me feel uncomfortable, that's all. Like you're criticizing everything here. Like you're storing it all up to write about in your blog: how boring we are, how suburban, how you can't wait to go again.'

Sophie guessed she deserved that one. 'I'm not . . . I don't think that,' she protested. 'I swear!'

Trish said nothing.

'Mum, I promise,' she said quietly. 'I wouldn't do that to you.'

The look in Trish's eyes said, *You already did.* 'Only it hurt me and your dad,' she said, spooning dollops of sticky dark mincemeat into the pastry. 'And while he might not admit as much, he's fragile right now. He couldn't bear to go through that again. It might finish him off.'

Sophie swallowed. 'I'm sorry. I'm not sure what else you want me to say,' she replied. 'I'm not going to write about you and Dad any more, okay? Look.' She took a deep breath. 'We've both upset each other over the years, we've both done things we shouldn't have.'

'Here we go. I've been waiting for this. I knew we'd get there sooner or later.'

'Well, it's true! I'm not the only one who's behaved badly here, am I?'

'Any chance of a cup of tea around here?' There was Jim, desperately trying to curtail the start of World War Three.

The room simmered with the unspoken argument. 'I'll make it,' Sophie muttered.

At least she had a good excuse to get out of the house frequently now. After two days' searching, she'd picked up a job at the café down the road six days a week, serving coffee and cake to yummy mummies who said, 'I really shouldn't,' then tucked into enormous flaky almond croissants with gusto. The pay wasn't great but she reckoned that by February she'd have enough money for a plane ticket somewhere new. If she could survive that long at home without nuclear meltdown, that was.

Obviously this wasn't good enough for her parents, as

Trish arrived home from work triumphantly one night with the news that she'd 'got Sophie a job'.

'Er, hello? I've already *got* a job,' Sophie reminded her. 'At Nico's Café. Where I was all day today. Remember?' Anger sparked inside her. Pushy parents never changed their spots, did they? They just lulled you into a false sense of security then started shoving again. *You're doing it wrong. You should do this. We think business studies is the best option. Drama School won't lead to any kind of stable job. You're making a big mistake, my girl . . .*

'I know, love. But this is an evening thing, teaching "Conversational Italian" at the Hurst. I reckon you'd be a shoo-in.'

Sophie felt like screaming. Oh, she could see it now – her mum flicking through the newspaper for job listings on the quiet, signing her up with recruitment agencies, trying to micro-manage her daughter's life just like before. 'Mum, I can look after myself, you know. You don't need to go around finding other jobs for me.'

'I know I don't. Tina's husband did it for you.'

'*What?*' Now she was really incensed. Had her mum sent the word round her friends and colleagues that her little girl needed a leg-up in the job world? Oh, brilliant. Her fists tightened into knots and it was all she could do to remain in the room rather than storm upstairs and pack up her belongings. She'd been here before, with her parents trying to dictate her life. She wasn't going to let it happen again.

'Calm down, for heaven's sake. I only mentioned to Tina that you were back for a while, that's all. Her hubby is the course director over at the college, and it just so happens that the woman who teaches the Italian classes is going off on maternity leave. So Tina, being really kind and helpful, put two and two together, told him that you're here, fluent in Italian, looking for a job, and . . .' Trish spread her hands wide. 'Bob's your uncle. He's asked you in for a chat.'

'But I . . .' Her anger was deflating.

'I'm not interfering,' Trish went on. 'I don't care if you get it or not. You've made it clear you don't want to stick around here – that's fine.'

'She's doing you a bloody great favour, although she's too polite to point that out,' Jim growled, looking up from his newspaper. 'And teaching Italian sounds a damn sight more interesting than waiting tables. Even you, stubborn as you are, have to admit it.'

'Sorry,' Sophie said grudgingly after a moment. 'You're right. That does sound interesting. I won't get it, though.'

'Why the hell not? Bright girl like you, you could do anything.' That was Jim again, voice raised.

'You can't do meaningless jobs all your life,' Trish suddenly burst out. 'Life's not a rehearsal, Sophie.'

Sophie glared. 'That's an unfortunate choice of phrase coming from you,' she muttered before she could stop herself.

'And that's uncalled for, dragging up ancient history,' Trish retorted, turning pink.

She was probably right. 'Sorry,' Sophie mumbled.

'Right,' Jim said. 'Does that mean you're going to give this a go, then?'

'I've never done any proper teaching before though, Dad,' she replied, then paused, thinking about it. 'Well, a bit, I suppose, teaching English to businessmen in Venezuela, but it was a total blag, cash in hand, no contract or anything. The only references I've got are from foreign employers.'

'Even better. With a bit of luck Tina's husband won't be able to understand a bloody word of 'em.' Jim chuckled at his own wit. 'I bet you're a great teacher, Soph, blagging or not. You've got excellent people skills – except when you're arguing with your parents, that is – you're patient, you're articulate . . .'

Sophie scuffed her toe along the ground, not knowing what to say. Her dad wasn't one for needless gladhanding; he would call a spade a bloody great shovel rather than soft-soap anyone. His praise made her feel disconcertingly warm and fuzzy inside. 'Thanks,' she said.

'You could do it,' her mum agreed. 'Think about it anyway. Tina said he'd love to chat with you if you're interested. Starts January. What have you got to lose?'

Er, my freedom? Sophie thought immediately. Being a teacher, even if it was only a maternity cover, was way more of a commitment than wiping tables in a café or pulling pints in a bar. Before, she'd always moved on whenever she'd felt like it, giving notice on a whim, jumping on a bus to someplace new if she had the urge. Even in Caracas, she'd taught English for . . . what? Three weeks or so to raise funds for the next leg of her trip. It was never serious.

Irritatingly, her dad's words kept coming back to her. *Sounds a damn sight more interesting than waiting tables . . .*

He had a point, if she was honest. She could waitress and clean tables with her eyes shut; it was an uncomplicated way to earn money. But much as she liked café camaraderie and talking to new people every day, it was boring at times. Plus the pay wasn't brilliant either, and you spent most of the time on your feet. She'd worn out that many pairs of shoes waitressing, it was a crime against footwear.

'Not scared, are you?' her dad teased, seeing her lost in thought.

'Of course not!' Sophie retorted, taking the piece of paper with the phone number on. 'I'll phone him tomorrow.'

Hurst College was in town, a short walk from the station – an unprepossessing sort of place, which wouldn't win any architectural prizes for its 1960s blocky design and tired interiors. Still, there were all sorts of interesting courses running, according to the college brochure: ceramics, cookery, modern languages, engineering, drama . . . Her gaze latched onto the course description of the latter and she found herself reading the details with a sort of hunger: acting and technical theatre skills . . . vocal techniques . . . characterization and script analysis . . .

'Sophie Frost?'

She was jolted out of her thoughts at the sound of the voice and looked up to see a lady in a navy twinset in front of her. Sophie rose to her feet, trying to smooth out the creases in the skirt she'd borrowed from her mum. 'Yes, hi. That's me.'

'If you'd like to come this way?'

'Sure. Thank you.' Her heart jumping with a sudden attack of nerves, Sophie followed the woman along the corridor. *You can do it,* she could hear her dad say. Well, it was time to find out, wasn't it?

Alan McIntyre, Tina's husband, was tall, slightly stooped and spoke with a soft Scottish accent. He also had a crushing handshake which nearly broke her fingers. Remembering her dad's advice – *Strong handshake, strong character* – Sophie took this as some kind of initiation test and squeezed back as hard as she could. Alan gasped in shock and dropped her hand, shooting her an *are-you-crazy* look. So that got things off to a good start.

'Have a seat,' he said, examining his fingers with a frown. 'So. The Italian job.'

'Oh, I love that film,' Sophie said with a grin, feeling that she had to make up for the handshake debacle. 'Hang on a minute, lads . . .'

'. . . I've got a great idea!' he finished. They both laughed. 'Brilliant stuff. Love Michael Caine.'

'Me too. Total ledge.'

'Now then.' He rifled through some papers on his desk. It was a tip, to be frank, with folders and files in assorted heaps. 'Tell me about yourself. How's your Italian?'

'Pretty good. I've lived and worked there for the last two years,' she told him. 'I took a crash course in Rome when I got there but there's nothing like living in a place to force you to learn a language really quickly.'

'Absolutely,' said Alan McIntyre, and gave an envious sigh. 'Lucky you. You know, that's one of my big regrets in life, never living anywhere but this country. Now I'm far too old and have far too many children and a far-too-big mortgage to even *think* about it. Just a little retirement dream to while away the godawful British winters . . . Anyway. Yes. Sorry. Whereabouts in Italy were you?'

'Rome for a year and more recently Sorrento, down on the west coast.'

'Oh, I know Sorrento. Beautiful place. Amazing beaches. And the food . . . My God. Best I've ever tasted.'

Sophie laughed again. This interview was turning out to be more like a chat with a jolly uncle. 'The food's pretty good,' she agreed.

'Must go back there sometime, escape from the kids for a few days with my wife. Definitely. Anyway. Interview. Yes. The class I would like you to teach is . . . let me see. Tuesday evenings, six-thirty to eight-thirty, complete beginners. I've got eight people booked on already and I'd hate to have to cancel. It's a ten-week term, with half-term in the middle. How does that sound?'

'Fab! I mean, yes, very good,' Sophie replied, trying to sound professional. She cleared her throat and drew herself up. 'I've already been thinking about lesson plans . . .' She dug out the piece of paper torn from her waitress notepad where she'd jotted down ideas during a quiet moment in the café. 'The first one could cover greetings and introductions, then basic conversational questions and answers, such as "How old are you?" and "What do you do for a living?"'

'Excellent, excellent. And you've done this before, I'm told?'

'In Venezuela, yes. Teaching English. Although it was a few years ago now.' She cringed, ready to see his enthusiasm screech to a halt.

He leaned back in his chair, eyes narrowing slightly as he considered her. 'Sophie, I'll be straight with you. You don't have much experience, I'm taking a bit of a punt here. But I like you. And I need an Italian teacher. So the job's yours if you want it.'

She tried her best not to look too astonished, but it was

a struggle. Oh my God. Had that actually just happened? 'I want it,' she assured him, beaming. 'I won't let you down.'

They shook hands on it – very carefully this time – and she walked out of there with a brand new job. The Italian job. She had a good feeling about this.

FACEBOOK STATUS: Sophie Frost – December 25
Merry Christmas, everyone! I'm at home in Sheffield for the first time in years – bit weird! Sorry I haven't posted anything for ages – things have been hectic. Hope you all have a great day xxx

She pressed 'Post' and watched as her message updated. Then she scanned through her timeline to see what her friends were up to, scattered as they were around the world. Lydia, her old flatmate in New Zealand, was on holiday in Fiji with her boyfriend. *Smooching in our hammock. Merry Xmas y'all!*, she'd written. Flamboyant, beautiful Harvey was still working in Berlin and spending the day with Kurt, his new man, in their modernist white flat in Leipziger Strasse. And Marta and Toni, two Dutch friends, had been to Manly Beach for the day, along with half the backpackers in Sydney, no doubt.

Sophie felt a pang, remembering her own Christmas Day in Sydney with Dan. They'd gone to Bondi with a disposable barbecue, a box of wine and all their mates. Music had played. Everyone danced on the sand. The sun shone the entire day. Then, that night, she and Dan had sat out in the tiny courtyard garden of the flat she was renting, and toasted one another with glasses of Australian bubbly. 'Happy Christmas,' he murmured as he leaned in for a kiss.

Still. She wasn't going to think about that now. Especially as she was totally over him. She hardly even stalked him on Facebook these days. He was probably married with babies and a fat Labrador by now – not that it was anything to her, obviously.

'Sophie! Breakfast!' her mum called at that moment. Sophie quickly dabbed her eyes – she wasn't *crying*, she must be allergic to something – and hurried downstairs.

Two bacon sandwiches later, plus a Mars bar from her stocking, she felt a lot better. She and her parents sat around the kitchen table peeling vegetables for lunch while her dad's *Now That's What I Call Christmas* CD blasted from the stereo. 'Present o'clock!' Jim announced every now and then, sending Sophie to the tree to bring back gifts for them all to unwrap. 'Gin o'clock,' he'd add at intervals too, uncapping the Gordon's and sploshing generous measures into everyone's glass.

'Easy on the booze, you,' Trish reminded him. 'You're still meant to be watching your cholesterol, remember?'

'Ah, bollocks to the cholesterol,' he replied. 'It's Christmas Day, woman! Nobody should deny themselves on Christmas Day.'

Aunty Jane, Uncle Clive and Sophie's grandma turned up

at midday, just as the potatoes went sizzling into the tray of hot oil. The house was full of noise and exclamations and the clink of ice as new drinks were poured. Grandma was stooped and gnarled these days, stone-deaf to almost everything unless you bellowed into her ear, but she remained beaming and jovial throughout, joining in with the words to Slade and Wizzard with surprising vigour. Aunty Jane was pissed and giggling after two swift sherries, leaving Uncle Clive to bore on about politics to anyone who would listen (nobody) until Jim challenged him to help finish the jigsaw of Dovedale he'd abandoned in the living room. 'Happy to oblige,' Clive boomed immediately. 'I'm a dab hand at jigsaws, you know, Jim.'

'Of course you are, Clive,' Jim replied with a wink at Sophie.

After a humongous and raucous lunch, more visitors arrived: Sophie's cousins Samantha and Richard with their respective families – four children, a babe in arms and an overexcited Yorkshire Terrier between them. The house was now bursting at the seams and getting a seat on the sofa was harder than securing a ticket for the Men's Final at Wimbledon. The living room was a melee of chocolate-fuelled children and flying wrapping paper and the noise levels were firmly at 'rowdy' . . . and Sophie was having an utterly brilliant day. Forget Bondi Beach and Berlin, this was the real deal: playing charades with your grandma and cousins, pulling crackers, eating Roses by the handful and laughing like a drain as your uncle Clive fell asleep in front of the Queen's speech and snored louder than a wild boar.

She looked round at her mum, whose turn it was to act something out in the highly competitive game of charades. Even Trish looked flushed and happy, in her best dress and a touch of make-up, making a rectangle shape in mid-air with her forefingers.

'It's a TV programme. One word.'

Nod. Trish counted on her fingers then held up four of them.

'Four syllables.'

Nod.

'First syllable.'

She pinched her earlobe then pointed at Sophie's grandma.

'Sounds like . . . grandma. Gran? Gran.'

'Man.'

'Ran.'

'Tan.'

Headshakes to them all.

'Ban?'

'Can.'

'Fan.'

More headshaking.

'Give us another one, Trish.'

'Third syllable. Arm? Arm!'

'Nan something arm something.'

'Second syllable. Sounds like . . . walk. Stroll.'

'Flounce.'

'Stride.'

'Go.'

Vigorous nodding.

'Go! Nan – go – arm – something. What the hell . . . ?'

Jim jumped to his feet, eyes dancing. '*Panorama!*' he yelled. 'Got to be!'

'Is correct!' beamed Trish, applauding him. 'Well done, Jim!' Then her face fell. 'Jim? Are you all right, Jim?'

Sophie turned in slow motion from her mother's face to her dad as if in a bad dream. He was clutching his chest and gasping for breath, his mouth working but no sound coming out. 'Oh Christ,' she cried fearfully. 'Call an ambulance. Somebody call an ambulance!'

Chapter Eleven

Riunione – Reunion

Catherine had always loved Christmas: the tree, the presents, the excitement. But this year it was all overshadowed by the lies, the deceit, the ex-bloody-husband. Faking happy families with Mike was like starring in a very bad farce. It was the most enormous strain, having him back in the house.

How, for instance, had she put up with that throaty walrus snore night after night for their entire marriage? He was a duvet-hogger too, forever rolling over and pulling it with him so that she woke up several times a night freezing cold and had to yank it back. She'd forgotten his other little faults, too: the way he swallowed so loudly when eating a meal. How he'd never rinse the bath out after using it. The way he could see a stack of washing up or a heap of dirty clothes and not think for a second that it had any part in his world. As for the TV remote, you'd think it was surgically attached to his hand. He ruled the evening viewing like a tyrant, marking up the Christmas *Radio Times* and consulting it constantly.

He didn't seem to notice her discomfort. In fact, he didn't

seem bothered at all. It probably felt like a holiday to him after fending for himself in his rented flat for the last two months. There he was, lord and master, whistling in the shower, taking Matthew to the football and renewing his role as Emily's personal taxi driver with annoying good humour. Every few days he would vanish for the evening, presumably to ravish wretched Rebecca on his rented sofa. When he came home and slipped into bed with her afterwards, Catherine could still smell the other woman's perfume on him. It made her feel sick. Why had she ever thought this stupid charade was a good idea? There was no way the Catherine from her diary would have put up with this kind of shenanigans. She'd have poured a pint over his head and told him where to go.

Catherine was sorely tempted. She was *this* close. But she owed it to Matthew and Emily to give them one last perfect Christmas, didn't she?

That was one silver lining at least: having her children home again. Mind you, they didn't seem quite the same teenagers who had left ten weeks earlier. Matthew now sported a tattoo on his forearm, a really horrible one, of a skull with flames bursting from its eye sockets. Meanwhile, Emily had had her beautiful hair peroxided white and cut very short, and a purple stud glittered in one nostril.

Catherine tried to hide her dismay, but it wasn't easy. 'They're growing up, finding their own identities,' Mike said impatiently when she raised the subject.

'I liked their old identities though,' she replied helplessly. 'Now I feel as if I don't even know them any more.'

In fact, Catherine thought, putting yet another load of laundry into the washing machine, she had barely seen them since they'd been home, let alone had the chance to indulge in the lovely, intimate mother-child chats she'd hoped for. They treated her just as Mike did: as a skivvy expected to clean up after them, keep the fridge well-stocked with their favourite treats, and provide dinner on the table at six o'clock every evening. Was that all she was to them?

Still, she reminded herself, they'd have a wonderful Christmas together. That was the main thing.

By eleven o'clock on Christmas morning, a hysterical scream was rising inside Catherine. She'd been up at the crack of dawn grappling with the turkey, then had peeled and chopped a mountain of potatoes, carrots and Brussels sprouts. She'd made a chestnut stuffing with her own bare hands, set the table with her best tablecloth and the nicest silver cutlery, and polished all the wine glasses. Meanwhile, Matthew and Emily battled on the Xbox and Mike got stuck into his new political biography, flanked by the tin of Celebrations and his trusty TV remote. Nobody lifted a finger to help her. Nobody even made her a cup of tea. But then again, she realized, they never had. For all these years, she'd allowed this to happen: she'd waited on them hand and foot as if that was all she was good for. To them, this was simply a perfectly ordinary Christmas Day.

Perfectly crap, more like, she thought darkly, pouring herself a large glass of wine.

When it came to present-opening, Matthew apologized sheepishly for not having bought her anything. 'I haven't had time,' he said, even though he'd done nothing but slob around since he'd been home. Emily, meanwhile, gave her a grannyish toiletries set which Catherine had seen on special offer in the village chemist. Mike, of course, hadn't maintained the charade of happy families as far as actually shelling out and buying her anything. God, no. Catch Mike wasting any of his precious hard-earned money? That would be the day.

Shirley and Brian, Mike's parents, arrived fresh from church. 'Catherine, dear, you're looking very pink,' Shirley exclaimed, then bit her lip and asked, 'Going through the change, are we? Hot flushes?'

Emily tittered, Matthew looked embarrassed and Mike popped another mini Mars bar in his mouth. I'll flush you in a minute, Catherine thought savagely. 'Just busy in the kitchen,' she said. 'Mike, maybe you could get your parents a drink?'

'Ooh, no, Mike, you stay where you are, I know how hard you've been working,' Shirley said before he could move a muscle. Not that he looked as if he was about to move anything, except perhaps his hand back into the Celebrations tin.

'Well, I'll have a brandy,' Brian said jovially. 'Seeing as it's Christmas.'

'And I'll have a sherry,' Shirley said. 'Just a little one. Seeing as it's Christmas.'

And I'll have a nervous breakdown, Catherine thought, whisking back into the kitchen before anyone else could put in an order. Seeing as it's effing bloody Christmas.

Half an hour – and another glass of wine – later, the meal was ready. Catherine set out the dish of buttered vegetables, the crispy roast potatoes, the gravy boat, the bread sauce and the wine. Meanwhile, Mike, Emily, Matthew, Shirley and Brian sat around the table while she fetched and carried, none of them offering to help. Any minute now a chorus of 'Why Are We Waiting?' would go up, Catherine thought furiously.

'Here it comes!' cheered Emily, eyes lighting up as Catherine brought in the turkey, bronzed and glistening on its platter, with juicy, bacon-wrapped chipolatas nestling around it.

'Come to papa,' Matthew said, rubbing his hands together.

'Best meal of the year,' Mike said, licking his lips.

'Oh,' said Shirley, sounding puzzled. 'Did I forget to mention we've become vegetarian?'

Something snapped in Catherine. Happy families, my arse, she thought. She'd had enough.

'Do you know what?' she heard herself saying in a high-pitched voice. 'This Christmas day is the worst one ever. You lazy lot don't deserve any of this.' And before she could stop herself, she raised the turkey platter above her head and hurled it at the wall.

Emily screamed. Mike shouted. Shirley shrieked. Matthew gave a nervous laugh. 'What the ruddy hell . . . ?' cried Brian as the huge turkey splattered against a framed family photo, smearing it with grease.

The turkey bounced off the radiator and down to the carpet where it landed inelegantly, feet sticking up in the air. Chipolatas rained like meaty bullets against the wallpaper, leaving oily blotches in their wake. The photo fell off its hook and down the back of the radiator with a muffled clang.

'*Catherine!*' Mike exclaimed. 'What on earth are you *doing*?'

'She's drunk,' Shirley muttered to Brian, looking appalled.

'She's flipped,' Brian murmured back, jaw sagging.

They were all staring at her in astonishment. Now she'd got their attention at least. Now they'd bothered to look at her. The worm turns, she thought, clenching her fists. 'I'm not drunk or mad or flaming menopausal, thank you very much,' she snapped. 'But I've had enough, do you hear me? Enough. Make your own bloody Christmas dinner, I'm off to Penny's. At least I might get some respect over there.'

'But Mum!' Emily protested, eyes suddenly swimming with tears. 'It's Christmas *Day*! You can't go!'

'Mum, we're sorry,' Matthew said. 'Sit down, let me sort out the turkey.'

Too late. Too bloody late. Catherine was hardened to any tears or protestations. 'Don't worry, *Daddy* will sort it out,' she sneered. 'He's good with birds, isn't that right, Mike?'

Mike had gone very white. 'Catherine . . .' he implored.

'This is ridiculous,' Shirley spluttered.

'Oh, fuck off, Mike,' Catherine replied, ripping off her apron. 'And you,' she added to her mother-in-law. She threw the apron on the table where it landed on the roast potatoes. 'Happy fucking Christmas,' she said, then turned on her heel and left them to it.

Penny answered the door in a purple party hat and gold lamé dress. 'Oh, love,' she said in alarm. 'What *happened*?'

'I just threw the turkey at the wall,' Catherine sobbed. 'And told Shirley to fuck off. Worst Christmas Day EVER!'

Penny pulled her in for a massive perfumed hug. 'Well, that's bogging Christmas for you,' she said, patting Catherine's back soothingly. 'Come and have some of ours. We were just about to start and there's enough food here to sink the *Titanic*.'

'Are you sure you don't mind?' The realization of what she'd just done hit her. Oh my God. All she could think of was the turkey's little legs sticking up, that oily splotch on the wallpaper, the shocked faces around the table. *Happy fucking Christmas.* SLAM.

'Course I don't mind, Cath, the more the merrier. Now then, what are you drinking, hon?'

'Large amounts.'

'I'm on it.'

Half an hour later, the doorbell went again and Emily appeared, white-faced and tear-stricken. 'Just in time for the Christmas pud, love,' Penny said, not batting an eyelid. 'Have a glass of wine and give your mum a cuddle, for goodness sake.'

'Are you all right, Em?' Catherine asked, hugging her tipsily. Christ, that brandy chaser and then the Pinot Grigio had gone straight to her head. 'I'm sorry about the turkey, and . . . well, everything.'

'There's a drumstick or two left here if you're peckish, Emily,' said Penny, whose party hat had slipped rakishly over one eye. 'Or you can go straight to the pudding. Dazza's just heating up the custard now.'

'What's happening at home?' Catherine asked. 'Is it okay? Are Shirley and Brian still there?'

Emily looked dazed. 'Dad told us everything,' she said, her voice catching on a sob. 'About this Rebecca woman. He said he's in love with her and you two are splitting up.' Her voice rose to a wail. 'Why did you have to tell us this on Christmas Day? You've ruined everything!'

'I'm sorry,' Catherine said, wanting to cry herself. 'We didn't mean you to find out like this.'

'*What* did she just say?' asked Janice, Penny's mum, cupping an ear. 'That nice Mike's left you? On Christmas flipping Day? What a tosser.'

'Mum! Don't be rude. Drink your Babycham and shut up,' Penny hissed.

'Mum! Don't understand it meself,' said Darren, Penny's boyfriend, coming into the room with a jug of custard and an aerosol of double cream. He shook up the aerosol and squirted two great clouds of cream straight into his mouth. 'Quality-looking bird like you, Catherine. What's the man thinking?'

'Who's for Christmas pudding then?' Penny asked, trying to change the subject. 'We've got custard and brandy butter and— Darren! Stop that! More wine, Cath?'

'Yes please,' Catherine said. 'I'll have everything, please. I'll die of a heart attack before the day's over.'

'And why the hell not?' said Janice. 'You bloody well tuck in, duck. Not every day you find out your bloke's a scumbag, is it? Men!'

'Oi,' Darren said, good-naturedly. 'We're not all scumbags, Janice. In fact, I've got something to say. This'll cheer everyone up.' He fumbled in his pocket, then dropped into a kneeling position in front of Penny. 'Penny, will you do me the honour of—'

'YES!' Penny screamed before he could finish his sentence. She dropped the serving spoon and grabbed the little box from his hand. 'Yes, Dazza, I bloody well will!'

'Here we go again,' muttered Tanya, Penny's eldest daughter.

'Aww,' sighed Janice. 'Isn't that romantic?'

'Ooh, let's see,' Emily said, perking up a little.

'It's lovely, congratulations,' Catherine said, trying to be pleased for her friend. She *was* pleased for her friend. Totally.

Out of the window, she could see the front door of their house opening, and Shirley and Brian marching out huffily, followed by Mike in an apron looking contrite and harassed.

This was one Christmas Day none of them would forget in a hurry.

Chapter Twelve

Emergenza – Emergency

'Call an ambulance!' Sophie screamed again, as Jim toppled to the carpet, clutching his chest. His face was frozen and an awful groaning sound gurgled up from his lungs. In a single moment, Christmas was over.

There was a beat of stunned silence then the room erupted into full-blown chaos, voices rising in uncontrolled hysteria, the children bursting into frightened tears. Trish and Sophie rushed to Jim's side. 'He's not breathing,' Sophie cried urgently, putting a hand on his chest and finding it unmoving. Her dad's face was shockingly white and lifeless. Had they lost him, just like that? Was it already too late?

Trish looked terrified. 'What should we do?' she gulped. 'Jim! Can you hear me, love? JIM!'

Sophie thought frantically. Back when she'd worked at Val Thorens, the staff had all undergone an obligatory first aid course. She and her friends had been squeamish about it at the time, not wanting to try mouth-to-mouth on the course leader's plastic dummy with the grotesque face; more interested in making plans for that evening's drinking session. But thankfully – miraculously – some of the information had stuck, filed away in a crevice of her brain under 'Might Come In Handy One Day'.

She put a hand on her dad's breastbone and pumped hard, twice, remembering that sometimes this was enough to start the heart beating again. The clock on the mantelpiece ticked a cruel imitation – one, two, three . . . Nothing happened. Shit. 'Make sure the paramedics know he's not breathing,' she shouted over her shoulder. 'Come on, Dad,' she urged. 'Come on.'

There was still no flicker of life. Her own heart thumping, she knelt beside him, put her left hand over her right and laced her fingers together on his chest. Thirty compressions, firmly and quickly, she remembered the course instructor telling them. 'One, two, three . . .' she counted under her breath.

'What's happening?' Trish cried. 'Where's the ambulance?'

'Two minutes away, apparently,' Richard said from somewhere behind her. 'Let me know if you want me to take over, Soph.'

Sophie had no intention of letting anyone take over. She would save her dad's life or die trying. 'Twelve, thirteen, fourteen . . .' she puffed urgently, pushing hard and wishing she had concentrated better that day back in the French Alps. What next? You had to tip the head back when it came to the mouth-to-mouth, she recalled. Pinch the nose, then put your mouth on the other person's and breathe into it, twice. Thirty compressions, then two breaths. Repeat until they started breathing independently. *If* they started breathing independently.

'Come on, Jim,' Trish sobbed, clutching his hand and weeping onto his shirt. 'Please, Jim, come back. It's Christmas,' she added plaintively.

'Twenty-eight, twenty-nine, thirty.' Sophie took a deep breath. *Ready, Dad?* She tipped his head back, pinched his nose shut, then put her mouth to his and breathed out slowly, feeling his chest inflate. His stubble grated against her face; such intimacy felt horribly wrong. Any minute now, she thought, I'll wake up and this will have all been a terrible nightmare.

Two breaths, but still nothing. *Please let me wake up now, please.*

She began the chest compressions again, shot through with adrenalin and anguish and desperation. *Come ON, Dad. Stop messing around. PLEASE.*

'They're here!' came a shout from the window – Julian, Samantha's husband – as the ambulance drew up. He ran to the front door and, seconds later, the paramedics were striding in, a man and a woman with bags of kit, immediately assessing the situation and taking control.

'Well done, love,' the man said to Sophie, kneeling on the other side of Jim. 'I'm Will – let me take over here now.'

'How long has he been out?' the woman asked Trish, taking Jim's wrist in her hand as Will began pumping his chest.

Sophie sat back on her knees, watching helplessly as the paramedics got to work. She could hardly breathe herself, it was such agony. 'Is he . . . ?' she croaked. 'Is he going to be . . . ?'

She couldn't finish the sentence. Trish was crying into her hands and Sophie went over and put her arm around her. 'Come on, Dad,' she said again, tears spilling from her eyes. 'You never even had a slice of our . . .' She could hardly speak, her throat felt so tight. '. . . of our Christmas cake.'

Such a stupid, trivial thing to cry about. So pathetic. But all she could think about was that magnificent cake she and her mum had made together, still in the kitchen, uncut. Jim had been joking all week that he was going to start on it, that he couldn't resist another day without a piece, until Trish had ended up hiding it from him. More tears fell. Dad made things so much easier in the house with his banter and teasing. And now . . . And now he . . .

'Okay, I've got a pulse,' said the woman just then. 'He's breathing.'

Trish sobbed even harder and clung to Sophie.

'He's alive,' Sophie gasped breathlessly through her tears.

'You saved his life,' Trish cried, choking on the words. 'You did it, Sophie.'

Jim was breathing but unconscious, and the paramedics announced they would take him into hospital. Trish immediately started flapping about the Christmas buffet tea, of all things, but Samantha put a calming hand on her arm and spoke, mother to fellow mother, one organizer of many buffet teas to another. 'Now don't you worry about anything except Jim,' she ordered. 'We'll manage perfectly well here. Trish, you're going in the ambulance with Jim, I take it? Sophie, I'll drive you there – I haven't had anything to drink so I'm perfectly safe. Why don't you grab a few things for your dad then we'll head off.'

'Thanks,' Sophie said numbly as Jim was stretchered out to the ambulance. She leaned against the banister in the hall, feeling for a moment like collapsing herself, then managed to get upstairs to gather some toiletries and pyjamas for him. Once in her parents' bedroom, she saw the remains of his Christmas stocking at the end of the bed where he'd unwrapped it that morning – a chocolate orange, a packet of luminous golf balls, a new diary, some ridiculous reindeer socks, a miniature of Famous Grouse . . . Tears stung her eyes. She loved that her parents still did each other stockings after all these years. How sweet was that?

Sniffing, she packed a bag for Jim, adding the reindeer socks in the hope that they'd make him smile. If he ever came round, that was. If she ever saw him smile again.

Jim was in the operating theatre when she arrived at A&E. There was tinsel draped across the computer screens and colourful cards pinned around the reception area, but Sophie felt completely detached from everyone else's Christmas celebrations now, as if happiness was something that belonged to other people.

Trish was in the waiting area, her face greenish-pale. She seemed to have shrunk since Sophie had seen her last: a small, scared woman in a navy-blue anorak who twitched whenever a doctor walked by. 'He's still unconscious,' she told Sophie. Her voice shook. 'They said something about putting him in a medically induced coma while they sort him out.' She clutched at Sophie blindly. 'A coma, Sophie. That's bad, isn't it? What if he doesn't wake up?'

'He will, Mum. He will wake up.' If she kept saying it, she might be able to convince herself, too. 'We've just got to wait it out. You know Dad. Strong as an ox.'

'But what if he dies? What will I do? I won't be any good on my own.' Fresh tears welled in her eyes. 'What am I going to do without him?'

Sophie eased Trish into one of the chairs and took her hands. 'Don't think about that now,' she said. 'Let's wait and see what the doctors say. Come on, Mum, we have to stay positive. He wouldn't want us sitting here upset.'

'I should have been stricter with him,' Trish said, not seeming to hear. 'All that booze he was necking today! I did tell him he shouldn't. I kept telling him! What was I supposed to do, snatch the bottle away from him?'

'It's not your fault, Mum, nobody's to blame.' She felt a pang of guilt, remembering how she'd clinked her glass against her dad's over lunch. *Cheers!* Why hadn't she thought to police his behaviour better as well? 'You did tell him, I heard you. He just got overexcited, didn't he? Couldn't help himself. Bloody big kid, that's what he is.'

They sat there together in silence, both still in their coats. Cliff Richard warbled from the radio and Sophie, who'd never been remotely religious, found herself praying for a Christmas miracle. *Please let him live,* she thought desperately. *I'll do anything. I just want more time with my dad. I want him to see me make a go of something for once, to be proud of me. Is that too much to ask?*

Hours later, the two of them were still in the same seats with only a collection of ghastly half-drunk machine teas and coffees to show for themselves. Samantha, bless her, reappeared with a Tupperware box of turkey sandwiches, Twiglets, scotch eggs and two slabs of the Christmas cake. 'Everyone sends their love,' she informed them, getting a thermos flask from her bag and then, after a furtive glance up and down the corridor, a bottle of brandy. 'Any news?'

Trish shook her head wearily. 'Not really. He's in surgery now. Nobody's telling us anything.'

'Are you going to stay here for the night? I can bring you toothbrushes and things if you want?' Samantha offered.

'Thanks, love,' Trish said. 'We'll stay but there's no need to come back. You've got your kiddies, and it's Christmas after all.'

'They're fine. I'll come back when they're in bed. Text me if you think of anything else.'

Sophie felt bad now for ever turning her nose up at Sam, calling her a goody two-shoes in private. She'd never criticize her again, not after so much kindness. 'Thanks, Sam,' she said, hugging her. 'That's really thoughtful. You're a star.'

Then there was just her and Trish, and the interminable waiting once again. They munched their turkey sandwiches together, both suddenly hungry, although neither of them could face the Christmas cake. 'It doesn't feel right having it without him,' Sophie said.

Trish surreptitiously poured them each a tot of brandy in plastic cups from the coffee machine. 'Sophie,' she said suddenly. 'I want to say I'm sorry.'

'What for?'

'For . . . You know. For what I did. The Drama School thing. I shouldn't have done it. I really regret it.' Her eyes leaked with fresh tears. 'I've not been the best mother I could be, I know that.'

'Oh, Mum.' The brandy surged around Sophie's bloodstream like an electric current and she shut her eyes for a moment, unsure if she was up to this conversation in a dismal hospital waiting area, of all places. 'You don't need to say this. Really. It was a long time ago.'

'But I do need to say it. I should have said it back then. I know you've never forgiven me.'

Sophie realized she was gripping the plastic cup so tightly the thin sides were crackling. It looked as though they were finally going to have the Big Chat, then. She'd thought about it enough times, fired herself up with rage and incredulity. Who wouldn't?

The whole toxic row had centred on her second year of sixth-form college, when she and her parents had undergone an epic saga of disagreement over 'What Sophie Should Do Next'. Against their wishes she'd applied to study drama in Manchester. Against *her* wishes (and completely unknown to her), they had filled out application forms for her to take a business studies course in Sheffield, so they could keep her where they wanted. Increased job prospects, they said. More options. Well, bollocks to that.

The interview and audition at Manchester went better than she could have wished for, and she returned home triumphant and excited about the direction her life would (hopefully) take. Unfortunately, to her great disappointment, no offer of a place arrived. They didn't even bother sending her a rejection. Had she really been that bad?

Of course, her parents were as smug as a rich bloke on a yacht. *Lucky that we came up with a fallback plan, isn't it?* they'd said, brandishing the business studies prospectus.

Sophie said no. They told her it was the best option. Sophie said no again. They said they'd pay for it. No. But—

No.

A stand-off ensued until Sophie finally plucked up the courage to phone the college in Manchester and ask why she hadn't been good enough for a spot on the course (she figured she might as well know if she was hopeless). It turned out that they *had* written to offer her a place after all. 'Yes, you scored very highly in the audition process,' the receptionist told her. 'Although according to our records, you turned down the place back in February.'

'But I didn't,' Sophie stuttered in disbelief. 'I never received the letter! But I *do* want to come!'

It was too late, of course. The college had filled the place – *her* place – with some other student by then. Shaking with rage, Sophie confronted her parents, and it all came out. Her mum had taken it upon herself to reject the place at Manchester on Sophie's behalf – 'I did it for your own good!' she cried shrilly. At which point Sophie stormed out of the house, slamming the door behind her.

For her own good, indeed. Unable to believe that Sophie might actually want to make her own decisions about the future, more like. It was the straw to end all last straws. There and then, Sophie abandoned sixth form, even though she only had two months left, packed up some belongings and walked out, staying on friends' sofas and camp-beds and doing cleaning and waitressing jobs around the clock until she'd saved enough money to go away for good. She was not going to have her life dictated by Jim and Trish any longer, and that was bloody well that.

'Look,' she said now, forcing herself back to the present day. 'That whole Drama School thing . . . it doesn't matter any more. I probably never would have made it as an actor anyway. Maybe you just saved me a lot of heartache.' She didn't mean a single word of this, but had no energy for an argument.

'It's not too late,' Trish said timidly. 'I mean . . . You could reapply now, you know.'

Sophie shook her head. The thought had occurred to her in the past but a lethal combination of pride and paltry finances always stopped her. 'I couldn't afford it, Mum,' she said. 'Let's just leave it. It doesn't matter.'

'It was only because I never really had much in my life,' Trish went on, scrubbing at her eyes with a well-used tissue. 'I wanted you to have all the choices I didn't. I can see now that we should have trusted and supported you, gone along with whatever you wanted to do, whether we agreed with it or not.' She poured them each another tot of brandy. 'I'm sorry, love. I let you down.'

Sophie took a deep breath and stared unseeingly at the vending machine. 'I always felt I let you down too,' she said honestly after a while. 'I felt like I was a disappointment to you and Dad.'

Trish shook her head. 'A disappointment? You? Oh no. We've been so proud of you – all those amazing things you've done.' Her hands shook on her plastic cup. 'Our Sophie, seeing the world, having so many adventures. We loved reading your blog – well, not all of it, not the bits about us. But my goodness! The places you've been! I'm in awe of you, really I am. So's your dad. I couldn't have done half the things you've done.'

Sophie felt dazed at such an unusually emotional outpouring. 'Oh, Mum,' she said, touched. 'Thank you.'

They looked at each other and smiled. It was the nicest moment of the whole day. For a split-second, Sophie even forgot why they were sitting in the hospital as she basked in what definitely looked like love shining from her mother's face.

'Now pass us those Twiglets, will you, I'm still ravenous,' Trish said, sounding more like herself.

'Here,' Sophie said, handing over the box. Maybe miracles *did* happen on Christmas Day after all, she marvelled, biting into a scotch egg. If only there could be one more miracle, please, in the operating theatre . . .

Chapter Thirteen

La vigilia di Capodanno – New Year's Eve

'Ten . . . Nine . . . Eight . . .' boomed the man with the microphone, his florid face filling the TV screen.

Anna glanced over at Pete who had his head back on the sofa, mouth open, eyes shut. He looked as if it would take a bag of Semtex to budge him.

'Seven . . . Six . . . Five . . .' chanted the enormous crowd massed around the London Eye and along the riverbank. There was a sea of tiny lights from their phones and cameras, held up as secondary witnesses to the event.

'Pete,' Anna hissed, elbowing him. 'Pete!' His head joggled with the impact of her nudge but his eyes remained closed. A tiny glistening stream of dribble escaped the side of his mouth and made a break for his jawline.

'Four . . . Three . . . Two . . .' There was the obligatory shot of Big Ben with an enormous countdown timer projected onto its side, the Houses of Parliament lit up like a fairytale castle.

'Pete!' Anna said, digging her elbow in. 'Wake up!'

'One . . . Happy New Year!' yelled the presenter, gurning. The crowd cheered and hugged each other. A thousand new photos flashed into existence. Fireworks exploded over the Thames, bright showers in the sky reflected in the black water below. 'Auld Lang Syne' played while New Year messages scrolled along the TV screen.

Anna huffed a sigh and scowled at Pete. Great celebration this was. On the telly, everyone was dancing and kissing. Here in the flat, Pete had started a low, whistling snore. She gave him a shove. 'PETE!'

His eyes jerked open, a bewildered look on his face. 'What? What's happening? What d'ya do that for?'

'Because it's New Year!' Anna told him exasperatedly. 'You missed it!'

'Oh! Already? I must have dropped off.'

'Yeah,' she said witheringly. 'You must have.'

'Give us a kiss then. Mmmm. Happy New Year, love. I reckon it'll be a cracker.'

'Yeah.' This is the year I'll find my dad, Anna thought. I will. I'm going to do it. 'I reckon you're right,' she added with a bit more enthusiasm.

She knocked back the last mouthful of her prosecco, which was warm by now. 'Want another drink? There's that weird liqueur Mum and Graham gave me.'

'Go on then. Be a devil.'

Anna went to unearth it from the pile of presents yet to be put away amidst their crumpled wrappings. New Year's resolution alert, she thought to herself. Get organized. Clear this dump up a bit. It was absolutely going to happen this year.

'Do you think you're meant to drink it with ice?' she asked, looking dubiously at the bottle. Her mum had brought the liqueur back last summer after a fortnight caravanning around Spain, and the bottle's label was printed with lurid pictures of palm trees and a spurting volcano. It was the sort of thing you'd only touch if you were already completely lashed.

'Yeah, if you've got any.'

Anna opened her tiny freezer compartment to find half a packet of fishfingers, an ancient Cornetto and some frozen peas. The ice cube tray was also in there but unhelpfully empty. 'Actually, let's drink it as it comes,' she decided, uncorking the bottle and sniffing, recoiling at the sharp, sickly aroma that stabbed her nostrils. Bloody hell. Resolution number two: stock up on a classier drinks cabinet. She couldn't imagine her Italian father going anywhere near crap like this. An image popped into her head of fireworks crackling over the Colosseum. *Happy New Year, Dad.*

She eyed the Cornetto, suddenly peckish, then shut the freezer door before she could start scoffing it. Resolution number three: eat more healthily. Nourishing soups and vitamin-packed smoothies. She'd definitely gained a few pounds over Christmas with all the cooking she'd done. Resolution number four: start running again. She, Chloe and Rachel had gone along to the Endcliffe Park Run religiously through the summer, but had slacked off when the weather turned chilly.

'Got any resolutions?' she asked Pete, bringing two glasses and the bottle back over to the sofa. She poured them each a measure and sat down, curling her feet underneath her. The heating had gone off ages ago and the temperature had plummeted outside. (Resolution number five: sort out the timer on the boiler, or at least find the instruction manual.)

'Well . . .' He slid his arm along the top of the sofa behind her head and gazed solemnly at her. Then he made the mistake of sipping his drink and promptly went into a paroxysm of coughing, ruining what had almost become a romantic moment. 'Jesus Christ! What *is* this stuff? Is your mum trying to poison us or something?'

Fearing the reason behind that soppy look he'd just been giving her (what on earth was he building up to?), Anna spoke over his coughs. 'I've got a few. Resolutions, I mean. Find my dad – obviously. Sort my flat out . . .' She gazed around critically. 'Actually, maybe I'll move somewhere new,' she said with a sudden flare of optimism. 'It's a bit of a pit, this place. I only ever meant to be here six months.'

'I was going to talk to you about that,' Pete said. His

earnest gaze was back, his drink safely abandoned on the table. He took her hand in his and played with her fingers. 'Maybe this could be the year we start living together, Anna.'

'Start living together?' Yikes. She hadn't seen that one coming.

'Yeah. Me and you. Maybe I could move in here first, then we could look for a place together. What do you think?'

What did she think? Her instinct was to leap off the sofa and make a cross with her fingers, as if warding off a peckish vampire. No way. He would drive her absolutely mad. He'd want to have sex every night for starters, his feet smelled terrible whenever he removed his socks, his stereo would dwarf her living room, space would have to be found for his lifelong collection of Sheffield United programmes . . .

'Um . . .' she began, not wanting to hurt his feelings. 'I hadn't really thought . . .'

'We've been together *years,* Anna. All our friends are settling down. Plus we'd save a fortune. I reckon it would be good, don't you?'

No, she thought vehemently. No, she didn't think it would be good at all. His annoying little habits would have her climbing the walls within two days.

So why are you still going out with him then, if you feel like that? a voice piped up in her head.

'Er . . .' she said, swigging her drink, forgetting they'd moved on from nice bubbly to vile hell-liqueur. Her throat burned with the alcohol and she spluttered, retching. 'I don't think we should rush into anything,' she managed to say when she'd recovered.

'We're hardly rushing,' he protested. 'Seems like the right time to me, that's all. I'm not saying let's get married or anything.'

'Good,' she blurted out before she could stop herself. Aargh. That was the volcano-juice talking. 'I mean . . .'

'But maybe it's time we stepped up our level of commitment,' he said, clasping her hand.

She stared at him. Where was he getting this tosh from? It sounded like a sentence whipped straight from a bad magazine article.

'Besides,' he said, pulling his hand away all of a sudden and fidgeting. 'I'm getting kicked out of my place next month.'

'You're getting . . . Oh.'

So that was what this was all about. Typical, thought Anna, gritting her teeth. Bloody typical. He couldn't even manage a romantic gesture without cocking it up, for heaven's sake.

'Right,' she said when he didn't say anything else. 'I see. Look, we're both a bit pissed right now. Let's talk about it another time, when we can think straight, yeah? I'm going to bed.'

He put his hand on her thigh and leered. 'You read my mind, babe. Let's see in the New Year properly, shall we?'

*

On New Year's Day, Anna peeled herself thankfully away from Pete, picked up her nan from Clemency House ('Hello, Violet', 'Happy New Year, Elsie', 'Hello, Mrs Ransome!'), then drove up to Skipton with her mum and Graham to visit her aunt Marie and her partner Lois. Anna had been so busy with work lately that she hadn't made any progress with her Gino-hunting, but this, she realized, might be a chance for further investigation. Marie had been on that fateful Rimini holiday with her mum all those years ago, hadn't she? Maybe she could provide the next clue in the search.

Marie was a tall, droopy sort of woman whose mouth turned down at the corners, as if life was a perpetual disappointment (poor Lois, Anna always thought), but her eyes lit up when Anna cornered her in the kitchen under the pretence of helping clear up, and asked her about the holiday.

'Rimini?' said Marie, clingfilming the ricotta and lentil terrine distractedly. (Anna already knew her grandmother would be farting the whole way home after a single slice.) 'Oh my goodness! I haven't thought about that summer for years. It was such a scream. Me and your mum, we really let our hair down.'

And your knickers, by the sound of it, Anna thought, filling the sink with hot, soapy water. 'Sounds brilliant,' she said casually. 'I was thinking of going there for a holiday myself. I don't suppose you've got any old photos to show me?'

'Ooh, yes, probably.' Marie popped a leftover mini sausage

roll into her mouth as she thought. 'Now where might those be? It's probably all changed from our day, mind, but I did have some somewhere . . .'

'You don't need to find them today,' Anna said. The last thing she wanted was for her mum to get wind of her mission. 'Maybe you could post them to me if you do come across them?'

'Yes, of course,' Marie said. 'I've been meaning to sort through my photo albums anyway. It'll give me something to do, won't it?'

'Thanks,' Anna said, trying to hide her glee. Who said private detective work was difficult? So far, everything was falling straight into her lap.

A few days later, Anna headed for Hurst College after work, her head still full of the yummy recipes she'd been researching that afternoon: slow-cooked lamb tagine, a spicy bean and orzo stew, bread and butter pudding with cinnamon custard . . . God, she was starving. Luckily she'd thought ahead and made herself a cheese sandwich that morning. It was now slightly squashed in the depths of her handbag, but she was so famished, she didn't care.

Inside, the college was a bustle of students, old and young, checking lists of classes on a noticeboard. Anna's spirits lifted. She was so glad she was here. Look at all these people on a cold, dark winter's evening, gathering to learn, questing for knowledge! It was quite awe-inspiring. She might just find somewhere to sit and have that sandwich first, though.

A frizzy-haired woman with a large mole on her chin and a clipboard came over, two seconds after Anna had perched on the steps to unwrap her foil parcel. 'Sorry, health and safety regulations, you're not allowed to sit there,' she said. 'Are you here for a class?'

'Yes,' Anna said, standing up again. 'Beginners' Italian.'

'You're in C301,' the woman told her, consulting her clipboard. 'Take the lift to the third floor, follow the signs to C block and it's the first door on your left.'

'Thanks,' said Anna, too distracted by her hunger to pay much attention. What had she said? Third floor, then . . . something. She went to the lift and pressed the button marked 3, then peeled back the foil on her sandwich and took a sneaky bite. Yum. Sod it, she'd eat it in the lift if she had to.

A red-haired woman appeared beside her. 'You're not going up to Italian, are you, by any chance?' she asked. She had pale, freckly skin and wide-spaced blue eyes that gave her a startled air. Late thirties at a guess.

Anna chewed hurriedly, aware that she had shed several bits of grated cheese around her boots. Not a great look. 'Yes,' she replied.

'Oh good. Have you got any idea where we're meant to be going?' The woman paused as if remembering her manners.

'Hello, by the way. I'm Catherine.' Then her forehead puckered. 'Wait – do I know you?'

'I don't think so,' Anna said, then added, 'I'm a journalist, so we might have met while I was covering a story near you, I guess.'

The lift doors pinged open and they stepped inside. Anna's tummy rumbled. 'Sorry,' she said, waving the sandwich. 'That was me. I'm starving. Excuse me.' And she'd just stuffed another bite in her mouth when Catherine's face cleared.

'Ahh! Got it. You're the chef, aren't you? The cookery lady. I never forget a face.'

The chef! The cookery lady! Wow. Recognized in public – how cool was that? But how *un*cool to be recognized while scoffing a grated cheese white bread sandwich. Surely this never happened to Nigella? She swallowed her mouthful quickly and beamed. 'Yes,' she said. 'That's me. Although I'm not a chef, I'm a total novice. But . . . you read the column?'

'*Read* it? I love it. I've been clipping your recipes out and saving them because they're always so good. I made your chestnut stuffing for our Christmas dinner. Not that I got to taste it, mind.'

'Oh?'

'And your mince pies were fantastic. Even better than Delia's, and that's the recipe I've been using for years.'

'Thank you!' Anna couldn't help a dizzying rush of pleasure. Receiving emails and letters from readers was one thing, but to actually meet someone – a real person! – who had used her recipes was amazing. 'Better than Delia, eh? Wow. I'm totally getting that carved into my headstone.'

Catherine smiled shyly. 'Delia who? That's what I say.'

Anna laughed. 'Exactly! I might get a tattoo of that. Good one!'

Ping! 'LEVEL THREE,' droned the lift voice just then, and the doors jerked apart.

Anna threw the rest of her sandwich in the bin as they went into the corridor and looked up and down. 'Aha. Beginners' Italian that way,' she said, pointing at a sign on the wall.

Catherine seemed hesitant now that they had stepped out of the confined space of the lift. 'God. I feel a bit nervous about this,' she confessed. 'I'm so going to be the thick one at the back of the class.'

'No way!' Anna said. 'Or rather, if you are, I'll be with you. I haven't got a clue. Pizza. Spaghetti. That's about my limit.'

'Prosecco,' Catherine ventured.

'Yeah, that too.' Anna grinned. 'Just listen to us, we're practically fluent already.'

The classroom, when they found it, was already full of people. A slight blonde woman perched on a desk at the front – the teacher, Anna presumed. Sitting facing her were two young Asian women who just had to be sisters, one with pink streaks in her hair, the other with a rather sullen mouth. There was also an older lady with extremely glam scarlet cat-eye glasses, knitting something in sparkly pink wool, an older man next to her (husband and wife?), as well as two men – one young and mixed-race, who was playing some kind of game on his phone and not making eye contact with anyone, and another who was slightly older (thirty-something) with a scruffy mop of sandy-brown hair and an open, friendly face.

'Is this the Italian class?' Anna asked.

'*Si,*' said the lady at the front. Nervous energy crackled from her as she stood up. There was something elfin about her, with her pointy little chin, green eyes and blonde bob. '*Buonasera, mi chiamo* Sophie – my name is Sophie.'

Oh. She was English. Anna had assumed that the teacher would be Italian, but she actually sounded as if she was from Sheffield, rather than anywhere more exotic.

'I'm Anna, and this is Catherine,' Anna said hastily, hoping the disappointment didn't show on her face.

'Wonderful,' Sophie said. 'Have a seat. I think everyone's here now. Let's get cracking!'

The lesson began with a round of introductions, first from Sophie. 'I might not seem very Italian to you,' she said apologetically with a glance at Anna – damn, her dismay must have been obvious after all – 'but let me assure you that I have been travelling and working in Italy for the last few years and love the language and culture almost as much as a real native. Perhaps we could start by going around the class with everyone saying their name and a little bit about why they're here tonight.'

The elderly couple went first. 'I'm Geraldine and this is Roy, my husband,' the lady began, putting her knitting down and smiling at everyone. 'We're due to celebrate our ruby wedding anniversary this summer and have booked a package tour around Italy.'

'We've always wanted to see the frescoes in Florence,' Roy put in.

'Pisa, Rome, Pompei, Naples . . . we're doing the lot,' Geraldine said. 'It's going to be our trip of a lifetime, isn't it, Roy?'

His eyes shone adoringly at her through his thick spectacles. 'It certainly is, love.'

'Wonderful,' Sophie said. 'Well, welcome to the class, both of you! I'll make sure you're equipped with all the vocabulary you need before you go.'

'As long as I know how to ask for a glass of port, I'll be all set,' Geraldine said, twinkling like a naughty schoolgirl.

Sophie grinned. 'I think I should teach you how to order champagne if it's your ruby wedding anniversary,' she replied. 'Who's next?'

'I'm George,' said the guy with sandy hair. 'And I'm here because of my New Year's resolution – to use my brain a bit more. I don't have any plans to go to Italy just now, but it would be great to order dinner in an Italian restaurant and understand what I was actually asking for.'

'Sounds good to me,' Sophie told him. 'Nice to have you here, George. How about you?'

She turned to Catherine who blushed scarlet. She had the sort of fair complexion in which colour rose very quickly. 'I . . . I've got a bit more time on my hands now that . . . um . . . at the moment,' she stammered. 'And like George, I haven't used my brain much recently.'

Everyone laughed, assuming she was joking, but Catherine clapped a hand to her mouth and looked mortified. 'Oh gosh, I didn't mean . . .' she cried, as George pretended to look indignant. 'I only meant . . . Oh, sorry.' She gave a nervous giggle. 'I'm sure you're incredibly brainy, George. I'm the dunce around here. I can't even speak English, let alone Italian, who am I trying to kid?'

'Hey, I've been called worse,' George replied easily. 'You'll have to try harder than that if you want to offend me.'

Catherine put her hands up to her red face. 'You can tell I don't get out much, can't you? Hopeless!'

'Not at all,' Sophie told her kindly. 'And it's good to challenge yourself – *brava*! Who's next . . . Ahh. Anna, is it? I recognize you from somewhere.'

Anna smiled. 'I'm a journalist,' she replied. 'In my dreams I'm a *Newsnight*-standard political investigator, but in the real world I write the cookery column for the *Herald*.'

'Of course! I knew there was something familiar about you. My mum loves your column,' Sophie said. 'And you're here because . . . ?'

'Because I recently discovered I have some Italian ancestry,' Anna said. 'And I want to explore that; to look into the culture, learn the language. I've been trying my hand at Italian cookery too,' she went on, feeling unusually shy as everyone gazed at her. 'Working my way round to Prada and Versace,' she joked. 'Maybe via a Ferrari . . . I've got to embrace my inner Italian, right?'

Everyone laughed. 'Too right,' said the girl with pink hair, grinning.

'Thanks, Anna,' Sophie said. 'Have you any plans to go out and meet your Italian family?'

Anna didn't really want to get into the nitty-gritty of not exactly knowing her father yet, let alone any wider family. 'Not at the moment,' she said cagily.

'Well, keep us posted,' Sophie said, seeing her hesitation. 'Who's next? Freddie, is it?'

Freddie was the young dude, Mr Cool, sitting on his own at the back of the class. Very handsome in his black shirt, with the collars ironed into proper points, Anna noticed. Either he was still living with his mum or he was one of those rare guys who had high standards in personal grooming. Pete could do with a few hints there, she thought to herself. 'I'm Freddie,' he said in a husky drawl. 'And I'm here because . . .' He paused, suddenly looking shifty. 'Um . . . Do I have to say? It's kind of lame.'

Anna's ears pricked up. Oy, oy. Mystery man, eh?

'Of course you don't,' Sophie replied. 'If you'd rather not tell us, that's fine.'

Geraldine leaned over inquisitively. 'Is it a girl?' she asked.

Freddie's coolness vanished in an instant and he shook his head, staring down at the desk. Anna exchanged a knowing smile with Catherine and Geraldine. It so *was* a girl, judging by the way Freddie pointedly refused to answer.

Sophie was frowning. 'Freddie . . .' she muttered thoughtfully. 'Do I know you from somewhere? You're not a famous journalist too, are you?'

He shook his head. 'Nah. Still a student,' he said.

'Do you live near Ranmoor?' Sophie tried. 'I've definitely seen you around . . .' Her face cleared. 'Ahh – could it have been in the Gladstone Arms?'

He grinned sheepishly. 'Probably,' he said. 'My parents live near there so I've been known to pop in.'

'That must be it,' Sophie said. 'And snap – mine live round there too. Small world.' She turned to the sisters. 'And finally,' she said. 'Ladies?'

'I'm Nita,' said the rather sulky-faced girl, 'and this is Phoebe, my sister. We're here because . . .' They exchanged a glance. 'We think Italian is a beautiful language,' Nita said unconvincingly.

Phoebe gave a snort. 'Speak for yourself,' she said. 'I'm only here because *she* talked me into it. And she's only here because she wants to meet sexy Italian men!'

It made everyone laugh, even Freddie, and any remaining ice was immediately broken. Sophie's lips twitched. 'Your secret's safe with me,' she promised Nita, who was now giving her sister total evil-eyes. 'Don't worry – what happens in Italian class *stays* in Italian class.' She clapped her hands together. 'Right – I'd better teach you how to say hello to your sexy Italian men, then, hadn't I? Let's not waste any more time. Good evening and welcome!'

Anna arrived home that night tired but exhilarated. She'd really enjoyed the class. Sophie had seemed nervous at first, but quickly got into her stride once she started teaching them some vocabulary. Soon everyone was practising short, halting conversations in small groups. They'd learned basic greetings and introductions, numbers, days of the week and months, before finishing off with the words for different members of the family.

Anna had relished telling the class, '*Mio padre si chiama* Gino.' It felt liberating saying the words out loud when she'd had to be so cloak and dagger around her mum and aunt recently. '*Mia madre si chiama* Tracey.'

'*Brava*,' Sophie smiled. 'Your father is called Gino, your mother is called Tracey. Geraldine? How about you?'

All the way home, Anna let the new, unfamiliar words singsong through her head. *Buongiorno. Come stai? Sto bene. Mi chiamo Anna. Come ti chiami?*

As she let herself into the communal downstairs area of the building, she saw a small package addressed to her in the pile of post on the shelf. Her heart gave a jolt as she recognized her aunty Marie's handwriting. Was it the photos from Rimini? She charged up the steps to her flat and let herself in before ripping through the carefully sellotaped packet.

It *was* the photos. Oh my goodness. Actual evidence of that Italian summer. She lowered herself onto the arm of the sofa and rifled through them shakily. One photo made her gasp out loud.

There was her mum in a bright red dress, posing with her arm around a man in a beachside restaurant. It was evening, her mum had lipstick and heels on, and looked young, pretty and extremely happy nestled against the man. He, meanwhile, was dark-haired, olive-skinned and smoulderingly handsome, with one hand resting possessively on Tracey's waist.

Anna practically stopped breathing as she stared at him. He looked so like her she couldn't drag her eyes away. It had to be her father. It just had to be.

'*Buonasera,* Gino,' she whispered, drinking in every detail of his face. She was almost afraid to blink in case the picture vanished while she wasn't looking. '*Buonasera, Papa.*'

Chapter Fourteen

Che lavoro fai? – What do you do for a living?

Catherine had really enjoyed her first Italian lesson. Well, apart from insulting poor George by saying he hadn't used his brain recently, of course. Thankfully she managed not to put her foot in it for the remaining time, and her classmates were all still speaking to her by the end. Over the next few days, she practised her new vocabulary around the house, in the car, and while she was mulching the garden. She even surprised the postman with a bright '*Buongiorno!*' when he knocked with a parcel.

By the time a week had gone by and she was on her way back to the college for lesson number two, she felt quite excited about learning more.

'*Buonasera!* ' cried Sophie as Catherine walked into the classroom. '*Come stai,* Catherine?'

'*Sto bene, grazie,*' Catherine replied shyly. *I'm well, thanks.* 'How are you? I mean, *Come stai?*'

'*Sto bene,*' Sophie replied. 'Have a seat while we wait for the others.'

Sophie looked very fragile, Catherine thought in concern. She'd noticed last week as well. There were dark rings under her eyes and her wrists were too thin, poking out of her jumper sleeves like knobbly twigs. She was just about to ask if everything really was *bene* when the rest of the class began arriving.

'Evening, ladies,' said Geraldine, coming in on a waft of Chanel. Geraldine had style, with her lovely cobalt-blue coat and heels, and a huge glossy black handbag, the sort that would knock out any would-be muggers with a single wallop. 'Goodness, it's chilly out there, isn't it? Meant to snow tonight, according to the radio. I think we'll have to get the extra duvet out later, Roy.'

'I think you're right, dear,' he said, following in her wake. He winked at Catherine and Sophie. 'I agree with everything she says, you know,' he whispered loudly. 'That's how come we're going to be celebrating our forty years this summer.'

'That's the secret, is it?' Sophie laughed. 'I'll bear that in mind if I ever find myself a husband. As long as he knows he has to agree with everything I say, we'll be laughing. Hello, Anna! Hi, George, come on in.'

Once everyone had arrived, exclaiming over the cold and taking off their coats and scarves, the second lesson began.

'Tonight we're going to learn a few more Italian words and

sentences so that you can start having longer conversations,' Sophie said. 'And we'll all find out a bit more about each other in the process.' She turned to the board and chalked up some words. '*Che lavoro fai?*' she said. 'This means, what job do you do?'

Catherine's stomach gave a lurch. What *job*? She didn't have a job! What was she supposed to say?

'So, Phoebe, let's start with you. *Che lavoro fai?* What job do you do?'

Phoebe twiddled a long strand of hair around her finger. The pink streaks had gone, Catherine noticed, replaced by a striking dip-dye look, with red now colouring the lower six inches of her hair. "I'm a hairdresser," she replied.

'Ahh, *una parrucchiera,*' Sophie told her, writing up the words. 'I should have guessed. So you would reply "*Sono parrucchiera*" – that means "I am a hairdresser". Who's next?'

They went around the class with everyone telling Sophie their occupations. Of course, the other students had far more interesting lives than Catherine. Anna, as she already knew, was a *giornalista.* Nice George who she'd insulted was a gardener – a *giardiniere.* Nita and Freddie were students, Roy was a retired teacher, and Geraldine had been a nurse. 'I'm doing a bit of am-dram now though, to keep myself busy,' she told the class, eyes twinkling. 'So tell me, Sophie, how do I say, "I am an actress"?'

As everyone spoke, Catherine felt herself grow hotter and

hotter and was hardly able to concentrate on what they were saying. Help! What on earth was *she* going to reply? Oh, me? I'm a divorced housewife. Too stupid to get a job. Who'd employ me?

'And finally, Catherine,' Sophie said with a smile. 'Tell us what you do for a living. *Che lavoro fai?*'

Catherine opened her mouth, wishing she could come out with something impressive. 'I'm . . .' A string of lies popped temptingly into her head. *I'm a trapeze artist. I'm a surgeon. I'm an astronaut.* But no. Her poker face was terrible. They'd all think she was mad if she started lying so blatantly. 'I'm just a mum,' she said in the end, with a little laugh. 'I don't really . . . I haven't actually . . .'

Geraldine leaned forward, trying to catch her eye. 'Hardest job in the world,' she put in staunchly, rescuing her. 'No "just a mum" about it.'

'Too right,' Sophie said. 'My mum says the same. Especially having had a daughter like . . . Anyway.' She stopped herself. 'So you can say "*Sono madre*" – I am a mother. How many children do you have, Catherine?'

'Two,' Catherine mumbled, feeling a complete loser. Any minute now Sophie would ask how old they were and she'd have to say eighteen, nearly nineteen, they've left home actually, and everyone would know she wasn't some nice stay-at-home mummy doing the school run and baking biscuits with her tots.

'*Sono madre,*' Sophie wrote on the board. '*Io ho due bambini.* Okay? I am a mother. I have two children.'

Catherine's face flamed as she repeated the Italian words. She wished now she'd mentioned her voluntary work, instead of being so apologetic about her life. It was all about the manner, she reminded herself. Penny didn't have a job – she looked after the house and kids and dogs, in between tennis, shopping trips and lunches. Would Penny have spoken like that, so self-effacing, so weak? No way. Penny would have made everyone laugh with her answer. Penny would probably have asked Sophie to translate 'party animal', or called herself a 'domestic slave' with a comical, long-suffering look. She wouldn't have made excuses for her life.

After conversing about their jobs in small groups, Sophie moved the lesson on to something even more excruciating.

'So, we've found out that Catherine has two children,' she said, flashing her a smile. 'What other questions can we ask each other?'

'Are you married?' Roy suggested, putting up his hand.

'Where are you from?' said Anna.

'Are you single?' said Nita.

'All good questions that might come up in conversation,' Sophie said. 'Let's start with marital status. *Sei sposata?*' She wrote the words up on the board. 'That means "Are you married?" To say "Yes, I'm married" is . . .'

Oh help. This was a nightmare! Was she really going to have to answer this? *No, I'm not married. My husband walked out on me. Never loved me, apparently. Yes, I might have a wedding ring on my finger but it turns out the whole thing was a sham!*

Catherine stood up abruptly. She didn't mean to but her legs suddenly pushed the chair back and she was on her feet. 'I'm just nipping to the loo,' she lied, rushing towards the door.

'Oh,' Sophie said in surprise. 'Well, we've got a coffee break coming up in ten minutes, so . . .'

Catherine didn't stop. 'I'll be right back,' she called over her shoulder, making her escape.

Out in the corridor she leaned against the cool wall and put her head in her hands. What would Penny do now? she wondered desperately. Her friend would probably brazen out the whole 'Are you married?' question in typical Penny style, she thought. 'What's the Italian for useless bastard?' she'd quip, making everyone laugh with her withering eyes-to-heaven look. She might even flash her blingy new engagement ring around. 'What's the Italian for third time lucky?' she'd say, wiggling her fourth finger.

Catherine couldn't do that, though. Penny was Penny, and Catherine was Catherine, both cut from different cloth. She should just go back in there and face the music. She didn't even have to tell the truth about this stupid 'Are you married?' question anyway. What did Sophie and the rest of them care? She could jolly well say, 'Yes, I'm married,' without having to go into the grisly details.

Just do it, she told herself fiercely, pushing the classroom door open again. 'Sorry,' she murmured, taking her seat. 'Needed to blow my nose.'

'No problem. So, Catherine, *Sei sposata?*'

Catherine gripped her hands beneath the desk and did her best to look normal. '*Si*,' she said through gritted teeth, reading the words on the board. '*Si, sono sposata.*' *Yes, I'm married.* If only they knew.

'*Brava!*' said Sophie. 'Let's take a quick break. Back in ten minutes, please.'

Chapter Fifteen

Il bar – The bar

'Thanks, everybody, you're all doing brilliantly.' Sophie stacked up her spare handouts at the end of the lesson and smiled around the room. Two weeks in and she was enjoying her Beginners' Italian class very much, even if Catherine had gone a bit strange on her halfway through tonight. Had Sophie unwittingly put her foot in it somehow? 'Don't forget your homework for next Tuesday,' she added. 'I'll see you again then. *Ciao!*'

After a rocky few weeks, Sophie's life was cautiously returning to a more even keel. Her dad had spent a week in hospital, undergoing bypass surgery, but was back home now and gradually regaining his strength. Her parents had had to postpone their planned holiday to the Canaries, but it seemed a small price to pay.

The Cold War between Sophie and her mum had seen a recent thaw, beginning with a tentative defrosting during Christmas night and becoming a full torrent of melting ice in the following days. Both overwrought and exhausted while

Jim's health seesawed so terrifyingly, they leaned on each other in a way they had never done before, finding comfort in one another's company. The trauma of Jim's collapse and its aftermath had rebooted their relationship, taking them back to square one. A new start.

It was the strangest badge of honour, having saved her own dad's life. Trish made a point of telling every friend and neighbour in full technicolour detail; it was the first part of the story she'd recount each time. 'She was amazing,' she'd marvel to whomever she had captive. 'Like something you might see on *Casualty*. He'd be six feet under if it wasn't for our Sophie, mark my words.'

If her mum was treating her like Florence Nightingale crossed with the Angel of Mercy, her dad was even worse. 'I owe you one, girl,' he said earnestly more than once, clutching her hand in his, moist-eyed. Mind you, if he was feeling less sentimental, he would ring the little brass bell by his bed and shout, 'Nurse Frost! Nurse Frost!' when he was after something.

'I won't bother resuscitating you next time,' she'd grumble as she went to see what he wanted.

Smiling to herself as she thought of his grin – God, but it was good to see that grin again! – Sophie put her notes into her big black tote bag, dimly aware of Geraldine's voice in the background. 'Does anybody want a quick drink? Me and Roy have set *Holby* to tape tonight, so we were thinking of popping to The Bitter End if anyone wants to join us.'

The Bitter End was a pub a short walk from the college, Sophie remembered distractedly, putting on her coat and slinging her bag over her shoulder. She hadn't been in – she hadn't been anywhere lately, let's face it – but it looked a proper old boozer, one that hadn't yet been gastro-pubbed to death.

'Sophie? Are you coming?' Geraldine was suddenly right in front of her, beaming hopefully. For a pensioner she was surprisingly nifty on her feet.

'Oh . . . me?' Sophie said, taken aback.

'Yes, you,' Geraldine replied. 'I'd ask you in Italian except I don't know how yet. What do you reckon? Quick snifter before we go our separate ways?'

'You don't have to,' Roy added in the next breath, as if he was used to deflecting his wife. 'I'd love to pick your brains about Italy, though. Places you've been, tips for beginners . . .'

'Better buy her a drink, love, if you're going to be badgering her all night,' Geraldine warned, with a fond smile at her husband. 'What do you say? The others are coming – well, except Freddie. He's busy, apparently Maybe next time, he said.'

Ahh, thought Sophie, remembering the romantic scene she'd witnessed in the Gladstone – Freddie and the pretty girl in the bomber jacket rushing towards each other. Maybe she was the reason Freddie was learning Italian in the first place, so he could impress her with his cultured ways.

Geraldine was still waiting for an answer. 'Well?' she asked.

'Go on, then,' Sophie said. It had been ages since she'd been out for a drink with anyone. 'That would be lovely.'

'So we've got a red wine for Anna, orange juice for Catherine, Guinness for George, a port and lemon for Geraldine, a . . . What was this one again?' Roy squinted at the lurid red drink in the shot glass.

'It's a Sourz, Roy,' Phoebe replied, smiling up at him. 'Thanks, that's mine. Nita's having the cider.'

'Thanks,' Catherine said shyly.

They had found two large tables in a cosy corner of The Bitter End, an old-fashioned sort of pub with dark-wood panelling on the walls, horse-brasses nailed to the black beams and a roaring log fire.

'A diet Coke for Sophie and a bitter for yours truly. There!' Roy placed the last drink on the table with a flourish and tucked the tray beside the table. 'Well, cheers everybody. Nice to come out like this together for a proper chat. We don't have to speak in Italian now, do we, Sophie?'

Sophie grinned. 'Certainly not. Now you can all relax and be yourselves for another week.' She raised her glass. 'Maybe I should just teach you how to say "Cheers" in Italian though, then I'll switch off teacher mode. It's *salute!*'

'*Salute!*' everyone chorused, clinking their glasses against each other.

'God, I feel dead cosmopolitan now,' Phoebe said, sipping her drink. 'I'm telling you, my boyfriend loves all these words we're learning. He made me keep whispering "*Tuuutti Frrrruuutti*" into his ear the other night while we were . . .' She blushed violently, suddenly remembering she was with a group of relative strangers, then coughed. 'Um . . .'

Nita elbowed her. 'Pheebs! We don't want to know your dirty little secrets!' she cried, horrified, but everyone was laughing.

'Now there's an idea,' Geraldine twinkled, nudging Roy. He looked startled for a moment, then raised an eyebrow so impishly that they all laughed again, even Phoebe.

'It's such a gorgeous-sounding language, isn't it?' Anna sighed. '*Mamma mia!* I can't wait to go.'

'Have you booked a trip?' Sophie asked, vaguely remembering Anna saying something about having family in Italy.

'Not yet.' She looked furtive. 'I'm still trying to decide where to go. I was thinking maybe Rimini. Has anyone been?'

Sophie shook her head. 'It's north, isn't it? On the east coast. I haven't been though.'

Nobody had, it seemed.

'I've been to Sicily,' George offered. 'Had a fantastic time there. I've still got a guidebook if you want to borrow it.'

'I was working in Sorrento before I came here,' Sophie

added. 'That's a great place to base yourself for a holiday. One – it's absolutely gorgeous, and two – it's dead easy to get out to Pompeii and Naples for day trips, as well.'

Anna didn't seem quite so enthusiastic about Sicily or Sorrento. 'I kind of need to go to Rimini,' she said mysteriously. 'I'm on a mission, you see.'

'How intriguing!' Geraldine said, leaning forward and setting her glittery earrings swinging. 'What kind of a mission? Tell us more!'

Anna sipped her wine. 'It's a long story,' she said. 'I don't want to bore you all with it.'

'Oh, you wouldn't be,' Geraldine assured her, but Roy put his hand over hers warningly. 'Don't nag,' he said. 'She'll tell us if she wants to.'

Anna looked really on the spot now, Sophie thought. 'Well . . . It's just . . . I'm looking for my dad,' she said.

'Is he lost?' Phoebe asked in confusion.

'Shut up, you spanner,' Nita hissed. 'You're drinking too quickly.'

'Ahh,' Geraldine said, looking uncharacteristically awkward. 'Sorry, dear – that was nosey of me. None of my business.'

Anna shrugged. 'No, it's cool.' Her mouth twisted as if she was debating whether or not to go any further, but then out the words tumbled in a rush. 'I've never known him, you see. Mum wouldn't even tell me his name. Then my nan let it slip. He's called Gino and he's Italian. And I think he and Mum got together when she was on holiday in Rimini.'

There was a general chorus of oohs and ahhs. 'Wow,' Sophie said. 'That's pretty massive.'

'Have you got anything else to go on?' George asked. 'I mean, have you tracked him down any further?'

'I've got a photo,' Anna said. 'But that's it, basically. I know it's a long shot, but I was thinking of going over and just showing it to people – everyone I can. I'm a journalist, I'm used to pursuing a lead, so . . .' She spread her hands out in front of her. 'What else can I do? I really want to meet him. I've got to try.'

'Hence you learning Italian,' Sophie realized.

'Yes.' She grimaced self-consciously. 'So please make sure I can say "Do you recognize this man?" by the end of the course, Sophie. I need the full Dad-finding vocabulary so that I'm tooled up and ready for action.'

'Good for you,' Catherine said.

'Yeah, fingers crossed,' George put in.

Geraldine leaned over and patted Anna's hand. 'I'm sure you'll find him,' she said. 'And when you do, won't he be thrilled to meet a lovely daughter like you.'

Tears appeared in Anna's eyes and she blinked them away with a watery smile. 'Oh Geraldine . . . thank you,' she said.

'Now look what you've done!' Roy exclaimed. 'You've gone and set her off! Honestly, I can't take her anywhere. Sorry about my wife, everybody. Can you believe I've put up with this sort of shenanigans for nearly forty years? It's no wonder my hair's white.'

Sophie chuckled. Roy reminded her of her dad, pretending to be long-suffering, yet it was clear to anyone he adored his feisty wife.

Geraldine swatted him playfully then raised her glass. 'To Anna's mission,' she pronounced.

'To Anna's mission,' everyone chorused.

'And a happy ever after,' Nita said. 'An Italian dad, that is so cool. Hey, and let us know if he has any fit sons, won't you?'

'I thought you liked Freddie!' Phoebe blurted out, and received a whack from her sister in return.

Catherine cleared her throat and went bright pink. 'Can I get anyone another drink?' she asked.

As the first drink turned into a second, and then a third, the group split into smaller clusters of people, and more intimate conversations developed. Sophie was sitting near Geraldine and Roy, and listened as Geraldine began asking Phoebe's advice about her hair.

'It's for the production,' Geraldine said, rather grandly. 'Remember me saying I do a bit of am-dram? If you could give me some pointers about the look I should go for, that would be splendid, dear.'

'What's the play?' Sophie asked curiously. It had been years since she'd been to the theatre. 'And have you got a good part?'

'She's the star, of course,' Roy said loyally.

'Give over, Roy Brennan, I'm no such thing,' Geraldine scoffed. 'I've only got two lines, love. The play's called *Money Talks,* and I'm an estate agent. Two lines, that's all I get, trying to sell a mansion to this daft bint who's won the lottery.' She pursed her lips and spoke in a hoity-toity voice. 'Can I help Madam with anything?' she said. 'That's my first line. I haven't learned the second yet. Pacing myself, you see.'

Sophie laughed. 'You can't rush these things,' she agreed solemnly. '*Money Talks,* did you say? I don't think I know that one.'

'Oh, you wouldn't. The director wrote it and it's a pile of you-know-what, to be honest.' She rolled her eyes, and Sophie couldn't help thinking that Geraldine was wasted in a two-line part. She had 'leading lady' written all over her. 'So, Phoebe, as I was saying. Estate agent hair . . . What would you advise?'

Phoebe looked a bit tipsy and swayed slightly on her stool as she spoke. 'God, I dunno, tidy and neat, nothing dead flamboyant or wild . . .'

Geraldine seemed dismayed by this advice. 'Oh,' she said, her mouth pinching together.

'Unless she's a rebellious sort of estate agent,' Phoebe added quickly. 'Y'know, like, she's a bit edgy.'

'Edgy, yes.' Geraldine nodded. 'I like the sound of that.'

'In which case I'd say, try adding a thread of colour. Not a blue rinse or anything naff, just a gorgeous stripe of lilac or something.'

'Hmmm.'

'*Or*,' Phoebe went on, seeing that this suggestion had gone down like a punctured dinghy, 'I could do you a lovely chic bob. Maybe a bit choppy. Swingy at the front, quite glam. Yeah. How about that?'

'Splendid!' Geraldine pronounced. 'That sounds just the ticket. Thank you, Phoebe. I shall book myself in nearer the time and you can do me over.'

Phoebe spluttered on her drink (this one was lurid green and looked positively radioactive). 'You mean *make* you over,' she said.

'Make me over! Oh dear, I've had one too many,' she giggled. 'Roy, keep an eye on me, will you? I'm going to get myself in trouble at this rate.'

Phoebe opened her purse and pulled out a business card. 'Here you are,' she said, passing it to Geraldine. 'Sophie, do you want one too? Anyone else? Cath, can I just say, you'd look awesome with a fringe. Thought it as soon as I clapped eyes on you.'

'Oh!' said Catherine, looking startled but pleased. 'Do you think so?'

'I know so. Give me a bell if you want me to work some magic for you, yeah?'

'I will.'

'We all will,' Sophie promised, and slipped Phoebe's card into her purse, planning to treat her mum as a surprise. After all the running around Trish had done for Jim lately, she could do with a bit of pampering. 'So, Geraldine,' she went on, 'when can we expect to see you in your play? I hope you realize we're all going to be getting seats in the front row now.'

Geraldine clapped her hands together and gave a squeal of excitement. 'You must! Roy, when is it? I'm hopeless with dates. Sometime in February anyway. But do come along. It'll be a hoot!'

It was nearly ten o'clock before Sophie's class disbanded and stumbled away in different directions, calling goodbyes into the frosty air. A biting wind stung her face as she walked the short distance to the bus stop, but she couldn't stop smiling. They were all so nice, so interesting! Even Nita, with the permafrown, turned out to be charming after a drink, and extremely intelligent too, judging by the sound of the PhD she was halfway through. Sophie and Geraldine had talked about acting for ages, then Anna had picked her brains about travelling around Italy. George had made everyone laugh, telling them about some terrible band he used to be in, and Catherine was so sweet and nice to everyone, even though she didn't seem to have a single shred of self-confidence.

Sophie was used to striking up conversations with people she didn't know; she'd become an expert after years of travelling. There was a standard pattern of conversation with fellow travellers – where you were from, how long you had been travelling, where you'd been, key highlights of your trip (magic mushrooms on beaches featured heavily), key lowlights of your trip (dysentery and mugging featured heavily), where you were going next. What struck her about tonight's conversations was how deeply rooted they all were in Sheffield. Nobody was talking about moving on, or competing about the most remote place they'd ever visited. Instead, they seemed happy to be right where they were. Interesting.

She got on the bus and sat upstairs, still thoughtful. Then, as they drove past the cathedral, lit up against the dark sky, she couldn't help remembering all the school Christmas concerts held in there, the way your footsteps would echo when you walked around, the dusty smell of the old building. There were so many memories in this city, ambushing her at every turn, reminding her of times gone by.

What are you running away from, Sophie? her dad had asked back in the hospital. It was becoming hard to remember the answer any more.

Chapter Sixteen

Una scoperta – A discovery

'Look, stop freaking out, it's like falling off a horse,' Penny hissed, uncorking a bottle of red wine with a soft pop. 'You need to get straight back in the saddle. Trust me.'

Catherine glared at her friend, but unfortunately she had her back turned – deliberately, no doubt – and was filling four wine glasses with Merlot. Falling off a horse, indeed. She felt like pushing Penny under the thundering hooves of a horse at that moment. *Come over for dinner on Saturday*, she'd said. *Just me and Dazza*, she'd said. *I'll get rid of the kids, we can chill out and have a laugh together.*

How kind, Catherine had thought gratefully, knocking on the door at seven o'clock that evening with the Merlot and a box of Bendicks. How thoughtful.

She should have known from Penny's shifty expression that there was a catch.

'Catherine – this is Callum, a mate of Darren's,' she said as they went into the living room. The dogs were doing an impression of a patchwork fur rug in front of the gas fire, as usual, and Tanya, Penny's eldest, was sprawled in the armchair having a loud phone argument. Rising from the caramel leather sofa, an expectant smile on his ruddy, porcine face, was Callum, a vision in a pea-green Fred Perry shirt and beige chinos.

You conniving cow, thought Catherine, stunned into panicky silence. In the dining space at the back of the long room she could see the table had been set for four, with candles and wine glasses. I'm going to kill you for this, Penny.

'Nice to meet you,' Callum said, his voice surprisingly high pitched. He was probably mistaken for a woman all the time on the phone, Catherine thought distractedly.

'Hi,' she said, fully aware of her old jeans, the red smock top she'd had on all day, the fact that she hadn't bothered putting on make-up *because this was only meant to be a casual dinner with Penny and Darren.* She turned to Penny and asked in a strangled voice, 'Need any help in the kitchen?'

Callum was five years younger than her and at least an inch shorter. He operated a fork-lift truck in a warehouse, he told Catherine when she asked him about himself.

'Ahh,' she responded politely. 'Um . . . What sort of things do you lift?'

'Crates, mainly,' he replied, forking a huge dollop of mash into his mouth as if demonstrating the skill involved.

Crates, mainly. God almighty. Where did they find this one?

Catherine scowled at Penny, who, to be fair, was starting to look extremely apologetic.

'I thought he'd be all right,' she whispered guiltily in the kitchen, when the two of them cleared the dishes and plates from the main course (a slab of gammon, with mash and peas; Penny was never going to be a contender for *MasterChef*). 'Darren's always saying what a laugh he is down the pub.'

'Well, I'm not laughing now,' Catherine replied. Sitting on her own lonely sofa like a Saturday night loser was starting to look a lot more appealing than being stuck here with Pigboy.

'Sorry, love,' Penny said, getting a stack of bowls out of the cupboard. 'I just thought you could do with some fun, that's all. I'm not matchmaking or anything.'

'Course you're not, Pen.'

Penny had pushed the boat out and defrosted a Sara Lee gateau for pudding, although when she served it, there turned out to be slivers of ice still lurking in the sponge which made it unpleasantly cold and crunchy.

'So,' Catherine said gamely, wincing as an icy shard made her fillings tingle, 'how are the wedding preparations going?'

'I'm thinking Amsterdam for the stag weekend,' Darren said, winking at Callum.

'Sick,' Callum replied enthusiastically. 'I went there for my brother's stag do, saw this wicked stripshow. Those Dutch birds will do *anything*.'

'We've booked a nice pub for the reception,' Penny said quickly, noticing Catherine's face. 'Invitations go out next week.' She jumped up to grab a magazine from the sideboard and flicked through to a Post-it-marked page before shoving it in front of Catherine. 'What do you think for the bridesmaids, by the way? Pink or lavender flower garlands?'

'Oh! Tanya's agreed to be a bridesmaid?' Catherine asked in surprise. Penny's daughter had flatly refused earlier that month, saying that she'd already been her mum's bridesmaid twice and she wasn't going near a stupid dress again, thanks very much. After much begging and pleading, she had 'compromised' by saying she would only be a bridesmaid if she could wear black, knowing full well that Penny would never agree to this. (Tanya was going through an all-black phase which involved lots of eyeliner, death metal and bad poetry. She no longer did colours.)

'No. I've given up on Tanya, she said she'd rather die than wear a ruffle. The dogs are going to be my bridesmaids.'

'The *dogs*?'

'Yeah, I'm getting little flowery things made for them to wear around their necks. They're going to look so adorable.'

'Lovely,' said Catherine, wondering if her friend was joking.

She wasn't. 'I know! As long as they don't pee in the register office, that is. Can you imagine? More cake, by the way?'

*

At the end of the evening, Callum insisted on walking Catherine home, even though you could see her front door from Penny's. 'I'm fine,' she said, putting on her coat (her knackered old gardening coat with one pocket hanging off because she hadn't thought she needed to dress up for a quiet night in at Penny's). From now on, she'd never knock at her friend's house again without a) full make-up b) clean clothes and c) peering through the lace curtains to suss out any so-called eligible bachelors who'd been invited along too.

'As a gentleman, I insist,' he slurred.

A gentleman? When he'd been wittering on about the glories of unrepressed 'Dutch birds' and lapdance clubs half the evening?

'As someone who is perfectly capable of crossing the road unescorted, *I* insist,' she retorted.

He took a few seconds to process the long words in the sentence. Then he beamed. 'I like a clever bird,' he told her. 'Come on, gorgeous. Let's get you home. Hey, we could even have a nightcap, what do you say?'

Was he insane? Catherine looked beseechingly at Penny for assistance.

'Callum, love, she's fine,' Penny told him. She'd been at the Dubonnet and her eyes were starting to cross. 'See you both soon, yeah?'

'Thanks, Penny,' Catherine said, hugging her. Despite the matchmaking, it had been nice to spend the evening away from her own telly. She'd only have ended up watching something crap like *Ice Road Truckers* left to her own devices.

'Thanks, babe,' Callum said, putting his fat arms around Penny and squeezing. He was shorter than her and his head rested cosily on her shoulder. He was looking straight down Penny's top, Catherine noticed with revulsion.

'Run,' Penny mouthed over his head, and Catherine slipped out of the door, with a last wave to Dazza, and trotted hurriedly across the street.

Not fast enough, though. 'Wait!' came a yell, seconds later. 'I thought I was going to . . .'

Catherine broke into a run. She opened her door as fast as she could and practically fell into the hallway, double-locking it and putting the chain on for good measure. Then she peeped through the spyhole and watched as Callum veered in zigzags down the road. 'Show me the way to go hoooome,' she heard him singing a moment later, and wasn't sure whether to laugh or cry.

She slid down the radiator until she was sitting on the carpet, head on her knees, arms wrapped around her legs. If she'd wanted to, she could have invited him in for a 'nightcap' – and the rest. They could have been having sex right now on her hall carpet if she'd given him the slightest encouragement.

The thought made her feel like throwing up her boiled gammon and chocolate gateau. It had been so long since she'd so much as *looked* at another man; she'd always been loyal through and through. Just the idea of letting someone other than Mike undress her, touch her, kiss her . . . Would she ever be ready to do that? Was she destined to spend the rest of her days alone?

'Get a cat,' her mum had advised sympathetically the last time they'd spoken on the phone. 'They won't muck you around like a bloke, and they're a damn sight cleaner.'

If the alternative was men like Callum, then Catherine was starting to think her mum had a point.

On Sunday, Catherine drove out to the care home for her lunchtime shift, helping in the kitchens and with the never-ending laundry. This was one of the many voluntary turns that she'd ended up being roped into: she was a sucker for a good cause. Mike hadn't been very keen on the idea of her getting a job ('Your job is being my wife,' he'd always told her), so she'd gradually accumulated ways to fill her empty days: listening to infants read at the local primary school, shopping for elderly neighbours, working a couple of mornings in a charity shop, walking dogs at the nearby animal rescue shelter, litter-picking with the Woodland Trust group . . . 'Oh, Catherine will do it,' people tended to say, and she always found it difficult to say no.

She was fond of her ladies at Clemency House, though, as well as the scant few male residents, of course. The stories you heard there! The lives that had been lived! Violet Wickes, for instance, had been a dancer in her day – showgirl rather than prima ballerina – and had hoofed it around the world. She could still give you a few steps on a good day. Then there was Alice, who might look sweet and doddery now, but who had been a firebrand political activist in her youth – camping at Greenham Common for months on end and leading marches on Downing Street. 'I've been arrested that many times for breaching the peace, they joked about building me my own cell,' she told Catherine cheerfully. And of course there was Nora, who had the naughtiest stories about her exploits back when she was a gorgeous young thing. She was a total scream.

All these amazing women. Catherine hoped she'd have something interesting to say for herself if she lived long enough to end up in a place like this.

She was still thinking about it later in the afternoon as she drove on to the animal shelter and took two of the dogs out for a tramp in the woods. Violet, Alice and Nora might all be old and shaky now, with clumpy orthopaedic shoes and occasional forgetfulness about what year it was, but whenever they talked about the past, their eyes lit up and you could see a flash of how they must have been in their prime: young and vibrant and making their mark on the world.

What was *her* mark?, she wondered, hardly noticing the dogs frenziedly pulling on their leads as a squirrel leapt up a tree in front of them. What would she look back on in years to come and recount with pride?

There had to be something, she thought to herself. There must be something noble and brave and exciting she could do. Mustn't there?

The heavens opened while she was out and she ended up running back to the shelter with the dogs, all of them dripping wet and muddy. The dogs didn't mind a bit – a quick shake and a rub down with the blanket and they were fine. Catherine, meanwhile, squelched back to the car, feeling cold and sodden. She'd jump straight in the shower when she was home, she decided, already envisaging the hot chocolate and toast she'd make for herself afterwards.

Such plans went out of her head, however, when she turned into their road and saw Mike's Peugeot sitting there in the driveway. Her knuckles whitened on the wheel as she parked beside it. What was he doing here? He'd kept his distance since Christmas and the awful turkey-flinging incident; he certainly wouldn't have dropped round for a pleasant chat and a slice of cake. Something bad must have happened. Something major. Oh God, please not the children.

Yanking on the handbrake, she hurtled from the car like an Exocet missile, fumbling with her keys at the front door. 'Mike? Is that you? Is everything all right?' she called.

He emerged down the stairs, looking irritated. 'Where on

earth have you *been*?' he cried. Then he stopped midway down and stared at her. 'Jesus, Cath, what have you done to yourself?'

'Wh-what?' she gulped, forgetting for a moment just how bedraggled she must look. 'I've been out. What's going on?'

'God, look at the state of you. You're dripping all over the carpet, for heaven's sake.'

How did he do that – make her feel small within a few seconds? She meekly took her coat off and hung it up, feeling as worthless as ever. Rebecca never looked anything less than perfect, no doubt. 'What are you doing here?' she asked, trying to wrest back control of the conversation. 'You haven't answered me. Is something wrong? What's happened?'

'I've been phoning you all day,' he said impatiently. 'When you didn't bother replying, I let myself in. I needed to get the mortgage documentation so we can get the ball rolling here.'

Get the ball rolling? She stared at him dumbfounded. 'What do you m-m-mean?'

He couldn't look her in the eye, she noticed. 'What do you think I mean? Look, Cath, you've got to move on. We're splitting up. And – not to put too fine a point on it – this is my house.'

'But . . .'

'I bought it, I've made all the mortgage payments. And now I want to buy a place with Rebecca, so . . .' He shrugged. 'I'm going to put this house on the market.'

'But what about me?' she croaked. Her heart was pounding. 'This is my home.'

He looked away. 'That's your problem, I'm afraid,' he said. 'I'm sorry, but I can't afford to keep two houses going. I'll send a few estate agents round in the week, okay?'

'Wait, Mike! We need to talk about this,' she said, but he was already pushing past her and walking to his car. Without another glance, he started the engine, reversed out into the road and drove away.

Shit. She had been dreading this: moving out of her home, having to start again somewhere else. She still didn't have a job or any kind of income, no savings fund or plan B. Wild, desperate thoughts hurtled through her head. Should she crawl back to her mum's in Reading? Ask to lodge with Penny? Prostrate herself to the council, beg for some temporary accommodation? Would she end up sleeping on the streets?

No. Of course she wouldn't. Mike was a good man, he wouldn't throw her out with nowhere to go. Would he?

The front door was still wide open and she closed it with a shaking hand, imagining a different woman standing here soon, closing the same door. Another family would move in, attracted by the generous-sized rooms, the lovely garden, the proximity to a great primary school and local amenities. Meanwhile, what was to become of *her*?

It was then she noticed the document case abandoned in

the hall; Mike had forgotten to take it with him. She picked it up, wondering what he'd put inside. All their mortgage statements, no doubt, and other house-related paperwork, so that he could 'start the ball rolling'. A cannonball, smashing straight through her life.

Her fingers hesitated on the metal catches. Would it be snooping for her to read through them?

No, she decided. They had both lived here for ten years. He might have paid for everything, but this was still her *home.*

The catches made loud clicking sounds as she opened the case and lifted the lid. Inside were a number of clear plastic document wallets, neatly labelled MORTGAGE, HOUSE and SP. She frowned. SP? What was SP?

She lifted it out from under the other wallets, but in her haste she dropped it and papers fanned everywhere on the hall carpet. Crouching down to pick them up, she froze as she saw a number of bank statements from Barclays Bank. Weird. A buzzing sense of déjà vu started up inside her as she stared at the papers. Since when did Mike have a separate account? She'd thought everything went through their joint Co-op account. What was going on?

Then she picked up one of the statements for a closer look and her mouth fell open in shock. Breathing hard, she read the figures again, wondering if her brain was deceiving her.

But no. It was all there in black and white. Almost one

hundred thousand pounds in a separate account for Mike, with every payment listed as a transfer from CENTAUR.

Catherine's mouth was dry. She didn't understand. It didn't make sense. Who or what was Centaur, and why had they been paying her husband so much money?

Chapter Seventeen

Il foglio di calcolo – The spreadsheet

'You don't mind, do you? It'll only be for a few weeks.'

Anna did mind. She minded a lot that Pete had taken it upon himself to use her flat as storage space for umpteen boxes of his crap while he negotiated some new living arrangements. 'No,' she said through gritted teeth as he dumped a box of lurid-covered fantasy novels on her bed.

'Great. Put the kettle on, will you, babe? I'm dying of thirst here.'

Can you not try dying a bit quicker? she felt like snapping, but curbed her tongue at the last second. Clambering over a wobbling tower of boxes and crates – why was a boomerang sticking out of one? Since when had Pete ever been near the southern hemisphere? – she swore under her breath as she entered the kitchen. She'd been trying out different varieties of ginger cake that evening for her next column and had left two dark, sticky beauties cooling fragrantly on a rack, only Pete had now shoved a box marked 'Kitchen Stuff' on the worktop, and in doing so had somehow showered dust and God knows what all over the top of them.

This was a terrible mistake. Letting him store his wretched football programmes and sci-fi videos in her flat was the start of the slippery slope. She'd managed to put off co-habiting for the time being at least, but for how long? She really had to put her foot down, make a clean break, get rid of Pete *and* all his stuff. Otherwise, before she knew it, years would go by and she'd wake up an old woman, still here with him. She'd hate herself for it.

'I've got to,' she muttered.

'Got to what, love? Give us a flash of your boobs?' There he was, popping up in the kitchen with that annoying cheeky-chappy smirk. 'Cor, now you're talking. And you baked me a cake and all. Two cakes! How's that cup of tea coming on, then?'

She took a deep breath. Now was as good a time as any. However terrified she was of becoming a lonely, dried-up old spinster, the alternative – this – seemed worse by the minute.

'Pete,' she said, trying to keep her voice neutral and calm. She put down the bottle of milk and folded her arms. 'Listen . . . I've been thinking.'

'Whoa!' He pretended to fall over in shock. Very funny. 'Well done and everything, babe, but I was just coming to say, I've got to move my car. I double-parked and your neighbour's just come out and had a go at me.' He pointed both index fingers at her like a cheesy gameshow host. 'So hold that thought, babe. Don't let it go to waste. I'll be right back.'

Said the man with so few brain cells you could give each one a name, Anna thought as the door slammed. She accidentally-on-purpose sloshed too much milk in his tea, just to annoy him, then gazed at the picture of Rimini she'd stuck on her fridge and sighed, wishing she could be there right now. Far away, feeling the warm sunshine on her bare skin, wearing sunglasses and flip-flops and exchanging life stories with her father. Instead she felt nothing but advancing claustrophobia as Pete's possessions invaded her space.

Meeting her father in Italy *would* happen, she was determined. The other people in her Italian class had looked at her as if she was some kind of nutter the other night, when she'd admitted her plan to them in the pub. They probably all thought she was barking, haring off on some mad hunt for him, with only a single photograph in her armoury. She wouldn't give up, though. No way. She'd regret it for the rest of her life if she let this lead go unexplored.

Her phone buzzed. *Might as well pick up a load more stuff now I'm in the car,* read the text from Pete. *Back in an hour or so x*

More stuff? How much stuff did he actually have? It had never looked that much when scattered messily around his place, but overnight he seemed to have turned into the male equivalent of Imelda Marcos with a vast array of possessions. There would be no room left for her to move at this rate.

Scowling at the dust-covered ginger cakes, she cut herself a slice of Christmas cake instead (two weeks into January and it still tasted fabulous) and took it and her mug of tea into the living room, planning to catch up on some emails while Pete was out.

A single step into the living room though, and she saw that he'd managed to completely fence in her PC on the tiny corner table with a blockade of boxes and a suitcase. Anna let out a groan of exasperation. Brilliant. How was she meant to get any work done now?

Cursing ferociously, she squeezed herself into the small space left on the sofa and flicked on the TV instead while she munched her cake. Nothing on. Then her gaze fell on Pete's laptop bag, balanced on one of the boxes. Sod it, she'd use that instead. She reckoned he owed her a few favours.

Opening it up and guessing at the password (Blades: bingo. Football and sex tended to be uppermost in Pete's mind; it was always going to be one or the other), she went online and began replying to the most recent comments and emails from her readers. Her latest recipe had been a hearty vegetarian stew to warm even the coldest of evenings. It featured squash, chickpeas, home-made roasted tomato passata, and various other vegetables and herbs, and had been utterly gorgeous, even if she said so herself. From the numerous emails she'd received, her readers seemed to like it just as much, apart from a few diehard carnivores who'd emailed in to say it would have been nicer with some pancetta or diced chicken. There was always someone who thought they could do it better, but Anna didn't let it bother her. She had never claimed to be anything other than an amateur.

Thanks so much, everyone, she typed. *Your comments are always welcome, and there are some great suggestions here. Meanwhile, I've got a couple of different ginger cakes cooling in my kitchen . . . I'll give you the recipe of the yummiest one later this week. Keep on cooking!*

Time passed so pleasantly that she completely lost track of the evening. When she next glanced up at the mantelpiece clock she realized that a) she had a horrific crick in her neck from peering down at the laptop and b) it was ten o'clock and Pete still hadn't returned.

As if he was reading her mind, her phone buzzed just then with another text. *Decided to stay at Mum's after all. See you tomorrow? P x*

Okay, see you then. Night x, she replied. Was it wrong that her first reaction was one of relief that she'd have her bed to herself tonight? Yes, she decided guiltily. Nice girlfriends were not supposed to rejoice at their boyfriend's absence.

She was about to close Pete's laptop when she remembered with a shudder of distaste the spreadsheet of doom she'd once stumbled upon – 'Sex With Anna' – and all the marks out of ten he'd ever given her. Did he still keep it up to date? she wondered. It would be easy enough to find out . . .

Spreadsheets. Most Recent. 'Sex With Anna'. Yep, there

she was, between his monthly outgoings document and his catalogued science-fiction and fantasy book collection. The sweet spot indeed. Cringing at what she was doing, she clicked it open to see his latest remarks.

She claimed to have a headache. Again – 5

A wearing granny knickers, nearly lost my stiffy. Definitely put on weight over Xmas – 6

Boring. Had to shut eyes and think about the fit one off Downton – 5

What the hell . . . ? Anna's eyes widened as she scrolled through the list of complaints: a litany of bad sex and fast-dwindling romance. The best score she'd had in the last three months was a solitary seven back in December. A seven! Meanwhile, he criticized her boobs, the size of her thighs, her kissing . . . It was so out of order. *Everyone* put on weight over Christmas, that was the law! And so what? A few pounds here or there didn't matter. He was hardly Mr Muscle himself, anyway, with that soft, spongy belly of his. The only six-pack he could claim was the six-pack of Boddingtons he'd left in her kitchen. Who was he to judge?

She closed the laptop, heart thudding, not wanting to read any more. Why hadn't he dumped her if he thought she was that unattractive? Why bother going through the motions?

She put her head in her hands, knowing how hypocritical she was, that she should ask the same questions of herself. The two of them had been on borrowed time for the last six months; they were a habit, a convenience to each other. Well, not any more. The soonest chance she got, she'd break it off. A mercy killing.

Her phone buzzed again, making her jump. She opened the text to see another message from Pete. This one was more unusual though.

BigBoy is throbbing 4 u. Feeling horny? ;-0

Underneath was a photo of his erect pink penis.

Anna stared at it for a full five seconds, her eyes out on stalks. Oh my God. What the . . . ? Was this his idea of reigniting the spark? Sexting her from his mum's spare room?

She licked her lips, wondering how to reply. Should she even reply at all? Maybe she should pretend she'd been asleep when the text arrived, make some apology in the morning. But what would he write on the spreadsheet then? *Frigid cow, wouldn't even indulge me in a bit of phone-wanking.*

She stuck her tongue out at the laptop. Oh, so what if he did? Let him write what he wanted, she was going to dump him by the end of the week anyway and he could slag her off to his heart's content afterwards.

All the same, she couldn't help feeling a strange frisson of curiosity. She and Pete had never actually had phone sex. Come to think of it, she'd never had phone sex with anyone. What exactly were you supposed to do? Should she spell out some sordid fantasies in a text? Or shove the phone in her knickers and take a photo for him in return? (Better not, actually, it was looking a bit unkempt down there. He might think he was looking at a snap of some jungly undergrowth in Borneo.)

Maybe she should just go along with it as a sort of social experiment. She might even get an anonymous feature out of it for a glossy magazine – they were always printing that kind of muck.

Three minutes had gone by and she still hadn't replied. He'd either have 'lost his stiffy' or he'd be wanking over 'that fit one from Downton' by now. Had she missed her moment?

Dripping wet for you, she typed back, half-thrilled, half-aghast at her own daring. *Give it to me hard, BigBoy.*

Her finger hovered on the 'Send' key and she hesitated. Oh God, she thought, looking at the words and wrinkling her nose. It was such a cliché, wasn't it? Straight out of a low-budget porn movie. *Give it to me hard, BigBoy,* indeed. So unoriginal.

Even worse than her unoriginality, she realized in the next moment, was the knowledge that Pete was sure to store any smutty texts on his SIM card and show all his mates. She'd once overheard Pete's mate Andy Gordon (Flash, as he was known) boasting in the pub about his girlfriend Kirsty 'taking one up the back alley', complete with lurid details. There was no way Anna wanted to end up the subject of a similar conversation. She imagined walking in with Pete one evening and seeing the knowing looks and smirks. Ugh, no thanks.

Delete, delete, delete. She typed 'SAUCY!' instead, with a winking emoticon. Was it better to be a cliché or sound like Kenneth Williams? She was too confused to decide. She sent it off and sat there breathlessly for a few minutes, waiting for him to respond.

When no reply came, she guessed she'd missed the moment. Knowing Pete, he'd be passed out snoring under the brushed nylon covers of his mum's spare bed, soggy tissues in the bin, a satisfied smile on his face. Feeling an odd mix of disappointment and relief, she got into her pyjamas and went to bed herself.

'So what have we baked this week?' asked Marla on Thursday. 'Please not more of that vegetarian stuff,' she added brightly, her smile so toothy and dazzling it almost fooled Anna into thinking she was being nice. 'I can't be doing with rabbit food, do you know what I mean? How do people *survive*?'

'Cake,' Anna replied briefly, looking up from her computer. She was typing up the nicest ginger cake recipe, feeling confident that her readers were going to enjoy this one. Once she'd cut the dusty bits off, it had been spicy and moist and magically seemed to get better with every passing day.

'Ahh,' said Marla, sounding doubtful. 'Hmmm.'

'What do you mean, *Ahh, hmmm*?'

Marla cocked her head on one side, eyes wide. 'Well, I don't want to criticize, obvs, but are you sure that's wise? Because it's, like, *January?* And everyone's totally watching their weight, with New Year's resolutions and that?' If you didn't know better, you'd think Marla was deeply worried on Anna's behalf.

Luckily Anna did know better. 'Not everyone's on a diet,' she replied, typing quickly even though she was making spelling mistakes.

'Oh, I know! I mean – *I'm* never on a diet, thank God! I'd die if I was fat, I would totally, like, shoot myself. But I know not everyone is blessed with an athletic metabolism, like *moi*.' She gave a tinkling laugh. 'Not that I'm saying *you* should be on a diet, Anna.'

She so *was* saying Anna should be on a diet. 'God forbid anyone should think *that*, Marla,' Anna said with admirable restraint, and went on typing crossly at an unsustainable speed. *Combinge the floor with the bakisng wperowe*, read the second line of her recipe.

'People always say when they meet me, no *way* are you a restaurant reviewer! You're so slim! Do you actually, like, *eat* the food, or do you just look at it and smell it? It's so funny! Hashtag hilarious!'

Hashtag liar, more like, Anna thought, typing even faster. *Beat the eeggs and stirs intoa the mizgture.* She was just wondering how she was going to unclench her jaw and squeeze out a reply when the telltale clip-clop of power heels came from behind her.

'Ladies, good morning,' said Imogen, arriving on a waft of Dior. Today's suit was funereal black because the newspaper's proprietor, Dick Briggs (or Big Dicks as everyone called him), was expected in for a meeting. 'Marla, Anna, do you have a minute? I've had one of my brilliant ideas, if I say so myself.'

'Super!' simpered Marla, batting her long eyelashes like an ass-kissing faun.

'You're on holiday next week, am I right?' Imogen asked her.

'Yes – sorry to rub it in, guys, but I'm off to Malaysia for a bit of winter sun,' Marla announced to the office at large, like anyone was remotely interested. 'I promise I won't go on about it *too* much, but can I just say, five-star hotel, thank you very much, and one of those infinity pools and—'

Imogen spoke over the boasting. 'So while you're away, I thought Anna could step in and write your column,' she said. 'Is that all right with you, Anna? Only I thought it would be the perfect next step for you, already being our foodie expert.'

The silence that followed was so absolute you could have heard a raindrop splash into an infinity pool.

'Oh,' Anna said in surprise. 'Really? That would be great.'

'No!' Marla protested, barely disguising her fury. She made a valiant attempt to recover herself, but her smile looked as strained as Big Daddy's wrestling pants. 'I mean . . . Sadly, I'm not sure Anna would be *quite* right,' she said. 'The thing is, you need experience to be a restaurant critic. No offence, Anna, but this is an exacting skill, and . . .'

Imogen narrowed her eyes. 'I think she'll do a very good job,' she said in her most severe take-no-prisoners sort of a voice. 'Marla, if you could brief Anna and give her some handover notes before you go . . .'

'But—'

'Thank you, Marla. Thank you, Anna. Look forward to seeing how you get on. Splendid!'

Marla stared after her with undisguised contempt. 'The readers aren't going to be happy about *this*,' she said bitterly, before turning back to Anna, thin-lipped. 'Don't get me wrong, Anna, you're a great little journalist . . .'

Great little journalist! Patronizing cow. Anna had been working at the paper years longer than Marla.

'And you've done a very nice job on the old *baking* . . .'

She said it as if Anna had been writing about dogshit.

'But, you know, my readers are very fond of my particular style of writing. It's quite witty and clever . . .'

First I've heard of it, Anna thought darkly.

'So, no offence, but . . .'

Anna had heard enough. 'It's a sodding five-hundred-word

restaurant review, Marla, it's not exactly the Opinion page in the *Guardian*. I'm sure I'll manage.'

Marla gasped in outrage. 'Well, if that's the way you feel about it, maybe somebody *else* should fill in for me,' she snapped. 'I'm sorry to hear you're so *dismissive* of the central part of the entertainment round-up.'

'For crying out loud!' roared Colin, like a bear woken from hibernation. He banged a fist on his desk. 'Will you just put a sock in it? Some of us are actually trying to work around here.'

Marla swung round to her desk and began a furious assault on her keyboard, her mouth as tight and puckered as a cat's bum. Anna couldn't help a secret smile to herself. Stand-in restaurant critic, eh? 'Our foodie expert,' Imogen had called her. That was definitely what you called a result.

Chapter Eighteen

L'agenzia di lavoro – The employment agency

Catherine barely slept a wink on Sunday night. The few dreams she had were threaded through with anxiety: someone else living in the house, her looking in from the outside, unable to open her own front door . . . Then she'd wake up in a cold sweat and feel sick that it might actually come true.

When she wasn't stressing out about being homeless, her brain was trying to unravel the strange mystery of all that money in Mike's account. Something was definitely fishy there. Sure, he was on a good salary as a senior GP with various responsibilities at the surgery, but it wasn't *that* good. Not good enough to have squirrelled away thousands and thousands of pounds in a secret bank account anyway. So where had the extra money come from?

All the crime novels she'd ever read started jostling to the forefront of her mind. Was he blackmailing somebody? Was he involved in some kind of fraud case? Had he . . . Her eyes boggled. Had he been killing off pensioner patients and somehow doctoring their wills?

By the time dawn broke, she knew she wasn't going to get any more sleep, so she got up and made a strong coffee. Then she retrieved the document files and spread the papers out on the kitchen table. No, she definitely hadn't imagined it. According to the bank statements, Mike had been receiving regular large sums of money (five or ten thousand pounds a time) for the last year and a half, always from the same company – Centaur. He probably wasn't bumping off little old ladies, then, unless Centaur was an evil mastermind intrinsically linked with the plot.

She dusted off the old laptop (Mike had taken the newer, whizzier model with him) and turned on the wifi. If he was up to something dodgy, then she was going to discover exactly what, she thought with a sudden burst of energy. Hell, she was still his wife, wasn't she? His soon-to-be-destitute wife. She had a right to know.

'What are you hiding from me, Mike?' she muttered under her breath as she opened up the browser.

Despite her best attempts, she didn't get very far with her internet sleuthing. According to Google, there were hundreds of companies all around the world called Centaur, none of which she could imagine having any connection to Mike, however hard she tried. She frowned hopelessly at the bank statements while her second cup of coffee cooled, knowing that she was missing something crucial but unable to work out what it might be.

She was just about to go and have a shower when a thought struck her. Whether she could solve the mystery or not, with Mike threatening to sell the house from under her, she was really going to have to get a job soon. Like, maybe today.

Later that morning, Catherine walked into Jenny Hayes Recruitment in town, dressed immaculately in her one and only black suit. She was ready to do battle. How hard could it be?

'I need a job,' she said bluntly to the woman behind the reception desk. 'Anything. I'm not choosy.'

The receptionist didn't react for a moment. She was about Catherine's age, with black-rimmed, oversized glasses that made her head look slightly pinched. (Had she been a forceps birth? Catherine found herself wondering.) There was a mug on the desk which read 'Don't Worry Be Happy', which was kind of ironic as the receptionist looked less like cracking a smile than anyone Catherine had ever seen.

Catherine was about to attempt communication a second time when the receptionist spoke. 'You need to send in a CV,' she said in a bored monotone, her eyes still on the screen in front of her. She typed something quickly, her polished nails flashing over the keyboard. 'Then we'll put you on our database and contact you if something suitable comes up.'

'Yes, I've done that,' Catherine said politely. She'd sent out about twenty in the first week of January in a flush of New Year optimism. 'But I haven't heard anything back from you. So I was just wondering—'

'Name?'

'Catherine Evans.'

The receptionist sighed as if this was all completely pointless, then typed in Catherine's name. 'Mill Cottage, Forge Lane?'

'Yes, that's me.'

'No. We've got nothing. Sorry.'

Catherine gritted her teeth. 'There must be something I can do. Honestly, I don't mind, whatever it is.' Out of the agency window her eye was suddenly caught by the sight of a young man embracing a much older woman. The woman was very glamorous, in a classic fawn trench-coat and just-blow-dried blonde hair. As they pulled apart, smiling, Catherine realized with a shock that the young man was Freddie from her Italian class. Whoa! She hadn't expected him to be dating a woman like that.

The rude cow behind the counter was coughing pointedly. 'I *said*, any office experience?'

'What? Oh, sorry. Office experience. Well, I've done a bit of filing and what-not for my husband.' She crossed her fingers surreptitiously.

'Any data-entry experience?'

'Um . . .' What the hell did that mean? 'I'm a quick learner?' she ventured.

'Can you type?'

'Kind of. Not . . .' She mimed fast-typing fingers. 'More like . . .' She mimed hunt-and-peck-typing fingers. 'But I do get there in the end. And I'm good at spelling. And punctuation. I got an A in my English Language GCSE.'

The receptionist's nostrils twitched as if she could smell something disgusting.

'So yes is the answer,' Catherine babbled. 'Yes. I can type.'

'But not . . .' Now the receptionist was miming fast-typing fingers with a look of contempt.

'No. Not . . .' She decided not to do the mime again. 'Not like that.'

The receptionist shook her head. 'Sorry. We don't have anything right now,' she said again.

'I can get faster!' Catherine cried. 'I promise. I'll practise all day until I'm . . .' She gripped her fingers into fists so they couldn't embarrass her with any more stupid mimes. 'Until I'm really amazingly fast. Until I'm scorching keyboards with my incredible typing.'

There was a terrible, slap-in-the-face sort of silence for a few moments, then the receptionist began typing pointedly again. Fast, proper typing, without looking down at the keyboard, Catherine noticed glumly.

'*Was* there a job, then?' she persisted. 'If I'd been able to type quickly, would you have given me details of a job? I can do it, whatever it is. Why can't you just give me a chance?'

The receptionist fixed her with a steely glare. 'I'm sorry,' she said for the third time, not sounding very sorry at all. 'We. Don't. Have. Anything. Right. Now.'

Chastened, Catherine dropped her head. 'Thank you anyway,' she found herself saying meekly, before scuttling away.

Outside, she leaned against the wall, feeling humiliated. Well, that had gone about as embarrassingly as humanly possible.

'One down, nine to go,' she muttered under her breath. She dug out the list of agencies she'd contacted and scribbled a line through Jenny Hayes Recruitment so hard the pen tore through the paper. Jenny Hayes and the snotty little madam who worked for her could shove their data entry somewhere painful. Things could only get better, right?

Wrong. Things only got worse. Selective Recruitment were . . . well, too bloody selective to want her. Crown Appointments did not give her the royal welcome. Even Domestic Goddesses, who specialized in cleaning work, didn't have anything suitable. She was starting to feel desperate. Didn't anyone want her? Was there nothing she could do?

'Hey! Catherine!' She was just walking up Pinstone Street towards the last agency on her list, when she heard her name.

Turning blankly, she noticed Phoebe, from the Italian class, leaning out of a nearby hairdresser's and waving.

'Hi,' she said, glad to see a friendly face at last. 'Hair Raisers – is this you, then?'

'Certainly is. What are you up to? Bit of shopping?'

Catherine pulled a face. 'Trying to get a bloody job,' she said. 'And failing horrendously. There's just nothing out there.'

'I know.' Phoebe nodded sympathetically. 'My fella Liam's trying to find something too. Pants, isn't it?'

'Totally pants. Great big horrible stained old pants.'

Phoebe giggled. 'Hey, why don't you come in, have a cup of tea? I haven't got a client for another hour and you look like you need a break.'

Catherine's feet were killing her. The thought of sitting down and having a drink was too tempting to resist. 'That would be brilliant,' she said gratefully. 'Thanks.'

Phoebe considered her for a moment. 'Tell you what,' she said. 'As I'm free, why don't I give you a quick cut and blow-dry? On the house.'

'Oh, I couldn't.'

'Course you could. Come on, let me take your coat. I'm telling you, a fringe would totally suit you . . .'

Before Catherine knew it, she was having her hair washed with sudsy apple-smelling shampoo, a steaming cup of coffee beside her. 'Now, then,' Phoebe said afterwards, guiding Catherine to a large comfortable chair in front of a mirror and combing out her damp hair. 'I'm thinking a bit more shape around the front, maybe some layers to add some weight at the back, and you've got to let me cut you a fringe, Cath. Trust me on this, it will revolutionize your face.'

'Er . . .' Catherine wasn't entirely sure she wanted her face revolutionized, but Phoebe was so charming and persuasive (and the coffee was so bloody lovely) that she felt powerless to refuse. And it had been ages since she'd thought twice about her hair, other than shoving it into a ponytail. Maybe a change would do her good.

Just as Phoebe was getting to work with her scissors, a platinum-blonde woman in a white coat walked through the door. Catherine jerked in her chair. Oh no. It wasn't, was it? It couldn't be. Please, no!

'Ooh Gawd, nearly took your ear off there, Cath,' Phoebe yelped. 'Are you okay?'

Catherine barely heard. She was too busy staring at the new arrival. Pristine white trench-coat. High black heels. A well-cut tan leather bag. Of course, she hadn't had any of that lot on when Catherine had last seen her. Only the red lipstick was the same.

'Cath?' Phoebe was saying, puzzled. 'What's up? You've gone really pale. Have you changed your mind about the fringe?'

'I've got a two o'clock appointment with Melissa,' the woman announced to the receptionist. 'Rebecca Hale.'

Rebecca. It *was* her. Last seen stark naked with her legs wrapped around Mike. That nasty smirk. *Oops.*

'Shit,' Catherine muttered, twisting her head to hide her face as Rebecca was helped into a black protective gown. 'Oh God. I need to go.'

'Why?' Phoebe sat in the chair next to her. 'What's happened? Are you not well?'

'That woman who's just come in – don't turn round – Rebecca, she's called. My husband left me for her.'

'Oh bloody hell,' Phoebe said. 'Oh no. That's awful.' She lowered her voice. 'She's a right bitch, and all. In here every few weeks to get her roots done, never leaves a tip.'

Catherine's hands were shaking in her lap. She felt as if she might be sick. 'I just want to get out of here. I don't want her to recognize me.'

'Don't you worry,' Phoebe said, patting her arm. 'By the time I've finished with you, you won't even recognize yourself. Sit tight and I'll crack on.'

Catherine held her breath as Rebecca was led away to a chair nearby and the hairdresser started talking to her about what she needed. Then Rebecca pulled out an iPad and started tapping away on it with an air of self-importance. To Catherine's relief, she seemed engrossed in whatever she was doing and didn't pay any attention when the hairdresser began separating her hair into sections to be coloured.

Phoebe, meanwhile, was snipping away, pausing now and then to check the lengths matched on either side. She perched in front of her to cut the fringe and Catherine shut her eyes as soft hair dropped into her lap. A mobile began ringing somewhere and she stiffened as she heard Rebecca's voice.

'Yeah,' she said. 'Well, can he come back at four o'clock? I did say I had a meeting this afternoon, Paul.'

'Meeting, my arse,' Phoebe muttered, leaning close as she evened up the ends of Catherine's new fringe. 'She's always bunking off to come here. Never gets her hair done at the weekend, like most people with a job. Oops, sorry, no offence, Cath.'

'None taken,' Catherine told her.

'There,' Phoebe said with satisfaction after a moment. 'You can open your eyes now. Tell me what you think of the length. Is that okay?'

Catherine opened her eyes cautiously and stared at the woman in the mirror. Her forehead had vanished. So had the straggly long locks and split ends. Instead, she had a neat shoulder-length bob that fell around her face, with a blunt fringe that ended just above her eyebrows.

'I told you it would suit you, didn't I? You've got such great cheekbones, Cath, your face is perfect for this style. And it'll look even better when I blow-dry it. What do you think?'

'Wow,' Catherine said, still fascinated by her own reflection. She looked about five years younger. 'It's so different. I don't look like me any more.'

'Let me dry it for you. It's going to be awesome. I'll just find some glossing spray, hold on.'

Phoebe hunted through a collection of bottles and Catherine smiled tentatively at the woman in the mirror. She looked like a different person. Maybe even a more confident person.

'I don't care!' Rebecca's voice rose crossly in the background. 'Just do it. And make sure that Centaur payment has gone through, will you? I don't want any more complaints.'

Catherine gave a sharp intake of breath as the words rang around her head. A Centaur payment? Rebecca was connected to Centaur?

'Here we go,' Phoebe said, spritzing lotion onto Catherine's hair and setting the hairdryer roaring. Then Catherine could hear nothing but her own thudding heartbeat.

Back at the house, Catherine went straight up to Mike's office. Now that she knew there was a connection between Mike, Rebecca and all this money, she had to search through everything again. There must be a clue somewhere.

She pulled out the bank statements. The first payment had

been made in June 2011, the year before last. What else had been happening then? Maybe if she could find an old appointments' diary of Mike's she might be able to trace his steps in the weeks leading up to that initial juicy ten-thousand-pound deposit. I'm on to you, Mike, she thought.

She searched through his desk drawers, looking for anything that might give her a lead. She worked cautiously at first, as if he might appear behind her and start shouting at her, but soon speeded up, driven on by curiosity. Pension folders, minutes from various meetings, car insurance – it was all here. There was also a plethora of pens and notepads with pharmaceutical logos, a sheaf of the twins' university bumph, conference brochures and . . .

She paused as a business card floated out of one of the conference packs. It was headed Schenkman Pharma, followed by *Rebecca Hale, Client Liaison Officer.* Underneath was an office telephone number and a personal extension number. Someone had added a mobile number in black biro. Schenkman Pharma. SP.

Her mouth went dry as she held the card for a moment. A little piece of history. They must have met at one of these dreary conferences, she realized. Oh, she could see it now. Take one bored GP, add foxy Rebecca, then mix with late nights in the conference hotel and flowing alcohol. Now stir.

Pens and notepads and crappy mugs weren't the only little extras he'd come away with, then. A business card pressed into his hand, red-manicured nails lingering a shade too long on his. *Here's my mobile number. Call me.* The oldest cliché in the book.

Her lip curled as she imagined drunken fumbles in the lift, his sweaty paws on her silk blouse. *What goes on tour stays on tour. What's your room number? Fancy a nightcap?*

Then she frowned. Hold on. Rebecca had been talking about Centaur payments in the hairdresser's earlier – yet this card said she worked at Schenkman Pharma. Were there two Rebeccas? A Rebecca in every port? What was going on?

Gingerly, as if it might be radioactive, she picked up the brochure from which Rebecca's business card had fallen. April 2011, a Schenkman Pharma conference at the Bartlett hotel in Blackpool, she read on the cover. Oh, the glamour.

She flicked it open and skimmed through the first page. *Welcome to Schenkman Pharma – a rising star in the pharmaceutical industry*, blah blah blah. God, even the itinerary was enough to put you to sleep: talks about the benefits of their new wonder drugs, an overview of recent MedTech innovations, their research techniques and trial case studies. She almost felt a nagging sympathy for Mike, having to sit through a weekend of sales talks from nerdy drug reps. Then she remembered the five-star dining and luxury hotel facilities which must have gone some way to ease the boredom. As had the free bar and Rebecca Hale, no doubt.

Frowning, she stared from the business card back to the

brochure, trying to tally it with what she'd heard earlier. Then she glanced up at the clock: six-thirty. Too late to start making any office phone calls now.

She put all the files and folders away where she'd found them. The last thing she wanted was for Mike to know she'd been snooping around. The business card, however, she left on the desk. 'I haven't finished with *you* yet,' she said under her breath.

Chapter Nineteen

La fotografia – The photograph

Something was different about the *Herald* office on Monday morning when Anna arrived for work. Everyone seemed unusually calm and relaxed. Two of the secretaries were giggling in a corner about their weekend shenanigans and there was a delicious smell of fresh coffee wafting out from the kitchen. Colin was actually whistling.

She cocked her head as she stared around, trying to detect what was different. Then her eye fell on Marla's empty chair and she remembered. Oh yes! Marla was on holiday. All week. Five whole days without any snarking or sniping, without any insults poorly disguised as innocence. Heaven. Who knew Monday mornings could feel so blissful?

She sat at her desk and switched on her Mac, then noticed a pile of papers on her desk with an acid-yellow Post-it note on top. *Restaurants to be reviewed herewith,* read a hasty scrawl. *Take your pick. 500 words to Imogen by Thurs 4pm.*

A sinking feeling went through Anna. Was this seriously the extent of the handover notes Imogen had asked Marla to provide? One crappy Post-it – that was *it*? Oh, great. Thanks a bunch. Any other self-respecting journalist might have actually filed an extra review in advance rather than dumping work on a colleague. Not Marla. Knowing her, she'd be stretched out on a sunbed, oiled and glistening right now, smiling to herself and hoping that Anna would come a total cropper this week. Then, of course, Imogen would be furious and Marla could be all, *Well, I didn't like to say, but . . .*

She realized she was making a faint growling noise under her breath and stopped hurriedly before she spoiled the new-found newsroom chill. Dirty tricks, Marla Tucker? You picked the wrong person to try it on with. Just for that, Anna was going to write the best restaurant review *ever*. That would show her.

Scrumpling the useless Post-it into a ball and tossing it in the bin, Anna leafed through the papers: all invitations from city restaurants and country hotels with new menus they wanted the paper to sample. There were loads of them! No wonder Marla always looked so smug – you could dine out every night of the week with this lot, plus a few free lunches thrown in for good measure, too. The question was, where should she try first? She might as well make the most of this. Which was the nicest-looking, the one she'd never usually be able to afford?

Ruling out the gastro-pubs and cheap pizza places took away quite a number of options. Some chancer had even sent in a flier for a new kebab place on London Road. In your dreams, love!

Thankfully, there were classier choices. Anna lingered over the menu of a fancy new French restaurant just off Leopold Square – that could be worth a punt. A fine-dining place near the Peace Gardens? Hmm, it looked worryingly posh. You could never relax in those places, in Anna's experience – *and* the portions were always tiny. What else was there? Ahh.

Yes. Enrico's Italian Kitchen – now *this* was more like it. She glanced through the sample menu stapled to the invitation, her mouth watering: risotto, pasta, dishes *al forno* . . . She licked her lips and picked up the phone.

'Hiya,' she said when Pete answered. 'What are you up to on Wednesday night?'

'Oh, hi, love,' he said, sounding surprised. It was only then that she remembered she was meant to be in a massive huff with him still. He'd blown her out at the last minute on Saturday night when he was meant to be coming out with her to her friend Chloe's birthday drinks. Some mate's stag do, he'd said at eight-fifteen, two minutes before she was about to leave the flat. Even worse, he hadn't even phoned to apologize the next day. Rude, that's what it was. No wonder he was taken aback to hear her sound so friendly now, asking him for his midweek plans, no less. 'Um . . . playing football with the lads,' he said after a moment. 'Why?'

'I thought football was Thursday?'

'It got changed. Why? What are you up to? How are you, anyway?'

'I should be asking you that. What happened on Saturday? Did it get messy? I tried ringing you, you know.'

'Sorry about that, babe. I couldn't hear my phone in the club, that's why I didn't answer.'

She twisted a pen between her fingers, not sure she believed him. And they still hadn't mentioned last week's sexting. What was going on?

'Oh, right,' she said. 'How about Tuesday then?'

There was a pause. 'Er . . . I've got this work thing.'

'Have you?' Pete never had work things. He escaped from his desk at five-thirty on the dot every night.

'Yeah. It's . . . Someone's leaving. They're having a do.'

'On a Tuesday?'

'Yeah! It's allowed, isn't it?' Now he was getting defensive.

She sighed impatiently. 'When *am* I going to see you, then?'

'You've got the hump with me now, haven't you?'

'No, I—'

'I knew it. That's why I didn't ring you, because I knew I'd get it in the neck.'

'Pete, I'm only—'

'Look, babe, I'm at work. Let's talk about this in our own time, yeah? I'd better go. See you.'

She heard the connection click off and gaped in disbelief.

What the hell had just happened? She'd been ringing to invite him to the nicest new Italian restaurant in Sheffield, yet somehow he'd managed to turn the call into her being the nag who cramped his style. 'Unbelievable,' she muttered crossly. 'Absolutely unbelievable.'

'What is?' asked Joe, coming in just then. 'The number nineteen bus? Tell me about it. Twenty minutes late again. A wheelbarrow could go faster than that useless piece of crap.'

Anna was still fuming about Pete. '*You* wouldn't turn down a night in a gorgeous Italian restaurant, would you, Joe?' she asked crossly.

'Course I bloody wouldn't,' he said. 'Why, are you offering?'

She laughed. 'No, but . . .' This was the moment where he was supposed to laugh too and say, Only joking, he didn't really think so. Instead, he was standing expectantly as if he was seriously waiting for an offer to be made. 'Well . . .' she said hesitantly, 'I do need someone to go with me, actually. It's a restaurant review – remember I'm covering for Marla? I just asked Pete, but he can't make it.'

'I can,' he said promptly. 'Unless it's tonight or Thursday.'

'I was thinking Wednesday.'

'Cool.'

'What – really?'

He shrugged. 'Why not? Could be a laugh.'

She thought about it. Why not indeed? It wasn't like a date-date. He was a fellow writer, they could bounce ideas off each other. And he was right – they could have a laugh together, too. Even better, it was a chance to practise some of her Italian.

'All right, let's do it,' she said. 'I'll book us a table. Cheers, Joe.' Then, just so that he wouldn't be in any doubt about this unexpected arrangement, she added, 'You're a real mate.'

The following evening, it was Italian class again, and Anna was pleased to see the other students. After a single night in the pub together the week before, she now felt as if they were her new friends. 'Hi, Geraldine, how are rehearsals going?' she asked, walking into the room. (Wonderful, she was word-perfect and now trying to wangle a new outfit for the show.)

'What happened on your blind date?' she whispered to Nita, opening her textbook. (He was late and had a moustache, came the answer, complete with pulled face. His number had already been deleted from Nita's phone.)

'Lovely hair – wow!' she marvelled to Catherine. 'Pheebs, did you do that?'

'I totally did,' Phoebe said, looking chuffed. She was wearing her hair in two plaits tonight – the demure schoolgirl look. 'Looks mint, doesn't it?'

'Thanks,' Catherine said, blushing. 'I'm really pleased. Everybody – get Phoebe to make you over this week. She's a miracle worker!'

Phoebe leaned forward, eyes gleaming. 'By the way, Cath,'

she said. 'Sad news. After you left, there was a terrible accident with Rebecca's white coat. Coffee all down it. No idea how it happened.'

'No!' breathed Catherine in shocked delight, then giggled, her hand flying up to her mouth. 'Seriously?'

'Yep. She said she wouldn't come to us any more. We're all so upset. Really gonna miss those non-existent tips.' She winked naughtily.

George raised an eyebrow. 'Blimey, your salon sounds like it needs its own TV show,' he said. 'Your hair looks great, by the way, Catherine.'

'Thank you!' she said, turning bright red.

'If you ever want a little trim, George, just pop in,' Phoebe said instantly, brandishing one of her business cards. 'I could do you a wicked boyband cut, one of those big floppy fringes and . . .'

He shook his head, grinning. 'I'm happy with the shaggy, unkempt kind of look, thanks,' he replied, running a hand through his sandy hair and batting his eyelashes. 'But I'll bear that in mind, Pheebs, if I ever want a change.'

As their homework the week before, Sophie had asked each of the students to prepare a few sentences about themselves, featuring the phrases they'd learned so far in Italian. The lesson began with them taking it in turns to read these aloud, occasionally stumbling over some of the pronunciations, although a couple of students – well, Geraldine – threw themselves very theatrically into the accent, complete with rolling 'r's and flamboyant hand gestures.

After Sophie had praised them for their efforts – even Phoebe, who giggled every time she had to say '*Ho*' – she went on to teach them the vocabulary for features in a town (market, cathedral, tourist office, etc.) and nationalities. Anna felt a thrill run through her as she imagined herself arriving in Rimini and asking directions in fluent Italian. She was so going to sort that trip out. Any day now.

As usual, the two-hour lesson went by in a flash. 'Well done, everyone, you're all doing great,' Sophie said at the end. 'See you next time. *Ciao!*'

'*Ciao!*' the others all chorused enthusiastically.

Sophie beckoned Anna over as she was about to go. 'Can I have a quick word?' she asked.

'Sure,' Anna said.

'It was Rimini, wasn't it, where you thought your mum had met your dad?' Sophie asked without preamble.

'Yeah, that's right. Why?'

'Only I've had an idea. A mate of mine's working there at the moment, according to Facebook. I was thinking . . . If you let me borrow that photo of your dad, I can scan it in and email it to my friend, see if he recognizes where it was taken,' Sophie said. 'It would give you somewhere to start looking, wouldn't it, if he can pinpoint the exact place? He might even know him!'

Anna's heart quickened. 'That would be brilliant,' she said. 'Thank you!' She thought of the photo propped up on her bedside table, wishing she could hand it over there and then. 'How can I get it to you? Are you in town at all during the week? I work at the *Herald* office, so could nip out and meet you any time.'

'I'm popping into town on Thursday,' Sophie said. 'How about grabbing a coffee sometime then?'

'Perfect,' Anna said. 'Do you know Marmadukes? I'll meet you there at around eleven. Thanks!'

Outside the classroom, Catherine was waiting for her. 'Um . . . Anna, can I ask you something?'

'Course you can,' Anna said. 'Shall we walk while we talk? My parking ticket runs out in fifteen minutes.'

They went along the corridor. 'I've found something out,' Catherine said bluntly. 'Something a bit weird, that I don't understand. I know journalists are experts at getting to the bottom of a story, so I just wondered . . .'

Anna's polite smile froze on her face. This happened every now and then – she'd be asked to investigate a missing will, or people would tell her indignantly about some injustice they'd suffered at work in the hope that she would highlight it in the newspaper. Axes to grind, usually. She was glad now that she'd given Catherine a fifteen-minute time limit. Some people could go on and on and on, given half a chance.

'Well . . . It's a GP, basically. He's a good GP, but I know that somebody's been giving him thousands and thousands of pounds – nearly a hundred thousand in the last year and a half. And I don't know why.'

Anna frowned. This wasn't the usual fare, admittedly. 'And you don't know who this mysterious donor is?'

'No. That's the thing. What would you think, as a journalist, if you knew those two facts?'

'What, that a GP had been receiving secret payments?' Anna said, walking through the revolving door at the front of the college and stepping out into the cold, dark night. She shivered as she waited for Catherine to emerge, shoving her hands into her coat pockets for warmth. 'I'd think the GP was being bought off,' she replied. 'Blackmail or bribery. Sounds dodgy to me.'

'That's what I thought,' Catherine said. Despite the cold, there was a sort of glow about her, as if she was burning with nervous energy.

'Who is it? What's the story?' Anna asked, unable to help her interest.

'Um . . . It's complicated.'

Damn. And now she was clamming up, just as Anna's appetite had been whetted. 'Well, if you need my help with any digging around, just drop me a line,' she said, taking a business card from her bag and handing it over. 'I can do investigative journalism as well as cooking, and I'm happy to help.'

Catherine pocketed the card with a nod. She seemed to be thinking hard about something. 'If the GP in question *was* involved in some racket or other, what do you think would happen to them if they were caught?'

'Depends on what they'd actually done. I mean, might they have been left this money by a grateful patient?'

'No,' Catherine said. 'It's regular payments from a company. It's not a grateful patient.'

Intriguing. 'Well, in that case, assuming some kind of fraud or corruption, the GP might go to prison,' Anna said. 'They'd almost certainly be struck off too, if it was extortion or bribery. Hard to say without knowing the full story, but there would definitely be repercussions.'

'That's what I thought.'

Anna paused at the edge of the car park. 'Sure you don't want to talk to me about it now? I promise it'll be confidential.' Hey, I'll even blow another quid on the parking, she thought to herself.

Catherine shook her head apologetically. 'Better not,' she said. 'Maybe another time.'

Anna shrugged, trying to mask her disappointment. There was nothing worse than having a juicy story dangled under your nose then snatched away. 'It's your call,' she said. 'But obviously, if you suspect wrong-doing – and you have some proof – you should really go to the police. Because if you don't, you might get done as well for being an accessory to the crime.'

That startled her. Anna had meant it to, of course. If anything was going to persuade quiet Catherine to talk, it was the prospect of being in the dock herself for keeping schtum.

Catherine's expression was hard to read in the dim glow of the lamppost, but she looked pretty uncomfortable. 'I'll bear that in mind,' she said. 'Thanks, Anna. It's all a bit . . .' Anna found herself leaning in closer. *Come on, Catherine, spill the beans.*

'It's complicated,' Catherine said again. 'Sorry.'

'No need to apologize.' She wasn't going to get anywhere now. Anna put her hand up in a little wave and pressed the remote unlocking button on her car key fob. 'I'll see you next week.'

She glanced over her shoulder as she opened the car door to see Catherine looking deep in thought as she went on her way. The mystery tugged at Anna's mind and a whole raft of new headlines sprang to life.

UNCOVERED Local GP exposed as fraud.

IN THE DOCK Blackmailing GP weeps in court.

DOCTOR, NO Dodgy Doc struck off for embezzlement.

It had all the hallmarks of a headline story, no doubt about it, thought Anna, starting her engine and cranking up the poxy little heating dial to maximum. She drove away, her mind ticking over with questions.

Chapter Twenty

Cosa stai facendo? – What are you doing?

FACEBOOK STATUS: Sophie Frost
I'm . . .

It was Wednesday evening and Sophie was lying on her bed with her laptop, her brain turning like a hamster wheel as she tried to think of something remotely interesting to write.

I'm restless.

She deleted it. It was true, but sounded too negative, too whingey. Nobody liked a whinger on Facebook.

I'm planning my next move.

She wrinkled her nose. That was true too, but then someone was sure to respond with *Where are you off to next, Soph?*, and she'd be forced to admit that she didn't quite know yet. She deleted that, too.

Feeling as if life has ground to a halt. ☹

Definitely not. Whinging again. Come on. Pull yourself together. Be positive.

Glad my dad is on the mend. Go Jim!

That was an improvement, although not exactly the sort of thrill-seeking update she was used to posting. Ever since she'd first joined Facebook, her timeline had been like a magical mystery tour – here, there and everywhere, with the photos and suntan to prove it.

Sunrise in Byron Bay!

Sampling cocktails with Dan in Darling Harbour. You know you want to!

Swam with dolphins in Kaikoura today. AMAZING.

Buongiorno amici! Now in Rome, working as an English tour guide – love it.

The view from my balcony . . . Don't hate me ☺

It seemed like another life now, a life she'd abruptly left. What did she have to say on her updates these days, after all?

Another scintillating shift in the café. Made approx. 9,000 lattes and got a massive £2.75 in tips. WHOOP!

Took Dad to his doctor's appointment. Rock on!

Watching Corrie with my parents. Living on the edge.

The view from my bedroom . . . gotta love a cul-de-sac.

It felt as if her world had shrunk on a huge scale in a matter of months: from oceans, mountains, beaches and rainforest, all the way down to the dimensions of a detached house in the suburbs, a crap café two streets away, and the bus route into college once a week. She kept imagining herself as a digital map that someone had focussed in and in and in, so that the rest of the planet was no longer visible. Distant horizons and adventures now seemed as unattainable as a January heatwave.

Even though these days she actually quite enjoyed her parents' company, being in their house was starting to wear a bit thin. She badly missed her independence – not only the travelling lifestyle, but also the little things: going out on a whim and not having to explain what time she'd be back, cooking when she felt like eating rather than fitting in with her parents' mealtimes, not having to ask before she changed the channel on the TV . . . It was hard work living *chez* Mum and Dad, even when they insisted on cooking and ironing everything for her. All that chit-chat and housekeeping stuff:

Has anyone seen my glasses?

Tea's ready!

Put something decent on, will you, love, Grandma's popping round in a few minutes.

How long are you going to be in that shower?

She seriously missed having something exciting to put up on Facebook now and then, too.

Sophie Frost . . . is well jel of what you lot are all up to.

Sophie Frost . . . will need to blow the dust off her passport at this rate.

Sophie Frost . . . has nothing to say.

The worst bit was, she couldn't imagine things changing any time soon. To put it bluntly, she was skint. Even if she knew where she wanted to go next (not a clue), she didn't have the funds for an airfare yet, nor enough for a place of her own in the meantime. Besides, she was signed up to teach the Italian class until Easter at the earliest and couldn't bail out now.

Maybe this was growing up – real life. Maybe she just had to knuckle down and get on with it, suck it up. She glanced back at her friends' Facebook updates with a pang of envy. Everyone else seemed to have exciting things to report:

Matt Howard: Learning to scuba-dive. Get in!

Nell Shepherd: I'm a proud aunty again. Josie and Rob had baby number two yesterday. A boy! Flying over to see them next week.

Ella Fraser: Off to Marrakesh in two weeks. Anyone fancy meeting up there?!

Dan Collins . . .

She stared at the screen as a new update appeared. Dan Collins? A shot of adrenalin pinballed around her at the sight of his name. She couldn't help a muffled scream of excitement as she read his words.

Dan Collins: I'm back in Manchester. Did you miss me?

Her breath came rapid and shallow and there was a pain in her chest as she stared at his avatar, a picture of him grinning with a pint in some bar or other. Then she shut down the laptop before she typed something she'd regret (*WHEN CAN I SEE YOU AGAIN???*) and went to make herself a cup of tea. Everything felt unreal and floaty; the kitchen floor seemed to lurch and tip as she walked across it, the words still echoing around her brain.

Dan Collins: I'm back in Manchester. Did you miss me?

Dan Collins. Manchester. Miss me? Miss me? Miss me?

Oh my goodness. She'd last seen him through streaming tears at Sydney Airport three years ago as he jetted out of her life. Yes, Dan, of course I've missed you, she thought wretchedly. I've never stopped missing you, you idiot.

I don't want you to go, she'd sobbed as they embraced one last time.

We'll meet again, he'd said into her hair. *I've just got a feeling.*

He probably said that to all the women. He'd managed to peel himself away and fly to Auckland, after all. Thanks and goodbye; it was fun but now I'm moving on.

Fun. It had been more than fun. It had been the best seven months of Sophie's life, travelling around Australia with him. They'd supported each other through terrible temporary jobs (her worst: a banana farm in Queensland where snakes and cockroaches were regular visitors; his worst: a door-to-door sales job in Brisbane where he had to dress as a strawberry and try not to get beaten up). They'd hired a car and explored the Blue Mountains, Fraser Island and Noosa; they'd freaked out on bad mushrooms in Nimbin and laughed through boozy Sydney nights together. They had gone skinny-dipping together on Coogee Beach on New Year's Eve. She had said 'I love you' and meant it for the first time in her life.

Then, one bright Saturday afternoon, he had told her he was going. His Australian visa was running out and he had a plane to catch. It had been a blast, but . . .

'I could come with you,' she blurted out, a single heartbeat later. They had come to Glebe market and the air was full of drumbeats and the scent of frying onions. Stalls nearby offered Tarot readings, second-hand Levi's, head massages and soya ice cream.

'You don't have to do that,' he said.

Someone was juggling fire clubs a few metres away; a crowd had gathered around, clapping enthusiastically. 'I know I don't,' she said.

He turned to face her, his expression rueful. 'Maybe we should just . . .' he said and shrugged.

An elderly Chinese woman grabbed Sophie's arm. 'Hey, Miss, you want massage?' she asked, gesturing to her nearby stall.

Sophie ignored her. 'What do you mean?'

'Well . . . I didn't come travelling to get in a relationship. And it's been brilliant, don't get me wrong, I've loved being with you, but . . .'

'You want massage?'

'No!' Sophie almost screamed at the woman, yanking her arm free. She was trembling, the market before her kaleidoscoping into fractured pieces. 'We don't have to be in a *relationship*,' she said, wishing she didn't sound so desperate. 'We can just . . . hang out.'

'Mister? Hey, Mister. You want massage?'

'No, thanks.' He grabbed Sophie's hand and they strode further into the market. 'Look, you're really cool. You are totally awesome and fun and gorgeous. And if we were in Britain right now and living ordinary lives, I'd probably want to . . . I don't know . . . marry you or something crazy. But . . .'

She shut her eyes. Why did there have to be a but?

'But this trip was meant to be for me. Does that make sense? Me, Dan, going round the world on my own. And that's kind of how I want to be.'

They were standing near a drumming workshop and the sound seemed to make every bone in her body vibrate. He was almost having to shout to be heard. She stared at him, trying not to cry, wondering how she could have got this so wrong.

'But I thought . . .' she managed to say, then swallowed. The incessant drumming made her head spin and she raised her voice. 'But I thought WE LOVED EACH OTHER!'

Just as she was shouting the words, the drums fell silent. Heads turned and everyone stared at the red-faced, bellowing Pom as she burst into tears and ran away, barging through the market unseeingly.

Ugh. Unhappy times. Despite all of her crying, sulking

and then, when she'd completely lost her dignity, out and out begging, he'd gone a week later with an unsatisfactory hug and nothing more.

She was left bereft and confused, missing him so much she couldn't think straight, unable to eat, sleep or even string a sentence together. It was all so wrong! It was all so unfair! He'd actually said he'd *marry* her if they were in the UK, hadn't he? She'd heard him with her own ears. How could anyone *say* that to a person then fly off to another country without them? It didn't make sense.

Eventually she broke all her own rules and bought her own plane ticket to Auckland, flying out ten days after him in the hope that she could track him down.

Unfortunately, within that time, he had completely vanished, swallowed up in New Zealand without a trace. However many messages she left him, however much she embarrassed herself, traipsing around the backpacker haunts showing everyone his photo (*Have you seen this man?*), she received only silence from him, and negative responses and pitying looks from everyone else.

He had gone. Long gone. And never seen again, even though she always kept an eye out for his freckled face and broad smile, cocked an ear for that distinctive too-loud laugh of his. They were still supposedly Facebook friends but that meant nothing; he hardly ever updated his status, and had over 600 'friends' listed the last time she looked.

She had once drunkenly scrolled through them all, torturing herself by wondering how many of the women he had slept with. Had he enjoyed a passionate fling in every continent? He hadn't seemed that kind of bloke, but maybe she was just naïve.

'Everything all right, love?' her mum said, coming in and seeing her motionless by the worktop, her mug still empty bar the dry teabag.

'Um . . . yeah,' she replied distractedly, lost in a loop of sun-tinged memories.

Dan Collins was back in the same country as her. Forty miles away, no less, just the other side of the Peak District. She had to see him again.

'Mum, can I open a bottle of wine?' she asked, suddenly feeling the need to blur the edges of this almighty shock. Tea wasn't going to cut it.

'Of course,' Trish said. 'Help yourself.' She hesitated. 'Are you sure you're all right?'

Sophie gave her a small, determined smile. 'Everything's fine,' she said.

The next day, work was drearier than ever. It was pouring with rain and every customer seemed in a foul mood. Grant, her boss, was supposedly on a trip to the cash and carry, although she was sure she'd seen him slipping into the pub over the road half an hour ago. In the meantime, she was left running around doing everything herself. She'd already scalded her hand twice on the coffee machine, and then a rampaging toddler crashed into a table, hurting his head and spilling drinks everywhere.

As the clock dragged out every boring, mindless minute, she found herself glancing at the door, wishing Dan would burst in and take her away from all this.

I made a terrible mistake, he would say. *I have been scouring the world for you. Let's run away together and live happily ever after!*

The door opened just then and she swung round with an insane burst of optimism, but to her disappointment it was neither Dan nor Grant, back to help out, but a red-haired woman, struggling in with an umbrella and a freezing draught. Then Sophie realized it was Catherine, from her evening class. 'Oh, hi,' she said. 'How are you?'

Catherine folded her umbrella and dumped it behind the door. 'Hi!' she said in surprise. 'I didn't know you worked here.'

'Yeah, more's the pity,' Sophie grumbled before she could stop herself. 'Are you local, then? I haven't seen you around before.'

'I live in Wetherstone but I do a couple of shifts at the Cancer Research shop just a few doors down,' Catherine said, unwinding her scarf. 'I've just missed a bus and it's so horrible out there, I thought I'd treat myself to a coffee while I wait.'

'Good for you,' Sophie said. 'Take a seat and I'll bring one over. Can I get you anything else? Cake? Pastry?'

Catherine eyed the cakes on display then shook her head reluctantly. 'Better not,' she said. 'I'm watching the pennies. Still haven't found a job yet.'

Sophie lowered her voice. 'Actually, they're on special offer today. Free to members of my Italian class only. Come and choose what you fancy.'

'Are you sure? You won't get into any trouble?'

'Nah. My boss is in the pub and he won't know the difference by the time he gets back. Take your pick.'

Sophie made them each a coffee while Catherine deliberated over the cakes, eventually choosing a chocolate tiffin slice.

'Good call,' Sophie said, sliding it onto a plate. 'Mind if I join you? I haven't had a break all day.'

'Be my guest,' said Catherine with a smile.

They sat near the counter so that Sophie could leap up and serve any new customers if she had to, but the rain seemed to have emptied the High Street for the time being.

Catherine cut off a square of tiffin and popped it into her mouth. 'Yum,' she said. 'How long have you been working here, then? It can't be that long, you're still so slim. If I had to serve cakes like this all day, I'd be the size of a house within a week.'

'The novelty wears off, honestly,' Sophie said. 'I started just before Christmas. I was in Italy before then for a couple of years.'

'I remember you saying. Sorrento, wasn't it? Were you working out there, or studying, or just having a lovely long holiday?'

'Working. Bar and café jobs,' Sophie replied. 'Nothing very thrilling – but somehow better for being abroad, if you know what I mean.'

'God, yeah. I did some awful jobs when I was inter-railing. Chambermaiding, cleaning, bar work . . . You do what you have to, don't you?'

'Exactly. And who cares when you can clock off and hit the beach?' She gazed out the window as the rain continued to lash down. 'Doing the same work in freezing wintry Sheffield doesn't have quite the same appeal, funnily enough.'

'But you've got your teaching as well,' Catherine reminded her. 'Everyone seems to be really enjoying the class. I know I am.'

Sophie smiled at her. 'Thanks. Yeah, I'm enjoying teaching it too, but it's only a temporary thing, a few hours a week. After that ends I don't know what I'll do.' She fiddled with her teaspoon. 'Originally I thought I'd save up and go travelling again, but . . .'

'But . . . ?' Catherine prompted when she fell silent mid-sentence.

'But I'm kind of enjoying being back in this country. Oh, I don't know.'

'What's stopping you staying, then?' Catherine asked curiously. 'I mean, I know the weather's not exactly glorious right now – I think we're all tempted to jet off for some sunshine. But isn't there a part of you that wants to . . . settle down?'

Sophie wrinkled her nose and tried to assemble her thoughts into coherent sentences. 'The thing about settling down that freaks me out is that you're being honest,' she said haltingly. 'You're saying, this is me. This is what I can do. I am a teacher, or I am a doctor, or I am married with five kids. This is it.'

Catherine frowned, not following her.

'Whereas while you're travelling, nobody really knows. While you're travelling you still have the potential to do anything, be anything. It's only when you stop and actually try to do those things that you discover your own capabilities, I guess.'

God. This was turning out to be a very deep and meaningful coffee. She had never actually articulated that thought out loud – or even in her own head – before.

'That's all right, though, isn't it?' said Catherine. 'Everyone has to make decisions about what they're going to do eventually. Even me.'

'But what if I can't *do* any of those things? That's what scares me. While I was away, it didn't matter that I was only waitressing rather than anything more demanding, because it was like, oh, well, obviously I *could* have an amazing job in Britain if I wanted, I'm just choosing to travel around and see the world. And that was fine.'

Catherine nodded. 'And you're worried that being in Britain, people will start judging you if you're not doing something amazing; they'll assume that you're working as a waitress because that's all you can do.' She sipped her coffee thoughtfully. 'I'm kind of in the same boat. I've never had a proper job because my husband always . . . Well. Long story. But now I'm having to look for work, and it turns out there's not a lot out there I can do. A job – or not having one – can be such a defining thing.'

'Yes. That's exactly it. And working here – ' She waved an arm around the café – 'defines me as a loser.'

'Says who? Nobody in your class thinks that, Sophie. We all think you're brilliant.'

Sophie gave her a grateful smile. 'That's so kind of you, but it's not like I'm qualified or even very experienced. It's yet another Sophie Frost blag.' She heaved a sigh. 'I guess, if I'm really honest, I'm worried about what my parents think of me. They haven't said it out loud, but I know they wish I was doing something a bit more impressive.'

'Sophie. Listen to me. As a mum, all I want is for my children to be happy. That is my main wish for them. And I bet you anything your parents feel the same way.'

'Yes, but . . .' A familiar figure had emerged from the Hare and Hounds, staggering slightly on the pavement. 'Oh, knickers, here comes my boss. I'd better go.' She leaned across and gave Catherine a kiss on the cheek before hopping down from her stool. 'Thank you. You're the first person I've been able to talk about this with. I feel loads better for just getting that off my chest.'

'Good,' Catherine told her. 'And for what it's worth, you're not a loser. You so aren't. Your class is the highlight of my week. I mean it.'

Sophie was touched. 'Thank you. I'm glad to hear that.'

'Well, it's true. You've got tons going for you.' She glanced at her watch. 'I'd better go now too, my bus will be here in a minute. Don't worry about it though, eh? You'll find the right thing soon, I'm sure you will. Thanks for the cake!'

'Any time.' Seeing Grant approaching, Sophie quickly cleared away the cups and tiffin plate, hoping with all her heart that Catherine was right.

Chapter Twenty-One

La cena – Dinner

On Wednesday evening, Anna got ready for her dinner with Joe feeling rather strange about the whole thing. Going out to a restaurant with another man, even if it *was* for work purposes, made her feel as if she was betraying Pete. It wasn't a date though, she reminded herself sternly, blow-drying her hair into big waves and blotting her lipstick. Joe was doing her a favour, helping her out, that was all. No big deal.

She checked herself in the mirror critically. She didn't want to be too vampy and dolled up (Joe would be scared to death), but then again it *was* an upmarket new restaurant so she couldn't exactly rock up in her jeans and Converse either. She settled for an emerald-green tailored shift dress with cap sleeves that she'd picked up in the Reiss sale and black patent heels. Actually, maybe that *was* a bit much. She put on her high-heeled boots instead and nodded approvingly. Better. It didn't look as if she was trying quite so hard now. With a cute black cape and a shiny black handbag, she was all set.

Just as she was about to leave the flat, she remembered that a notebook might come in handy for jotting down menu and dinner details. Ahh, yes. Seeing as this was actually a work thing, and all. She stuffed one into her bag and hurried out.

She was meeting Joe for a drink beforehand in the Porter Brook, and he was already waiting at the bar with a pint of bitter when she arrived. Was she mistaken, or did his eyes widen a fraction when he saw her all dressed up in her best togs?

'Looking hot there, Morley,' he joked as she went over, pretending to pull on the collar of his shirt. 'I think the temperature just rose another notch in here.'

'Oh shut up,' she said, rolling her eyes. 'A glass of red wine, please,' she said to the barmaid, then perched on a stool next to him. 'How did your interview go this afternoon, then? Have you persuaded the Tigers to let you be their team mascot yet?'

'Not yet. The bastards. I would look so good in that tiger costume, and all.' He grinned at her. 'It went pretty well. I was meeting Sean Davies for a catch-up, remember him?'

'Never heard of him.'

'You have. Played for the Tigers as a teenager, signed up by Harlequins after a single awesome season. Marla's got a big poster of him by her desk. Looks like he should be in a boy band.'

'Oh, *him*. I know. The only rugby player who doesn't have a broken nose or mashed-up ears.'

'Give him time. Anyway, yeah, he's all right. Can actually string a sentence together, which is always a bonus. Reckons he's in with a shot of making the Welsh Squad for the Six Nations, too.'

'Wooo,' said Anna, paying for her drink. She wasn't exactly a fan of rugby.

'Big woo,' Joe agreed, ignoring her sarcasm. 'Because if he does, then I get to cover the matches with a legit Sheffield connection. Win!'

They took their drinks and sat down at a table. 'So,' Joe began conversationally, 'what's the latest with your dad, then? Found anything else out about him?'

Anna began telling him about the photo, and Rimini, and how Sophie might be able to help her. 'Once I get a bit more information, I'm hopping on a plane and I'll pound the streets until I've found him, you wait.'

'Good for you,' he said. 'I hope you do.'

'I've just got this feeling that I will,' she replied. 'I've dreamed about it, you know. Dreamed that I'm there in Italy and I see him across the street – just a glance – and then everything goes into slow motion. We look really alike in my dream, so I run towards him and he notices me and his eyes sort of light up because he can tell, he can just *see* that I'm his daughter – ' She broke off, feeling vulnerable laying her secret dream out in public like that, but he was nodding.

'That's the wish, is it? That he's just, like, there's my girl, and you have an instant connection?'

She shrugged. 'I know it's all pie in the sky. But yeah, something like that.' She sipped her wine – blood-warm and smoky. 'After that, I don't know. Maybe, if we get on amazingly, I might stay in Italy with him for a while.'

'You'd leave the *Herald*?'

'Well, you know. Maybe.'

'You'd seriously turn down a hard-hitting local newspaper in *Sheffield* for a chance to live in *Italy*? You'd give up all of *this*?'

She smiled. 'Imagine that, eh? But I might have a whole new family out there. I'd want to get to know them, wouldn't you? And I'd love to do something a bit different anyway. I reckon I could totally cope with the Italian lifestyle – all that sunshine and amazing food.' The latter reminded her of what they were meant to be doing and she glanced at her watch. 'Shit, we'd better go, we're going to be late.'

Winding their way through the chairs and tables towards the door, Anna suddenly noticed Freddie from her Italian class across the pub. Small world! She was just about to shout his name when he leaned forward in his seat and put his arms around the person opposite him at the table: a big guy in a paisley-patterned shirt. 'Oh!' she exclaimed. Freddie was gay?

'What?' asked Joe, almost cannoning into the back of her.

'Nothing,' she said, walking towards the exit. Nita was going to be gutted about that, she thought.

It was cold outside, with stars spangling the dark sky, and Anna found herself wishing she'd put on something more substantial than her cape. Luckily they didn't have too far to go, dodging a few noisy groups of students and clusters of girls' nights out tottering between wine bars.

Enrico's had been Mulligan's Bar until recently – an Irish pub famed for its rowdy nights and illegal lock-ins. Nowadays, it looked far more respectable with a smart new sign hanging from the front, freshly painted insides and tea-lights flickering on the tables. As soon as they walked through the front door, Anna smelled garlic and roasted vegetables and her tummy gave a happy growl of anticipation.

The *maître d'* showed them to their table and presented them with a leather-backed menu each, and the wine list. 'Good choice,' Joe said, glancing around at the soft lighting, the clean, pressed tablecloths and the open kitchen at the back of the restaurant where three chefs were in action. He picked up the wine list. 'I take it we won't be needing this? Got to keep a clear head for your review, right?'

Anna stared at him. 'You're joking, aren't you? Give it here. We're having the works, sunshine. Can't do a proper review without sampling the booze, can I?'

'Ever the professional.'

'You know it.' She ran her eyes down the list of vintages. White, red, rosé, fizz . . . She looked up and grinned at him.

'What's your poison? Only I was thinking I'd try the prosecco.'

'I like your style. Let's have a look.'

She held it away from him teasingly. 'I thought you wanted to keep a clear head?'

'Me? Never. I was worried about you. Can't have you getting trollied on the job now.'

She arched an eyebrow. 'Sounds like a challenge to me.'

They both laughed. 'Even if you get completely lashed, you'll write better copy than Marla anyway,' he said. 'So bottoms up, I say.'

Anna tingled at the unexpected compliment. 'Thanks,' she said. 'Do you know what, I'm going to go crazy and have a cocktail. Our readers would want us to sample a broad range of drinks for their benefit, wouldn't they? We can't just stick to boring old house white or whatever.'

'That's so considerate of you,' he said. 'And I will too.' He peered at the wine list. 'A Bellini, that's got my name on it.' He winked. 'When in Venice . . .'

'We're in Sheffield.'

'Don't spoil it. Come on, this is your chance to live your Italian dream, for one night only.'

She gave him a long-suffering look.

'Can't you hear the bells from the *campanili*? The sound of water slapping against the gondolas? The flap of a thousand pigeons taking off from St Mark's Square?'

'You sound as if you know it well,' she said in surprise.

'Yeah, I was there last year with Julia.'

'Ahh.' *Julia.* There was a conversation-stopper if ever she heard one. The famously beautiful Julia, Joe's long-standing girlfriend. 'What do you fancy to eat?' she asked, changing the subject.

They pored over the menus for a few moments. Everything sounded utterly delicious, but Anna couldn't help a sneaking disappointment that all of it was in English. Shame – she'd been hoping to impress Joe with her Italian vocabulary, translating various dishes for him. Was that a bit sad of her?

Yes. Because he had a girlfriend and she had a boyfriend, she reminded herself sternly. She wasn't supposed to be trying to impress Joe or any other man for that matter. What was wrong with her?

'Good evening. Are you ready to order drinks?' The waiter had appeared beside them from out of nowhere and stood attentively, his pen poised over the notepad.

'I think we might be,' Joe replied. 'Anna?'

She looked up at him and he was smiling at her in such a sweet, affectionate way, it made her brain scramble. 'Um . . .' she started, trying to pull herself together. 'I'll have a Spring Sling, please.'

'And I'll have a Bellini. Cheers.'

'Shall we share some bruschetta while we think about food?'

'Definitely. And some olives too, please.'

'No problem. Bruschetta and olives. Thank you.' The waiter was Italian and Anna thrilled to hear his accent. She only just managed to stop herself asking where he was from. *Di dove sei?* Give it a few drinks and she'd be whipping out her father's photo and passing it round the waiting staff, she thought to herself. *Have you seen this man?*

'Hey, cheers for this, by the way,' Joe said as the waiter vanished again. 'Total perk.'

'Thanks for coming,' Anna said. 'That reminds me.' She rummaged in her handbag for her notepad. 'I should probably jot down a few first impressions of this place before we drink too much.'

'Always on duty, Scoop.'

'Absolutely.' She began writing. 'Good service,' she murmured as she wrote. 'Candles. Decent menu – didn't you think?'

He nodded. 'Decent menu.'

'The waiter pronounced "bruschetta" properly,' she went on, her writing getting messier and more abbreviated as she went. 'Nice buzzy atmosphere – thirty-something crowd, would you say?'

'Yep. Music's a bit shite, if you ask me. I think the owner likes his soft rock by the sound of it.'

They listened to the background strains of a power ballad and Anna wrinkled her nose. 'Shite music,' she wrote, then stuffed the notepad away again as the waiter returned with their drinks. 'That'll do. The review's coming together.'

'It's practically written itself already,' Joe agreed as the waiter set their cocktails carefully down in front of them. 'Cheers!'

'*Salute!*' Anna said, clinking her glass against his. 'Up your bum.'

'Up yours and all.'

The waiter cleared his throat and they both jumped, having quite forgotten he was there. 'You are ready to order your main courses now?' he asked as Anna and Joe burst into giggles.

The world seemed to shrink around their candle-lit table for two as the evening went on. Anna couldn't remember ever laughing so much over dinner. They worked their way through the drinks menu, both deciding that PornStar Martinis (passionfruit, vodka and champagne) were the most amazing things ever, then forced down a pudding each. 'For the sake of the review' had become the catchphrase of the night.

The bill was pretty hefty when they finally declared themselves done, and Anna handed over her card hoping a) that it wouldn't bounce and b) that the newspaper would actually refund the full amount. Marla hadn't given her any indication of budget restrictions in her Post-it-handover and Anna hadn't thought to check with Imogen. Ahh, well. Even if she had gone wildly over the limit and had to cough up the extra, it would be worth it. She'd had *that* much fun.

Loath to end the evening, she took her time getting up from the table and fiddling with the button on her cape. 'Well . . .' she said reluctantly. 'That was lovely. But I guess—'

'We could go for a last drink,' Joe said, interrupting. 'If you want to, that is. It's only just after ten.'

Her heart leapt. 'Great idea,' she replied, feeling a warm glow inside. Joe didn't seem in any rush to hurry back to Julia, did he? And she only had her empty flat full of Pete's crap awaiting her. 'How about the Lescar for a quick one? Drink, I mean. Not . . .' Help. There was no filter on her brain any more. She started walking towards the door before he could see how flustered she was, how red in the face.

'Sounds good to me,' he said, following her.

The Lescar was five minutes up the road and on her way home; a stylish, dark-walled pub with a beer garden and great Sunday dinners. But before they turned off the main road towards it, they passed Nando's and Anna's eye was drawn to two people sitting at a table by the window. One of them was Pete. The other was a woman she didn't recognize, with chestnut hair cut in a pixie crop.

Anna stopped, wobbly on her high boots, and watched as

if in a dream while the two of them leaned across the table towards each other and kissed.

'Oh my God,' she gulped, unable to drag her gaze away. The red wine and cocktails and all that food started swirling unpleasantly in her stomach. Her head hurt. Who was this woman? Why was Pete snogging her? He even had his hand on her face now, their lips seemingly glued together in unstoppable passion.

'Are you all right? What's up?' Joe's words made her start. She'd forgotten he was even there.

'I . . .' She opened and shut her mouth feebly. None of it felt real any more – the laughter and great food of Enrico's, the review she had to write tomorrow, the vision of her boyfriend kissing another woman. She was freezing cold all of a sudden and pulled the cape tightly around herself. 'I've got to go,' she mumbled. 'Sorry. I – I just remembered . . .' All plausible excuses failed her. 'I'll see you tomorrow, okay?'

'I don't understand. What happened?'

'Sorry, Joe,' she said. Oh no. Was she actually going to cry? Please don't let her cry. 'I can't . . .' She held up her hands. 'Bye.'

He looked confused, bewildered even, but she just wanted to get out of there, had to escape before Pete turned and saw her. Joe was saying something but she didn't stop to listen, just began running. *Go.* Adrenalin spiked her bloodstream as she ran, breath juddering out of her with every step.

All of it was starting to make sense now. Perfect, horrible sense. It was like a veil lifting and revealing the truth in all its ugliness beneath. His excuses for not seeing her recently. Blowing her out on Saturday night. The change of football night – she should have guessed that was a lie. Football night was entrenched in Pete's week, an immovable boulder. As for that sex-text he'd sent the other evening . . . had it even been meant for Anna's eyes, or had he intended it for Pixie-woman?

She clutched a hand to her chest as she walked the last few steps to her building, feeling as if the bottom had fallen out of her world. How long had he been cheating on her anyway? Was he planning to dump her?

Back in the safety of her flat, she flopped onto the sofa and the tears fell thick and fast. She still couldn't quite believe it. And there he'd been on New Year's Eve talking about moving in with her! Maybe it was her fault for being so unenthusiastic and not cutting him a front door key with her own teeth, there and then. Maybe if she'd been nicer to him, more encouraging, she wouldn't have driven him straight into the (annoyingly thin) arms of Pixie-features . . .

She blew her nose and hiccupped, then wrapped her arms around herself. Then something occurred to her. Pete's spreadsheet. Was Pixie-chick on there?

Her heart galloped as she opened the laptop, not sure she even wanted to find out. With trembling fingers she clicked on his spreadsheets and scrolled through them.

Science-fiction and fantasy novels
Sex with Anna
Monthly outgoings
Blades team-lists and match-performance
Tax return . . .

Hmmm. Well, there was nothing untoward there. Nothing un-Pete-like whatsoever. Maybe this woman was a one-off. Maybe – her stomach lurched in panic – maybe he'd seen *her and Joe* in Enrico's, had jumped to conclusions and pounced on Pixie-chops as some kind of rebound thing.

She wrinkled her nose. Nah. Turning the other cheek was not Pete's style. If he'd seen them in Enrico's, he'd have blundered in there furiously, maybe even taken a pudgy swing at Joe. All the same, it did remind her that appearances could be deceptive.

Maybe there was some excuse, some perfectly good reason for Pete being with that woman. Perhaps she'd got it wrong, in fact, and it wasn't even Pete at all! She'd been meaning to get her eyes checked for months; she was certain she'd become more short-sighted recently.

The tiny flame of hope sputtered and went out as quickly as it had ignited. Don't kid yourself, Anna. You're not *that* short-sighted that you can't recognize your own so-called boyfriend snogging the face off some other bint.

She was about to close the laptop again when something nagged her about Pete's list of spreadsheets. How come

'Science-fiction and fantasy novels' was the most recently updated? She hadn't seen him read a book for weeks.

She clicked it open . . . and stared open-mouthed. The sneaky bastard. The cheating, lying, book-dodging git. Turned out, this particular spreadsheet wasn't a compilation of his favourite books at all. Once opened, the title was in fact *Sex with Katerina.* Anna's eyes boggled as she started to read through the entries.

Smashing blowjob in M&D's bathroom – 10

Quickie in Greyhound toilets. Dirty girl! – 9

BEST EVER. Her place. Tantric! – 11

Anna's eyes smarted and she let out a shocked sob. Oh, Pete. Oh, Pixie – or Katerina, rather. Oh no!

She pushed the laptop away but the words danced around her brain tormentingly. She'd have nightmares for the rest of her days. A quickie in the skanky Greyhound toilets, for heaven's sake. Yuck. As for her doing *that* to Pete in the 1970s avocado-green bathroom at his parents' place . . . Words failed her.

In a fit of anger, she snatched back the laptop and, with two clicks, deleted the entire spreadsheet. In another two, she deleted the one about her as well. And five minutes later, she'd created a brand new document. This one was called: *Pete, you spineless loser, consider yourself DUMPED.*

Chapter Twenty-Two

Il caffè – The café

On Thursday, Sophie braved the twisting flurries of snow and went to meet Anna in Marmadukes, a café opposite St Marie's Cathedral. It had felt like serendipity the week before when Sophie had spotted the Facebook update made by her chef friend Marco, saying he'd just spent a week at a trade fair in Rimini and was now visiting his parents nearby. She'd met Marco back when she'd worked in an amazing *pasticceria* in Rome, and they'd always got on well. If his parents were nearly-locals, he would probably know the area pretty well and she was sure he wouldn't mind helping out.

Marmadukes was small and cosy, with trays of yummy-looking pastries and cakes on the counter, and 'Cast No Shadow' by Oasis playing from the speakers. 'Cold enough for you, Alf?' the lad behind the till was asking the elderly man in the woolly hat he was serving.

'*Cold?*' scoffed the man. 'This is warm, this. Two foot of snow we've got up on the hills. Had to dig us way out just now. This is nothing!'

Sophie hid her smile. Yorkshire people were brilliant, she thought to herself as she squeezed through to see if Anna was in the back room. Warm, indeed. It was bloody Baltic outside, but there was a certain type of stubbornness here – amongst men, in particular, she'd noticed – that meant they steadfastly refused to acknowledge even a trace of weakness.

Anna had found a table round the back and waved as Sophie came in. Her long, dark hair was pinned up with a green pencil and she wore black-rimmed glasses and a spotty purple scarf around her neck, as well as the more conventional outfit of a black V-neck jumper and jeans. 'Hi!' she called.

'Hi,' said Sophie. 'Let me just grab a tea and I'll be right with you. Do you want anything else?'

'Those *pain au chocolats* looked pretty tasty to me,' Anna said. 'I will if you will . . .'

Sophie grinned. 'Two *pains au chocolat* coming up.' She dumped her coat on the back of a chair and went to the counter.

The tea arrived in Yorkshire Tea mugs (of course) with dinky old-fashioned bottles of milk, and they both set to work on the pastries. 'Thanks so much for doing this,' Anna said, dabbing a stray flake with her finger and popping it in her mouth. 'It's really kind of you.'

'No problem,' Sophie said. 'I don't know how much he'll be able to tell you, but I thought it was worth a go.'

'Any kind of information would be a bonus,' Anna admitted. 'According to the internet, Rimini itself is really long and stretched out – fourteen kilometres of beaches apparently, so there are just tons and tons of hotels and resorts. Mum could have been anywhere.' She slid the photo across the table in a plastic wallet. 'But if your friend has any idea about where this was taken then that would be a start.'

'Sure,' Sophie said. She looked at the photo of the dark-haired man in the centre, his arm around a beaming young woman. 'Wow. So this is your dad.'

'That's him. Gino.'

'I can see the resemblance,' Sophie said, peering closer. The photo didn't have the sharpest definition ever, but there was no mistaking the olive complexion and dark features that both Gino and his daughter shared. She tucked the plastic wallet carefully in her bag. 'How exciting. Leave it with me. Hopefully Marco will come up with something helpful.'

'Thanks. I can't wait to meet him – my dad, I mean. I don't even know if he knows I exist.'

'Are you still planning to go out to Rimini yourself, see if you can track him down?' Sophie asked.

'That's the plan.' Anna stirred her tea, looking more pensive. 'Although a lot of things are up in the air right now, unfortunately.'

'Oh. Good things or bad?'

'Bad.' Anna sighed. 'I found out last night that my boyfriend has been seeing someone else. Which was lovely.'

Her fingers trembled on the teaspoon and Sophie noticed the dark circles under her eyes. 'Oh shit. Are you sure?'

'Totally sure. Sure beyond doubt.' She pulled a face. 'For one thing, I saw them kissing in Nando's. And for another, I discovered he's charted the whole torrid thing on a spreadsheet.'

Sophie's mouth fell open. 'No! A *spreadsheet*?'

'Yeah. A sodding spreadsheet. Every bloody detail.'

'That's horrible. And at the same time, totally lame.' Sophie sipped her tea, then snorted. 'On a spreadsheet indeed.'

'I know, right? What kind of twat does that?'

'A twat who doesn't deserve you, that's who,' Sophie told her. 'Honestly. Does he catalogue all his books in alphabetical order as well?'

'Yep. And he's kept a detailed log of every financial transaction he's ever made,' Anna replied. 'Including – and I kid you not – the one time he actually gave a homeless guy a quid.'

'God. Last of the big philanthropists.'

'Yeah. Last of the flaming dickheads, and all.'

There was a pause. The two women on the next table were having a gossipy 'He didn't', 'He did!', 'Tell me he didn't!', 'I'm telling you he did!' conversation, which was rising in volume.

'So, what happens now?' Sophie asked Anna. 'Does he know that you know?'

'No. We've got that delightful conversation yet to come. I emailed him to say he's got to get all the stuff out of my flat by nine o'clock tonight or I'm chucking it out on the street, so he's probably got the hint that I'm a tad cheesed off.' She rolled her eyes. 'Although knowing what a plank he is, he might even have missed that clue, to be honest. Anyway. Sorry to bang on about it. Not your problem.'

'That's all right. I hope you sort things out.' Sophie eyed Anna over her mug. 'You know, in my experience, hopping on a plane for an adventure – like, to Rimini – is pretty much the best thing you can do after a broken heart. Maybe you should take off for a bit? Get away from it all.'

Anna raised an eyebrow. 'Yeah? That's what you did, is it?'

'Yeah.' Then Sophie stopped, feeling like a hypocrite. It had taken her three years and lots of plane journeys to even *start* getting over Dan – and look at her the other night, reduced to jelly at the news that he was back in the same country as her. 'Well, it helps in the short term, anyway,' she added after a moment. 'But I'm not exactly an expert. Whatever it takes, that's what I say.'

'What it took last night was dodgy liqueurs and cake. Today, it's review-writing and phone-ignoring. Tonight, it'll be flat-clearing and probably having a stand-up row with him on the pavement.' Anna screwed up her face. 'Anyway. It's probably for the best.'

'Yeah. Well, good luck.'

They were silent for a moment, both rather awkward at all these confidences when they barely knew each other. 'I don't believe it', 'Well, it's true!' screeched the women behind them. 'I knew he was up to something when he came home with those bungee cables. I thought either he's sorting out that roofrack at last, or he's going all fifty-shades on me.'

Anna giggled. 'The mind boggles,' she whispered, then drained the last of her tea. 'I'd better go. Thanks again for helping with the photo – and for the chat.'

'Any time,' Sophie replied. 'Here's my number,' she said, scribbling it down on a paper napkin. 'Ring me if you need a drink or a moan. Hey, and remember what I said about hopping on a plane if things get too complicated. It might be just what you need, a bit of Italian sunshine.'

'That's not a bad idea,' Anna said. She put the napkin in her bag and smiled. 'Look forward to hearing what your friend says in the meantime. See you soon.'

That afternoon, Jim had an appointment at the hospital and, as she wasn't working, Sophie decided to go along too. If she was at home she'd only be trying to think of something witty and love-me-ish to post under Dan's recent Facebook update, or checking out train times to Manchester.

She mustn't stalk the poor man. For all she knew, he was married with seven children by now. (He wasn't married with seven children though, as she knew damn well. Or, if he was, he hadn't thought to put it on his Facebook page anyway. She'd checked.)

They all hoped that this would be Jim's final appointment at the hospital. He was on new medication since the second heart attack and he no longer got so breathless or tired. Trish had even stopped raising a warning finger whenever Jim broached the subject of returning to work. Maybe, just maybe, life was about to take a welcome turn back to normal for him at last.

It was still bitter outside, with a raw, slicing wind, but as soon as you walked into the reception area of the hospital, the temperature soared and it was like stumbling into the tropics. As Sophie and her parents stopped to take off their hats and scarves, she glimpsed an unexpected face. 'Roy!' she exclaimed in surprise as he walked in. 'What are you doing here? Is everything all right?'

Roy's usual smile wasn't anywhere to be seen. In fact he looked downright terrible – pale and stressed, twisting his hands together as he replied. 'Geraldine's had a fall,' he said, his eyes great pools of anxiety. 'Yesterday. She's been in all night.'

'Oh, Roy,' Sophie said. 'Is she okay? What happened?'

'Black ice on the front path,' he said. His mouth trembled.

'She was wearing high heels, the daft thing. High heels with black ice, I ask you! I did tell her she should put on some wellies but she wasn't having any of it. Not Geraldine. "You'd have to chloroform me before you catch me wearing wellies in public," she said.'

Jim caught his eye. 'Women,' he said knowingly, earning himself a nudge from Trish.

'I'm so sorry,' Sophie said, putting a hand on Roy's arm. 'Is she hurt? What did the doctors say? Oh – this is my mum and dad, by the way. Mum, Dad, this is Roy, he's one of my students.'

Roy gave them a small, tense smile. You could tell his heart wasn't really in it, though. 'She's fractured her pelvis,' he said. 'They kept her in overnight. I've just been back to pick up some clothes for her. She's in a lot of pain.'

'The poor thing,' Trish said sympathetically. 'Is there anything we can do to help?'

'Yes, let me take your number, Roy,' Sophie said, pulling out her phone. He looked as if his world had been tipped upside down and shaken out of all recognition. She remembered Geraldine saying they had no children ('Not for want of trying, eh, Roy? But it wasn't to be for us') and wondered how they were going to manage. 'Have you got any family around, or neighbours who'll be able to help out?'

He was blinking as if the questions were all too much for him. He seemed so lost without garrulous, charming

Geraldine beside him – older and more feeble, standing there in his coat and scarf. 'Tell you what,' she said quickly. 'I'll walk round with you now, okay? Is that all right, Dad? Then I'll meet you two in Cardio.' She took Roy's arm. 'Come on. Tell me where we're going and I'll keep you company.'

Back home that evening, Sophie went straight to her laptop, determined to swallow her pride and respond to Dan's Facebook update. Seeing Geraldine and Roy holding hands in the hospital ward and smiling into one another's eyes, still besotted after all these years, had reminded her that true love did exist. It happened for some people – her parents were another shining example. Who was to say it couldn't happen for her, too? If anyone was worth fighting for, it was Dan Collins.

It had been a good day overall, she thought, as she waited for the home page to load. She'd enjoyed her chat with Anna. Then at the hospital her dad had been discharged and told that he could go back to work on Monday. He hadn't stopped smiling since. As for Geraldine – well, things weren't so bright for her, unfortunately, with several weeks of bed-rest ahead and definitely no high heels for a while. And bless her, she was hardly recognizable with no make-up and a pair of flannel pyjamas on. But Sophie was glad that she'd bumped into Roy and could offer some practical support and comfort. She was already planning how she and the other members of the Italian class might be able to rally round.

On the way home from the hospital, her mind had teemed with possible replies to her ex-boyfriend's *I'm back in Manchester. Did you miss me?* update. If she was going to reply (and she definitely was – faint heart never won fair bloke, and all that), then she had to come up with the perfect response: cool, funny, and just a tiny bit flirty, to let him know that *hello,* he was still in with half a chance. So what to write?

She discounted a blunt *HELL, YES* (too obvious), played around with a few witticisms punning on 'Down Under' (too crude), pondered on some in-jokes that nobody else would understand (up yours, Dan's other friends) before deciding to keep things simple.

A straightforward, grown-up *Dan! Welcome back. Hello from sunny Sheffield* – that kind of thing. That would do the trick, wouldn't it? Not a hint of bunny-boiler, yet subtly letting him know she was also in the UK.

Feeling quivery, she opened the browser and clicked through to Facebook. Back, back, back she scrolled through the timeline to find his message . . . there it was.

She frowned, the quivery feeling replaced by disappointment as she saw that twenty-three comments had already been left beneath his initial posting. Too slow off the mark, Sophie.

Gemma Blaine: Dude! Totally missed you. When can I get my hands on you again? ☺ *xxxxx*

Alice Harris: Dannyboy! Get your arse down the Tib pronto!

Eloise Winters: Course we did! RING ME!

Jade Nicholls: OMG DAN! Cannot WAIT to see you. Deffo missed you, babe. Big kisses.

Sophie couldn't read any more. Kisses. Capital letters. Babe. Dude. Who were these women and what claims did they have over him?

She shut down the web page, her hand shaking on the mouse. Gemma and Alice and Eloise and Jade . . . she bet they were just the tip of the iceberg. Easy-going, handsome Dan must have been fighting them off for the last few years. And why had she ever thought otherwise? She should have known.

Well, she was damned if she was going to add her name to the slavering harem. Dan had made it perfectly clear back in Sydney that all good things came to an end. He'd got it right first time.

Chapter Twenty-Three

All'ufficio – At the office

Trying to write a killer restaurant review with a hangover was one thing. Trying to write it with a hangover and an image of your boyfriend snogging another woman flashing through your brain approximately every thirty seconds was damn near impossible. Yet Anna's copy needed to be on Imogen's desk by four o'clock this afternoon: fact. And she knew that Marla, on returning to work, would go straight to Anna's review like a heat-seeking missile hellbent on racking up a long, critical list of its faults. If there was a single lame sentence, Marla would cite this as conclusive evidence that Anna just wasn't up to the job: fact.

Getting some fresh air and meeting Sophie helped some, especially as Sophie seemed so confident about her friend making a breakthrough when it came to the Gino-hunt. But all too soon she was back in her stuffy office, the screen in front of her maddeningly empty.

Enrico's, the new Italian restaurant on Ecclesall Road, has a great atmosphere and lovely staff, she began, then immediately deleted it. Ugh. Wooden and forgettable. Try again.

Love Italian food? Then you'll love Enrico's, the new Italian restaurant on Ecclesall Road, she tried next. Also awful, she decided in the next moment, backspacing through the lot. Now she just sounded like a cheesy advert.

This was harder than she'd anticipated. That all-important first sentence was eluding her. Anna knew from previous Imogen lectures that you had approximately three lines to grab a reader. If you hadn't hooked them in by then, they'd turn the page and ignore your carefully written piece. 'You can have the most fascinating, brilliantly constructed article ever,' Imogen liked saying, 'but if the opening is shite, nobody will bother discovering its magnificence.'

Anna swigged the rest of her lukewarm coffee, trying to get into the right frame of mind. She never had this problem usually. Bloody Pete and his wandering tongue. Not only had he made her feel like a complete idiot, he was now inadvertently wrecking her career by distracting her from the job in hand.

'Everything all right?' said Joe, walking past just then. His expression was wary, as if he half-expected her to freak out and sprint away like she'd done the night before.

'Yeah, fabulous,' she replied sarcastically. 'Couldn't be better.'

He put his hands up. 'Only asking,' he said, then walked off.

Oh great. Now she'd driven him away when he was only being friendly. She opened her mouth to say sorry, she didn't mean it, but then shut it again because he was already out of hearing range.

Heaving a sigh, she turned back to her computer, made the font of her title bigger, put it into bold, then made it smaller again and added the date. Then she put her name into italics and out again. *Come on, Anna. Make a start. You can always go back and edit out the crap bits later. Just write, damn it!*

Still her fingers hovered over the keys, refusing to tap out a single word. This was hopeless. Maybe she should just throw a sicky and go home. But then she'd have filed nothing for the review and Imogen would never give her another chance. Also, Marla would *love* it. Just imagine the gloating, the unbearable smugness. *More difficult than it looks, isn't it? Not everyone has the talent necessary for reviewing, unfortunately.*

Thinking of Marla gave her an idea. How did *she*, the self-proclaimed queen of the Sheffield restaurant scene, do it? Anna opened the newspaper's website and clicked through past reviews, hoping for inspiration.

Picture the scene: it's Saturday night, I'm in my new dress from Republic and some seriously mega heels, out with my three besties all looking their finest. Where's the best place in town for a group of women to go for some fabulous food in stylish surroundings? Well, funny you should ask that . . .

Anna pursed her lips. Marla's style was all me-me-me, but even she had to admit it worked in its own way. It was a damn sight better than the plodding opening sentences she'd already tried and rejected, that was for sure.

Come on, Anna. You can do personal. You can do bubbly. Just bloody start writing, for heaven's sake.

She lowered her fingers like a maestro about to launch into a difficult piano concerto, then at long last began to type.

'Anna, it's me. Pete.'

'Come in.' Anna held the door open for him then stepped back as he tried to put his arms around her. 'Don't.'

'Anna, love, you've got it all wrong.'

'I don't think so.' Her voice was Arctic, crackling with ice. 'What was it again – a blowjob at your mum's house? A quickie in the Greyhound toilets? That's lovely, that is, Pete. That's total class.' She folded her arms across her chest and stuck her nose in the air. 'Just take your stuff and go.'

Shock and fear filled his eyes. His jaw dropped. Gotcha. 'What do you mean? How did you . . . ?' he stammered.

'Your laptop,' she said curtly. 'All there in black and white for anyone to read. Anyone with half a brain cell who could guess your password, that is.'

His face sagged like a fallen cheese soufflé. 'I . . . I . . . I was only mucking around,' he pleaded. 'It didn't mean anything.'

'Don't make it worse.' She grabbed her handbag. 'I'm going out now. I'll give you half an hour to clear your stuff then I never want to see you again. Got that?'

'But Anna . . .'

'Bye, Pete.'

She walked briskly out of her flat and down to the Lescar, where for thirty torturous minutes she sat on her own at a corner table with a pint of Guinness and tried her hardest not to cry.

When she returned home, every last trace of Pete had vanished, bar a note on the table.

Sorry, Anna. Then he'd started writing *If you ever . . .* only to change his mind and cross it out. Huh. She could only guess at what he'd been about to say.

If you ever want a shag, give us a ring.

If you ever feel desperate, call me.

If you ever decide you've made a mistake, you know where to find me.

Yeah, right. Hell would freeze over first.

If Anna thought a line had now been drawn under the traumas of the week, she was sadly mistaken. As soon as she arrived at work the next day, before she'd even taken off her coat, Imogen was on her case.

'A word, please, Anna,' she said in that crisp, no-nonsense way that immediately struck terror into your soul.

Oh God, Anna thought, following her boss into her office.

Now what? It was that restaurant review, she could feel it in her bones. Imogen hated it. Imogen was regretting asking her to cover for Marla. Imogen was going to—

'It's the restaurant review,' Imogen began, as if reading Anna's mind. 'I'm disappointed, I must say. I was hoping for something zingier, with a bit more punch.'

'Zingier, with a bit more punch,' Anna repeated dully.

'Yes, Anna, the lovely zingy sort of punch that you manage in your cookery column. It's glaringly absent this time. What went wrong? Any clues? Were you ill? Were you drunk? Had someone slipped you some Valium? You blew it.'

Whoa. Why don't you just come straight out with it, Anna thought, wincing. She opened her mouth, wondering whether or not to pour out her lovelife sorrows on her boss's powder-blue padded shoulder. It took her less than a second to decide Not. Imogen was about as touchy-feely as an alligator. 'Sorry,' she said feebly. 'Must have been having an off day. I'll give it another try.'

'You do that. And bring in the personal touch this time. Less of the meh, give me your voice. Make it your story, okay? I've promised the subs they can have it by midday, so you'd better get on the case. Clock's ticking.' She spun on her chair to do something on her Mac, so Anna took the hint and scuttled away.

Yuck. It was like redoing homework. As a journalist, you could never be too precious about your writing – it inevitably got corrected, tweaked, cut – and that was fine; that was part of the job. Being asked to start from scratch on something was a completely different matter. Her sole consolation was that Marla wasn't there to witness this humiliating walk of shame back to her desk.

She re-read her rejected review, spirits sinking. In all fairness, Imogen was right to sack it. The whole thing was pretty turgid, reviewing-by-numbers at its worst: I ate this, my companion ate this, the restaurant was like this.

Okay. But that was yesterday's attempt. Today she'd crack it. In two hours and forty minutes, no less. If Imogen wanted zing and punch and the personal touch, she'd bloody well give her the lot.

If you've been reading my cookery column recently, she began, *you'll know I'm a sucker for Italian food. So when I was offered the chance to review Enrico's, the new Italian restaurant on Ecclesall Road, I'd booked myself a table before you can say 'bruschetta'.*

She paused. Good. That would do it. What next? *Make it personal,* Imogen had said. Personal. Okay. Then she remembered Pete's lie about not being able to come to the restaurant with her, and her eyes narrowed. Should she drag Pete into the review, make him part of 'the story'? Imogen might be furious with her for straying beyond her remit. *This is meant to be a piece about food, not your private life, for goodness sake,* Anna could imagine her snapping. But on the other hand, she might love it. And what better way to lure in a reader than with the added spice of some real-life gossip?

It sounded a perfect place to spend a romantic evening, but unfortunately my boyfriend claimed he was busy, Anna typed. *Shame! Just as well—*

She hesitated, knowing that Pete's mum read the weekend edition of the paper, cover to cover, as did his workmates. Oh, knickers to the lot of them, she thought. He'd brought this on himself.

Just as well a handsome colleague was free to accompany me, she typed. Read it and weep, Pete, she thought, stabbing the keys viciously as she went on. I don't need you anyway.

Unlike the first dreary affair, this review practically wrote itself. The cloud had lifted and she flexed her writing muscles with glee, knowing that her copy was witty and sparky, with truckloads of that elusive zing.

Will I go back to Enrico's? Hell, yes. And here's the acid test. As Handsome Colleague and I left, heads spinning from the dangerously moreish PornStar Martinis, I felt so deliciously full and content that not even the sight of my 'boyfriend' smooching the face off another woman in the window of Nando's could wipe the smile off my *face. Plenty more* pesce *in the* mare, *as they say!*

She checked it all through for any grammar and spelling mistakes, then copied it into an email and sent it to Imogen before she could change her mind. Sometimes, a girl had to do what a girl had to do. And a giant two-fingers up to Pete in the weekend review would do very nicely for starters.

On Saturday morning, Anna woke up early and reminded herself that this was the first day of the rest of her life. She dug out her sports bra then put on her tracky bottoms and running shoes and went dutifully to the weekly Park Run in Endcliffe Park. This was one New Year's resolution she had actually kept up so far, and she loved meeting her friends every Saturday to take part in the huge, everyone-welcome five-kilometre run that took place rain or shine.

A run with the girls followed by a hearty brunch in the park café was just what she needed. Her friend Chloe was recently single too, and over their plates of eggs and bacon they planned a few girly treats together to prop one another up. Afterwards, Anna headed back towards her flat feeling much better about the world. She had some new recipes she wanted to try for next week's cookery column and then she was going to spring-clean the flat from top to bottom. She might even look at flights to Rimini. Hadn't Sophie told her it was the best cure for a broken heart?

She grabbed a paper from the newsagent on the way home and flipped through the pages to find her review. Imogen had pronounced herself 'delighted' with the new, improved piece when she'd read it ('*That's* more like it!'), and Anna had glowed with praise (and relief) for the rest of the day. Ahh, here it was. She stood in the street while she looked at it appraisingly – then nearly dropped the newspaper in shock.

Wait – somebody had changed her headline. Like, totally rewritten it. She'd titled the review: MAMMA MIA! ENRICO'S GRABS A PIZZA THE ACTION, but now the lettering screamed: MAMMA MIA! ENRICO'S . . . THE FOOD OF LOVE?

Worse than that, one of the designers (who? Wait till she got her hands on them) had added a broken-heart image to the layout as well as . . . Oh no. A silhouetted image of Joe's byline photo with question mark graphics around it, clearly identifying him as the 'Handsome Colleague' of the piece.

Flaming hell. This was a disaster. This was spectacularly awful. Instead of two-fingers to Pete, the designer had made it look as if the piece was all about her falling in love with *Joe*. How had this happened? Had Imogen given the brief, or had the designer decided to make mischief?

Stuffing the paper under her arm, she ran all the way back to her flat and snatched up her phone. She had to warn Joe about it, tell him there'd been a terrible misunderstanding, let him know that this was not – repeat, NOT – her doing.

Too late. As she switched on her phone, she saw that he'd already sent a text, the cold unfriendliness of which left her chilled to the bone.

Just seen your review. WTF? Jules is fuming. Thanks a bunch.

'But I didn't mean . . .' Anna protested out loud, then slumped onto the sofa in dismay. Bollocks. Worse and worse. How was she ever going to dig herself out of this one?

Chapter Twenty-Four

L'abito nuziale – The wedding dress

'Ta-dah! What do you think?'

Catherine blinked her troubled thoughts away and lifted her gaze to see the vision that had just emerged from behind the velvet curtain of the Wedded Bliss changing room. Words failed her. 'Oh!' she said brightly after a moment. Was her smile staying on? She hoped it didn't look too forced.

Meanwhile, Carole, the hairsprayed, permatanned manager of Wedded Bliss, was clasping her hands together in what looked worryingly like a gooey-eyed orgasm. 'Ooh, it's absolutely *gorgeous,*' she breathed. 'Ooh, I'm tearing up here. Sensational!'

Catherine still hadn't managed to string a sentence together. 'Um . . .' she croaked.

Penny turned to the side and struck a pose, one white-gloved hand on her hip, the other pulling down the brim of her white-ribboned Stetson. She jutted her chin as if eyeing up a rodeo horse. 'Not what you were expecting, Cath?' she asked.

'Not exactly,' Catherine confessed. Truth be told, she wasn't quite sure *what* she had been expecting. Definitely not the fringe-edged, mid-calf-length dress coupled with white-sequinned cowboy boots, though.

'It's an excellent fit,' Carole went on enthusiastically, taking a step closer. 'Very flattering. This style has just come in, so it's very "on trend" as they say.'

Penny stamped a foot and pretended to swing a lasso above her head, admiring herself in the full-length mirror the whole time. 'It was Darren's idea,' she told Catherine, ignoring Carole's sales witter. 'I told you, didn't I, me and him have been going line dancing together? You should come, it's such a scream. And we thought, well, why not go the whole hog with a bit of a western theme? You know how he loves his cowboy films.'

'Right,' Catherine said politely. Darren was usually a jeans and T-shirt kind of bloke, occasionally donning a striped shirt and some aftershave for a night down the Plough. She couldn't envisage him galloping up to the register office in chaps and a black Stetson, silver spurs gleaming on his boots. Still, it would be original. 'So what's *he* going to wear?'

'We're not here to talk about *him*, love,' Penny snorted. 'What do you think of *this*?'

'I think it's very . . . you,' Catherine replied truthfully, taking in the lace sleeves, the tight satin bodice, the zigzag hem. 'I thought you'd decided not to wear white, though?'

'I know. But have you seen what most cowgirl dresses are like? There's a lot of fringed brown suede. And much as I love my Dazza, I'm not wearing brown suede to my own frigging wedding.' She eyed herself in the mirror and smiled. 'Whereas something like this definitely says *Bride*.'

'Oh yes, absolutely,' Carole agreed fervently. 'It says confident, modern bride, unafraid to defy convention.'

Penny stared quizzically at Carole as if noticing her for the first time, then turned back to Catherine. 'Cath?'

Catherine gave a weak smile. The dress definitely said *something*. 'Er . . .'

Penny tipped her head on one side and frowned. 'Is everything all right?' she asked. 'Only you seem a bit quiet. Not yourself.'

Catherine took a deep breath. 'I was going to tell you later,' she began, flicking a glance at Carole who took the hint and instantly pretended to be rearranging a tiara display. 'This morning I—'

'Sorry I'm late!' The door of the boutique crashed open just then and in strode Leona, Penny's sister. Catherine had met her at Penny's parties over the years, not to mention at her first two weddings; she was blonde and busty, with a cackle that could shatter glass and hips that could break a man's heart. 'Sweet Jesus, what are you *wearing*, doll?' she asked, throwing her hands up dramatically.

'This is our Savannah dress,' Carole interjected, her smile becoming slightly frosty. 'It's for the fun, romantic bride who wants an informal yet stunning design.'

'It looks shit though,' Leona said. 'Pen, are you out of your mind?'

'Oh, here we go,' Penny said, pulling a face. 'Wedding dress advice from my sister who's never actually been able to get her own husband.'

'Oi! Cheeky mare. Do you want my help or not?'

'Not if you're just going to start bossing me about, no,' Penny retorted. 'There's no need to be rude the second you get here.'

Catherine and Carole exchanged a glance. 'We do have a wide range of other styles,' Carole began tactfully. 'Perhaps you'd like to try something else?'

'Perhaps my *sister* would like to show a bit of gratitude,' Leona said, drowning out the rest of Carole's suggestion. 'Perhaps she'd like to say a word of thanks that I'm here yet again, helping to choose a third flaming wedding dress when we all know it'll be divorce papers six months down the line.'

'Oh, don't *trouble* yourself,' Penny said, her voice dripping with sarcasm. 'I mean it – if that's your attitude, just do one. I don't need your help anyway!'

'Ladies, *please*,' Carole said, wringing her hands.

'Great – so now I've come into town and paid an hour's parking for nothing,' Leona huffed.

'Oh Christ, Leona, two quid, are you seriously giving me grief about two poxy quid for the car park?'

'Just shut up! Both of you!'

Everyone fell silent at Catherine's shout. Penny looked startled, while Leona fixed her with a 'Who the hell are *you*?' kind of look. Carole, on the other hand, gave her a small smile of appreciation, then quickly resumed her poker face and pretended she was rearranging the tiaras all over again.

'Sorry,' Catherine said, blushing, 'but this is not getting us anywhere. Penny. No offence, but I'm with Leona on that dress. The zigzag hem is kind of weird, but the Stetson and boots actually look quite cool. Carole, is there another cowgirl-type dress she can try instead?'

'Yes, of course,' Carole said. 'We've got the MaryLou and the Sapphire. Let me just see if we have those in a ten . . .'

She bustled away, leaving Catherine faced with the sisters, both of whom were still staring at her. 'Sorry,' she said again. 'I didn't mean to shout. I'm having a bit of a strange day, that's all.'

'You're fine, love,' Penny said, recovering herself. 'And I'm sorry you got interrupted by my sister barging in. She was just about to tell me something,' she explained to Leona.

'Oh, right,' Leona said. 'Go on then, what is it?'

Catherine swallowed. This was not how she'd envisaged things panning out. Leona settled herself on a velvet banquette, crossed her thigh-booted legs and leaned forward expectantly, showing an inch of plump cleavage. Penny folded her lace-clad arms and nodded. 'Go on, Cath.'

'I phoned up Rebecca,' she said baldly.

'Her husband's fancy woman,' Penny added to Leona in a stage whisper. 'What did you say? I hope you gave her a piece of your mind.'

Carole came bustling back with a pair of white satin dresses, but melted discreetly into the background again as she took in the serious atmosphere. Years of dealing with brides-on-a-knife-edge, emotional mothers and uptight friends had given her a hyper-sensitive trauma radar.

'I've found something out,' Catherine said, not caring who heard any more. 'Rebecca and Mike – they're in it together. It's her who's been paying him all this time. Thousands and thousands of pounds.'

Carole tried and failed to suppress a gasp.

Leona's eyes bulged. 'She's been paying your hubby for sex?'

'*Mike*?' Penny was incredulous. 'I mean, no offence, hon, but he's hardly—'

'No, not for sex,' Catherine said. 'It's even worse.'

She had worked it out all by herself in the end: the payments, the conferences, the affair. All it took was a single phone call to the number on Rebecca's business card and everything fell into place.

'Schenkman Pharma, how can I help you?'

'Is Rebecca Hale there, please?'

'I'll just check, hold the line, please . . . I'm sorry, she's in a meeting, would you like to leave a message?'

Catherine held her nerve. Time for her shot in the dark. 'I was hoping to talk to her about a payment I received through Centaur,' she said crisply. 'Is there anyone else in the department who might be able to help?'

'Of course. Let me put you through to Rebecca's assistant, Paul.'

It had been as easy as that. Then she'd had a pleasant and very revealing chat with Paul, who sounded rather young and not the brightest bauble on the Christmas tree. He'd cheerfully assured her that yes, all their payments for this particular project did come from Centaur, rather than directly from Schenkman. 'I'm not sure why,' he added. 'I suppose it's easier for them to account everything separately.'

Guessing wildly here, Paul, but it could be something to do with the fact that this is all ethically suspect, Catherine thought grimly. 'Thanks,' she said at the end of the call. 'You've been very helpful.'

'Would you like Rebecca to call you back, Mrs . . . I'm sorry I didn't catch your name.'

'That's fine, Paul. I think I know everything I need to now.'

Penny frowned as Catherine finished recounting this. 'So what are you saying? The pharmaceutical company have been paying Mike? What for?'

Leona had slumped back on the banquette, clearly preferring this version of events less than the cash-for-sex one she'd originally anticipated.

'For prescribing their product,' Catherine replied, 'and advising other GPs to do the same at all these swanky conferences he goes to.'

'What product is it? Viagra or something?' Leona asked with a shade more interest.

'It's called Demelzerol, some kind of betablocker. Brand new on the market, from what I can find out, very little clinical research.'

'So? You've lost me.' Now even Penny had an *Is-that-IT?* kind of expression.

Catherine opened her mouth to reply, but Carole beat her to it. '*So*,' she said, as if speaking to a pair of idiots, 'it's a clear case of ethical conflict. Is he prescribing the drug because he genuinely thinks it will benefit the patients, or is he doing it to line his own pockets?'

'Exactly,' Catherine said.

'That's dodgy as fuck,' Penny pronounced.

'That's outrageous,' Leona agreed.

'I know,' Catherine said. She spread her hands wide and

gazed around at them. 'But now that I've found this out – what do you think I should do?'

Catherine's head had been buzzing with ideas of what she should and shouldn't do ever since she stumbled upon her new information. So far the list of possible courses of action went as follows:

One: she could report Mike to the General Medical Council. Carole (who seemed to know a surprising amount about medical ethics) thought he would face a disciplinary hearing and could possibly be struck off. He might even go to court if it was proved that patients' health had been affected by his actions. It would be justice, sure, but what would it do to the children? The shame would ruin their lives.

Two: she could blackmail Mike for a share of the money. This was Penny's idea. 'Tell him you're not moving out of the house either,' she added for good measure. 'That'll stick it to him.' It was tempting. Her money problems would be over in a flash. But could she live with her conscience? No. Never.

Three: she could blow the whistle on Rebecca and the dodgy pharmaceutical company *and* blackmail Mike. This was Leona's contribution. 'Let them both hang,' she said viciously. 'They've been in it together, they should go down together. And good riddance to the rotten pair of 'em.'

Or, of course, there was option four: do bugger all. That way, Matthew and Emily never had to know their father had tarnished his professional reputation. Plus, she would avoid a nasty confrontation with Mike. If she was honest, that was the part she was dreading most of all. He was not going to take any of this lying down, that was a given.

This last suggestion didn't go down too well with the other three, though. By now, Carole had made everyone a coffee and cracked open the Gypsy Creams (although Penny was refused either until she changed out of the Savannah dress and hung it safely out of spilling distance). To a woman, they all shook their heads when Catherine put forward the fourth option.

'Do nothing? You can't let him get away with this,' Penny told her.

'Do nothing? When you could bleed the bastard dry? Give over,' Leona said, spraying crumbs in her indignation.

'It would be morally wrong,' Carole said sagely. 'People might have *died* because of your ex-husband's greed.'

They were right. She had to do something. Besides, Anna had spelled it out only too clearly last week after Italian class: if Catherine did nothing with her evidence then she herself might be liable for punishment. She could be done as an accessory to the crime! The last thing she wanted was for the cell door to slam shut on *her.*

Oh, it was so difficult. So complicated. She wished she'd never come across the bank statements and the conference brochures and Rebecca flaming Hale's business card. But she had. And now she had to think very hard about what, if anything, she was going to do about it all.

By the time Italian class rolled around again that night, she was still to make any kind of decision.

'*Buonasera,* Catherine,' Sophie said, looking up from where she was going through some notes at the front of the room. '*Come stai?*'

'*Non c'é male,*' Catherine replied. *Not bad. Kind of confused. Not sure what to do. But overall, not bad.*

'Is everyone here now?' Sophie asked, counting heads.

'Roy and Geraldine aren't,' Anna said, twisting in her seat to glance around. Roy and Geraldine always sat in the same seats, on the left, but both were empty tonight.

'Ahh,' Sophie said. 'I've had a bit of bad news about Geraldine, actually. I'm sure Roy won't mind me telling you that she's in hospital with a fractured pelvis.'

A gasp went around the room. 'Oh no!' cried Anna. 'Is she going to be all right?'

Ouch, thought Catherine. As a doctor's wife – a doctor's ex-wife – she knew that a pelvic fracture was a very painful injury and took weeks to recover from.

'How is she?' asked Nita. 'What have the doctors said?'

'And how's Roy doing?' George put in. 'My dad fell apart when my mum was in hospital.'

'Geraldine's going to be in hospital for a while, I think,' Sophie said, 'so Roy is . . .' She paused diplomatically. 'Well, he's worried and upset, obviously. I thought I'd tell you guys in case there's anything we can do to help.'

'I'm happy to pop round with some dinners for him,' Anna said at once. 'I mean, with my column I'm cooking far more than I can possibly eat single-handedly.'

'I can help too,' Catherine blurted out. 'I can do some shopping for him, or drive him to the hospital if he needs it.' Still to find a job, she might as well make herself useful, she thought.

'I'm based near the hospital,' Nita added. 'If Geraldine's up for visitors, I could nip in and see her.'

'Oh, that's lovely of you all,' Sophie said. 'If anyone wants to pass on their phone numbers, I'll give them to Roy. I'm sure he'll appreciate every bit of help we can offer.' She took a pile of photocopies and began handing them out. 'Well, the class will certainly be quieter without those two, but let's get on with today's lesson anyway. I think you're going to like this one. We're going to learn how to order food and drinks, the vocabulary for different shops and also telling the time. Let's get started.'

'I'm starting to give up on Freddie *ever* coming out for a drink with us,' grumbled Nita, as they commandeered their usual tables in The Bitter End later that evening. 'I just don't understand it. I'm, like, totally getting these good vibes off him, but then he never wants to come out and have a drink with us.'

'Ahh,' said Catherine. 'I think I know why.'

Anna shot her a look that said, *You too?* 'Yeah,' she said. 'Nita, I've been meaning to tell you.'

'Bollocks,' Nita sighed. 'Go on. He's taken, isn't he? Typical!'

'Freddie?' Sophie asked, tuning in all of a sudden. 'Yes, he's seeing someone, didn't you know?'

'I saw him out the other night,' Anna said. 'I was a bit surprised, actually.'

'Me too,' said Catherine, remembering the chic woman she'd seen Freddie with in the street the other week. 'She's so much older than him for starters.'

'Is she?' Sophie asked, frowning. 'I didn't think so.'

'She?' Anna was frowning too. 'I saw him with a bloke. I thought he was gay?'

Phoebe laughed, nudging her sister. 'Out of luck, Neet,' she said.

'A bloke?' Catherine repeated. 'He was with this older woman when I saw him on Fargate. She was a right glamourpuss, too.'

'God, he doesn't half get around,' Sophie chipped in. '*I* saw him snogging the face off this foxy young thing—'

'Man or woman?' Nita interjected glumly.

'Woman,' Sophie told her. 'About your age,' she added.

'Flipping heck, how many has he got on the go?' Phoebe exclaimed. 'Hey! Maybe he's one of those male escorts!'

'You might still be in with a chance,' George teased Nita, winking at her.

'Yeah, if you're willing to cough up his fees,' Phoebe sniggered.

Nita looked fed up. 'I'm never usually wrong about these things,' she said. 'I so thought I was in there. And now I find out he's the Sheffield Casanova!' She drained her shot glass and got to her feet. 'Sod it, I'm going to get drunk. Who wants another?'

Catherine was sitting next to George, who was wearing a T-shirt which said ACE OF SPADES, with a picture of a garden spade. She was getting to like down-to-earth, friendly George, now that she'd got over the embarrassment of that first lesson. He was mid-thirties, she guessed, with shaggy, sandy-coloured hair and steady brown eyes that held your gaze.

'Are you able to do much gardening work, when it's been so cold?' she asked, making conversation.

'Not a huge amount,' he said. 'I'm a carpenter too, so I've been making a lot of bespoke kitchen units lately.' He grinned. 'I can do you a lovely table or bookcase though, if that's more your thing.'

'Nice,' she said approvingly, 'being able to work with your hands for a living.'

'Absolutely. I love it,' he said. 'Although nothing beats working outside, if you ask me. Planting stuff. Growing stuff. Eating stuff you've grown . . . That's what it's all about. Actually, I've been meaning to say . . .' He leaned forward and addressed the table. 'If any of you lot ever fancy it, I'm part of a community allotment, out past Hillsborough. We grow fruit and veg for a veg-box scheme, and we're always looking for volunteers on Sundays or Thursday mornings.'

Phoebe looked unimpressed. 'What, digging and stuff? Look at these nails, George. It's not going to happen, love, sorry.' She waggled her beautifully manicured hands, the nails gleaming with dark purple polish.

'I could lend you some gardening gloves . . .' George offered.

She shook her head. 'I don't like nature. Sozballs.'

'I'll come along,' Catherine offered. 'I help at a care home on Sundays but—'

'It *was* you!' Anna said suddenly. 'At Clemency House? I saw you leaving last week, just as I was coming to see my nan. Nora Morley, she's called. Says you make a cracking cup of tea.'

'I love Nora!' Catherine cried. 'She's so . . .' She stopped herself just before she said 'naughty'. Nobody wanted to hear that about their grandmother, did they? 'She's so much fun.

I do the garden there through the summer,' she added to George.

'Wow, you're busy,' Sophie commented. 'And there you were the other week in class, telling us you didn't work! When you're helping at a care home and working in the charity shop, *and* you've got kids.'

'She walks rescue dogs too, she told me when I was doing her hair. Didn't you, Cath?' Phoebe put in.

They were all looking at her with . . . Well, she could only describe it as admiration. 'Yes,' she said, feeling her cheeks turn pink. She wasn't used to being admired. It felt absolutely bloody wonderful.

'God, that's awesome,' George said. 'Good for you.'

'Yeah,' Anna agreed. 'Now I feel *really* lazy in comparison.'

'Well, I don't have an actual *job,*' she pointed out, 'so I have to do something all day.'

'Yeah, but even so. I feel bad for asking you now, when you're so busy,' George said. His eyes sparkled. 'Hey, if you're into gardening, you could always join us on a guerrilla run sometime. Fancy a spot of pavement-pimping?'

'Pavement *what*?' Nita asked.

'Pavement-pimping. A group of us do it now and then. Planting stuff around town to make the place look better. There's not that much you can do at this time of the year, but we've got a load of fruit bushes we want to plant in the city centre if anyone wants to give us a hand.'

'Ahh – guerrilla as in balaclava, SAS-styley,' Anna realized. 'Not gorilla as in King Kong.'

'That's the one,' George said.

'Is it legal?' Catherine could have kicked herself. She sounded so prim and proper. 'I mean, have any of you got into trouble doing it before?'

George's eyes crinkled at the edges. 'It's not *strictly* legal,' he replied. 'It's not our land so by rights we shouldn't be digging it up or planting stuff. But most council officials I've come across have turned a blind eye. It's not like we're doing any harm. We sneaked a whole bed of sunflowers into the Peace Gardens last year when the council had their budget cut and couldn't afford new plants. I don't know if you saw them? It looked amazing.'

'I did! I remember those,' Catherine said. 'It was like a corner of Provence, right here in Sheffield.'

He looked pleased. 'Yeah, that was us. And we put in a load of tulips and lavender in Fitzwilliam Street, and a whole mini vegetable plot at the university. Some of the students mucked in and kept it weeded through the summer – and then they got to help themselves to all the fruit and veg that grew.'

'That is so cool,' Sophie said.

'That's what guerrilla gardening's all about, really – turning boring, neglected land into something beautiful and useful.'

He paused. 'So if anyone wants to come out with us, let me know. The more the merrier.'

'I . . .' Catherine hesitated. Years of obedience and toeing the line ran deep in her. She had a sudden image of Mike being called out to where she'd been arrested and locked in a cell. What would he *say*?

'I'll come,' said Nita. 'Sounds a laugh.'

'Me too,' said Sophie. 'I reckon we'd rock the balaclava look, ladies.'

'I might come along as well,' Anna said thoughtfully. 'I reckon there's a magazine feature here just waiting to be written.'

George's brown eyes were still patiently on Catherine, waiting for her answer. 'Go on then,' she said, a thrill of trepidation running through her. 'Yeah, why not? Could be fun. Count me in!'

Chapter Twenty-Five

All'ospedale – At the hospital

'Here's the ward.' Sophie pressed the button beside the doors and addressed the small speaker. 'Hello, we're here to see Geraldine Brennan.'

'Come on in.'

The door buzzed and she pushed it open, Catherine and Anna behind her. It was Wednesday evening and the three of them had come to visit Geraldine in hospital, bringing an armful of magazines and some posh chocolates.

'My goodness!' Geraldine exclaimed, her hands flying up like birds when she saw them at the end of her bed. She was propped up against a mountain of pillows, resplendent in blue satin pyjamas and definitely looking more like her old self, Sophie thought, noticing the blusher and lipstick she had on. This was progress.

'What's this, the three good fairies come to visit?' Geraldine asked before they even had a chance to say hello. She wagged a finger. 'Taking it in turns, are you? I've already had

Phoebe pop in with her curling tongs to "do me over" as she put it. Very sweet of you, girls.'

'We were all so sorry to hear the news,' Anna said, putting the chocolates on her bedside table. 'Brought down by your glam heels, no less – that's so unfair. How are you feeling?'

'All the better for seeing you lot,' Geraldine replied. 'What a smashing surprise. Do sit down. They've only given me two chairs but one of you can perch on the bed. I did say to them, I hope you realize, I'm going to get a *lot* of visitors, you really should give me at least four chairs, but they didn't listen. Mind you, I'm not complaining. I'm grateful for what I can get. Anyway, listen to me going on. You can tell I've been bored out my mind lately, can't you?'

'Has Roy been in today?' Sophie asked.

'Roy's been in every day, bless his heart. I keep saying, Roy, don't put yourself out, especially when the roads are icy. We don't want two of us in here, crocked, like a matching pair. He insists though. Can't keep away.' She gave a naughty wink. 'What can I say? I've still got it, even in a hospital bed. He can't resist.'

They all laughed. 'You've definitely still got it,' Anna agreed.

'Anyway, it's very kind of you to come out here to visit an old fogey like me,' she went on. 'Six weeks' rest, the doctors have told me. Six *weeks*? I said, you're joking, aren't you? I can't rest for six minutes, let alone six weeks.'

'You're like my dad,' Sophie said with a grin. 'He was in here before Christmas and the most impatient invalid ever. Couldn't wait to get out of bed and back home.'

'He sounds a very sensible man to me,' Geraldine said. Her gnarled hands shook slightly on the covers and her mouth drooped. 'I could kick myself for winding up here, honestly, I could. Well, if I hadn't broken my ruddy pelvis, I would anyway. I won't be kicking much for a while now.'

'I bet the weeks will fly by,' Catherine said kindly.

'I bet they blooming won't,' Geraldine grumbled. 'I'm going to miss the Valentine's tea dance – me and Roy have been looking forward to it for weeks. And I'm going to miss your class, dear. Not to mention the play!'

'Oh no,' Sophie said. 'I'd forgotten the play. Do you have an understudy?'

Geraldine wrinkled her nose. 'They'll probably ask Brenda Dodds to step in. Got the acting skills of a stuffed fox, that one.' Then her face cleared. 'Unless . . . Well, why don't *you* do it, Sophie, love? I remember you saying you were a bit of an actor yourself, and I could put a word in with the director. You could wipe the floor with Brenda Dodds, believe me. She couldn't act her way out of a paper bag.'

Sophie assumed she was joking and laughed. But Geraldine had taken her hand and was gripping it with a new enthusiasm. Apparently she wasn't joking. 'Me? Well . . . I'm not in the drama group, am I?' she said uncertainly. 'I can't just parachute in and take your part.'

'Why ever not? Leave it with me. I'll talk to Max – that's the director. Ever so nice he is. Quite dishy too, I have to admit, although settled down with a lovely fella – Josh – so there's no chance for us girls, unfortunately. Still, you can't complain about a bit of eye candy, isn't that right?'

Sophie was starting to get a glimpse of why Roy had once confessed that he just agreed with everything his wife said. Geraldine was like an unstoppable force that swept you along, leaving you powerless to strike out in another direction. 'I . . . Well . . .' she stuttered. 'I mean, I haven't done any acting for years. Certainly nothing professional.'

Geraldine snorted. 'Professional? Give over. None of 'em are *that*, love, don't you worry. So I'll pass Max your number, shall I? He'll be so pleased. He popped in yesterday and, honestly, he looked stricken. Geraldine, he said, what *am* I going to do without you?'

'The show must go on,' Anna said demurely. 'I think you should give it a try, Sophie.'

'There you go! *She's* on my side.' Geraldine couldn't hide her triumph. 'And you are too, Catherine, aren't you? There, Sophie. You see? We all agree. You have to do it now!'

'Geraldine is absolutely gorgeous and I love her to bits, but it's kind of like trying to argue with a bulldozer,' Sophie said afterwards, when the three of them had escaped to a nearby pub. 'I almost feel sorry for that poor guy who's trying to direct the play. I bet she's always butting in with suggestions of how she thinks it should be done.'

'It was probably him icing up her drive that caused the accident in the first place,' Catherine joked. 'Poor Geraldine. Italian class is going to be a lot quieter without her, that's for sure.'

'Are you going to call this Max bloke, then?' Anna asked, sipping her beer. 'I couldn't tell from your face whether or not you actually wanted to, or if you were secretly thinking, *Noooooo!*' She made her fingers into a cross as if warding off a vampire, then nudged Sophie. 'I don't know about the rest of your acting skills, but your poker face is a bloody triumph.'

Sophie smiled. 'I did always love drama, as I must have told Geraldine one night down the pub,' she said. 'But I haven't been on stage for . . . what, must be eight years, when I was doing my A-levels.' She had a sudden vision of herself in a long velvet dress and bare feet. 'Lady Macbeth. *Take my milk for gall, you murd'ring ministers,* and all that.' God, she'd loved it. She'd known that play backwards by the time they came to perform it. Only a handful of performances for the school and parents, but still, she had thrown herself into the part, living and dreaming her character's deranged ambition and scheming.

'Looks like a happy memory,' Catherine said gently.

'Yeah. It was what I really wanted to do with my life, before I dropped out and went travelling.' She had tingles just remembering the electrifying moment at the end of the play before the audience broke into applause. And how, when she'd come on to take her bow, she was sure the clapping rose in volume. *This is for me,* she'd thought, swelling with joyful glory. *They're clapping for ME.*

'I think Geraldine might have made a good call here,' Anna said teasingly. 'She's weakening, Cath. Look how misty-eyed she's gone.'

Sophie laughed. 'Well, I'll give him a ring,' she said. 'He'll probably tell me to bog off and curse Geraldine for interfering, but you never know . . .' Mustn't get too carried away, she reminded herself. Two lines, Geraldine had said. All the same, the camaraderie of being part of a drama group and the adrenalin charge of performing on a stage was pulling her in like a tide. 'Anyway . . .' she said, trying to think of some other topic of conversation. Then she remembered. 'Oh God! Anna! I've got news for you. I meant to tell you earlier.' She rifled through the contents of her slouchy red bag, sending pens and lip salve flying. 'Where did I put it?'

Anna sat up immediately. 'Is this your friend in Italy? What did he say?'

Sophie pulled out a crumpled piece of paper, the printed copy of the email she'd received the night before. 'He says he reckons the picture was taken in Lungomare Augusto,' she read aloud, then handed the print-out to Anna. 'That's the real touristy bit, apparently, lots of hotels and bars. So if you're going off on a papa-search, that's the place to start looking.' She paused. '*Are* you still going, do you think?'

'Lungomare Augusto,' Anna said to herself, and grinned. 'Oh my goodness. This is so exciting. Thank you! And yes, I'd go tomorrow if I could.'

'Ahh,' Sophie said, remembering their conversation in Marmadukes. 'No improvements with the boyfriend?'

'Technically an ex-boyfriend now,' Anna replied.

'I saw your Enrico's review at the weekend,' Catherine said sympathetically. 'But I like the sound of this Handsome Colleague. What's happening there, then?'

Anna groaned. 'Me and my big mouth, that's what's happening,' she said. 'I wrote that as a dig at Pete, my ex, without thinking about how Joe – that's Handsome Colleague – would feel when he read it. Or how his girlfriend would feel, come to that. Honestly, he's just a mate, I never meant for it to sound anything more.'

'Oops,' said Sophie.

'Yeah, massive oops,' Anna sighed. 'And it's all my bloody editor's fault. She and the designer thought it would be *hilaire* to put that photo of Joe in and big-up this whole romance angle – which doesn't even *exist* – and now he's furious with me and I feel like I've lost a friend. Pete, obviously, couldn't give a toss. Probably too busy shagging his new bird to look at anything as boring as a newspaper.'

'Oh no,' said Catherine.

'Oh yes,' Anna echoed. 'Honestly, it's been a complete nightmare, the last few days. Joe's girlfriend has got a massive cob on apparently, accusing him of doing the dirty on her – which he didn't. And *he's* got a cob on with *me*, because he obviously thinks I'm some kind of stalkery maniac who is desperate to drag him into bed with me. When . . .' She hesitated ever so slightly. 'When I'm so not!'

'That *is* a nightmare,' Catherine agreed.

'Can't you explain to him?' Sophie asked. 'Like you've just done to us?'

'I've tried. He won't listen. He's been really cold and off-ish with me, says I've made him the laughing stock of the office. And the worst thing is, this total bitch we work with who usually does the restaurant reviews thinks it's the funniest thing ever, and will not shut up about it. So yeah, the thought of leaving the country is pretty appealing right now, I have to say.' Anna shuddered.

'Men,' Catherine said with surprising vehemence. 'Why do they have to make life so bloody complicated?'

'Hear, hear,' said Sophie, who still hadn't done anything about the Dan Collins conundrum. Then she registered the ferocity of Catherine's tone. 'Hold on – I thought you were a happily married woman?'

Catherine snorted. 'Yeah, I thought I was too. Right up until he went off with some blonde dolly bird who . . .' She clammed up. 'Never mind. But that's why I bolted from your lesson that time, remember, when you were teaching us *Sei sposata*? I didn't know how to reply.'

'Oh Catherine, I'm sorry,' Sophie said.

'It's not your fault.' Catherine swirled her wine around in her glass. 'I thought about asking you to translate, "Yes, but my husband's just left me", then decided it was probably a tad dramatic for an evening class. Which is why I just said, "Yes" and left it at that.'

'Is it definitely over?' Anna asked. 'It's not just a mid-life crisis or . . .'

'It's over,' Catherine replied. 'He said he'd never really loved me at all. It's kind of hard to come back from a statement like that. Besides . . .' Her mouth twisted in a grimace. 'After what I've found out about him, I wouldn't want him back anyway.'

'Why, what's he done?' Sophie asked, then felt nosey. 'Sorry. None of my business.'

Anna leaned forward. 'Does this have something to do with what you were asking me about the other week? The dodgy payments thing?'

Catherine nodded, twisting her hands in her lap, but said nothing else. Sophie glanced from her to Anna, not following what was going on. Dodgy payments?

Now it was Anna's turn to apologize. 'Sorry,' she said in the next breath, seeing Catherine's awkwardness. 'I swear I wasn't fishing. You don't have to say anything.'

'It's all right. I still haven't decided what to do about it.' Then, after a deep breath, Catherine launched into the torrid story of her ex-husband who seemed to have been taking backhanders from a drugs rep. 'What's really awful is that I Googled Demelzerol, the drug he's been prescribing, and discovered lots of internet forums where people were discussing how ill it made them feel,' she said at the end. 'I'm worried that he's been talked into prescribing this drug when it doesn't even seem to work properly.'

The name set a bell jangling in Sophie's head. 'Wait – did you say Demelzerol?' It was familiar for some reason, and then she remembered where she'd seen it: on a packet of pills in the bathroom cabinet at home. The name always made her think of a girl called Demelza, who'd been at her posh private school. 'Is it a betablocker? I think my dad was prescribed that after he had a heart attack.' Her own heart was booming suddenly and she began to feel uneasy about the way this conversation was going. 'Your ex isn't one of the doctors at the Risbury Road Medical Centre, is he?'

All the colour leached from Catherine's face. 'Yes,' she said hoarsely, her eyes huge and anxious. 'Yes he is.' They stared at each other for an awful moment loaded with accusation and apology. 'Oh God, Sophie. Is your dad all right?'

Sophie swallowed. 'Well, he is now,' she said, 'but the doctors at the hospital took him off Demelzerol the other week because he had a second heart attack.'

Catherine looked as if she was going to throw up. 'So it didn't work for him,' she said, her voice barely above a whisper.

'No. In fact, it might even have caused the second heart attack which he had at Christmas. He was really ill for days, he's only just been allowed back to work.' Tears brimmed in Sophie's eyes. If her dad's health had been put in jeopardy because of one greedy doctor thinking only of his own pocket, then she'd . . . she'd . . .

'Jesus,' gasped Anna. 'That's awful.'

Catherine's eyes were also glistening. 'It's horrible,' she agreed. 'Sophie, I'm so sorry. I hate Mike for doing this. I've got to stop him. I promise I will.'

'You must,' Sophie said, still light-headed with shock. 'Dad might have died. We thought he was going to . . .' She choked on the words. 'We thought we'd lost him.'

Catherine took hold of her hand and squeezed it. 'I'm so truly sorry that you've been through this,' she said. 'Honestly I am. And I'll be straight with you: I've been scared to confront Mike about what I've found out because . . . Well, he's always been a bit of a bully. I knew he'd be angry with me for poking around and . . .' She waved her hands. 'Whatever.

But now I know about your dad, there's no way I'm going to keep quiet any longer. No way.'

Even through the strong feelings churning inside her, Sophie could see that Catherine looked terrified at the prospect of confronting her ex. 'Do you want me to come with you when you speak to him?' she asked. 'For a bit of moral support?'

Catherine seemed tempted by the offer then shook her head. 'I need to do it alone,' she said. 'But thank you. I'll let you know what happens.'

As Sophie waited for the bus back to her parents' house, her heart was still pounding. She felt very much like tracking down this Doctor Evans and giving him a piece of her mind – not to mention a piece of her fist. Catherine might be scared of him, but she wasn't. She was livid. How could somebody *do* that? How could they live with themselves afterwards? Doctors were meant to be good guys, the saviours of others, not out for what they could get at the expense of their own patients.

The bus arrived and she paid her fare and found an empty seat on the top deck. It took her a moment to realize that her phone was ringing in the depths of her bag. An unfamiliar number showed on the screen. 'Hello?'

'Hi, is that . . . Sophie Frost?'

A male voice, not one she recognized. 'Yes?'

'Hi, I'm sorry to trouble you in the evening. My name is Max Winter, I'm calling on behalf of the Sheffield Players Drama Group.'

'Oh.' That took the wind out of her sails. Geraldine didn't waste any time, did she? 'Hello. Listen, I'm sorry if Geraldine has been badgering you about . . .' Then she stopped herself. Let the man say his bit.

'Not at all,' he said easily. 'She said you were looking to join a drama group and that you might be interested in our one.'

'She did? I mean – excellent. Yes.' Sophie couldn't remember actually saying such a thing, but now didn't seem the time to start quibbling.

'We're rehearsing Monday, Thursday and Sunday evenings at the moment, so maybe the best thing is for you to come along to our rehearsal tomorrow and we can have a chat. How does that sound?'

'That sounds . . .' Sophie hesitated, feeling that all of this had been very much thrust upon her, without her having much of a say. But it was only a tiny speaking part in a play – it wasn't as if she was auditioning for a Hollywood production. *Go for it!*, she heard Anna and Catherine say in her head. 'That sounds great,' she said eventually. 'Thank you.'

As she finished the call, she sat on the jolting bus, wondering what on earth she was letting herself in for. For all she knew, the Sheffield Players Drama Group was a bunch of bossy old biddies like Geraldine and the play would be absolutely awful. But then again, it might just turn out to be the best fun ever.

Screw your courage to the sticking-place, she thought to herself, remembering her old lines as Lady Macbeth. *And we'll not fail.*

Well, she wasn't sure about that, but it was worth a try, wasn't it?

Chapter Twenty-Six

Coraggio – Courage

The last time Catherine had felt so apprehensive was when Matthew and Emily were collecting their A-level results. But that was nothing on the dizzying, almost paralysing cold-sweat fear that gripped her as she walked into the Plough two days later to meet Mike. Here we go, round one, seconds out. Not literally, of course, although Penny *had* advised her to 'twat him one, for God's sake'. Still, she would say her piece if it was the last thing she did. She had to.

On the phone beforehand, she'd been deliberately vague, telling him that she wanted to meet up to discuss 'the future'. 'Fine, I'll drop by after work,' he'd said in that curt, too-busy-to-speak-to-you manner of his. No doubt he thought she was going to start weeping and begging to stay in the house again. Think again, Mike.

'Let's meet in the pub,' she'd suggested, and he'd agreed, thank goodness. She figured he wouldn't be able to go completely ape at her in a public place, although she wasn't taking anything for granted.

He was already there when she arrived, halfway through a pint. 'So what's all this about?' he asked as she slid into the chair opposite him, clutching a glass of wine.

Hello to you too, Mike. How are things, Mike? Whatever. They didn't have to bother with pleasantries, they could cut straight to the main event. She took a deep breath and dumped the pile of paperwork – bank statements and conference brochures – on the table. 'It's about this,' she said, adding Rebecca's business card on top with a final flourish.

He looked at the pile in front of him and then up at her, alarm in his eyes. Then, after a split-second of naked panic, a mask slipped back across his face. 'What do you mean?' he asked. 'And why the hell have you been going through my private papers when you have no right?'

'I mean, I know what you've been doing. All this money, the sweeteners from Schenkman,' she said, trying to keep her cool. She had never been good at confrontation and her instinct was to bolt, to scurry away, apologizing for poking her nose in. Then she thought of the anguish on Sophie's face and remembered how important this was. 'And I think it's *disgusting.*'

'I don't know what you're talking about,' he said, making a grab for the bank statements. 'I'll have those back, thank you very much.'

'I think you do know,' she said. It was like playing chess,

she thought, her heart thumping. Advance and block, advance and block. Mike had never been one to lose an argument willingly. 'I think you know exactly what I'm talking about.'

'Catherine . . . You've come out with some stupid things in the past, but this – *this* really takes the biscuit.' He was rattled, she could tell. She could almost see his brain whirring behind his eyes, trying to compute a feasible excuse. Forget it, sunshine, she wanted to say. There's no way you're sliming out of this one.

'Really? And how's that, then?'

'Because you've got it completely . . . You've jumped to the most insane conclusions,' he snapped. Any pretence of civility had vanished now. 'Thought you'd go snooping around, did you? The woman scorned and all that bollocks.' He glared at her. 'This is about the house, isn't it? You getting your knickers in a twist because I want to sell it.'

'It's not about the house,' she replied, trying to keep her tone even. She wished now she'd taken Sophie up on her offer to come along too and back her up. 'It's about you doing the wrong thing. Thinking of yourself before your patients. Nearly killing Jim Frost on Christmas Day.'

He jerked his head so fast he was in danger of giving himself whiplash. 'What do you know about Jim Frost?' he said, gripping her wrist.

'Enough to know that it's no thanks to you he's still alive,' Catherine said. 'Let go of me.'

'Is this some kind of blackmail?' he hissed, his fingers tightening. 'Is that what it is? Trying to play dirty, are you? Trying to get some of my money?'

'I don't want your stinking money,' she said, struggling to get her wrist free. 'Let go of me, I said.'

He shook his head, eyes narrowed. 'My mum always reckoned you were a gold-digger,' he said. 'To think I used to stick up for you!'

'I'm not a gold-digger,' she said, but her voice was wavering. Damn Mike. Damn his rotten mother. He could always push her buttons in the worst kind of way.

'Look at you, sitting there with your self-righteousness and your "evidence",' he said scornfully, flicking his other hand at the pile of papers. 'You thought you were so clever, coming here tonight, didn't you? So fucking clever! Well, I'll tell you something for nothing, Catherine. You're nothing but a—'

A white-hot rage suddenly burned through her as he ranted on. She had come here prepared to be reasonable but within five minutes he'd resorted to playground bully tactics. Let's put Catherine down again. Let's make Catherine feel stupid again. And she *had* felt stupid and worthless, the whole time she'd been married to him. But she wasn't with him any more – and she wasn't stupid either. The only stupid thing she'd done was not sticking up for herself sooner.

'One of my friends is a journalist,' she said, interrupting him. 'She already knows about this whole story. I've photocopied everything for her.'

That threw him off his stride. For about two seconds, anyway. 'Friends? You don't have any friends,' he sneered. 'Only Penny. And nobody in their right mind would ever take *her* seriously.'

'I do have friends,' she said quietly. 'And all I have to do is call the one who's a journalist and ask her to run this story. Now *let go* of me or I'm going to start shouting.'

He dropped her wrist as if it was burning him and her hand banged down on the table. The skin was chafed and red where he'd held it. 'I'm not going to let you hurt me again,' she said quietly. 'Not ever.'

'What? For crying out loud, Catherine. There's no need to be so dramatic about all of this.'

She raised her eyes to his and met his gaze full on. How she hated him. 'Oh, I think there is,' she replied. 'Now. Why don't you just admit you've done something wrong? Then we can talk about how you're going to put it all right.'

Mike hadn't exactly capitulated and admitted his guilt in the way she would have liked, but Catherine still felt the most enormous thrill of pride whenever she played the scene back to herself afterwards. She had done it. For once, she had actually stood up to Mike even though, surprise surprise, he'd tried his usual trick of knocking her straight back down. This time she hadn't let him, though. This time she'd won the battle.

'You've got to stop taking their money and speaking at these conferences,' she'd told him baldly once he'd realized that she was deadly serious about blowing the whistle on him. 'What's more, you've got to stop prescribing those bloody drugs! What if Jim Frost had *died*? You'd have blood on your hands, Mike. Is that what you want?'

'I did what I thought was best,' he said in a low voice, but she wasn't having any of that.

'You didn't, Mike. What's got into you? A few years ago you wouldn't have dreamed of prescribing drugs that you weren't completely certain about. You were always a good man. What changed that?'

He put his head in his hands, seemingly penitent at last. 'I don't know what to do, Cath,' he said in a muffled voice. 'I'll call off the estate agents, tell them I've changed my mind. Will that be enough?'

She stared at him, appalled that he still appeared to think this was all about her. *Enough?* she felt like saying. Enough for whom? Not for Jim Frost or any of the other poor buggers he'd fobbed off. 'Oh, wise up!' she snapped instead. 'Who's talking about estate agents? This is about *you* doing the right thing. I think you need to have a word with your own conscience before you make any decisions.'

He raised his head. 'And what about the journalist? What are you going to tell her?'

This was so weird. Mike – *vulnerable*? It had never happened before. 'I haven't decided yet,' she replied. 'Let's meet again in a few days and you can tell me your plans. In the meantime –' she got to her feet and picked up the pile of brochures – 'I'll leave you to it.'

And out she'd walked, head in the air, knowing he was watching her go. Knowing, too, that he wasn't feeling quite so cocky any more.

Since then, the buzz of self-respect and go-girl attitude had stayed with her, fizzling around her like some kind of power-shield. For the first time ever, she'd been brave, she hadn't let him trample all over her. It felt amazing.

Fired up with her new confidence, when she went to the garden centre the next day and saw a sign on the door advertising vacancies in the nursery, she didn't hesitate to pick up an application form. Why not? Nothing had come from the snooty suits in the temp agencies yet, and grubbing around with seed trays and plants was far more her style than high heels and make-up anyway. Growing things made her happy.

While she browsed around for the bits and bobs she needed, she remembered what George had said about his guerrilla gardening exploits. Before she knew it, she'd chucked some extra sunflower seeds into her basket and was wondering where she could secretly plant them. It was astonishing what beautiful flowers could grow from one tiny seed, she thought, as she queued up to pay. She hoped the tiny new seed of confidence inside her would flourish and bloom, too.

'When did you get into this – gardening, I mean?' It was Sunday, and Catherine had rearranged her other voluntary work to come along to the community allotment George had told her about. It was a vast space with an orchard, two fields of vegetables and an old Victorian glasshouse. There were loads of people there too, all working together while their children raced around playing tag. Catherine was helping George cover one of the vegetable patches with old tarpaulin to kill off the weeds, weighing down the corners with broken bricks. 'Have you always had green fingers?'

'Yeah, since I was a lad,' he replied. 'My dad had an allotment and I used to help him; it was our thing.'

'That's nice,' Catherine replied, with a sudden memory of Mike spending hours with Matthew, making and painting Airfix models together. *That was our thing,* she imagined Matthew saying fondly to some woman in the future. 'Does he live round here, your dad?'

'Not far,' George replied, heaving a log onto the edge of the tarpaulin with a thud. 'Bakewell way.'

'Lovely,' she said. 'And you're close, are you? Do you get to see him much?'

'Most weeks,' he said. 'He's on his own now – my mum

died a few years ago. I try to pop round when I can, help him out with little jobs, you know.'

'I remember you saying the other night, he struggled when she was ill,' Catherine said. 'That must have been hard. I'm sorry.'

He straightened up and gave her a small, brief smile but there was a flash of pain in his eyes. 'Yeah,' he said. 'Well, this is done. How about we start cleaning out the glasshouse next? Could do with a scrub down before we get the planting underway in a few weeks.'

'Sure,' she said, hoping she hadn't just put her foot in it somehow. Everyone had their fragilities.

The glasshouses certainly hadn't seen a lot of TLC recently. Grimy and cobwebby, the panes thick with muck, there was a graveyard of dead plants at one end, a couple of small citrus trees overwintering in pots and a lot of empty space besides. George filled a bucket with warm soapy water, and he and Catherine began cleaning the grubby panes, flicking away curled-up woodlice and dead spiders as they went.

'So when am I going to meet the rest of your family, Catherine?' George asked conversationally after a while. 'Do you think they'll come down here to help out one day?'

'The rest of my . . . Oh,' she said. *Er, never?* 'Well, my kids have both gone away to uni now, and my husband . . . He's left as well. Basically.'

'Ahh.' He looked mortified. 'Sorry. I didn't realize.'

'Yeah. I kind of downplayed the whole abandoned wife thing in Italian class,' she said, trying to sound breezy and upbeat about it. 'Doesn't tend to be a good conversation starter.'

'I bet.' They scrubbed in silence for a few moments and she felt awkward. The admission was a conversation ender too, clearly.

'It's fine though,' she said bracingly before the silence could open up too wide. 'I mean . . . you know. I'm getting on with it.'

'Good,' he said. 'What doesn't kill you makes you stronger, and all that.'

'Yeah,' she said. Time for a change of subject. 'How about you, are you married? Any kids?'

'Not any more,' he replied. 'No kids. My marriage broke up a couple of years ago, so I kind of know what you're going through.'

She concentrated on a particularly grubby bit of glass so that she didn't have to look at him. 'What happened?'

'We were living in London, both lawyers, can you believe,' he said, and she tried not to look too surprised. Dressed as he was now in faded black jeans, a thick blue fisherman's jumper and muddy wellies, with a day's stubble around his chin, she couldn't picture him in a sharp suit, addressing a courtroom. 'Then Mum became ill and I took some time off so that I could come up here and help Dad. There's only me, see. No brothers or sisters.'

'Ahh,' Catherine said.

'After Mum died, I felt torn in half. Dad was so helpless, didn't have a clue how to look after himself. Mum had always done everything for him,' he said. 'Meanwhile, there's Jess back in London, fed up with me not being there and asking when I'm coming home.'

Catherine felt for him. 'Impossible choice.'

'Yeah,' he agreed. 'We talked for a while about us both moving up here, relocating. A lawyer can work in any city, after all. But she . . .' He shrugged. 'Oh, I don't know. She's Home Counties, always was a bit patronizing about Yorkshire, reckons it's all flat caps and whippets. I guess it didn't fit in with the image she had of herself, of how she wanted us to be.'

'So you moved back up and she didn't?'

'Not immediately. We tried to carry on as we were but the writing was already on the wall. We started arguing all the time about stupid, trivial things that were just an excuse to shout at each other. Then she had an affair with one of my friends and . . .' He spread his hands wide, soapy water dripping from his sponge. 'That was that.'

'And how are you now?' Catherine asked tentatively. 'You seem pretty together to me, but I know it's tough.'

'Yeah. Well, it took a while. Moving away from my job, my

friends and my home and trying to get over a failed marriage all at once felt like falling down the rabbit-hole, you know? I was suddenly in this completely new world: back up north, single, a flatlining career . . . it was scary.'

'I can imagine.'

'But then again, it gave me the chance to re-evaluate everything, like a stock-take of my life. I realized that actually, I was never that happy being a lawyer. Some of the clients I had to represent – I knew damn well they were guilty as hell, but I still had to defend them, that was my job. Took me two seconds to decide I didn't want to do that any more once I'd moved up here. Got into carpentry instead. Now that's proper work. Making something with your hands, creating something lovely or useful with wood . . . That's bang on. That'll do me.'

'I know what you mean,' Catherine said. She sat back on her heels, not caring how filthy the ground was. 'Mike leaving made me have a long think about what I want to do, too. For so many years I was just somebody's wife, somebody's mum. I think I forgot how to be me, if that doesn't sound too mad.'

'It doesn't sound the slightest bit mad to me.' George smiled at her. He seemed to have forgotten about glass-cleaning now as well. 'And have you remembered how to be you yet?'

'I'm getting there,' she said. She remembered Mike's face,

his startled expression when she'd spoken up for herself so doggedly the other night in the pub – when she'd actually threatened him. 'Yeah,' she said, nodding. 'I'm definitely getting there.'

Chapter Twenty-Seven

Mi dispiace – I'm sorry

Anna was starting to think she was never going to live down the 'Handsome Colleague' thing. It was going to be carved on her effing gravestone at this rate. All week, work had been complete and utter pants, the Embarrass-Anna show. Colin, the old stirrer, kept wolfwhistling whenever Joe walked through the office, and Marla insisted on saying repeatedly what a lovely couple they made. 'I always had my suspicions,' she fluted.

'It was just a stupid nickname,' Anna growled approximately ninety-seven times a day. 'I was only trying to get back at my boyfriend. How was I to know that Imogen and the designers would sabotage it?'

Joe had been terse with her ever since publication. 'Next time, if there's trouble in paradise, don't drag me into it,' was all he said, flinty-eyed. She felt like the worst friend ever.

'I don't see what the problem is, the readers *loved* it,' Imogen said airily. She was applying lipstick in her office when Anna went in for a whinge. 'We've already had letters in asking when you and "Handsome Colleague" – ' she made quotation marks with her fingers – 'will be out on the town again. It's going to be like that Gold Blend ad all over again. Remember? You're probably too young. The sexual tension went on for *years*.'

Anna stared at her, not sure if her boss was serious, joking or just plain unhinged. 'What do you mean?' she asked. 'The restaurant review was only a one-off, wasn't it, while Marla was away. She's back now, so . . .' She tailed off, wishing Imogen would stop pouting at herself in the mirror and pay attention.

'Ahh, but the readers love a story,' Imogen replied, turning and dazzling Anna with her smile. 'It's what I've always said. I think I'm going to switch Marla onto something else for a few weeks – Ruth's maternity cover, that'll do it. I'll tell her she needs to help the new person settle in, show them the ropes.'

Anna didn't like the way this was going at all. 'But Ruth is one of the news reporters,' she said weakly.

'Yes,' Imogen said. 'And Marla's always telling me how flexible she is. I'm sure she'd love the chance to go out on the road and do some real journalism for a change.'

Anna stifled a snort. Yeah, and I'm Jarvis Cocker, she thought. Marla would have an absolute nervo at the thought of leaving her comfortable desk for anything other than a slap-up meal and another cushy review. Then she grasped the full implications of what Imogen was saying. 'Wait, so you mean . . .'

'Yes,' said Imogen. 'I do. You can write this week's restaurant review too; your second attempt was very good, you know. And make sure you invite Joe along again. I can't wait to see what happens next – and nor can our readers. They're going to love this!'

'She said *what*? Is this some kind of joke?'

'I wish it was,' Anna said miserably. She and Joe were in the little kitchen area and she'd just broken the news to him over the steaming kettle. 'I'm really sorry, Joe. I made a massive mistake. And you don't have to do it. In fact, it would make both our lives easier if you didn't. I'll totally understand if you say no.'

His expression was hard to read as he reached for the box of teabags and dropped one each into their mugs. 'Julia's going to go ape,' he muttered.

'Yeah. I know. Listen, don't worry, I'll go back to Imogen and say it's not possible.'

'But then again, I did have such a laugh with you in Enrico's last week,' he said unexpectedly. He raised his gaze to hers and she felt hot colour creeping into her cheeks.

'You did? I mean . . . yeah. So did I.'

'And to be honest, with Julia . . . we haven't been getting on very well for ages,' he said.

For some reason, Anna went all goosebumpy. 'Sorry to hear that.' But if she was honest, she didn't feel sorry in the least. She actually felt quite glad. Was that wrong of her? Did that make her a really terrible friend? Yes, she thought firmly. Yes, it did.

There was an awkward silence filled by the whooshing of the kettle and then an abrupt click as it finished boiling. 'If it makes things easier, I don't mind speaking to Julia,' Anna volunteered. 'I could say, you know, there's nothing going on, I just called your boyfriend "handsome" because . . .'

Joe was looking at her in such a strange, steady way that she lost her tack. 'Because,' she floundered, 'I was trying to wind up my ex.'

'Ahh,' he said. 'No other reason?'

She coloured. 'Well . . .'

'Ooh, here they are, the lovebirds in the kitchen!' Imogen sang just then, bustling in and switching on the Nespresso machine that only she was allowed to use. 'Planning your next date, are we? Plotting romantic instalment *numero duo*?'

'Imogen!' Anna practically shouted. God, she was embarrassing. 'It's not a date!'

'Course it's not,' said Joe. 'And we object to you setting us up in that way.'

Do we? Anna thought, crestfallen. 'Yes,' she added quickly. 'Absolutely. We do. Because the two of us . . . It's ridiculous to even *think* anything's going on. Like I would fancy Joe!'

Her words came out shriller and more indignant than she'd intended them to and she saw Joe wince. Argh. Now she'd gone and hurt his feelings again, just when they were getting somewhere.

'Exactly,' Joe went on. 'So if you're serious about us going along with this charade, Imogen, then we'll expect to be justly rewarded, considering the mental torture we're both going to suffer.'

Mental torture? Anna thought, wounded. There was no need for him to be quite so—

Then she noticed the gleam in his eye. 'Right, Anna?' he said with a surreptitious wink, while Imogen fiddled with her machine.

'Er . . . right,' she said, although she still didn't know what he was up to. 'Right.'

'Might I remind you two that I am your boss, and you'll jolly well do what I say,' Imogen told Joe in her most head-mistressy voice. Anna could tell she was more amused than cross, though. 'Go on then, what are you after? And don't say a pay rise, because we both know Dick Briggs is never going to swallow that one.'

'Well, as it happens, there is something I wanted to talk to you about,' Joe said. 'Sean Davies, our local rugby hero, is in the Wales squad, as you know, and hoping to be picked for the next Six Nations match. I've been meaning to ask if I can go along and watch it. If Sean ends up playing, I could get a wicked interview with him afterwards.'

Anna's shoulders sagged in dismay. Oh Joe, she thought crossly. Bloody typical man! Of all the things he could have asked for, and it was a flipping rugby match. She thought he had more chutzpah than that.

'And when *is* the next match?' Imogen asked, lips pursed.

'The twenty-third of February,' Joe replied. 'Wales versus Italy. In Rome.'

Anna's mouth fell open. *Rome?* Had she heard that correctly? Okay, rewind, she took it all back. He was a complete and utter genius, who'd just played Imogen brilliantly.

'And Anna was saying that there was an Italian cookery course she wanted to go along to as well,' he went on, nudging her. 'Also in Rome. Perfect for the travel section.'

Was she? Had she? He was so making this up. She loved it!

'Weren't you, Anna?' he asked, raising an eyebrow.

'Oh. Yes,' she lied. 'That's right.'

'Actually, it's the same weekend,' Joe said, and Anna felt a sudden dropping sensation inside and her legs went wobbly. Whoa. Joe was trying to wangle them both a trip to Italy. Together. No way was Imogen going to go along with this, but all the same . . . *Joe was trying to wangle them both a trip to Italy!* What did this mean?

Imogen laughed. 'The same weekend, eh?' she said. 'Now there's a coincidence.' She took her espresso cup and sipped it thoughtfully. 'Leave it with me,' she said. 'But in the meantime, book the next restaurant, please. And make it somewhere romantic, whatever you do.'

As she walked away, Anna and Joe both gaped at each other then burst out laughing. 'This is so not going to happen,' Anna gurgled.

'But it was so worth a punt,' Joe said, passing her her mug of tea.

'Did you really just make all of that up on the spot?' Anna marvelled. 'You're wasted as a sports reporter – you should write books.' She laughed again. 'Best blag ever. Cookery course in Rome, indeed. That was inspired. I'd better go and find one on the internet, just in case she calls our bluff.'

'I bet you could get a train from Rome out to Rimini, too,' he said. 'Wasn't that where you reckoned your dad was?'

'Oh my God, yes,' Anna breathed. 'I could, couldn't I?' She stared at him in excitement, unable to believe what might happen. And paid for by work, no less!

'Better brush up on your Italian,' he said, putting the milk back in the fridge. 'And book us another restaurant to review. It's worth faking a bit of romance for Italy, right?'

'Yeah,' she said, then found herself wilting a little. Faking a bit of romance? It wasn't that she wanted there to be a *real* romance . . . Well, she didn't think so anyway. Did she? 'God, yeah,' she added quickly, trying to sound more certain. 'Fake it till you make it. I can fake it with the best of them. I was with Pete for two years, after all. Total faker, me.' She seemed unable to stop saying the word 'fake' all of a sudden. 'So . . . Actually I think I'll just shut the fake up,' she said, trying to pull herself together. 'Thanks for the tea. And fingers crossed for Rome!'

Anna could hardly wait for Italian class the following week. 'You'll never guess what,' she said breathlessly as soon as she stepped into the classroom. 'I'm going to Italy – to Rome!'

'No *way*!' squealed Sophie. 'That's brilliant news. How come? And what about Rimini?'

'Yeah, I'm going there too,' Anna said, laughing at her own good fortune. She could still hardly believe that Imogen had agreed to it. 'In a few weeks' time! My friend at work wangled us both a trip.'

'Whoa! Lucky duck,' whistled Phoebe.

'That's smashing,' said Roy, who had come to the lesson alone, looking rather pale and tired but there nonetheless. 'Good for you, pet.'

Catherine gave Anna an arch look that said, *You're so sussed.* 'This wouldn't be anything to do with the Handsome Colleague, would it?' she asked.

Anna grinned. 'It's not like that,' she said.

'Oh, isn't it, Madam? Saturday's review sounded as if you

were getting on *very* well,' Catherine replied, eyes narrowing. 'There was practically steam coming from the page.'

'God, yeah,' Nita agreed. 'I was like, they are so going to kiss at the end of this dinner. Phwoarr!'

'I missed it, what happened?' Phoebe said. 'Was it footsie under the table, Anna? Smooching over the bread basket?'

Anna giggled. 'No, I . . .' she began, then glanced at Sophie, aware that she was swallowing up valuable lesson time with the details of her personal life. 'Sorry,' she said. 'I'm taking over the class here. I'll tell you all about it in the pub after we're done here, how about that?'

'God, cliffhanger,' Nita grumbled, rolling her eyes, but then elbowed Anna as she sat down. 'Good on you, girl. Bagsy me sitting next to Anna in the pub.' She glanced round at Freddie. 'And look, even Freddie's interested in the goss. Are we finally going to get you down the boozer, Fredster, or what?'

Freddie bit his lip. 'I'm meant to be meeting someone actually,' he said apologetically.

'Oh,' said Nita, drooping in her seat.

'Awk-ward,' sang Phoebe under her breath.

'You can always bring them along too,' Sophie suggested. 'Everyone's welcome. But anyway, shall we get on with the lesson? Today we're going to learn a few more verbs, and we'll start practising talking about our daily routines – getting up, having breakfast, going to work . . . that sort of thing.'

She grinned. 'And *then* we're going to get all the gossip out of Anna down the pub. Bring it on.'

The second restaurant-review dinner – not a date, Anna kept reminding herself – had taken place at Milton's, a new brasserie on Norfolk Street. With flickering candles and intimate booths for two, it was definitely a romantic venue, just as Imogen had requested, with modern French food and the most mouthwatering dessert list Anna had ever salivated over.

'Good call,' said Joe, looking around appreciatively while she took off her coat. 'Restaurant looks nice too,' he added.

'Ha ha. But thanks,' Anna said. She'd put on her favourite black boat-necked dress and rollered her hair so that it fell in big waves around her shoulders. At the time she'd been channelling an elegant *Mad Men* look, but on her way into town she'd started worrying that it was more Jessica Rabbit, all cleavage and hips – way too much for dinner with a colleague. 'So do you.'

'What, this old thing?' he joked, flicking his shirt. 'Thanks. So . . .' he said, picking up the menu. 'What are Anna and "Handsome Colleague" going to get up to tonight, then?'

She rolled her eyes. 'Just because I said that once doesn't mean I'm calling you it again,' she warned. 'You could be renamed "Annoying Colleague" by the time this goes to print.'

'Imogen wants romance,' he reminded her. 'And the readers of Sheffield are panting for some action, according to her.'

'So? The readers of Sheffield might have to lump it,' Anna replied, studying her own menu.

'Come on, I'm only having a laugh,' he told her. 'I think "Handsome Colleague" may at least lean in and try for a kiss later on. You know what he's like.'

The list of food began jumbling in front of Anna's eyes. Try for a kiss? Did he mean she should make this up for the sake of the column, or was he actually saying . . . ? The situation was getting very confusing.

'I think "Handsome Colleague" ought to remember that he's still got a girlfriend before there's any of that,' she said lightly, hoping he couldn't hear her heart pounding. 'I fancy the steak frites. How about you?'

It had been a very odd night. An enjoyable night, definitely, but nobody could have denied the peculiar undercurrent running through it all. Sitting in a romantic restaurant for the purpose of writing a fictional romantic review, feeling attracted to the man opposite you but not having a clue how he felt in return . . . It didn't half mess with your head.

'So nothing happened?' Sophie asked, when they were ensconced in their usual seats in The Bitter End after the Italian class.

'Not even a peck on the cheek,' Anna replied, trying not to sound too disappointed. 'Which is fine, obviously. Because he does have a girlfriend, after all, the beautiful yet mardy Julia.'

'Sounds like *she's* on the way out,' Phoebe commented.

'But you put in the review that there was "simmering tension",' Catherine said. 'I was hoping that bit was true.'

'Well, it kind of was,' Anna said, 'but I'm pretending I just made that up to get my boss off my case.' She pulled a face. 'It's all extremely complicated.'

'But you're going to Rome together at least,' George said.

'Yep,' Anna replied. 'He's going to see the Wales match and I've booked myself onto an Italian cookery course. I can't wait!'

'Wonderful,' Sophie said. 'And then on to Rimini? To Lungomare Augusto?'

'You bet. I'm going to hunt down that papa and we'll all live happily ever after,' Anna said. She raised her glass. 'Cheers to that!'

Everyone clinked their glasses together and chorused '*Salute!*'

'So you're really going then,' Catherine said to Anna, as George asked Roy about Geraldine and the others all leaned in to hear the answer. 'Wow, that's so exciting.'

Anna beamed. 'I know. I can't believe Imogen has given us the go-ahead. We've got to write at least two more restaurant reviews for her, though – that's the pay-off. The usual reviewer – Marla – is spitting feathers, I'm telling you.'

'And have you got a strategy when it comes to tracking down your dad? Have you been able to find out any more?'

'Well, I've been digging around online,' Anna replied. 'I've put his photo up on a couple of Rimini-based message-boards in the hope that someone will identify him before I go. I've been in contact with a lady at the tourist office who said she'd help me search through records in the town hall, too.' She sipped her drink. 'It's a bit of a needle in a haystack still, but I've just got to try.'

'It's a shame you can't find out his second name,' Catherine said. 'It would help so much in getting an address or phone number.'

Anna fiddled with a beermat. 'I know, but my mum is so stubborn. She's never wanted to talk about him. And God knows I've tried. My nan hasn't mentioned him again either. As for my aunt . . . She's so loyal to my mum, I know she'll never say anything.'

'It might be worth one last shot with your mum,' Catherine said. 'Seeing as you're going all that way. Don't you think?'

'Hmmm.' Anna bit her lip. Catherine was right, but what would it cost? A massive row? An icy months-long silence?

'Sometimes as a parent you keep things from your children because you want to protect them,' Catherine said. 'I've done it myself. But if one of them came to me and laid it on the line, saying *tell me,* I think I would. Especially if they were about to head off abroad on a quest, like you.'

Anna didn't respond instantly. She was trying to imagine what her mum would do if she laid her cards on the table and informed her she was going to Rimini, so there. Would Tracey help her or stand in her way?

'It's worth a go,' Catherine urged. 'Just be honest with her. It could make all the difference.'

'Hi Mum, it's me.' It was ten o'clock the same evening and Anna, with half a bottle of wine inside her, had decided to take action.

'Hello, love, I was just on my way up to bed. Is everything all right?'

'Everything's fine,' Anna said. She shut her eyes for a moment and willed herself to go through with this. 'Er . . . Mum. Look, I know this might be a shock, but last year Nan told me about Gino. My dad. And the thing is . . . Well, I'm going to Rimini to find him in a few weeks.'

There was a shocked silence. Anna cringed, waiting for the furious blast she knew was coming. 'Your dad?' Tracey said blankly. 'Rimini? Sorry, love, you've lost me. What are you on about?'

'I saw Marie's photos. Nan told me his name. I'm going to Rimini but I need more than a photograph. If you could just tell me his second name or anything else about him, it would be a massive help. Please, Mum. It's really getting to me. I just want to know.'

There was another long silence. '*Please,*' Anna repeated for good measure. 'Tell me, even if it's awful. I really want to meet him. I've been learning Italian and everything for this.'

Tracey's voice sounded shaky. 'Oh God,' she said. 'I don't . . . Oh, Anna.'

'Please, Mum. *Please.*'

'Okay,' she said eventually. 'But I don't want to do this over the phone. Why don't you come up at the weekend? Then I'll tell you everything, I promise.'

Chapter Twenty-Eight

L'attrice – The actress

Sophie wasn't sure what to expect when she went along to meet the drama group in their rehearsal area, a church hall in Broomhill. Would the other members all be gobby pensioners like Geraldine? she wondered doubtfully. Would Geraldine's nemesis Brenda Dodds shoo her off the premises with a Zimmer frame for her impertinence and presumption?

Oh well. Let her. Sophie was only here as a favour, she reminded herself as she walked up to the door. As long as she could honestly say to Geraldine that she'd come along and given it a go, that was what mattered. She probably wouldn't get the part anyway.

Geraldine had coached her on the play itself. 'A modern comedy of errors,' she'd grandly described it, before adding, 'Taking the mickey out of rich folk thinking they're better than what they are.' The plot seemed to revolve around a family winning the lottery and changing for the worse. Geraldine had been due to play the estate agent who showed them around a mansion they wanted to buy. To Sophie, there didn't sound a huge amount to go on in terms of character development. Even Meryl Streep would have struggled to make something of the tiny part.

But Meryl Streep wouldn't have stood dithering around on the doorstep like this, would she? She'd have pushed open the door, put on a big smile and walked in. So that's what Sophie did too.

'Hello, you must be Sophie! Come over and join us.'

Geraldine was right, Sophie thought: Max Winter, the director, was unquestionably gorgeous, with his shock of black hair and keen blue eyes that fastened directly onto you, even across a hall full of people. He also had a generous, wide sort of smile that made her feel instantly at ease.

'Hi,' she said, shaking his hand and smiling self-consciously at the other members of the group as they gazed at her. They were a mixed bunch, she noticed gladly – all ages from teenagers to oldies – and no little old ladies were advancing threateningly with any kind of walking aids raised as cudgels. 'Thanks for inviting me over. I appreciate that Geraldine rather thrust me upon you.'

'Not at all,' he said. 'It's always good to have a new person come along.' He gestured to some seats. 'Why don't you tell me a bit about yourself?'

They sat and chatted for a few minutes and she told him about her travels and the nomadic lifestyle she'd been living until autumn last year. 'But drama was always the thing I loved,' she said. 'And since I'm going to be staying in the UK for a while, I'd like to try my hand at it again.'

'Good, good,' he said. 'Excellent. Can I hear you read something?' He grabbed a dog-eared script from a nearby table and flicked through it. 'Here. Maybe you could be Rose in this scene. I'll be Mark. They're a married couple who are down on their luck. He's just blown the last of their week's money on lottery tickets.'

'Okay,' she said apprehensively. She glanced through the scene to get the measure of it. An argument, good. She sounded some of the lines out in her head, then did her best to put herself in the position of angry, down-trodden wife, imagining bitter years of disappointment and frustration stretching behind her. She gripped the pages tightly so that he wouldn't notice her hands shaking and hoped her voice would do her justice. *I want to do this,* she found herself thinking. *I want to impress him.*

She took a deep breath and threw her shoulders back. 'Ready when you are,' she said.

As an audition piece, it was a gift to an actor. There was everything contained within the lines of the script: confrontation, tension and pace, and Sophie gave it her all. At the end, she was surprised – and delighted – to hear a faint ripple of applause from the other people in the room. She'd forgotten they were even there. 'Oh,' she said, blushing. 'Thank you very much.'

Max clapped too. 'Very nice,' he said. 'Well, I'm more than happy for you to take the part of Wendy since Geraldine is out of action. I hope you'll want to stick around with us afterwards, too. We're planning to do *Saint Joan* next.'

'I love that play,' Sophie said. 'We studied it at A level.'

'. . . Is the right answer,' he replied with a grin. 'Let me introduce you to the others, then I'll give you your own script. It's a tiny part, yours, I'm afraid, but think of it as a warm-up for plays to come.' He put a hand up. 'Guys! Everyone, this is Sophie. Can we take turns standing up and telling Sophie a line or two about ourselves, please? Then we'll start the rehearsal.'

Sophie went home that evening on a massive high. It had been so much fun! Yes, her part was titchy with limited scope for actual acting, but that wasn't the point. It had been brilliant just reading from a script with the others, seeing their characters come to life off the page, and feeling like a cog in a fantastic machine that always became more than the sum of its parts. The first performance was only a few weeks away now, so there was an added giddiness and fretting about costumes and final stage positions. She'd forgotten how much she loved it all.

Back home, she went straight to her laptop.

FACEBOOK STATUS: Sophie Frost

Guess who's been treading the boards again? she typed with a grin. *Drama Queen . . . MOI?*

She scrolled through her timeline to see what her friends had been up to and let out a squeak of excitement when she read that Harry, a friend from the Aussie days, was back in the UK.

Prince H! she typed. *We need to meet up and drink schooners! Let's make a plan.*

A split-second after her message appeared under his, so did another one. From Dan.

PRINCE! he'd typed. *Mine's a VB, mate. Name the time and place.*

Oh Gawd. Awk-ward, as Phoebe would say. He must have been typing his message at the exact same time she was. She bit her lip, wondering whether to comment on this. *Great minds!* or *Jinx!* or *OMG, we were always on the same wavelength, Dan, we are destined to be together!*

Hmm, maybe not.

Before she could think of anything cool though, Harry had already posted a reply. *Hey guys! Good to hear from you. Are you two still together?*

What a question. *If only, Harry.* Her fingers hovered over the keyboard, debating how best to reply. *No* and a sad face? Definitely not. *No, he chucked me?* Ick. Harry didn't want the gory details. Maybe it was best not to reply at all.

She leaned towards the screen as a new message flashed up from Dan. And then all the breath seemed to be sucked out of her as she read, *No, mate. Sadly I blew it, like the prick I am.*

Christ. *Sadly I blew it?* Did that mean he regretted it? Or was he just being polite, to save her feelings?

You always were a prize tool, Harry replied cheerfully. *So – drinks, then? We should definitely get the Sydney crew together. Soph, are you in too?*

Her fingers froze on the keyboard. She felt totally thrown by the way this conversation had turned. Oh shit. Drinks with Harry and the Sydney crew – massive yes. Drinks with Harry and the Sydney crew including Dan – massive don't know.

Then she got a grip. Knowing what a flake Harry was, this whole meeting up thing might never get off the ground. And even if it did, she could always duck out at the last minute. No way was she going to say *No* on Facebook and have Dan think she still carried a torch for him.

Sure thing, she typed breezily. Then she turned off the laptop before she could get drawn into anything more definite.

'Here you go. Eggs, bacon, teabags, some mince. A bag of carrots, Cox's apples, milk and butter. That was everything, wasn't it?'

'Thanks, petal. Let me make you a brew while you're here.'

Roy shuffled towards the kettle while Sophie began putting his groceries away in the fridge.

She had been a frequent visitor to Roy and Geraldine's little two-up-two-down terraced house in Nether Edge recently, as had the other members of the Italian class. Catherine popped in regularly to whip round with the hoover. George had come by to mend a broken stair-rail, while Anna brought pies and cakes that she'd baked, claiming they'd only go to waste if he didn't have them. Phoebe, bless her, had borrowed a manicure set from the salon and gone into the hospital to paint Geraldine's nails a vampish shade of dark red, too. Three other ladies in the ward had already requested her return, apparently.

'. . . which I wasn't sure about,' she heard Roy say just then. 'What do you think?'

Sophie jerked back to the here and now as a steaming mug was plonked in front of her. 'Sorry, what? I was in my own world there,' she confessed.

'You do seem a bit distracted today, love,' Roy said, heaping sugars into his tea and stirring. 'What's up?'

Sophie sighed. 'Oh, it's just…' *Shut up,* she chastised herself before she could get any further. Roy didn't want to know the ins and outs of her lovelife. 'Just nothing,' she said lamely.

'Is it heck nothing. Go on, try me. I'm a good listener.'

Sophie smiled. 'Honestly, it's nothing.'

He raised a silvery eyebrow suspiciously. 'I've been married to Geraldine nearly forty years, pet, I've heard it all, you know,' he told her. 'Come on. Is it a bloke? Do you need me to go round and have a word with him for you? Used to be a good boxer, me, back in me army days.'

The thought of Roy throwing a punch at Dan on her behalf made Sophie's lips twitch. 'Don't tempt me, Roy,' she said.

'So it *is* a bloke. Giving you the run-around, is he? The swine.'

'Well . . . it's complicated.'

'The best ones always are,' he said sagely. 'Here, I've got some biscuits somewhere, Anna brought them round. Shortbread, very good.' He bustled about, finding the tin and some plates, and set them on the table. 'Tuck in.'

'Thanks.' All of a sudden, Sophie found that she did want to talk about the dilemma which had been buzzing around her head for the last few days. 'This guy, then,' she began haltingly. 'I thought he was the love of my life a few years ago, more fool me. We were in Australia together, and just so happy. I've never felt like that before – or since. Then he dumped me out of the blue, left the country, and that was that.'

'Sounds a bloody fool if you ask me,' Roy commented, dunking his shortbread.

'Only now he's got back in touch,' Sophie said. 'And I don't know what to do.'

I'm sorry, he'd written in a private Facebook message the day before. *I behaved like a self-centred prat. I thought I wanted freedom but I just missed you the whole time. I was so miserable without you.*

Maybe it's too late and you're with someone else now, in which case I hope you're happy together. Ah bollocks, of course I don't. I hope he's a twat and you're about to dump him. I would love to meet up anyway. What do you think? Have I blown it?

Love Dan x

'Hmmm,' Roy said, when she'd recounted the details to him. He chewed his shortbread thoughtfully. 'Well, we all make mistakes. Takes a certain kind of person to own up to them, though.'

'Yes,' she said. 'It's taken him long enough, mind. It's three years since I saw him, you know. He obviously wasn't *that* bothered.'

Roy shook his head. 'Me and Geraldine split up once,' he said. 'Back when we were courting. Had an argument over the daftest thing – she had borrowed my sister's bike and left it outside the library. Wasn't there when she came out. But would she say sorry when it were her fault it got pinched? No, she bloody well would not.'

Sophie smiled, loving the thought of a teenage Geraldine cycling around the city. 'I bet she was gorgeous when she was young,' she said.

'Aye, she were that. Gorgeous as a June rose, but stubborn as a one-eyed mule. We broke up over it, any road. I was getting it in the neck from our Janet, while Geraldine tried to blame *me* for lending her the bike in the first place.' He shook his head. 'I went out with Mary Gibbons instead but my heart was never in it. And Geraldine went off with Bobby Henderson, who everyone knew was a piece of work.'

'So what happened?'

'We were at a dance at Cutler's Hall, all four of us. She were in this dress – I'll never forget – white with pink roses, and her long hair all pinned up. Smashing, she looked. She'd got a job as a conductress on the tram at the time, so I went up to her and asked, "Can I have a return, please, Miss?" "A return?" she says, a bit snooty like. "A return to where?" "A return to where we were before that argument about the wretched bike," I said.'

'Aww,' Sophie said, wrinkling her nose. 'Roy, that's lovely.'

'And from that day on,' he said, 'we were never parted.' He drank his tea, misty-eyed with nostalgia. 'So you see,' he went on, 'if you both want to try again, you can. Don't let history muck things up.'

'Well, it worked for you,' Sophie said, remembering with a pang how Dan had been back then – tanned and carefree, always laughing. She could remember how his skin felt against hers as if it were yesterday.

'It did,' he replied. 'And it might work for you too, if you give it a go. What have you got to lose?'

'Pride, dignity, self-respect . . .' She ticked them off on her fingers.

'But it's worth a try, I reckon. The love of your life? Asking for another chance? You can't say no to that, Sophie.'

'No,' Sophie agreed. 'I guess I can't.' She drained the tea and got to her feet. 'I'd better get on, anyway, I'm meant to start work at the café in half an hour. Thanks for the chat – and you're right, by the way. You *are* a good listener.'

'You have to be, with a wife like mine,' he said, pulling a funny face. 'Thanks for bringing my shopping, duck. And good luck with this fella. If he has any sense he'll be grovelling for you to take him back.'

She smiled faintly. 'I'll let you know.'

Chapter Twenty-Nine

Il giardino – The garden

'So,' Mike said, leaning back in his chair and shooting Catherine a wary look. 'What happens now, then?'

It was Thursday evening and they were in the Plough again, their own personal Switzerland of meeting places. Time to lay those cards on the table, Catherine thought to herself. Time to nail this once and for all.

Tonight she'd come better prepared, having thought long and hard about what she wanted as well as how he could make amends. Mike had arrived looking pale and unshaven, with bags under his eyes and bad skin hinting at sleeplessness. Good, Catherine found herself thinking without much sympathy. If anyone deserved a few long, dark nights of the soul, it was him after his shabby behaviour.

Drinks on the table, she eyeballed him right back. 'I want to stay in the house,' she said.

'Here we go,' he said. 'I should have known you'd twist this around to you.'

Up yours, Mike. 'Not just for my sake,' she went on, as if he hadn't spoken, 'but for Matthew and Emily too. They need stability while they're at university; it's only right that they should still have their childhood home to come back to in the holidays.' She folded her arms. 'Three years, that's all, just until they've finished at uni. Four, if you think, as I do, that they might need a bit of time to sort themselves out afterwards and find jobs. Then you can sell it, if you want.'

'Hmm,' he said non-committally.

'It's not as if there's anything left on the mortgage,' she added, having undertaken a thorough sweep of all the household paperwork in recent days. 'And in the meantime I can manage the bills on my salary. It won't cost you a penny.'

'Your *salary*?' he scoffed. 'You've got a job?'

She knew he was being particularly vile because she'd rumbled him, but all the same, she wished he didn't have to say it as if the thought of her working was such a joke. 'Yes,' she replied tightly. 'I have, thanks.'

He snorted. 'First time for everything,' he muttered under his breath.

A tickertape flashed through her head of all the dinners she'd cooked him, all the baskets of laundry, all the bulging binbags and ironing and stair-hoovering. Then came a final image of her hands tightening around his meaty, ungrateful neck. 'I would have *loved* a job before,' she snapped, 'but you always told me my job was looking after you and the kids. Remember?'

'Bollocks,' he said unconvincingly.

'You wrecked my confidence. You told me I couldn't do anything, and said nobody would want me,' she went on, her voice rising. 'You were so macho about being the provider, the hero of the family who paid for holidays and treats, that you never once supported me when I talked about working or going back to college.' She glared at him. '*Now* do you remember?'

'No,' he replied, although the shifty look in his eyes told her a bell was ringing loud and clear in his head. He fidgeted on his stool. 'What's the job, anyway?'

Just look at that patronizing smirk; he couldn't wait to rip her and her mysterious new job to shreds. In Mike's opinion, being a doctor was the most noble profession out there; anything else was inferior. *Nothing very noble about taking backhanders though, is there, Mike?* she felt like saying.

'It's just a job,' she replied steadily, refusing to compete. Only, to her, it was more than that, of course.

The day before, she'd driven out to the nursery in Risbury with her job application form, only to be greeted by the manager, Maggie, who read it through there and then. Maggie showed her around the place and the two of them had a lovely chat about plants and gardening in general as they went. The nursery looked great: a large shed where three other women stood around a big table, a seed tray of vermiculite and compost each, planting seeds or thinning seedlings with the radio playing songs in the background.

I could do this, Catherine thought, her confidence crystallizing in a way that it never had in all the recruitment agencies she'd slogged around. What was more, the nursery ran an inspiring outreach programme, helping to train troubled teenagers in horticultural skills, and she was dying to get involved with that, if possible.

'It all looks great,' she said to Maggie at the end. 'Thanks for your time. Let me know if you'd like me to come in for an interview or anything.'

Maggie burst out laughing. She was a big buxom woman with auburn curly hair, dark blue eyes and soft freckled skin. In her fifties now, she must have been stunning in her day. 'What do you think *that* just was?' she said, a hand on her hip. 'That's as good as my interviews get, doll!'

Catherine felt such an idiot. Here she was in jeans and scruffy boots and not even any mascara on. 'I'd have put a skirt and heels on if I'd thought I was going to be *interviewed*,' she confessed. 'I'd have washed my hair and all.'

Maggie boomed with laughter again. 'You won't want heels in this place, chuck,' she said in a friendly voice. 'Besides, you look fine to me. Can you start on Monday?'

Catherine's mouth fell open. 'You mean . . . I've got the job?'

'Sure, if you want it. The pay's not amazing, I have to tell you, but it's a nice place to work. I suppose I'd better take a character reference and what-not, but you seem all right and I'm not usually wrong about people.' She held out a big freckled hand. 'So are you in?'

Catherine shook it in disbelief. 'I'm in.'

She felt joyful and excited for the rest of the day. Working in that shed with the women she'd seen, earth beneath her fingers, the radio playing . . . She could do that, she knew she could, way better than wrestling with a computer in an air-conditioned office. It would mean giving up most of her voluntary commitments, which was a shame, but she was sure they'd understand. It was time to start doing more for herself, rather than spending her life running around after everyone else.

'As for the money you got from Centaur,' she said to Mike now, changing the subject briskly, 'I think you should give it back.'

He was raising his pint to his lips as she spoke, but almost dropped the glass on the table as her words registered in his brain. 'Give it *back*?' he echoed.

'Not to the pharmaceutical company,' she said, straight-faced. She had given this a lot of thought. 'Back to the NHS. The Children's Hospital is running an appeal for funds, for instance – they'd welcome your guilt money. And maybe you should give some of it to the families affected by your decisions, too. Jim Frost, for example. Ten grand or so to him should make up for nearly killing the man and ruining his family's Christmas.'

He spluttered. 'I don't think—'

'Oh, I do.' She stared him down meaningfully. 'I think it's the least you can do, Mike. The very least. Otherwise . . .'

Her unspoken threat – *Otherwise I'll tell my journalist friend* – dangled weightily between them. *And you know I'll do it, Mike.*

His expression pained, he swallowed down a large mouthful of bitter without seeming to even taste it. Then he looked at her as if he no longer recognized her. 'You've changed,' he said accusingly.

Yes, Mike, I have, she thought. And it's a change for the better. 'You haven't agreed to my suggestion yet,' she reminded him.

He glared at her. 'Yes,' he muttered, beaten at last.

So it had all been bluff and bluster, she thought. Fight back and he turned out to be made of hot air and nothing more. She wished it hadn't taken her so many years to discover this – but she knew it now at least.

'Good for you, Cath,' said Sophie. 'Sounds like a brilliant week, what with your new job and all.'

It was Saturday now and Catherine had come to meet Anna and Sophie for the weekly Park Run; Anna's idea. It was a grey, drizzly morning but there were still a good hundred people there and a lively, cheerful atmosphere as they thudded around together.

'I have a feeling that your ex isn't the only doctor who's going to have to rethink their prescriptions in the future,' Anna said mysteriously and tapped her nose. 'Just a little something I saw on the news wires in the office yesterday.'

'What's happened?' Catherine asked.

'Schenkman Pharma, wasn't it? They're in all sorts of trouble. Forced to take Demelzerol and a couple of other drugs off the market because of the number of people suffering side-effects – and there's talk of them facing massive financial penalties too. Some of the trial data has been leaked and it looks as if a lot of negative results were concealed in the official reports.'

Catherine felt an enormous weight roll off her shoulders. So it was over. The secret was out, and the matter now completely out of her hands. 'Thank goodness,' she said. 'It's been on my conscience the whole time – wondering if I should take the story to the press, do more about it. But then I'd think of the children, and I just couldn't go through with it. I couldn't bring myself to shatter their image of Mike as a good guy.' She pressed her lips together, feeling overwhelmed by emotion and guilt. No doubt Sophie would disagree with her when her own father had suffered at Mike's hands.

But Sophie looked sympathetic. 'You were in an impossible situation,' she said. 'And for what it's worth, I think you were really brave, standing up to your ex and forcing him to act.'

'Absolutely,' Anna agreed. 'Don't beat yourself up, Cath. You did something at least. Other people might have buried their heads in the sand.'

Catherine gave a wan smile. 'I think it was the threat of "my journalist friend" that did it in the end. That's you, by the way.'

Anna laughed. 'Because I'm *so* threatening,' she said, pulling a face. 'I could totally . . . put him in my next restaurant column.'

'Handsome Colleague becomes Dodgy Doctor,' Sophie suggested, quirking an eyebrow.

Anna pulled a face. 'Not this week he doesn't,' she said. 'It's the Valentine's special, isn't it? I've been baking like a loon, trying to work out the best home-cooked dinner for two for my cookery column, *and* me and Joe have got to suffer the red roses and cheesy music of The White House on Valentine's night for the restaurant review. Imagine how thrilled his poor girlfriend is about that!'

'Shit,' Sophie said. 'Really? I'd be fuming if my boyfriend had to take someone else out for dinner.'

'Me too. I think the relationship is currently hanging by a thread, you know. I have to say, I do feel really bad about it.'

'You shouldn't,' Catherine told her, feeling the beginnings of a stitch. With all the tennis she'd played over the years, she'd thought five kilometres would be a doddle, but talking and running at the same time was starting to become a problem. 'He could have said no to the whole thing, couldn't he? *You've* done nothing wrong.'

'Yeah. Two more weeks and I'll be in Rome anyway, so it'll all be worth it,' Anna said, shrugging. 'Hey – and talking of epic journeys, I'm off to see my mum this afternoon in Leeds. She's finally agreed to tell me more about Dad.'

'Really? Wow, that's fantastic,' Sophie said.

'You must be so excited,' Catherine said.

'I know, I'm psyched. Well, psyched and bricking it, weirdly. I'm scared she's going to say something awful about him.' Anna's pretty mouth twisted, betraying her nerves.

'No,' Catherine managed to puff. 'I'm sure she won't. But either way, at least you'll know.'

'Yeah,' Sophie agreed. 'I bet he'll be great. You'll see.'

After the run, the three of them had coffee and brunch together in the cosy park café. Half-term had just started so there would be no Italian class during the week, but they agreed to meet again for the next Park Run the following Saturday. 'Oh, and did you two get the text from George about going guerrilla tomorrow?' Catherine asked as they said goodbye.

'I can't make it, we've got an extra rehearsal on,' Sophie said.

'And I'm snowed under with work,' Anna said. 'Are you going, Cath?' She winked. 'I think our George has got a soft spot for you, you know.'

'He hasn't!' Catherine protested. 'He's nice to everyone, not just me.'

Anna and Sophie looked at each other, eyebrows raised. 'Methinks the lady doth protest too much . . .' Sophie teased, and elbowed her. 'He's lovely anyway. You could do a lot worse.'

'I'm not really . . . I hadn't even *thought* . . .' Catherine began, struggling to get the words out. Oh God. Why had they said that? Now she was all flustered. 'Anyway,' she said, trying to change the subject, 'I'd better go. Good luck with your mum, Anna – and that Valentine's dinner. I'll be reading all about it.'

'And you too with the new job,' Anna said back, 'and with the play, Sophie. We all want to come and see you on stage so let us know about tickets, yeah?'

'Honestly, my part in it . . . blink and you'll miss me,' Sophie said, but you could tell she was chuffed. She hugged them both in turn. 'It's been a pleasure, girls. Have a good week!'

The following day, when it was time to meet George for their guerrilla gardening mission, Catherine kept remembering the way Sophie and Anna had teased her about him, and her nerve almost failed. They were only messing about, she told herself, as she dithered at the front door. They were just joking. She and George . . . Well, it was impossible. It was silly to even think about it.

George had told her the plan in the pub earlier that week: a group of them were clearing a patch of wasteland over near Fox Hill. This was no balaclava-wearing operation under cover of darkness, he explained. This was about the preliminaries: clearing the land then digging over the soil. 'The gardening's only half the story,' he said. 'It's more about transforming neglected spaces; retaking the land to serve the community.'

George was already there when she arrived, along with a tall Irish bloke called Cal and two women, Jane and Nicki. Armed with rubber gloves and bin bags, they set about clearing the ground of broken glass, empty cans, a couple of syringes, an old tyre, crisp packets and even some used condoms. Gross.

'What's the plan when this has all been cleared?' she asked. 'Are you going to plant vegetables and stuff here?'

'We want to create a community garden,' Jane told her. 'Nothing mega, just some lawn, maybe a wild flower garden and a vegetable plot . . . a place for people to hang out, basically. There are lots of flats around here, so not everyone's got their own garden. This could be their place.'

'I'd love to hold a big party here in the summer,' Cal said

dreamily. 'Maybe even a barbecue, invite the whole estate, get everyone together. That's what it's all about.'

Catherine gazed around, imagining music and dancing and the smell of sausages on a barbecue. 'I feel guilty for not doing more with my garden now,' she confessed. 'I've neglected it lately.'

'Sounds like you've been busy with lots of other things,' George said, picking up a pair of old Y-fronts with a grimace and stuffing them in his binbag.

'Yeah,' Catherine said. 'The annoying thing is, I've got a whole sackful of bulbs in the shed that I didn't plant last autumn. I kept meaning to, but then with . . .' She lowered her voice so the others wouldn't hear. 'With Mike going, I just didn't get round to it. I wouldn't mind, but I'd bought these lovely tulip bulbs – they're my favourites and they'd all be starting to come up soon. Oh well. Next year, I suppose.'

Once they'd cleared the site of rubbish, Cal marked out an area for a raised bed against the wall of a disused building. He'd brought along some old railway sleepers which they used to edge it, then they dug over the soil and mixed in bucketfuls of compost. Finally, they dug holes and planted some blackcurrant bushes, a small pear tree and a couple of plum trees.

'It looks so much better already,' Catherine said, standing back and marvelling at what the five of them had achieved in one afternoon.

'It's going to be great,' Cal agreed. 'Are you up for coming along some other time?'

'Definitely,' Catherine said. She grinned at George. 'Looking forward to it.'

Chapter Thirty

La verita – The truth

'So,' said Anna, staring intently at her mum. 'Tell me.'

They were sitting in Tracey's conservatory in creaky wicker chairs with fat, faded cushions and a coffee each ('Better make it a strong one,' Tracey had said, her smile not reaching her eyes). Thirty-two years of stubborn silence was almost over.

Tracey took a deep breath. 'Right,' she said. 'So. What's your nan been saying then?'

And they're off. 'She said my dad was – is? – called Gino and he's Italian,' Anna replied shakily. She could hardly believe they were having this conversation at last. 'She said he was nothing but trouble. And then you mentioned you went to Rimini as the last holiday before I was born, and I thought, Aha.'

'Yes, but—'

'Aunty Marie let me see her pictures of your holiday,' Anna went on, unable to stop now she had started, 'and I just put two and two together. Is this him?' She pulled out the photograph from her handbag, hands clammy. 'I've been told that this is Lungomare Augusto. Is that where you and Dad met?'

It was her Sherlock Holmes moment: evidence revealed, her hand played. Da-dah! In the car driving over here, she'd pictured Tracey's undisguised surprise at this point, and yes, sheer admiration that Anna had pieced together the puzzle. Elementary, my dear mother.

Yet her mum was looking from Anna to the photo and back again, her expression becoming increasingly bewildered. Then she shook her head.

'I'm sorry, love,' she said. 'You must have misunderstood. I've no idea who that bloke in the photo is, but he's not your father.'

'He's . . . not?'

'No. Tell me exactly what your nan said, if you can remember.'

Stunned by this setback, Anna tried her hardest to think. 'She said I looked like him,' she remembered. 'And then she said, *The Italian. Your father. Nothing but trouble.*'

There was silence for a moment save for the ticking of the oil heater plugged in nearby. Then Tracey sighed. 'When Mum said "the Italian",' she began wearily, 'she meant the Italian restaurant in Clay Cross where I worked as a waitress. I was eighteen and just out of nursing college. I worked evenings and weekends there that summer while I looked for a proper job.'

Anna stared at her aghast. What? The Italian was a *restaurant*?

'Gino's, it was called,' Tracey said. 'It's closed now. I think it's a Costa Coffee these days.'

Gino's. The *restaurant* was called Gino's. 'So my dad was Gino – your boss?' Anna asked, her mouth dry, her brain struggling to catch up.

Tracey shook her head. 'There was no Gino,' she replied. 'That was just a made-up name to sound authentic. The manager was called Bob Woldesley. Dirty old letch he was, too.'

'Oh no,' Anna said, besieged by visions of dirty old Bob Woldesley accosting her poor teenage mother in the stock room. (Even worse, her dad was called *Bob Woldesley*? He sounded like a wedge of stinking cheese.) 'So . . . it was him? And that was why you never wanted to talk about it?' She felt like crying. What had the bastard *done* to her mum?

'God, no, what kind of girl do you take me for?' Now it was Tracey who looked horrified. 'I told Bob where to get off. Catch me taking my knickers down for . . . Anyway. No. Your dad was the chef.' Her lips tightened. 'He was really nice. Funny. Handsome.'

Her dad was a chef. A chef! Hope suddenly lit up inside her. 'And was *he* Italian?'

'Tony? No, love. He was a Londoner.' She gave a sniff. 'Southern gobshite. I should have known he'd be no good.'

Anna was reeling. A *Londoner*? This didn't make sense. She had *felt* so Italian. She had come to love all things Italian! And yet her new-found knowledge of the culture, the language, the cookery . . . it had nothing to do with her. Not a drop of Mediterranean blood ran in her veins. 'So what happened?' she managed to say.

'It was only ever a fling,' Tracey said sadly. 'All on his terms, more fool me. We went out four or five times, then he said he had to stop seeing me because he was going to get married.'

'Oh, Mum.' It might have been thirty-two years ago but Anna could still see the hurt in her eyes.

'By then, it was too late of course. He moved away and I didn't realize I was pregnant until a few months down the line when I began to show. It's hard to believe now, but I was skinny as anything back then – until all of a sudden, I had these whopping great boobs and a belly poking out. Talk about a shock.'

'Did you let him know? Were you able to track him down?'

'Not at the time. I was too proud. Besides, I didn't have a clue where he lived. London's a big place. I went to the library and tried looking him up in the London phone book but got nowhere.'

Anna's head was whirling. She'd got it all so wrong. She

wasn't Italian. Her dad wasn't Gino. There would be no papa-hunt in Rimini. 'That must have been awful,' she managed to say.

'Yeah. Mum went ballistic at me – she'd always told me to keep my legs crossed until I was married, see, and . . .' Her mouth twisted in a grimace. 'Well, it wasn't the happiest of times.'

Anna reached out and squeezed her hand. 'I can imagine.'

Tracey's eyes were shining. 'I'm sorry that I can't tell you your dad was some gorgeous Italian fella,' she said. 'I really wish I could. I should have said something to you before now, but it's been difficult. I felt such an idiot.'

Anna put her arms around her mum and hugged her tightly. 'Don't worry,' she said. 'It doesn't matter. I understand.'

Dear Dad,

This is a strange letter to write, but . . .

She screwed up the paper and put it in the bin. No. She shouldn't even *say* 'Dear Dad' – it was too informal too soon. For all she knew, she might even have got the wrong Tony Sandbrookes, although as far as she could tell, there was only one person in London with that name. Maybe if she began with a simple 'Hello'—

'How much longer are you planning to do this anyway?' came an icy voice just then.

Or maybe she shouldn't be trying to write a letter introducing herself to her never-met father in work time in the first place. 'What was that?' She raised her head to see Marla glowering down at her.

'How much longer,' Marla repeated bitterly, 'are you planning to steal my column?'

Ahh.

'Because I hate being on the news desk,' she said, eyes blazing, looking very much as if she'd like to stamp her foot. 'And I think it's totally unfair that you just waltz in and take over behind my back.'

'It wasn't like that.'

'We both know it was. You and Joe, plotting together. Smarming up to Imogen. And now you've got the Valentine's dinner to review and—'

'Two more restaurants, that's all Imogen wants,' Anna said, trying to placate her. Two more restaurants, and then she was meant to be going to Rome, although even that felt like a slap in the face now that she knew her dad was more Rotherhithe than Rimini. She hadn't told Joe yet; hadn't told anyone. Maybe if she kept it in her head, it wouldn't really be true. 'Then the column's all yours again, I'm sure,' she added wearily. She didn't care any more.

Marla narrowed her eyes. 'You know he's tried it on with *me* before, don't you?' she snarled. 'Joe. At the Christmas meal.

Put his hand up my skirt during the dessert course, asked me if I'd be his little Christmas cracker.'

'No!' Anna didn't believe her. Did she? Marla seemed very certain of her facts.

Sensing she'd hit a nerve, Marla carried on. 'He does it to everyone. Didn't you know? He's one of those blokes who's just out for what he can get.' She smiled triumphantly. 'If I were you, I'd nip this sham romance in the bud before he makes his move on you. If it's not too late, that is.'

She swept away, nose in the air, and Anna watched her go. Stirring, that's what Marla was doing, she told herself. A transparent attempt to snatch back 'her' column. And yet . . . It couldn't be true about Joe being a ladies' man, could it? Sure, he'd always been charming and, yes, okay, a bit flirtatious too – but a hand up Marla's skirt? Christmas crackers? Doing it to *everyone*?

Gritting her teeth, she turned back to her computer. She didn't have time to think about this now that she had two columns to finish and a ton of correspondence to get through, not to mention the letter to her dad that she kept trying and failing to write. With the Valentine's review coming up, and Rome the following week, as well as the news about her dad – London Tony – to get her head around, she felt as if there were a lot of plates to keep spinning right now.

*

Thursday was Valentine's Day. For the first time in years, there was no daft card from Pete to open over breakfast, no smutty limerick to giggle over (he was proud of those; they had become a tradition) and no penis-shaped chocolate to unwrap (a blessing, admittedly). Shovelling muesli into her mouth, she thought of the umpteen romantic breakfasts taking place in bedrooms around the country and felt horribly alone, sat there in her threadbare dressing gown with only John Humphrys and the *Today* programme for company.

Pete had vanished out of her life astonishingly quickly, leaving no trace once he'd sheepishly picked up his belongings and removed them from her flat. No text messages, no sightings, nothing. Gone, just like that. Over. She thought of him writing a silly limerick for his new girlfriend (*There was a hot chick, Katerina . . .*) and was surprised by how much it made her want to cry.

She cycled into work trying to feel don't-care-ish and free, but the two garages she passed had buckets of cellophane-wrapped bouquets on the forecourt, and all the windows of the shops near the office were a riot of red and pink love-hearts. The rest of the country was carrying on with Valentine's Day regardless of her.

Still, at least she was going out that evening, even if it was only a pretend date for a restaurant review. Having slaved over her Valentine's cookery column, Anna would have been quite happy to sack the romantic element and go for fish and chips somewhere, but unfortunately they were booked in for a table for two at The White House, which had the naffest Valentine's-themed menu in the city. Normally, she would have steered several miles clear, but Imogen, buoyed by the success of Anna's last two reviews featuring 'Handsome Colleague', had decided to crank up the romance a notch and insisted on choosing the venue.

'Don't be a snob, I'm sure you'll have a great time,' she'd said bossily. 'And even if you don't, pretend you did; my husband plays golf with one of the owners.'

The White House, like many other restaurants with an eye on their profits, was running two dinner sittings for Valentine's night, so Anna had booked them in for the early slot at six-thirty. That way, she figured, Joe could at least go on to meet Julia afterwards like a proper boyfriend.

She had mixed feelings about the evening, she realized, as she put on her make-up and pinned up her hair in the office loos after work. Since her recent *contretemps* with Marla, Anna hadn't been able to look at Joe in the same way. Hearing that he'd tried it on with her – and countless others, by the sound of things – had totally spoiled all the vague fuzzy feelings she'd been having about him. She just hadn't figured him for the sleazy type – no way.

Marla was probably lying to spite her, she reminded herself as she added a last coat of mascara. All the same, she felt about as unromantic as it was possible to feel. She'd just got shot of one crap bloke. She sure as hell wouldn't let herself get tangled up with another in a hurry.

Joe was already at the restaurant, sniggering over the menu when she arrived. He'd spent the afternoon over at Hillsborough interviewing some of the Wednesday players, but had obviously found time to go home and get changed because he was now wearing full black tie as if he were expecting to dine at a glamorous banquet. She burst out laughing when she saw him.

'Nice togs,' she spluttered.

'Thought I'd dress for the occasion. Anywhere that has a dish called Salmon Caress on the menu has to be classy, right?'

She laughed again. 'Salmon *Caress*? You just made that up.'

'I did not.' He jabbed at the menu. 'Some other prat did. Apparently it's roasted salmon with "an embrace of salsa verde and parmentier potatoes".'

'Salmon Caress, indeed.' Anna snorted. 'Who in their right mind would want to be caressed by a *salmon*?'

'Another salmon might,' Joe replied, doing a fishface at her. 'It *is* Valentine's Day, Anna.' He glanced down at the menu again. 'Still, if that doesn't tempt you, there's always the Sole Seduction.'

'The Sole . . . ? Oh God. You're not even kidding, are you?' She glanced around, taking in the surroundings properly for the first time. Pink and silver helium balloons floated up as table decorations. A single red rose stood phallically in a stem glass on each table with a sprinkling of silver confetti around it. They were just missing the violin player and some lovebirds flitting about, and it would have been Full House on the Valentine's bingo card.

She sat down. Actually, the Valentine overkill was oddly cheering now that she was here; you could imagine the staff laughing uproariously as they put the whole thing together. 'Well, if there's not pink champagne on the wine list, there had better be a damn good reason why,' she declared. She snorted as she started reading the menu herself. 'I'm going to have to try the Prawn Pleasure Pinnacle just to see if I can order it with a straight face.'

'Now there's a challenge,' Joe said. 'Just think, when we're in Rome, eating boring risotto or cannelloni, we'll be wishing we could enjoy a Hopelessly Devoted Duck one last time.'

'A devoted *what?*' Anna was starting to feel slightly hysterical.

'Don't you start.' He grinned at her. 'Hey, I can't believe we've managed to wangle Rome, can you? It's going to be amazing.'

She hesitated, the laugh in her throat suddenly disappearing. 'Yeah.'

'I was looking at flights; there's a direct one from Manchester on Saturday morning but it leaves at seven a.m. which is a bit of a mare. So I reckon if we fly out the night before, we can have a couple of nights there, then there won't be any rushing around at the crack of dawn. When were you thinking of going to Rimini, by the way? Because I started looking at trains and—'

She held up a hand. Stop right there. 'I'm not going to Rimini any more.'

His forehead crinkled. 'You're not? How come? I thought . . .'

'He's not Italian after all. I got it wrong. There is no dad in Rimini.' To her horror, she felt tears swelling in her eyes and couldn't bring herself to look at him, fearful that he might laugh. 'What a pillock, eh?'

'Oh no.' He reached across the table and put a hand on hers. 'Are you sure?'

'That I'm a pillock, or that my dad's not Italian? Both. My mum told me.' She sniffed and wiped her eyes on the back of her hand. 'He's a bloody Londoner. Jellied eels and doing the Lambeth bleeding walk – that's my real heritage. So all my cooking, learning the language, going to Rome . . . it's been for nothing.'

'It hasn't,' he said gently. 'Because you've loved doing it all and seemed so happy lately. From what you've told me, your evening class has been brilliant, and the cooking has gone great guns too – *and* it got you your own column! Who cares where you're from? London Schmondon. You can still enjoy those things.'

He was being so sweet and kind that now she really *was* in danger of blubbing. 'Thanks, Joe,' she said with a watery smile.

'And we'll have a brilliant time in Rome too,' he reminded her. 'In fact, you might even enjoy it more – the pressure's off! You won't have this stressful trip to Rimini hanging over your head.'

'That's true,' she said. 'I can still do my course even if I'm not Italian.'

'Damn right you can. They're not going to be taking DNA samples at the door, are they?'

'Let's hope not.' She blew her nose. 'Thanks for being so nice to me,' she said. 'What a muppet, honestly. I can't believe I got it so wrong.'

'Don't be daft,' he told her. 'Who your dad is makes no difference anyway. You're still the same Anna – funny, lovely, a talented writer, a good friend, a genius chef . . .'

'Keep going.'

'. . . Who needs some pink champagne immediately. Let's order.'

Chapter Thirty-One

Il ragazzo – The boyfriend

'Mum!'

'Oh, Em! Hello, love! Come here!' Catherine hugged her daughter joyfully, breathing in the scent of clean hair and perfume. *Her girl.*

It was Friday afternoon and the end of Catherine's first week in her new job. The work had been simple but satisfying and her colleagues were lovely. Maggie was a great boss too, mucking in with them and jollying everyone along. (She had even arrived on Thursday with chocolates for the team, 'Just in case your fellas are as crap as mine about Valentine's and forgot to give you owt.' How lovely was that?!) And now it was the weekend, and here was Emily, come to visit for a full two days. Bliss.

Catherine had been looking forward to this all week. She'd already taken the liberty of booking them a cosy table for two upstairs at Browns on Saturday for lunch, with plans for a shopping marathon afterwards. If you couldn't treat your own daughter with your wages, then what was the point of earning them?

A split second later, she noticed the youth at the side of the porch – a tall, handsome guy in a biker jacket with an air of aloof insouciance, as if he'd rather be doing cool stuff with cool people somewhere way cooler than this. He was carrying two motorbike helmets and only then did Catherine see the gleaming chrome and black beast behind him. In the eyes of any mother with a teenage daughter, it was a death-trap.

'Oh,' she said, trying not to show her alarm. Emily hadn't mentioned a boyfriend. She certainly hadn't mentioned a motorbike. Didn't she know how *lethal* they were? 'Hello,' she added quickly. *Bang goes the girly weekend.*

'Mum, this is Macca. Macca, this is Mum. Catherine to you,' she added with a grin.

Mrs Evans, if you don't mind, Catherine felt like saying.

'All right,' drawled Macca, avoiding her eye.

'Nice to meet you, er, Macca,' Catherine said. She started putting her hand out for him to shake but he didn't seem to notice so she dropped it quickly to her side. 'Come in. Um . . . Are you staying for the weekend as well?'

'Uh . . . Yeah?' said Macca, as if he didn't care either way.

Catherine was still trying to come to terms with the fact that her daughter had been driven here on a motorbike.

Hideous, nightmarish images rattled into her head of them dodging around cars, leaning into hairpin bends, colliding with an oncoming lorry and being thrown into the centre of the road . . .

'Can I make you some tea?' she asked hurriedly. *Stop it, Catherine.* They'd got here in one piece, hadn't they? 'Coffee?' Clearly tea and coffee were the drinking choices of middle-aged fogies, judging by the look on Macca's face. 'Squash? Something stronger?' she said desperately.

'Mum, you devil, don't tell me you've been on the sherry already,' Emily laughed. 'We're all right, thanks. I said to Katy we'd meet her down the pub later. Come on,' she told Macca. 'I'll show you my room.'

The two of them thundered upstairs, laughing together about something, and Catherine drifted into the kitchen forlornly. Oh. Okay then. Dinner for two was suddenly dinner for three. She tried to banish the uncharitable thoughts from her head and look on the bright side. Emily was back, and they would still have a lovely time together. Wouldn't they?

'So, are you a student as well, Macca?'

She had managed to stretch the chicken pie to feed the three of them, by dint of adding mushrooms and carrot to the filling and serving it with the biggest baking potatoes in the bag. Not that this oaf looked grateful for her efforts, mind; he was shovelling in mouthfuls as if he was half-starved, one hand caressing Emily's thigh under the table as he ate.

'Having a year out,' he mumbled, a small blizzard of pastry flakes falling from his lips as he spoke.

'A year out? What, working or saving to go travelling, or . . . ?' she asked, although she was pretty sure his answer would be neither.

'Just a year out,' he said, not meeting her eye.

'Macca's a musician,' Emily said, shooting him an adoring look.

'Oh. What do you play?' God, this conversation was hard work. Clearly Macca hadn't been honing his social skills during his year out.

'Guitar.'

'Are you in a band?'

'Mum – give him a break,' Emily protested. 'It's not an interview!'

Catherine saw her rolling her eyes at him and felt betrayed. 'I'm only taking an interest,' she said, wounded.

Emily began chatting to Macca about plans for the evening and Catherine tuned out; miserable images flashed up in her head of her daughter hanging out in squalid basement flats with unsavoury men, dirty windows never letting in any light, the sweet cloying smell of cannabis, the plaintive sound of a strummed guitar.

Look at Emily, so bright and fresh and clean, with her

plump pink face and the pony-riding rosettes still on her wardrobe. The thought of this cretin opposite her daring to tarnish her daughter's sparkle made Catherine feel like killing him.

'Morning!' Catherine called, jogging across the frosty grass to Sophie and Anna the next day. She'd woken early and decided to come out to the Park Run, certain that Emily and Macca would be snoozing for a few hours yet. It was a clear, cold morning and she zipped her tracksuit top up as high as it would go, her breath puffing out in little clouds as she ran.

Sophie was doing jumping jacks to keep warm and Anna was stretching out her hamstrings, a blue beanie hat on her head. 'Hey, I thought you were going to drag your daughter along this morning,' she chided as Catherine approached.

'I was,' Catherine replied, 'but she brought this bloke back from Liverpool with her last night, out of the blue. They were both spark-out when I got up so I thought I'd leave them be.'

'Ooh. Serious boyfriend, then, if he's come for the weekend,' Sophie said, raising an eyebrow.

Catherine pulled a face. 'I hope not,' she confessed. 'He's completely bloody gormless. And so rude.'

Sophie laughed. 'You should talk to my mum. I brought home a few horrors in my time,' she confessed. 'You could compare notes.'

'Didn't we all,' Anna said. 'Shame you didn't get your nice weekend together, though. I remember you were looking forward to that.' She peered towards the start line. 'I think they're calling us over,' she added.

Catherine tried to put things in perspective as they jogged across to join the other runners. Maybe the girls were right, she told herself firmly, as they set off along the path. Everyone went through their share of terrible boyfriends, didn't they? She'd certainly had a few. Perhaps she'd been a bit harsh on old Macca.

But then she remembered the way he'd spoken to Emily last night and her charity shrivelled back to nothing. She'd been on her way upstairs with a basket of laundry when she heard Emily's voice float out from her bedroom.

'What do you think – this blue top with my jeans, or my black dress?'

Catherine had paused, thinking for a moment that her daughter was addressing her. Then Macca spoke.

'That top's a bit tight, isn't it?'

'Do you think?' Emily sounded doubtful.

'Yeah. Way too tight. I don't think you've got the figure to carry that off. No offence.'

It was the longest speech Catherine had heard him make, and she didn't like a word of it. No offence indeed, when he'd just criticized her figure like that. Who was he trying to kid?

'Oh,' said Emily uncertainly, and Catherine winced, imagining the crushed expression on her daughter's face. 'Should I wear the dress then?'

'It's kind of short. Haven't you got anything less . . . slutty?'

It was like going back in time, hearing Mike say similar things to her. She could remember the anxiety fluttering inside as she paraded outfit after outfit before him only to see the shake of his head, lips pursed together in disapproval. Oh, Emily. Don't put up with this rubbish like I did.

'Um . . . I suppose so.' Emily sounded chastened now; Catherine could hear the coathangers rattling in her wardrobe as she went through it.

Been there, done that. She hesitated on the landing, not knowing what to do. Her instinct was to leap to Emily's defence, but she knew her daughter might not thank her for it.

'Cath? Are you all right?'

Sophie's voice dragged her back to the present; they were running alongside the playground but she'd been miles away. 'Sorry,' she said. 'Not awake yet.'

'Still thinking about the pratty boyfriend?'

'Yeah.' In the end, she'd said nothing, just made a point of telling Emily how gorgeous she looked when she finally emerged in a long-sleeved smock top and jeans. Emily's smile hadn't quite reached her eyes though, and Catherine could tell she didn't feel very gorgeous at all.

'How did it go with your mum?' Sophie asked Anna in the next moment, and Catherine felt bad for being so wrapped up in herself.

'Oh God, yeah!' she cried apologetically. 'What did she say? Have you found out any more about your dad?'

Anna's face went a bit pinched. 'No,' she said. 'Not really.'

'Oh,' said Sophie, glancing sideways at her. 'But I thought she was going to tell you . . .'

'Mmm,' Anna replied. 'It was a bit of a weird conversation actually. I'm still trying to get my head around it.' She grimaced. 'Not what I was expecting.'

Catherine had never seen bubbly Anna so reticent. 'Are you okay? You don't have to tell us if you don't want to,' she began, but Anna was already changing the subject.

'Anyway,' she said, lengthening her stride slightly, 'how are you two? How's the play coming along, Soph?'

Sophie flicked a glance at Catherine and Catherine shrugged. Whatever had happened between Anna and her mum was clearly not up for discussion. Not yet anyway.

Catherine arrived home feeling full of energy after the run. She'd knocked two minutes off last week's time and her skin tingled from all the fresh air. As she kicked off her trainers in the hall though, she heard Emily's voice from the kitchen, high-pitched and defensive, and her mood deflated almost immediately.

'He's just a friend, I've known him for ever. Honestly, there's no way he's interested in me.'

Catherine pricked up her ears but could only make out a surly mumble from Macca in reply. Then came Emily again, protesting tearfully. 'I *didn't*! I swear! I don't even really *like* him!'

Catherine held her breath as she heard that low mumble in reply once more. What was he *saying* to her?

'It's not like that!' cried Emily wretchedly, and something inside Catherine snapped. Whatever it was, she had to stop this. She was damned if she was going to let history repeat itself.

Her hands curling into fists, she strode into the kitchen. 'What's going on?' she asked.

Emily was at the cooker, poking bacon around the frying pan with a fork and jumped as Catherine spoke. She was only wearing a long T-shirt and there was something hopelessly vulnerable about her bare pink legs, mottled with gooseflesh, and the damp spikes of her eyelashes. 'Oh! Mum. It's nothing.'

'It didn't sound like nothing to me. You sounded upset. Again. What's happening?'

Emily shrank into herself, glancing nervously over at Macca and then back to Catherine. 'Honestly, Mum, it's fine. We were just talking.'

'Talking? Is that what you call it?' Catherine put her hands on her hips and glared at Macca. 'Well, let me tell you something for nothing, sunshine. I'm not having you putting my daughter down in my house,' she told him. 'I heard you last night as well, making her feel bad about what she was wearing.'

He curled his lip at her, scornful and disbelieving. 'You what?'

'You heard me. Nasty, that's what it is. Nasty and rude. My ex-husband used to put me down in the same way. Years and years I put up with it until my confidence was in shreds. So believe me, I'm not standing here and watching you do the same thing to my daughter. She's worth more than that.'

'Mum!' Emily hissed, mortified.

'I'm deadly serious,' Catherine snapped. 'So you'd better start treating her with a bit more respect, pal – otherwise you can get out of my house. Understand?'

He stared back at her, eyes limpid. 'Whatever.'

'I'll take that as a yes,' she snapped. 'I'm going to have a shower now. You just think about what I said.'

Upstairs in the safety of the bathroom, she leaned giddily against the tiled wall and let the water pour down on her. Oh my goodness. Had she actually just *said* all of that, hands on her hips like a tongue-lashing fishwife? She couldn't quite believe her own daring, nor her ferocity. But she had meant every single word. No way would she let her daughter put up with the same kind of treatment she'd had from Mike: a sarcastic put-down here, a 'no offence' there, a drip-drip-drip of snide remarks that resulted in an imbalance of power, a bullying tyrant, a woman with zero confidence.

All the same, would Emily ever forgive her for it?

'So what happened? Did he go?'

'Yeah.' It was the next day, and she had driven over to the allotment after a sleepless night, hoping that some hard work and fresh air would sort her out. The weather was unexpectedly mild and she was helping George dig over a vegetable plot. 'The only problem was, she went too.'

'Your daughter? What, they both just upped and left?'

'They'd gone by the time I got out of the shower. Didn't even eat their breakfast.' She leaned heavily on her spade, remembering the shock of the empty house, her running from room to room calling Emily's name, the bacon abandoned in the pan. Too late. 'I feel terrible, George. The first proper boyfriend she's ever brought home and I bollocked him and sent him packing.'

'And you were right to, by the sound of it,' he told her. 'The guy sounds a total jerk.'

'He was. The sort of jerk I married, so I should know.'

'Well, then, I reckon you did her a favour.' He turned the

fork in the soil vigorously a few times. 'What has she said about it since? Have you made up?'

'Me and Emily? No. She won't even answer my phone calls,' Catherine said unhappily. 'Honestly, George, it's so unlike me, shooting off at the mouth like that. I don't know what came over me.' Even as she said the words, she knew they weren't strictly true. She'd known exactly what had come over her: a terrible premonition of the future, of Emily going down the same wrong path she'd done, letting a man crush her spirit until she hardly recognized herself.

'Give her a few days,' George advised. 'You probably dented her pride, blowing your top in front of this bloke. Called her allegiances into question.'

'That's what I'm worried about: that she's decided her allegiance is with *him*, not me. You know what it's like at that age – passions run high. And parents know nothing, obviously.'

'I'm sure deep down she knows you were only trying to protect her,' George said, and she smiled at him gratefully. He was so easy to talk to; she was so glad she'd decided to come here today. 'Just like I'm sure deep down you know you're meant to be helping me dig this vegetable plot over.'

Catherine laughed, despite her anxieties. 'Sorry.' She plunged her spade into the hard ground, standing on it until it sank all the way in. She hoped George was right and that Emily would know in her heart that Catherine had acted out of love. Surely she would?

The sun chose that moment to peer out between two thick cotton wool clouds and Catherine turned her face to the sky, appreciating the feeble warmth it provided. In a few weeks it would be spring, she thought, digging at the soil with a new burst of energy. The days would become longer and lighter, the trees would be in bud, snowdrops and primroses would give way to daffodils and blossom. It had been a long old winter, all in all.

'You know, you're a really nice person, Catherine,' George said, out of the blue.

She glanced up in surprise to see him leaning on his fork, smiling at her, his eyes crinkling at the edges. 'Oh! I am? Thank you,' she said, taken aback.

'I hate imagining your husband treating you in the way that you've talked about,' he said. 'I'm glad you're not with him any more.'

'Me too,' she said, feeling self-conscious.

'And I was thinking,' he went on, 'maybe we could go out some time. Just the two of us.'

Just the two of them . . . Oh my goodness. Was he asking her on a date? Her initial feeling was one of panic. 'Well . . . I . . . Gosh,' she said stupidly. Colour rushed into her face. 'I'm a bit out of practice,' she said, and then blushed even harder. Oh God. That sounded like she was talking about sex. 'With going out, I mean. Going out with men.' As opposed to what? Badgers? 'It's been a while.'

'Well, you don't have to go out with *men,*' he pointed out mildly, 'just me. And only if you want to.' He unearthed a huge bramble root and chucked it behind him. 'We could go for a drink tonight if you fancy it.'

'Tonight?'

'Yeah, if you're not busy.'

Of course she wasn't busy. She was never busy. But going for a drink, with him? Tonight? *I'm not ready to go on a date,* she thought uncertainly. Would she ever be ready for it?

She glanced across at him and he smiled – a proper, warm smile. She smiled back. Well, why not? It was George. He was lovely. And in the next moment, an unfamiliar girlish excitement began spiralling up inside her at the thought of going out with him to a pub somewhere. Talking. Having a drink. Getting to know each other. *It's just like getting back on a horse,* Penny had said. 'Okay,' she blurted out.

'Really? Great,' he said. He grinned at her and her tummy did a strange kind of flip that left her breathless. 'You're on.'

Driving home later, she felt elated by this new development. Who would have thought it? Her and George, going out for a drink together. She'd half-expected him to elbow her and tell her he was only joking, he hadn't meant it like *that,* but the last thing he'd said as she'd kicked the mud off her wellies that afternoon was that he'd see her at eight o'clock in the

Walkley Arms, a pub near the allotment. So it was game on. An actual *date.* Oh-Em-Gee, as her daughter would say.

Would he try and kiss her, she wondered, feeling hysteria bubble up inside her as she turned off the main road into the village. Would this be the start of an actual relationship? Would he want to go to bed with her? Were they going to fall in *love?*

Oh gosh. It was terrifying, frankly. She needed some advice from Penny or – no, not Penny. She'd only advise Catherine to pounce on him in the pub and stick her tongue in his mouth. The Italian class girls, then, Sophie and Anna. What would they say if they were here now?

She could almost hear their voices ringing through her head. *Yay! Go for it, Catherine!*

She indicated left to turn into her road and then almost stalled the engine as she saw the forlorn figure sitting on her front doorstep. After the most atrocious, hurried bit of parking ever, she scrambled from the car. 'Emily!' she cried, rushing over. 'I thought you were back in Liverpool! Are you okay?'

Emily burst into tears as Catherine wrapped her arms around her. 'I'm sorry, Mum,' she sobbed. 'I'm really sorry.'

'Oh, sweetheart.' She held her close, Emily's face cold against hers. 'Come inside, let me make you a cup of tea. How long have you been sitting there?'

'About an hour. I forgot my key and Penny was out.' She

wiped her eyes on her sleeve as Catherine let them in. 'Macca dumped me.'

'What an idiot,' Catherine said staunchly, her heart breaking at the sight of that tear-stained face and puffy cheeks.

'I know you didn't like him, Mum, but I really d-d-did. I loved him.'

'Oh, darling, come here.' Emily had always been one to wear her heart on her sleeve and now her face was twisted with raw pain and misery. Catherine just wanted to wrap her up in her own fierce love and never let anyone hurt her again. She could *kill* Macca, the bloody great oaf. She *would* kill him if she ever saw him again.

'He said . . . He said I was too *ordinary.*' She choked on the word, fresh tears spilling down onto Catherine's jumper.

'Ordinary? Rubbish! You're the most lovely, special, beautiful girl on this planet,' she said. 'And don't you dare let anyone tell you otherwise.' She gave another fierce hug. 'Ordinary indeed. As if! Now come inside this minute and let me sort you out.'

Emily blew her nose and trudged into the house, letting Catherine fuss over her with some hot chocolate and a packet of Jaffa Cakes. 'Thanks, Mum,' she said with a feeble, pink-eyed smile. A last shuddery sob shook her shoulders. 'I'm sorry I just ran off like that yesterday. He was so angry I didn't know what else to do. He said if I didn't go with him he'd leave me there and then.'

Catherine sat down next to her at the table and stroked her cheek. 'I'm sorry I put you in that position,' she said. 'I probably shouldn't have bawled him out like that. It just got to me, seeing the way he was treating you. I didn't like it.'

Emily blew on her hot chocolate. 'He was really nice to me sometimes,' she said defensively, eyes lowered.

'Sometimes isn't enough,' Catherine said. 'People who switch their niceness on and off are not to be trusted. Take it from me.'

There was a small silence as she thought of Mike. They hadn't spoken since that showdown in the pub and she wondered uneasily if he'd kept his word about the money, or if he'd already changed his mind.

'We didn't have that much in common, I suppose,' Emily admitted after a moment. 'I mean, he's really fit, but, you know . . . We never really *talked*, not properly. And he was always getting jealous of other men looking at me.'

'Sounds like he was insecure. One of those people who put you down to make *themselves* feel better. Like . . .' she said, then stopped.

'Like Dad did to you?' Emily prompted.

Catherine folded her hands in her lap. She didn't want to slag off Mike to Emily; he was her dad, her hero. 'Sometimes,' she said quietly.

Emily leaned her head against Catherine's shoulder. 'I actually kind of loved it when you shouted at Macca, you know, Mum.'

There was a lump in Catherine's throat. 'Did you?'

'Yeah. I was like, Go Mum! for sticking up for me.' She nibbled another Jaffa Cake. 'I'm glad you were on my side, not his.'

'I'm always on your side, Em. Always. Don't ever forget that.'

'Thanks, Mum.' They sat there in companionable silence for a few minutes and Catherine felt lightheaded with relief that they were together again. Allies.

'I'm sorry it wasn't a very good weekend,' Emily said after a while, 'but I don't have any lectures until tomorrow afternoon, so I can stay tonight if that's okay. Maybe we could go out somewhere together and have tea.'

'That would be lovely,' Catherine agreed, but then George's smiling face appeared in her mind and she remembered that she already had plans. Her date. 'Ahh,' she said. 'Um . . . I kind of said to someone I'd go out this evening. I'm sure I can rearrange it, though.'

Emily moved away from her – just a fraction but Catherine felt it. 'Who?' she asked. 'Penny?'

'No, not Penny. Just someone I met from the allotment. That's where I was today.'

'Oh.' A new chill entered Emily's voice. 'Is it a man?'

'Yes, but . . .'

'Does Dad know?'

'It's not like that, Em.'

'Isn't it?'

Wasn't it? Catherine hated the coolness that had appeared between them all of a sudden. 'It doesn't matter. I can put him off,' she said quickly.

'I feel a bit weird, you going out with another man.'

'I'm not going *out* with him.'

Emily studied her, a small frown appearing. 'Isn't it kind of soon? I mean, Dad was only here at Christmas. I don't think you should rush into anything, Mum.'

Said the girl who had just thrown her heart at a moron like Macca. 'I'm not rushing, Em. Anyway, me and your dad had already split up by Christmas, remember. He walked out the day you and Matthew left home.'

But Emily didn't seem to be listening. 'Have you kissed him? Have you *slept* with him?'

'Emily! What sort of question is that?'

'Does Matthew know? Has he met him?'

'No! There's nothing *to* know!' Her tiny fledgling relationship, fragile as a dandelion clock, had been blown up into something ugly and sinister within seconds. 'Look, it's not a big deal. I'll see him another time, okay? I'd rather go out with you anyway.'

'Would you?'

Would she? Catherine tried to block out that fluttery, excited feeling that had whipped up inside her as she came home earlier. Emily . . . George . . . Oh, it was unfair that she had to choose between them. Of course her daughter would win every time – especially when she was vulnerable and clingy like now.

'Yes,' she said firmly. 'Of course I would. Let me change out of these muddy jeans and we'll have a lovely girly time together.'

Emily smiled – finally – and it all felt worth it. 'Thanks, Mum,' she said.

Text to: George
From: Catherine
Hi George, v v sorry but can we rearrange drink? Emily (daughter) has turned up, dumped by crap boyf, needs me here. Really sorry. Do you mind? C

Text to: Catherine
From: George
No worries. Hope she is OK. G

Text to: George
From: Catherine
Maybe we can do it some other time instead?

'Mum? I said, are you going to have a pudding?'

'Oh. Er . . . No. I'm full, thanks.' Catherine checked her

phone again as Emily deliberated over the menu. Still no reply.

'Mmm, melting chocolate fondant, that sounds amazing. Sure you're not tempted?'

'No. But you have one. It sounds lovely.'

There was still no reply from George by the time they got home later. Had he gone off the idea already?

Text to: George

From: Catherine

Sorry again re tonight. And thanks 4 the chat earlier anyway. Really helped. See you at Italian 2moro x

Catherine and Emily sat down to watch a rom-com together with a bottle of wine, but Catherine couldn't concentrate. Maybe his phone was out of battery. Maybe he was out of range. But maybe the silence was because he was cross with her for cancelling the date. She had explained though, hadn't she? It wasn't anything personal!

Her phone buzzed with another text and she almost spilled her wine in her haste to read it. But it was from Anna.

Text to: Catherine

From: Anna

Just heard on local news there's been a massive donation to the Children's Hospital fund – like, really massive. Mysterious donor, they said. Don't suppose this has got anything to do with you, has it?! A xx

Catherine gave a small smile. So Mike had actually done it – given away the money, wiped the slate clean. This was really good news. Mind you, it also meant that her phone was still working perfectly well. *Come on, George, talk to me.*

She tried to get into the film but her mind kept drifting elsewhere, wondering what might have happened in a parallel universe where she had put on some perfume and a nice dress and then, knees knocking with nerves, gone to meet him. Now she might never know.

Chapter Thirty-Two

Il spettacolo – The performance

'Well, I'll be buggered.'

'Jim! Language!' Trish tutted as she stacked dirty coffee mugs into the dishwasher.

'I can't buggering well believe it.'

'JIM!'

'It's not April Fool's yet, is it? What the devil . . . ?'

Sophie looked up from her breakfast to see him staring down at a bank statement, his blue eyes boggling in their sockets. 'What is it, Dad?'

Jim passed a hand over his brow and shook his head. 'It must be a mistake,' he said hoarsely, shaking his head. 'Must be. Because how else has ten thousand flipping quid ended up in our bank account?'

'What? Let me see.' Sophie had never seen her mum move so quickly. 'Oh my God, Jim. Look at that. Ten thousand pounds!' Trish sank into a chair as if the shock was too much for her. 'How on earth did that get in there?'

'No idea,' Jim said. 'Funds transfer – that's all it says. The bank will have cocked up, you wait. Someone with fat fingers pressed a wrong number is my guess. I suppose I'd better give them a ring and fess up.' He held the statement up in the air. 'Take a good look at it, girls. Chances are that ten grand will be whisked away again quicker than you can say "spending spree".'

During a lull that morning at the café, Sophie nipped out to the back yard on the pretext of putting the bins out, and phoned Catherine. 'It's gone in,' she said. 'The money. Thank you.'

'Oh good. I'm really glad. Thanks for getting me the account details. I wasn't sure if Mike would actually go through with it. His conscience must have been giving him hell, though.'

'Ten thousand pounds he paid,' Sophie said, with a flicker of glee as she remembered the shocked delight of her parents. 'It was so hard to keep a straight face this morning. My mum and dad think it's some kind of a mistake; they haven't realized that it's actually theirs yet.'

'Well, I hope they enjoy spending it. And I'm sorry to put you in the position of having to keep a secret from them, but . . .'

'It's fine. I understand.' Sophie knew that was the condition Mike had imposed on Catherine, scared that if his cover was blown, it would be the end of his career.

'Thanks. Well, I'm glad it all worked out in the end anyway. Hey, any word from Dan yet?'

'Not a sausage. I'd better go. Thanks again, Cath. See you soon.'

Any word from Dan yet? If only. Sophie had almost given up hope of hearing from him now. There were only so many times you could hit refresh on Facebook and email before you felt like hitting yourself. After her carefully worded reply to him, which had taken the best part of an hour to construct, she had received precisely nothing in return. Why did men *do* that – make you think there was a chance, a future, only to completely ignore you when you responded to them? Hell, it wasn't as if she was asking *him* to send her ten thousand pounds. Ten lines of text would do. Even 'Hi' would be a start.

Had she put him off somehow? She had read and reread her message, trying to decipher it forensically, looking in vain for what she had said that could have frightened him off.

Don't worry about it, she had written, *I'm fine. Good to hear from you.* (Obviously she'd omitted all the bits about stalking him hopelessly around the world, the broken heart that lasted months (years), the fact that she'd never fallen in love again.)

Give me a shout if you're ever over this way, she'd finished breezily. *Love Sophie.* She hadn't said *Ring me* or *Let's meet up!* or *Let's get back together!!!,* even though she was convinced those thoughts must have been practically audible, humming across the Peak District to him in the form of rippling soundwaves.

Maybe it was the 'Love Sophie' that had scared him. But then, he'd written 'Love Dan', hadn't he? He'd said he hoped she wasn't seeing anyone, that he missed her, that he had been miserable without her!

Still. Whatever. She'd been over him for three years, so a brief Facebook exchange was not going to change anything. Besides, she was far too busy to think about him now anyway, what with working all hours in the café, planning her next half-term of Italian classes, and the play to worry about this week as well. She certainly didn't have time to agonize about lines of text on a computer screen. So there.

She would be sorry when the play was over. She'd only been rehearsing with the group for a couple of weeks, but felt as if she'd bonded with them all already. She loved enigmatic, sexy Max whose passion for theatre rubbed off on everybody. She adored Ruby and Gareth, who played the two main characters. They were twenty-somethings like her and great fun. There were a couple of teenagers, Beth and Alys, both shy emo types who hid behind their fringes and too much make-up, but who were awesome in character and really came alive when speaking their lines. The pair of them were hopelessly in love with Jonty, who was twenty, dark and dimpled, with the dirtiest laugh Sophie had ever heard. And the oldies were fab too: Valerie, who made all the costumes on her Singer sewing machine; Patrick, dapper and twinkly with his Brylcreem and shiny suit; Meredith with the elegant silver bun, who did everyone's make-up; and Dickie, who'd once been an extra in *Emmerdale* and name-dropped like there was no tomorrow. As for Brenda Dodds, she was a total pussycat who always brought home-made brownies along to rehearsals. It was a mystery why Geraldine had taken against her.

The play was on for two nights – Thursday and Friday – and according to Max, both were pretty much sold out. The company didn't have their own theatre but had links with a nearby secondary school who were letting them use their stage and facilities for a small fee. It wasn't exactly The Crucible, but hey, you had to start somewhere. And now the costumes and props were all ready, and everyone was pretty much word-perfect. Show-time.

Sophie hadn't really made a big deal of her part in the production, but when she peered out from behind the curtains before the opening performance, her knees buckled in surprise to see her parents sitting expectantly in the second row, and Anna, Catherine, Phoebe, Nita and Roy further back in the audience. Her eyes felt swimmy with emotion suddenly, and she had to take three deep breaths. They'd all come. They'd all bothered to get tickets and sit here in the chalk-smelling hall on a plastic chair, for her sake. When Sophie checked her phone she saw that Geraldine had remembered too, and sent a text. *Knock 'em dead, kid,* it said.

'Two minutes,' Max said just then and a twitter went around everyone backstage. Beth started having palpitations about her hair, Ruby had a wardrobe malfunction that required three of Valerie's safety pins, and Jonty locked himself in the toilet to do some unusual voice exercises that sounded as if he was gargling and being strangled at the same time. Sophie felt dizzy with fright, her throat horribly dry. Oh God. She was actually going to have to walk out onto that stage in front of all those people and speak. And act! Why had she ever thought this was a good idea? Why had she let Geraldine talk her into it?

Max came up behind her then and squeezed her shoulder. 'You'll be great, doll,' he told her. 'As soon as you get out there, the adrenalin will take over and you'll fly through it. No probs.'

'No probs,' she echoed jerkily, her breath feeling tight in her lungs. And then the lights went down through the hall, a hush descended and the curtains opened to reveal Ruby and Gareth on the stage.

'Let's do this,' said Max under his breath.

It was over before she knew it – her feet carrying her to her spot on stage, her lines spoken without pause or error, a hand on the hip, an exasperated face at the audience (that got a chuckle) and then clip-clop, clip-clop, back off stage. It was more than that though: it was the roaring sensation that buzzed through her, almost uncontainably; the surge of pride at the end when the audience clapped them through two curtain calls, and the joy of seeing her parents' beaming faces, Phoebe giving her the thumbs up and her friends all applauding. It was like the rush of a drug, a pure high of happiness and relief and *I-did-it*!

And then she happened to glance back through the audience and saw another familiar face right at the back, his hands high as he clapped, his mouth stretched wide in a smile. It was Dan. As their eyes met and shock ricocheted through her, he put his forefingers between his lips and gave a wolfwhistle.

How did he . . . ? she wondered in a daze, then remembered that she'd posted a link to the play on Facebook. That was how. And now he was here, actually here in the same room as her again. It was all she could do to walk off stage as the curtains closed for the final time.

The cast squealed and hugged each other as they went backstage. 'Fabulous, guys, you were fabulous,' Max cried, slapping each of them on the back as they went past. 'Ruby, you totally nailed that ending. Gareth – magnificent, my friend. The audience loved you all. Well done. Amazeballs!'

Sophie could hardly hear anything anyone was saying. She was rushing hot and cold all over, still stunned by the sight of Dan in the audience. She hadn't just imagined him, had she? No – he really had been there. Clapping. Smiling at her. Wolfwhistling. Actions spoke louder than words, as every drama student knew. And right now, his actions were speaking pretty damn loudly.

'Are you okay, Soph? You look a bit flushed.'

It was Ruby, one hand on her back, her eyes brilliant with energy.

'I . . . Yeah. Fine. You were great by the way.'

'Thanks! So were you. I think Max has got some bubbly in the fridge if you want a glass?'

'Sure, yeah.' She swallowed, aware that she was acting oddly. 'I'm just going to powder my nose and see my friends. Back in a minute.'

They were all there, clustered around the stage door: her Italian class friends, her parents, Dan. Three satellites of people who meant so much to her. She wasn't sure who to greet first.

Anna and Catherine burst forward to hug her, solving that problem. 'Hey! You were ace!' cried Anna.

'The whole play was great,' Catherine enthused.

'Geraldine will be so proud when I tell her,' Roy said, moist-eyed.

'That dark-haired guy was fit, wasn't he?' Nita was saying. 'Is he single, do you know?'

'Well done, darling,' her mum said, coming forward next and kissing her. 'You did so well.'

'You were the best one in it,' Jim said gruffly. 'You *were!*'

'Oh, Dad,' she said fondly. 'I hardly think—'

'Well, I do,' he said. 'You sparkled up there, like a real star.'

'You totally did,' Anna agreed. 'I think a new career beckons, you know.'

Dan, she noticed, was standing back behind everyone else, smiling as he watched her accept all the compliments. God, he was still as handsome as ever, with those melty brown eyes and the dimple in his cheek; his hair was a little shorter than in the Australia surfie days, less boy-band, more grown-up somehow. A black coat was slung over one arm; she'd never seen him in winter clothes, she realized. 'Hi,' she mouthed, feeling breathless to be sharing the same airspace with him again.

His smile broadened. 'Hi,' he mouthed back.

Other people were saying stuff – Roy was introducing everyone to her parents and Phoebe was making some comment or other – but she was deaf to it all. Blind to everyone else. The hall seemed to shrink down and down around her until the world consisted only of her and him.

She stepped forward and so did he. Then they both rushed together at once and practically fell into each other's arms. She was half laughing, half crying, and she could smell his scent (just the same) and was being crushed by his embrace (just the same), and it was, without any doubt, the single best moment she'd had in years.

'Are we going to the pub then, or what?' she heard Jim's voice after a while. 'I want to drink a toast to my talented daughter.'

'And I want to know who this bloke is,' she heard her mum murmur in reply. 'Where's she been keeping *him* all this time, then?'

Sophie separated herself from Dan and stood next to him, beaming at them all. 'Mum, Dad, this is Dan. We were together in Australia a few years ago.'

The men shook hands solemnly and Trish looked all fluttery and excited. 'Hello! How exciting! So – you're Australian, are you?'

'Am I heck. I'm from Manchester,' he said, and everyone laughed.

'And these are some of the people I've been teaching Italian to,' Sophie went on. 'Catherine, Anna, Roy, Phoebe and Nita – this is my mum and dad, Trish and Jim. And Dan.'

Roy was looking Dan up and down, sizing him up. 'Is this the one who . . . ?' he asked.

Sophie coloured. 'Um. Yes. Yes, Roy. That's him.'

Roy leaned forward and shook hands with Dan. A tight handshake by the looks of things. 'I've heard about you,' he said, with a warning edge to his voice. 'And I don't want there to be any messing about, not with our Sophie.'

'Roy, you don't need to—'

'Understand?' Roy asked Dan.

'Absolutely,' Dan said, with a sideways glance at her.

Sophie's head was starting to swim. She still didn't quite know what Dan was even doing here. It was definitely time to go to the pub. 'Come on,' she said. 'I think the whole cast are going to the Queen's Head if you all fancy it?'

'I hope this is okay, me just turning up,' Dan said to Sophie as they left the school hall and went out into the night. 'I was going to reply to you on Facebook but then I thought, well, actually, it might be better face to face. I kind of forgot that you might have other people here as well though.' He lowered his voice. 'I thought that bloke was about to deck me one back there.'

Sophie laughed. 'Roy? He's lovely,' she said. 'Although he did tell me he'd been good at boxing, back when he was in the army. Probably not one to get on the wrong side of.' She kept having to look at Dan to make sure she hadn't just conjured him up from the depths of her imagination. Tall, lean body, rumpled hair, sexy deep voice: yes, it was definitely him. 'It's so weird doing this, walking down the street in England together, I mean,' she said. 'How long are you back for?'

He was like her, she knew: a traveller with a passport full of stamps. So she nearly stumbled on the pavement when he replied, 'I think I'm back for good now.'

'Oh. Seriously?' She hadn't been expecting that.

'Yeah. Don't get me wrong, I've had an amazing time. Great people, great memories, great times – nuclear dysentery in India aside. But it was all so temporary, you know? I just want to unpack now – not just my rucksack, but mentally too. Have a front door and a key again, have an address where people can find me. Make a new go of life here.' He laughed rather self-consciously. 'God, that was a bit pompous. Did any of it make sense?'

'Yeah. It did actually.' They walked for a moment in silence. 'What do you think you'll do now you're back?' she asked. 'Because that's my problem: finding the thing I want to do here.'

'I've got a place at uni for September,' he said as they reached the pub and waited for the others to catch up. 'A PGCE – I'm going to be a music teacher.' He grinned. 'How grown up does that sound?'

'Scarily grown up,' she replied, pushing open the pub door and feeling a tinge of envy. Even Dan knew what he wanted to do with his life. When would she?

Max insisted on buying the whole cast a drink, while Jim, the tightest man in Yorkshire, insisted on getting a round in for

Sophie's friends. 'Not every day you have a windfall, is it?' he said, patting his wallet.

'Take a photo, someone, quick,' Sophie joked. 'This is the first and last time you'll ever see my dad buying drinks without a gun to his head.'

Trish, meanwhile, made sure she had a seat next to Dan when they commandeered two big tables. 'So,' she began, fixing him with a very direct, curious gaze. 'What do you do then, Dan?'

Sophie groaned inwardly. *Are you good enough for our daughter?* was the subtext, loud and clear. But this was Dan, she reminded herself: charming, easy-going, friendly Dan, who had trekked across India with only two pairs of pants and a penknife. If anyone could handle her mother, it was him.

'I'm going to be a music teacher eventually,' he replied. 'My course starts in the autumn. So, in the meantime, I'm working in a music shop in Manchester and teaching a bit of guitar on the side.' He grinned his wide, affable grin, the one that nobody with a pulse could resist. 'So basically I'm going from lazy traveller to penniless student,' he said cheerfully. 'I think my parents will be hanging the flags out the day I actually get a proper job with a pension and all that.'

'Does that sound familiar?' Sophie asked Jim and Trish.

'Of course not,' said Trish loyally, but Jim guffawed. 'Bloody right it does,' he said. 'Although me and your mum have been thinking.'

'Oh God, here we go,' said Sophie, pulling a face.

'Well, it's just, with that money coming out of the blue the other day,' Jim said (and Catherine, overhearing, turned pink), 'we thought we'd like to spend some of it on you. College, or whatever you want to do. We know we mucked up your chances first time around, you see. So if Drama School still appeals . . .'

'Oh, Dad!' She felt choked with emotion. She almost couldn't speak. 'Do you mean it? Seriously?'

'Course we mean it! Your mum doesn't mind downgrading her five-star holiday to camping in the Lake District . . . I'm joking. We're still going to have a bloody great holiday. But we want you to have the freedom to make choices too.'

'And we won't interfere this time,' Trish said. 'That's a promise.'

Dan squeezed her hand. 'There's a good Drama School in Manchester, you know,' he said.

Sophie caught her mum's eye. 'We know,' they said together.

Her new friends were beaming at her. 'Do it!' Anna urged.

'Sounds perfect,' Catherine added.

'We'll all come and see you when you're in the West End,' Jim teased. 'I can see it now, your name up in lights – SOPHIE FROST. Our girl.'

'Stop it, Dad,' said Sophie, but she couldn't help smiling. She'd long since put her acting dreams aside, filed them away under 'Never Going To Happen'. And now she was being offered a second chance – a dazzling, golden ticket of a second chance. *At last,* she thought, *this is what I really, really want to do. What I've always wanted deep down.* 'Cheers everyone,' she said, a lump in her throat as she raised a glass. 'Here's to whatever happens next.'

'Cheers!' they chorused.

Dan had to leave at about ten-thirty in order to get the last train back to Manchester and Sophie was seized by a sudden anxiety that she wouldn't see him again as he made his good-byes. 'Do you have to go now?' she asked, as she went with him to the door. She deliberately kept her hands by her sides so that she wouldn't clutch at his coat sleeves in desperation. 'I mean . . . can we meet up some other time?'

'God, I hope so,' he replied, and hugged her in that lovely crushing grip again. Then they stood apart, smiling at each other, suddenly shy. 'So . . . can I ring you?' he asked. 'Is this okay? Can we . . . start again?'

A mad rush of happiness began starbursting inside her. *Yes. Yes! Are you kidding me? Yes!* 'I'd like that,' she replied.

He kissed her, gently at first, then more passionately, and she swayed against him, giddy with longing. She just wanted to drink him in, to stay like this forever. 'Why don't you come over to mine this weekend?' he said eventually, his voice soft against her ear.

'This weekend?' Her heart leaped.

'I'm renting this flat in the city centre; it's a bit of a shoebox but it's dead handy for everything. We could spend some proper time together.'

Goosebumps broke over her skin even though the pub was toasty warm. Proper time together. Drama School. His face in the audience, his hand in hers. The evening already felt like a greatest hits compilation; there were so many moments which she was going to run and rerun in her head later on.

'I've always loved shoeboxes,' she told him, then kissed him again.

Chapter Thirty-Three

Due notti a Roma – Two nights in Rome

On Friday morning, Anna sat crosslegged with her laptop on her bed, preparing to write what was probably her last ever restaurant review for the *Herald.*

She was working from home as she had to pack and be at the airport for her afternoon flight to Rome, but had promised she'd email her review to Imogen first thing. Signing off her final column would be a relief in some ways: Marla would be off her back, Imogen would have to stop all her heavy-handed stirring, and of course she and Joe would no longer be flung together in such a ridiculous, embarrassing situation. To say it had been a strain was the understatement of the year.

So why didn't she feel happier to be washing her hands of the whole shebang?

For the last review dinner out together, two nights earlier, she and Joe had gone to Maxwell's, a new steak house in town, and had laughed themselves stupid, discussing how she could go out in spectacular style for this final column. Joe had suggested an unfortunate choking incident involving 'Handsome Colleague', a fishbone and a trip to A&E – 'Well, it'll be good copy, won't it?' – but Anna had demurred, fearing a possible lawsuit from Maxwell's, as well as the immediate removal of further freebies. Marla would not thank her for *that.*

'Maybe Handsome *Rival* turns up, proclaiming his undying love for me,' Anna said. 'He and Handsome Colleague come to fisticuffs over the starters, wine is thrown, tears are shed—'

'I'm not sure Handsome Colleague is much of a fighter,' Joe interrupted. 'He's legged it out the back, whimpering and fearful for his life.'

'All right, let's big up the romance then,' Anna said. 'A proposal over the dessert course. *Our eyes locked across the tiramisu . . .*'

'Steady on,' Joe said. 'Handsome Colleague isn't the kind of maniac who rushes into something like that. He hasn't even got his leg over yet, remember.' His eyes glinted wickedly. 'Now there's an idea . . .'

'What, Handsome Colleague gets his leg over with me? Right here in Maxwell's?' She could feel herself blush just at the suggestion. Okay, so he was obviously only joking, but all the same . . .

Joe waved a hand dismissively. 'God, no, he's far too classy for that,' he replied. 'He waits until you're walking home together then finds a convenient bus shelter.'

'Oh, that's just lovely,' Anna said, rolling her eyes. 'I think he'd find himself getting pushed under the next convenient bus then, for being such an unromantic jerk.' She made a squishing noise as she pressed her hands together. 'Flat Handsome Colleague, end of.'

'Only trying to help.'

Yeah, right. She wished he wouldn't. Trying to work out whether or not he was actually flirting was killing her. 'Maybe, rather than passion, we need the opposite,' she said, trying to steer the conversation to safer ground. 'Huge drama: Handsome Colleague tells her he's in love with someone else.'

'As long as it's not their boss. And definitely not Colin. I'm not sure the readers are ready for a gay love triangle.'

'No, I've got it: he's in love with the former restaurant reviewer,' Anna giggled. 'It'll make Marla's day, can you imagine? A columnist showdown.' Oops, she probably shouldn't have said that, she thought in the next moment, remembering how Marla had boasted about Joe making a pass at her. *You know he's tried it on with me before, don't you? Put his hand up my skirt, asked if I'd be his little Christmas cracker.*

'Absolutely not,' Joe said, putting his menu down in horror. 'Don't even joke about it.'

The devil was in Anna now. 'Ahh, too near the knuckle, eh? I heard you two had had a little moment together.' Shit. She must be drinking too quickly. She wished she hadn't said *that,* either. Not only did it make her sound jealous, but now he looked appalled.

'What, she told you, did she?'

He does it to everyone. Didn't you know? He's one of those blokes who's just out for what he can get.

'She said something about you making a move on her . . . Sorry. None of my business. These things happen, right?' She looked down at her menu hastily as he glowered. 'What are you going to order?'

'The lying cow,' he said, annoyed. 'For fuck's sake. It was *her,* trying it on with me, pouncing on me when I came out of the gents' at the Christmas party. I can't believe she told you otherwise. You believe me, don't you?'

'Of course.' She did as well. It was all perfectly clear. Why had Anna wasted a single second taking Marla seriously?

'I'd never . . . Ugh. Did she really say that? I'd *never* make a move on her. I so wouldn't.'

He looked so uncomfortable that Anna began to feel bad. 'Sorry I mentioned her. Really. Consider her banned from the rest of the evening. Now, let's order, shall we? That waiter's going to get a rejection complex if we send him away again.'

*

When she began writing her review, Anna had chosen to ignore all their daft ideas and played it straight, barely mentioning Joe at all. Description of décor – check. Description of food – check. Description of wine list – check. Very informative but deliberately bland.

Forty minutes after receiving it, Imogen promptly sent the document back with one single comment: SEX THIS UP. It was kind of inevitable really. So, with a small sigh, Anna had reopened the file this morning and stared at it until the words became meaningless. How could she describe their last dinner together without copping out? How could she do it justice?

Of course it had been wrong to leave out Joe from her earlier attempt. The evening *was* Joe – their easy banter, their stupid jokes, the way they'd laughed and talked. The way, every now and then, there had been a look between them, an electrifying, intense sort of look. *Do you feel this too?* she had wanted to ask. *I'm not imagining this, am I? Because it feels so damn good, being with you.*

She stared at her laptop then deleted the last effort entirely. Sod it, she thought eventually. Maybe it was seeing Sophie and her ex, Dan, snogging like that after the play last night and feeling a burn of envy. Sometimes you just had to follow your heart, even though it was terrifying as hell. It was a risk she had to take.

She took a deep breath and started typing, tentatively at first, but then with more conviction, her fingers flying over the keyboard. Her coffee cooled beside her as the words poured out faster and faster. Then she read the whole review through, her heart thumping. There it was in black and white: the most honest thing she'd ever written. Could she seriously send this to be published?

The front door buzzer went just then. 'It's the postman,' she heard when she answered the intercom. 'I've got a letter here, needs signing for.'

'Thanks,' she said, and pressed 'Send' on the email before she could change her mind. Let's see what Imogen makes of *that*, she thought, hurrying down to open the door.

She signed for her letter and had a little chat with the postman, then came back upstairs and made herself a strong coffee. Her phone pinged with an email from Imogen. PERFECT, was all it said.

Anna gulped. Too late to change her mind now. She ripped open the envelope distractedly, hoping she hadn't just made an enormous mistake. Then she started reading the letter and everything else was forgotten.

Dear Anna,

Thank you for your letter. It came as quite a shock to me, but I do remember Tracey, and working at Gino's so you've definitely got the right man. I'm just sorry I haven't been part of your life for the last thirty-two years. My wife and I – Dina, she's called – were not able to have children, and this has been a great sadness to us. Please believe me when I say I am delighted to know I am a father after all. I would love to meet you if that is possible?

You asked about my life after I left Yorkshire. I married Dina and we rented a little flat off the Clerkenwell Road in London. We have been very happy there, working at what used to be my grandparents' restaurant, called Pappa's. I am the head chef and Dina still works at front of house. Pappa's is in an area called 'Little Italy' (my mother is Italian) and the customers and staff have become like our family over the years.

Thank you for sending the clippings of your work. I am so pleased that my daughter is a food writer! I tried your zabaglione recipe and even my mother – your 'nonna'! – said it was the best she had ever tasted. I would love to cook for you one day. Please come and visit us. Everyone is so excited to hear about the new addition to the family.

I am enclosing a photo of Dina and I, and another of my parents. We all hope we can meet you very soon.

With much love,

Your father, Antonio

Tears brimmed in Anna's eyes as she reached the end of the letter. Happy tears. Tears of delight and wonder. She read the whole thing through again, and then a third time. Wait until she told Joe about *this*!

Eight hours later, she and Joe were sitting in a trattoria in Piazza di Spagna, at the base of the Spanish Steps. In Rome!

The sky was a velvety black above them but the square still bustled with tourists climbing the famous Scalinata (the widest staircase in Europe, according to Joe's guidebook), admiring the beautifully lit bell towers of the church at the top, and taking photographs of each other around the fountain below. Inside her, a deep pride stirred. This *was* her country; hadn't she known all along?

She had hugged the secret to herself for the rest of the day, not wanting to tell Joe her news in such boring surroundings as the airport or the bus into the city centre. A brilliant story like hers deserved the best kind of setting for its telling. She waited until they were sitting in the restaurant with a glass of prosecco each, then told him everything.

Joe's mouth fell open. 'So he *is* Italian after all,' he laughed. 'Wow, Anna. You were right the whole time!'

'I can't quite believe it,' Anna admitted. 'His family are Italian, he's a chef at their Italian restaurant . . . I mean, how perfect can you get?'

'That's amazing,' Joe said. 'Totally cool. And your mum had no idea?'

'As far as she was concerned, his name was Tony Sandbrookes – his dad's English, you see. Except really he was – is – Antonio, with an Italian mum and grandparents. Which, in my book, is even better than having a dad actually living in Italy, who I probably wouldn't get to see all that often, and who might not even understand English.' She hugged herself, beaming. 'Now I can hop on a train to London whenever I want to see him. Just like that!'

'Well, cheers to you,' Joe said, refilling their glasses. 'What great news, Anna. Here's to family, and new beginnings – and being in Italy, land of your father.' They clinked their glasses and he grinned. 'I'm still in shock that we're actually here at all, you know.'

'Me too. I kept expecting Imogen to pop up at the airport and haul us back to the office.' Anna breathed in the scents of tomato, oregano and wine, enjoying the sound of Italian voices all around her. 'This is all down to you. Thank you to the power of a billion for having the nous to even suggest this to her.'

'Well, thanks to you for writing such fantastic restaurant reviews that she actually went along with it,' he replied.

'What a team,' she said, savouring the creamy bubbles of the prosecco as it fizzed on her tongue.

'Go us,' he agreed and they smiled at each other. He really was extremely handsome, she thought to herself. What a stroke of luck, her getting the restaurant gig in the first place, and him coming along like that. Never in her wildest dreams could she have imagined that they'd end up here together.

'Talking of London,' he said just then, looking rather awkward, and she jerked out of her reverie. London? 'I was going to tell you – I'm going down there myself in a couple of weeks. I've got an interview for a job.'

She spluttered on her drink in shock. 'What, you? In London?'

'Yeah. They're looking for a new sports writer at the *Guardian*. I just chucked them a CV, not really holding out much hope, but they've asked me to come in.'

She felt as if she'd had a bucket of cold water tipped over her. 'Wow. So . . . you'd move down there?'

'Well, yeah, if I get it. I reckon it would be a bit of a bastard commute from Sheffield.'

Her good mood had evaporated just like that, replaced by an ache of loss. The office would be rubbish without him. Her *life* would be rubbish without him, she realized. 'I'd really miss you,' she blurted out.

He pulled a face. 'I haven't gone yet! I might not even get the job. It just seemed like a good opportunity. The next step up.'

'Absolutely,' she said, trying to sound jovial. 'Well, best of luck.' She managed a faint smile but couldn't help feeling gutted at the thought of him going. Then she remembered her last restaurant review, due to be published tomorrow, and cringed. Oh no. Why on earth had she decided to make it so personal, so candid? It crossed her mind to dash to the loo and make an urgent call to Imogen, begging her to pull the piece, offering her anything: money, the rest of her writing career, her soul . . . but it was already too late. The newspaper would be printing right now.

'You'll have to pop in and see my dad while you're down there. Check out Pappa's,' she said brightly as the waiter put some bruschetta and black olives between them. '*Grazie.*'

'Definitely,' he said, popping an olive into his mouth. 'How about you anyway, what are your career plans? Surely we're due a cookery book soon, or your own TV series. You could be the next Nigella, licking wooden spoons in your kitchen and giving smouldering looks to camera.'

'I don't think so,' she replied, rolling her eyes.

'The brilliant thing about writing is you can do it anywhere,' he reminded her. 'You've got solid reporting experience as well as the cookery and restaurant reviewing. And you're good. You're really good, Anna. What's to stop you writing for magazines now, or a bigger newspaper? What's to stop you taking the leap too?'

She realized she'd eaten an entire piece of bruschetta without even tasting it, breaking the first rule of food writing in three bites. She couldn't look him in the eye. He might not think she was all that good a journalist any more when he read her Maxwell's review the next day, let's face it.

'I don't know,' she said warily. 'Inertia, I guess. Fear of the unknown.' She swallowed. 'Joe, there's something I should tell you. About tomorrow's paper.'

'Hmm?' A large group of Welsh rugby fans chose that moment to walk past the restaurant window, draped in red-dragon flags, with two of them wearing huge daffodil heads around their faces. Joe was distracted watching them, then turned back to her. 'What were you saying?'

She drained her prosecco in a single glug. Sod it. He'd find out for himself soon enough. She wouldn't ruin the evening. 'Never mind,' she said. 'Shall we order another bottle?'

The newspaper had paid for them to stay in a basic hotel near the Spanish Steps – two rooms, obviously – and Anna felt incredibly drunk as they trailed back there after dinner. She hadn't managed to bring up the subject of her review again, but in her mind it had overshadowed the rest of the evening. What had she *done*? For all their talk of inertia and finding it difficult to leave their current jobs, the idea of handing in her notice on Monday morning and never coming back was becoming more appealing by the minute. The first Handsome Colleague review had been bad enough. How would she ever live this one down?

'Well,' he said, when they got back to the hotel and up to their floor. 'I know you've got an early start in the morning . . .'

'Yeah, I'd better call it a night,' she said quickly before he did.

'Oh,' he said. 'Can't tempt you with a nightcap?'

Tempt her? If only he knew. But she was already sloshed and if she had any more to drink, she would probably make a gigantic fool of herself. 'Better not,' she said, slotting her key-card into the lock of her door and jiggling it until a green light appeared. 'Night then,' she said. 'Hope it goes well tomorrow.' Hope you don't get an avalanche of texts from your mates taking the piss out of you because of me. She sighed. Oh bollocks. She couldn't just say *nothing.* 'Listen, Joe. I'd better warn you,' she blurted out. 'The review tomorrow . . . I'm sorry, all right? I hope it doesn't piss you off.'

His eyes were liquid black in the dim light of the corridor; it was hard to read his expression. 'Why, what have you said?'

She looked away. 'You'll see. But I'm sorry, okay? I hope that . . . we're still cool.'

'God. What on earth have you . . . ? Wait, Anna, you can't just—'

She pushed her bedroom door open and scuttled inside, letting it shut behind her. Then she stood there in the darkness, heart pounding, wishing she hadn't been so impulsive earlier. *Perfect!*, Imogen had said – and it had seemed perfect at the time. Only now . . .

Joe was knocking at the door. 'Anna! Let me in.'

It was excruciating. What should she do? She shut her eyes and willed him to go away. What a mess she'd made of everything! 'I'll see you tomorrow,' she said eventually. *Please go now. Just go.*

There was a pause. 'Okay,' he said uncertainly. 'Listen, don't worry about it. I'm sure whatever you've said is fine.'

Wanna bet? she thought miserably. She sat down on the saggy single bed that gave a little sigh of escaping air. Oh well. At least she'd warned him. What was done was done. And tomorrow was another day . . .

Restaurant Round-Up: Maxwell's Steak House

By Anna Morley

On paper, Maxwell's looks like a smart new addition to the Leopold Square set; a sleek, elegant restaurant that punches above its weight with a range of prime dry-aged steaks and seafood, a decent wine list and cocktail menu, and classy, upmarket décor. Handsome Colleague and I scrubbed up accordingly, reckoning we might just be in for a treat.

But here's where I need to make a confession. This is my last review for the Herald *and I wanted to go out with a bang. And so, as we sat nibbling our starters (mine: a delicious crab and avocado salad; his: two gorgeously crispy goats' cheese medallions with baby spinach), we began plotting together, both suggesting ways to make this a truly memorable piece of writing. We joked about inventing a love rival, a dramatic hospital dash due to an errant fishbone (note to the lawyers: this did not happen), even some spontaneous passion between us. From the comments I've received after previous reviews, I know that readers of the* Herald *do love a bit of intrigue across a restaurant table, after all.*

We moved on to our main courses, still discussing how to angle the review. I went for a 10 oz rib-eye super-marbled steak with gratin dauphinoise and a side salad (amazing), whereas Handsome

Colleague professed to be starving and ordered the 16 oz Porterhouse steak with the truffle Parmesan fries (he devoured the lot). And then it struck me. Why was I trying to trump up some silly story to please you, my readers, when I was in denial about the best story of all? Why didn't I just come out and be honest with myself, and everyone else: I was (still am) in love with Handsome Colleague.

There. I've said it. Maybe you'd guessed it from the start, but believe me, I hadn't. Over the last four weeks, as we've dined out together around the city, we have talked and laughed and had so much fun, I couldn't believe I was getting paid to do it. Reader – I'm nuts about him. The only trouble is, I've no idea if he feels the same way.

Anyway. Back to the restaurant. The food was fantastic – I couldn't fault a thing. The staff were friendly and helpful, the ambience was warm and buzzy, and in short, this is a great place to come either for a romantic meal for two, or with a group of friends. Thank you, Maxwell's, for an excellent night out – and for helping me realize what was under my nose all along.

When Anna's alarm sounded the next morning she felt fuzzy and disoriented for a moment, until the fragments of the day before rattled into her head with dizzying speed. Her dad's letter. The flight to Rome. Dinner with Joe. Her restaurant review . . .

Shit. Suddenly she was wide awake, throwing off the baggy T-shirt she'd slept in and leaping into the drizzly shower. *Her restaurant review.* She had to get out of here and off to her course before Joe had a chance to see it.

Five minutes later, she was dragging a comb through her wet hair and throwing on her clothes, then she grabbed her handbag and headed downstairs. The cookery course began with a trip around a food market, Trionfale, to buy ingredients with Stefano, their chef, before returning to Stefano's kitchen near the gardens of the Vatican City to cook a feast together. She'd ordered a taxi to take her to the market but had fifteen minutes to grab some breakfast before then. Luckily for her, Joe had a more leisurely start as the match didn't start until two-thirty that afternoon. He'd still be in bed, blissfully unaware of what she'd done.

The hotel restaurant was small and rather dingy but smelled reassuringly of coffee and toast. After loading up her tray with breakfast, she sat at an empty table and took her first sip of coffee. Yum. Even hotel coffee from a machine tasted better in Italy.

She unfolded the print-out of her itinerary and read it for the hundredth time. It was going to be a great day, cooking with a real Italian chef, learning from a master. Hopefully it would be so interesting and enjoyable she wouldn't have time to think about Joe the whole day. As for tonight . . . Well, tonight she'd find out if Joe was still talking to her. She'd have to worry about that later.

'Mind if I join you?'

She almost jumped out of her skin at the voice, then Joe sat down opposite her, his hair still wet from the shower.

'Oh,' she gulped. 'I wasn't expecting to see you this morning.'

'I saw the review,' he said without preamble. 'Looked it up online last night. Talk about leaving a guy wondering.'

'Oh God.' She buried her face in her hands. This was exactly what she'd hoped to avoid. Her and her big gob! 'I'm sorry, Joe. I don't know what came over me. You must think I'm such a—'

'Did you mean it? Or did Imogen put you up to it?'

Her eyes were still covered; she couldn't bring herself to look at him. But he'd handed her an escape route if she wanted it. She could say yes, Imogen put me up to it, she told me what to write . . .

She swallowed. No. That would be a lie. Slowly she peeled her hands away and looked at him. Then she took a deep breath and told him the truth. 'I meant it,' she said, her voice shaking. 'And I know you've only just split up with Julia and you're probably not interested and—'

'Thank God for that,' he said and took hold of her hands across the table. 'Because I feel the same way about you.'

Her breath caught in her throat. 'You . . . You do?'

'Isn't it obvious? Of course I do. Have done for ages. I think you're gorgeous and funny and clever . . .'

She laughed in delight. The world was spinning. 'Really?'

'Definitely. Why do you think me and Julia split up? I knew that I didn't feel the same way about her.'

They beamed at each other for a giddy, breathless moment. Her heart boomed. 'Does that mean . . . we can kiss each other?' she asked recklessly.

'When in Rome . . .' he said. 'You bet.'

Chapter Thirty-Four

Qual è il tuo numero di telefono? – What is your telephone number?

George seemed to have vanished from Sheffield, much to Catherine's dismay. He hadn't appeared at the Italian class on the Tuesday after their non-date. He hadn't made it to Sophie's play two days later, even though Anna had bought him a ticket. And then when Catherine went along to the Fox Hill estate on Sunday to help with the new community garden, he wasn't there either. 'George?' Cal repeated when she asked about him. 'Haven't seen him all week. Must have a lot of work on or something.'

Now it was Tuesday evening again and time for Italian. She found she was holding her breath as she walked into the classroom – only to exhale in disappointment when he wasn't there. She wished now that she'd phoned him rather than texted the week before. You could misread a text so easily, couldn't you? If she'd just spoken to him, he would have heard the regret in her voice. Oh, why did it all have to be so difficult?

Phoebe, Nita, Sophie and Roy were clustered around Anna, she noticed in the next moment, and Catherine remembered that her friend had just come back from Rome. Oh, and of course – she'd written that amazing review in the *Herald*, where she'd poured her heart out about Joe! 'Anna!' she exclaimed, hurrying over to join them. 'How was Rome? Did you have a good time?'

Anna looked radiant, there was no other word to describe it. 'The best,' she replied, her face shining with happiness. 'I've got so much to tell you all, please say we can go to the pub after this lesson?'

'Definitely,' Catherine and Sophie chorused.

'We'll *all* go,' Nita said, glancing pointedly at Freddie, who'd just arrived in the classroom. 'I can't wait to hear all about it.'

Later, at their usual tables in The Bitter End, everyone – even Freddie – listened, rapt, as Anna described her Italian weekend to them: the fantastic-sounding cookery course on Saturday and the few hours' sight-seeing she and Joe had squeezed in before their plane home on Sunday. '*And* I managed to speak loads of Italian too,' she said proudly.

'And what about you and Handsome Colleague?' Catherine asked. 'Come on, don't keep us in suspense!'

'God, yes,' Sophie said, agog. 'I read your review on Saturday – whoa. It totally gave me goosebumps.'

'Me too!' Phoebe cried, clutching her chest dramatically. 'So romantic. What did he *say*?'

Anna beamed. 'He said he feels the same way. And so he's Handsome Boyfriend now, not just Colleague.'

'Whoop!' squealed Nita. 'God, it's all happening for us ladies, isn't it? First Sophie and *her* hunky man. Now you, Anna. Who's going to be next?' She batted her eyelashes. 'Surely *moi*?'

'Well, I don't think it'll be me,' Catherine said with a little laugh.

'No?' Anna looked at her quizzically. 'I thought maybe . . .'

'No,' Catherine said, her heart thumping. She saw Anna and Sophie exchange looks and prayed fervently that they weren't about to mention George's name. Not out loud, to the rest of the class. The last thing she wanted was for anyone to get the wrong idea or start gossiping about her. *Oh dear. Did she have a bit of a thing for him, then?*

'I had a text from George earlier, saying he wouldn't be here tonight,' Sophie said quietly, as Phoebe started telling the others a funny story about one of her customers. 'Apparently his wife's been involved in an accident and is in hospital. He's gone down to see her.'

'I didn't know he was married,' Anna said.

'He's not any more,' Catherine said, but she felt as if her heart was being clenched in an iron grip. George dropping everything and rushing down south to be at the bedside of his ex . . . What did that mean? 'Did he say anything else?'

'No, just that. Sounds pretty serious.' Sophie paused, eyeing her over her wine glass. 'Are you okay, Cath? Did something happen between you two?'

'Not really. He asked me out for a drink the other week—'

'I knew it!' cried Anna.

'But I said no. Or rather, I said yes, but then had to cancel. My daughter was . . . Well, she needed me.' She bit her lip. 'I haven't heard anything from him since then and thought maybe he was being off with me. Sounds like he's got other things to worry about right now, though.'

'I reckon. Well, hopefully . . .' But Sophie didn't get very far with her sentence because Anna was suddenly nudging them both and indicating that something far more interesting was occurring on the other side of the table.

'My phone number?' Nita was saying.

Freddie coloured slightly as he realized that everyone else appeared to be listening in, but ploughed on. 'I was thinking maybe we could go out one night,' he asked her. 'Practise our Italian in an Italian restaurant somewhere?'

There was a flash of triumph on Nita's face but it vanished almost immediately. 'Hold on a minute,' she replied. 'I'm not sure I want to be just another notch on your bedpost.'

'My bedpost? What?' he asked, puzzled.

'I've heard about all your conquests, Freddie. I'm not stupid, you know!' Nita said witheringly.

'Conquests?' Freddie echoed. 'What do you mean?'

Sophie gave a little cough. 'Well, I mentioned to Nita that I saw you with a dark-haired girl in the Gladstone just before Christmas,' she confessed.

'And I saw you hugging a gorgeous older woman in town one day,' Catherine said, feeling like the biggest gossip ever.

'And I saw you with a bloke in the Porter Brook last month,' Anna added. 'Sorry, mate.'

Freddie's jaw dropped lower and lower with every revelation. 'Hold on,' he said. 'The dark-haired girl in the Gladstone – that must have been Maria. My ex-girlfriend,' he added to Nita. 'Her family are Italian, and that's why I started the course, because we were meant to be going to a big wedding in Tuscany in June and I wanted to learn a few phrases.'

'Aww, that's nice, Freddie,' Phoebe said sympathetically, earning herself a glare from her sister.

'Only we split up two weeks later,' Freddie admitted. 'So I'm not with her any more.'

'What about this older woman then?' Nita asked, lips pursed. 'And this bloke Anna saw you with?' She wasn't letting him off the hook that easily.

Freddie looked flummoxed. 'Well, I'm not gay,' he said, 'so

the bloke must have been a mate of mine.' His forehead creased as he thought. 'The Porter Brook, did you say? A couple of weeks ago? It might have been my mate Lee. He'd just lost his job and was in bits. We had a bit of a manly hug, but that was it. I didn't start snogging him or owt.'

'Sorry,' said Anna, shame-facedly. 'I totally jumped to the wrong conclusion.'

'As for the older woman . . .' Freddie looked blank. Then his face cleared. 'Ahh. Was she wearing a long blue coat, by any chance? Silvery blonde hair, maybe swept up in one of those bun things?'

'A chignon,' Phoebe said helpfully. 'Very elegant.'

'Yes, I think so,' Catherine said.

Freddie nodded. 'That's my mum,' he said. 'And I definitely didn't snog *her* either.'

Catherine blushed. 'Oh sorry, Freddie,' she said apologetically, 'you must think we're a right nosey lot.'

'It's only because you're so gorgeous,' Anna told him. 'We couldn't help noticing you, that's all.'

'Well, I'm not going out with Maria any more, or my mate Lee, or my mum,' Freddie said, his cheeks turning pink. 'So, Nita, let me try again. Would you like to come out for dinner with me one night?'

'For the love of God, say yes,' Roy begged. 'The poor lad. Put him out of his misery, Nita!'

Nita beamed. 'Yes,' she said with a grin. 'I'd bloody love

to!' She smirked at her sister. 'I *told* you!' she said before leaning over the table and giving Freddie a great big kiss.

Phoebe cheered, and Sophie, Anna and Catherine all clapped. Roy banged Freddie on the back. 'No wonder you've never come out to the pub with us before,' he said with a laugh. 'Bloody lions' den, this, isn't it? Let me buy you a drink, son. Let me buy you *all* a drink. Geraldine's going to love this!'

Text to: George
From: Catherine
So sorry to hear about your wife. Is she ok? Are you? Ring me if you need to chat. C

Text to: Catherine
From: George
Thanks. She came off her bike, hit by a car. Bad head injury, internal bleeding, broken bones. Has been in intensive care all week. ☹

Text to: George
From: Catherine
Oh God, how awful. So so sorry. Hope you are hanging in there. Am here if you need to talk. x

But he didn't ring. He didn't even reply. So that, thought Catherine sadly, was that.

Chapter Thirty-Five

Due settimane dopo – Two weeks later

Anna walked past the cascading waterfalls and fountains of Sheaf Square, her overnight bag on one shoulder as she approached Sheffield station. Next stop, London, she thought, and a thrill rippled through her. All that searching she'd done, all that wondering and imagining . . . it was coming to an end today. After nearly thirty-three years in the world, she was at last going to meet her father.

They had spoken on the phone a few days ago and a weight had lifted from her; a weight she hadn't even realized she'd been carrying until it was gone. He was real. She had talked to him. He had a London accent and a husky chuckle and said he couldn't wait to meet her.

'Me too,' she managed to say, unexpected tears pricking her eyes. 'Oh, me too.'

'I hope it's okay, but everyone's very excited about you coming down. My wife, my mother, all the relatives want to see you. If it's too much, I can hold them at bay, so just say if you'd rather not . . .'

'I'd love to meet them,' she said, happiness bubbling inside her at the thought of this big Italian family waiting for her. 'The more the merrier.'

She had spent the night before baking a cake for him – well, for all of them, really. It had taken her a while to choose the right recipe, but she'd settled on a layer cake, Dolce alla Napoletana, with pastry cream and flaked almonds. She hoped they would approve of it, and her too, more importantly.

Her phone bleeped in her bag suddenly and she stopped to read the text. *Hope it goes well today, love. Thinking about you. Mum xx*

Anna was grateful that her mum was taking this new relationship with her dad so well. Tracey had become quite emotional when she'd at last revealed the truth. Never usually one to wear her heart on her sleeve, Tracey had burst into sobs, berating herself for not trying harder to find him, admitting how difficult it had been as a single mother, apologizing if she'd let Anna down in any way.

'Oh, Mum,' Anna said, choked up herself, her head whirling with all these confessions. 'You haven't let me down. I've never thought that for a minute!'

Tracey was still in full flow though. 'And I know I've been hard on you sometimes, but I just didn't want you to . . .' Her words were drowned out in a new gale of sobs. 'I didn't want you to make the mistakes I did. Not that *you* were ever a mistake . . .'

'Honestly, Mum, you don't have to say this.'

'You were – are – the best thing that's ever happened to me. And I mean that. I might not have said it enough . . .'

'Mum, it's fine.'

'But I hope you know I mean it.'

They held each other for a few minutes until Tracey gave a spluttery sort of laugh and wiped her eyes. 'Sorry about that. I don't know where it all came from.'

Anna gave her a last squeeze then let go, just as Lambert, the enormously overweight ginger moggy, strutted into the room, demanding attention with a loud meow. Both women laughed and the conversation turned to more mundane things: work, and Anna's nan, and the weather forecast for the weekend (brightening up, according to Tracey), but Anna felt there was a new understanding between them, a new depth of closeness. No more secrets keeping them apart. It was all good.

Another text had come through. *PS Take a photo of him for me, will you? He was a right looker back in the day.*

Anna laughed as she stuffed her phone back in her bag and went on towards the station, waving as she saw Joe waiting for her outside.

'Whoa, get you,' she teased. 'Savile Row?'

'Yeah, right,' he scoffed, glancing down at his suit. 'Marks and Spencer's more like.' He leaned in to kiss her. 'You all right?'

She kissed him back, feeling the usual swooping sensation inside that came whenever she was with him. 'Raring to go. How about you? Practised all your difficult interview questions? Where do you see yourself in five years and all that bollocks?'

He arched an eyebrow. 'Sitting in the boss's chair, running the show, of course,' he said. 'Come on. We've got ten minutes before the train. Let's grab a coffee and find our seats.'

She grinned at him and they went into the station together, her own question running through her head. So where did she see *herself* in five years? Well, that was impossible to answer. Right now, she felt as if anything could happen.

The simple answer was just two words though: with Joe. As long as she was with him, she knew she'd be happy.

Epilogue

Io ricordo – I remember

The Italian sky was a bright, cloudless blue and the scent of the hot pink bougainvilleas around Lucca's poolside bar mingled intoxicatingly with the tang of coconut sun oil and cigarette smoke. Catherine was twenty years old, with a well-stamped inter-rail ticket, a red dress and the best tan of her life. The air had shimmered with heat and a million possibilities. Anything might happen.

And then there he *was, Mike, pulling himself out of the pool, water streaming down his muscular arms: he was tall and athletic, with golden skin and a crooked smile. As he straightened up, she couldn't help noticing the way his swimming shorts just revealed the tops of his hip bones and she shivered with sudden desire.*

He walked over, beads of water still clinging to his body, his eyes never leaving hers. 'Ciao, bella,' *he said, his voice low and husky.*

She turned hot all over. Her breath caught in her throat. It felt as if this was the moment she'd been waiting for. She raised an eyebrow flirtatiously and smiled back at him. 'Ciao,' *she said.*

What a summer that had been. Catherine and her friend Zoe had gone backpacking together during the university holidays and ended up chambermaiding in a lively hotel in Lido di Jesolo on the Venetian Riviera. One day after their shift, she'd come down alone to the pool and there he'd been. *Ciao, bella,* he'd said in his best Italian accent. She'd fancied the pants off him from the word go.

He was there for ten days with a group of mates, and the two of them had a good time together, dancing at the resort disco, sinking lurid cocktails, kissing passionately as the sun went down . . . and the rest. Neither of them had thought it was anything other than a holiday fling: two young things swayed by the heat of the Mediterranean sun and their own dizzying lust. The pregnancy test proved otherwise, though.

Funny how life turned out, wasn't it? Sometimes you seemed to complete a full circle. Because now, almost twenty years later, Catherine was back in Venice, a short boat ride away from where it had all started.

'*Una spremuta, per favore. Grazie,*' she said to the waitress who came to take her order. It was a glorious sunny April day and she had arranged to meet the others in a café overlooking the Grand Canal. From here you could see the watertaxis and gondolas, the slow-moving crush of tourists, cameras flashing as they attempted to capture small slices of the city's magnificence.

'*Uno momento,*' the waitress replied with a smile.

A fortnight earlier, term had finished at Hurst College and the ten-week Italian course had come to an end. All of the class – well, almost all – had gone out for an Italian meal together afterwards to celebrate and say goodbye. And then, the very next day, on a whim, she'd booked return flights to Venice and an apartment a stone's throw from the Frari Church. Well, why ever not? You could do these things when you were footloose and fancy free, after all.

Venice was stunning, every bit as beautiful as she remembered. More so, in fact, because as a twenty-year-old she hadn't appreciated the sheer majesty of the Rialto Bridge, St Mark's Square, the Palazzo Ducale and, oh, all of it. She'd forgotten, too, how one stumbled upon astonishing piazzas and ancient churches around every corner, all the bright red geraniums that bloomed on windowledges, the skinny stray cats slinking around dusty alleyways, strings of chilli peppers and bowls of fat lemons, Murano glass twinkling in every shop window . . .

Oh yes. Well, she appreciated it now. Every last ravishing bit of it.

Her juice arrived and she thanked the black-clad waitress and sipped it, enjoying the warm spring sunshine on her face. She still couldn't quite believe she was back here, just a few miles from the spot where her life had swerved off course so dramatically nearly twenty years earlier. Well, it was back on track now at least, that was for sure. Full steam ahead.

The last Italian lesson had felt quite sad, as if something really significant was drawing to a close. Over the ten weeks of the course, the class had become more than just a learning experience for her. Every single member of the group had given her something precious in their own way: friendship and new confidence in herself, not to mention the best haircut ever. She planned to keep in touch with all of them.

Phoebe had been promoted recently and Catherine was booked in for another cut with her soon. Freddie and Nita were an item, and already planning a weekend away in Milan. Geraldine had been allowed home again, on condition that she stayed in bed. She was hoping to be up and about on crutches within a few weeks, and she and Roy were still going ahead with their Italian holiday of a lifetime in September.

Anna had recently met her dad and nonna, and received a rapturous Little Italy welcome, by the sound of things. She and Joe were still very much together and Anna positively glowed with happiness whenever she talked about him. Over their class meal out, she had broken the news that Joe had been offered a job in London and had accepted it – and that she had decided to move down with him. She was going to continue her cookery column on a freelance basis while looking for work in the capital. 'And my dad says there's always a job for me at Pappa's if I get stuck,' she said with a grin.

Catherine was going to miss her but knew that this was the right thing for her friend. 'I hope you'll come back and visit us loads,' she said when they hugged goodbye at the end.

'Of course I will,' Anna said. 'I'll be back all the time to get my Yorkshire fix, you wait.'

Sophie, too, was making big plans for her future. Now that she'd discovered what she wanted to do with her life, she wasted no time in auditioning for the Drama School in Manchester and was offered a place. This time around, nobody intercepted the offer and she accepted it happily. Before term started in September, she and Dan were saving up to go inter-railing around Europe together as a last blast of freedom. Catherine was glad that Mike's guilt money was being put towards such brilliant purposes, and no longer sitting like a bad smell in his own account.

As for George, well, he had never made it back to the class, sadly. She guessed his head was all over the place. But even though nothing had quite happened between them, becoming his friend had been a wonderful, rewarding thing in its own right, she realized. She carried a packet of wildflower seeds with her at all times now, sprinkling them between her fingers whenever she walked along a grotty street or neglected patch of wasteland, just in case one seed was to find its way into a crevice and bloom there. Like George and his guerrilla friends, she couldn't help seeing the city as one big garden, just waiting to be filled with flowers and fruit. It was astonishing how quickly an unloved place – or even a person – could be transformed.

A voice interrupted her just then. Two voices. 'Hey, Mum!'

'*Ciao!*'

They were back, Matthew and Emily, sliding into seats opposite her at the table, both in sunglasses and T-shirts, their arms already turning brown from the sun.

'Hi,' she said, happily. Look at them both, so gorgeous and confident. What more could a mother wish for? 'Find anything nice while you were shopping?'

'I bought this sick carnival mask,' Emily said, pulling it out of a carrier bag and holding it up against her face. The mask was ghostly white with gold and peacock blue swirls around the eyes and cheeks. 'Awesome, isn't it? I'm totally going to wear it to the uni masked ball in June.'

'Lovely,' said Catherine, smiling. Emily had a new boyfriend these days, who was a marked improvement on Macca, she was pleased to say.

'And we both chipped in to buy you this, Mum,' said Matthew, passing her a small bag. 'To say thanks. It's so cool being here.'

Catherine couldn't help remembering the non-presents at Christmas, and felt as if her heart was expanding as she pulled out a small, pink tissue-wrapped parcel. 'Oh, guys, thank you,' she said, opening it to find a blue Murano glass heart on a delicate silver chain. 'It's beautiful,' she said, fastening it around her neck. 'Really beautiful. Thank you.'

'Well, thank *you* for bringing us,' Emily said affectionately, squeezing her arm. 'I love Venice. It's, like, the coolest place ever!'

'I agree,' Catherine said. 'And it seems only right that you two should come here. After all, it's where you both started off your lives.'

'Where we both . . . ? Oh.' Matthew looked grossed out. 'Right.'

'You mean, you and Dad . . . ? Here?' asked Emily.

'Just a few miles away,' Catherine replied. 'And we were only a bit older than you two are now. That's a weird thought, isn't it?'

'It's a bloody terrifying thought,' Emily said with a shudder. 'Contraception all the way for me, thank you very much.'

Matthew was still looking pained. 'I think I need a drink,' he mumbled, gazing around in vain for any waiting staff. 'What do you want, Em?'

'Diet Coke, please. Unless anyone's starting on the booze yet, in which case I'll have a Peroni.'

'Good one,' Matthew said. 'We're on holiday, aren't we?'

Catherine pulled a twenty-euro note from her purse and handed it over. 'Here,' she said. 'Make that three Peronis.'

As Matthew loped away in search of sustenance, Emily flipped her sunglasses onto her head. 'Are things all right with you and Dad these days?' she asked. 'I saw him last week and he said he was moving in with this woman, whatever her name is. I still haven't met her but he wants me and Matthew to go round to their place. Is that okay with you?'

'That's fine,' Catherine said, because it truthfully was. She and Mike were so different, she had realized; she couldn't imagine them ever being a pair again. She had seen him a few weeks ago, on Penny's hen night of all occasions, and he'd been in the same club, dad-dancing badly on the dancefloor. People were nudging each other and smirking, and Catherine had felt sorry for him at first . . . right up until the moment she saw him man-handling a girl who was definitely not Rebecca. No, she was well rid of him. He and Rebecca deserved each other in Catherine's opinion.

'Do you think you'll ever fall in love again, Mum?' Emily asked, looking concerned. 'What happened to that guy, the one you were meant to be meeting for a drink that night?'

'Beers are on their way,' Matthew said just then, rejoining them at the table. He leaned back in his chair, hands behind his head, and grinned contentedly. 'Please tell me you've stopped talking about our immaculate conception now.'

'Yeah, Mum's just about to tell us about this guy she likes,' Emily told him, and his face fell.

'Oh,' he said, 'I'm not sure I want to hear this.'

'Ignore him,' Emily urged. 'Go on, Mum. What happened? Is he still on the scene?' She fiddled with her sunglasses, looking less sure of herself all of a sudden. 'I'm sorry about that night, you know. I felt bad about it afterwards. Making you stay in with me instead of going out with him – especially when you'd been so cool and brave about Macca.'

Catherine gazed at her fondly across the table. Emily had grown up so much since she'd left home. 'It's fine,' she said. 'Thanks, though.'

'*Tre* Peroni?' the waitress said just then, producing three bottled beers on a tray. She set them down with a glass each.

'*Grazie*,' Catherine said.

'*Prego*.'

'Mum?' Emily prompted. 'What happened?'

Catherine poured the beer into her glass, not wanting to reply immediately. 'Well . . . nothing,' she admitted. 'He's had a hard time lately. His wife just . . . Well, she died actually. Sounded awful.'

'His *wife*?' Emily sounded scandalized. 'You didn't say he was married!'

'They split up a few years ago,' Catherine replied. 'She was with someone else. But still – you don't stop caring about someone just because you're not together any more.'

She sipped her beer, wondering for the millionth time how he was doing. They'd texted a few times when he was at a low ebb, and as far as she knew he was back in Sheffield now, but he seemed to have gone to ground. She missed his cheerful nature, she missed talking to him, and she missed the prickling nervous excitement that had coursed through her when he'd asked her for a drink. But she knew that such a shocking, sudden bereavement would have hit him hard. She hoped he was okay.

'So . . . what? That's it?' Emily asked, sounding disappointed.

'Well . . .' Catherine took another mouthful of cold Peroni, which was slipping down very easily. 'Actually I'm not sure. Ages ago I mentioned to him how much I love tulips. Months ago, this is. And I said how cross I'd been with myself because I was in such a flap all autumn with your dad going that I left it too late to plant up any tulip bulbs.'

'Riiiight.' Emily was frowning, as if she couldn't see where this was going.

'And then I came out of the house the other morning and two pots of tulips had appeared in the front garden. Gorgeous red and yellow ones, really beautiful.'

'What, and you think he put them there?'

'I don't know. But then I got to work and there were more tulips in pots outside the front gate. Purple and white ones this time. My boss, Maggie, said she hadn't a clue where they'd come from.'

'Aww, that's lovely!' Emily cried.

'Bit creepy if you ask me,' Matthew muttered.

'So I can only assume it's a message to me. A friendly, thank you sort of message. From him.'

'It's *totally* a message,' Emily said enthusiastically. 'A lovely, beautiful, romantic message. God, I wish someone would do that for me.'

'They will,' Catherine assured her. Then she paused. 'The question is, what do I do now?'

'You phone him, you dingbat,' Emily told her.

'And you wouldn't mind? If anything happened between us?' The million-dollar question. The reason she'd hesitated to respond immediately to him.

'Of course we wouldn't! Would we, Matt?'

Matthew shrugged. 'I suppose not. As long as he's a decent bloke.'

'He is. He's really lovely.' An excited, heady feeling rushed through her. 'Are you sure this is okay? Because I want you to know, you two come first and always will. You know that, don't you?'

'For heaven's sake! Of course we know it. You don't have to say all this.' Emily grabbed her hand and squeezed it. 'Go for it, Mum. We're happy for you. Aren't we, Matt?'

'Yeah. It's cool, Mum. As long as he knows he'll have me to deal with if he ever mucks you around.'

She laughed. 'Penny said the same thing. She also told me she's already put him in her seating plans for the wedding breakfast at the end of the month, and won't take no for an answer.'

'There you go then,' Emily told her. 'There's no escape for the poor bloke. God help him.' She grinned. 'Seriously, though, I'm pleased for you. Really pleased. So do you think you'll ring him when we get back?'

A bubbly feeling of anticipation spiralled up through Catherine. She was *happy*, she realized. Happy to be here with her children in such glorious surroundings; happy with life itself and how wonderfully everything had turned around. She was ready to try again, and her children's blessing was the missing piece of the puzzle, the last bit of confidence she'd been seeking.

'Yes,' she said, her voice catching. 'I think I will.'

There must be something about Venice and her lovelife, she decided, as the conversation moved on to Matthew's forthcoming exams, and then Emily's plans for summer. *Thank you, Venice,* she thought to herself with a smile. Grazie. *I don't know what's around the corner for me this time . . . but I'm very much looking forward to finding out.*

Italian Words and Phrases

If reading *One Night in Italy* has inspired you to take an Italian holiday yourself, you're in for a treat! Here are a few essential words and phrases that you may find useful. Happy travels!

Hello/Good morning	*Buongiorno*
Goodbye	*Arrivederci*
Hi/Bye	*Ciao*
My name is . . .	*Mi chiamo . . .*
What is your name?	*Come si chiama?*
Excuse me	*Scusi*
Thank you	*Grazie*
Please	*Per favore*
I don't understand Italian	*Non capisco l'italiano*

Where is . . . ?	*Dov'è . . . ?*
The nearest beach	*La spiaggia più vicina*
The castle	*Il castello*
The pool	*La piscina*
A nice bar	*Un locale simpatico*
How much does . . . cost?	*Quanto costa . . . ?*
I'd like . . .	*Vorrei . . .*
A coffee	*Un caffè*
A beer	*Una birra*
A glass of white wine	*Un bicchiere di vino bianco*
Some paracetamol	*Del paracetamolo*

Anna's Recipes

If you can't make it to Italy this summer, then you can at least eat like an Italian with the following recipes, inspired by Anna's cookery column. *Buon appetito!*

Focaccia

This basic recipe can be adapted to taste – try brushing with garlic and rosemary-infused olive oil or adding cooked red onion and olives before baking.

Makes one loaf

250g strong white bread flour
1 tsp salt
one 7g sachet dried yeast
1 tbsp olive oil
200ml cold water
olive oil and sea salt for the finishing touches

1. Place the dried ingredients in a bowl, then add the olive oil and 150 ml of the water. Stir to form a dough, then knead for ten minutes while you gradually add the remaining water. You can also do this in a food mixer using the dough hook if you prefer.
2. Lightly oil a work surface then tip out the dough and knead for a further five minutes. Now oil the inside of a clean (large!) bowl and put the dough inside. Cover with a tea towel and leave in a warm place until the dough has doubled in size.
3. Once the dough has risen, you need to 'knock it back' which basically means punching it a few times – extremely satisfying. Then tip the dough onto a large baking sheet lined with greaseproof paper, flatten it and pull it into the corners so that it's the right shape. Leave to prove for about an hour.
4. During that time, preheat the oven to 220°C/425°F/gas mark 7. Before baking, press your fingers into the dough to create dimples, then drizzle the loaf with olive oil and sprinkle over the sea salt. (If you're adding cooked red onions etc., now is the time to do that.)
5. Bake in the oven for 20 minutes. (Your kitchen will smell amazing!)
6. Best served hot, with an extra drizzle of olive oil.

Tiramisu

Love coffee? Love chocolate? Then you'll love this easy Italian classic . . .

Serves 6

568 ml double cream (i.e. a large pot)
250 g mascarpone
60 ml marsala
5 tbsp caster sugar
300 ml strong coffee (made with 2 tbsp instant coffee and 300 ml boiling water)
170 g sponge fingers
30 g dark chocolate
cocoa powder for dusting

1 Whisk the cream, mascarpone, marsala and sugar together in a large bowl until combined.
2 Divide the sponge fingers into two piles, then dip one pile in the coffee (use a shallow bowl or dish to make life easier), turning them so that they are soaked through, then arrange in the bottom of your serving dish.
3 Spread half of the cream mixture over the coffee-soaked fingers, then grate the chocolate and add most of it to the top. (Save approximately 5 g for later.) Soak the

remaining sponge fingers in coffee then place on top of the cream layer, then add the rest of the cream mixture to cover.

4 Cover with clingfilm and put in the fridge for a few hours (or overnight). To serve, add the remaining grated chocolate and dust with cocoa powder. The tiramisu will keep for up to two days – but will probably vanish much sooner!

If you enjoyed

One Night in Italy,

you'll love these other books
by Lucy Diamond . . .

The Secrets of Happiness

The best things in life can be just around the corner

Rachel and Becca aren't real sisters, or so they say. They are step-sisters, living far apart, with little in common. Rachel is the successful one: happily married with three children and a big house, plus an impressive career. Artistic Becca, meanwhile, lurches from one dead-end job to another, shares a titchy flat and has given up on love.

The two of them have lost touch but when Rachel doesn't come home one night, Becca is called in to help. Once there, she quickly realizes that her step-sister's life is not so perfect after all: Rachel's handsome husband has moved out, her children are rebelling, and her glamorous career has taken a nosedive. Worst of all, nobody seems to have a clue where she might be.

As Becca begins to untangle Rachel's secrets, she is forced to confront some uncomfortable truths about her own life, and the future seems uncertain.

But sometimes happiness can be found in the most unexpected places . . .

Summer at Shell Cottage

A seaside holiday at Shell Cottage in Devon has always been the perfect escape for the Tarrant family. Beach fun, barbecues and warm summer evenings with a cocktail or two – who could ask for more?

But this year, everything has changed. Following her husband's recent death, Olivia is struggling to pick up the pieces. Then she makes a shocking discovery that turns her world upside down.

As a busy mum and GP, Freya's used to having her hands full, but a bad day at work has put her career in jeopardy and now she's really feeling the pressure.

Harriet's looking forward to a break with her lovely husband Robert and teenage daughter Molly. But unknown to Harriet, Robert is hiding a secret – and so, for that matter, is Molly . . .

'Stuffed with guilty secrets and characters you'll root for from the start, this warm and emotional novel about a family in crisis makes for delicious summer reading'

Sunday Express

'Enthralling drama about family secrets' *Heat*

The Year of Taking Chances

It's New Year's Eve, and Gemma and Spencer Bailey are throwing a house party. There's music, dancing, champagne and all their best friends under one roof. It's going to be a night to remember.

Also at the party is Caitlin, who has returned to the village to pack up her much-missed mum's house and to figure out what to do with her life; and Saffron, a PR executive who's keeping a secret no amount of spin can change. The three women bond over Gemma's dodgy cocktails and fortune cookies, and vow to make this year their best one yet.

But as the following months unfold, Gemma, Saffron and Caitlin find themselves tested to their limits by shocking new developments. Family, love, work, home – all the things they've taken for granted – are thrown into disarray. Under pressure, they are each forced to rethink their lives and start over. But dare they take a chance on something new?

'Well-written, full of humour and filled with a reminder about what it means to be kind' *Closer*

'Warm, witty and wise – perfect for lazy afternoons on the sofa' *Daily Mail*

Me and Mr Jones

Three charming brothers – which would you choose?

Meet the women in love with three very different brothers . . .

Izzy's determined to escape her troubled past with a new start by the sea – but flirtatious Charlie Jones is causing complications.

Alicia's been happily married to loyal Hugh for years but secretly craves excitement. Maybe it's time to spice things up?

Emma's relationship with David was once fun and romantic but trying for a baby has taken its toll. Then temptation comes along . . .

As the future of the family's B&B becomes uncertain, Izzy, Alicia and Emma are thrown together unexpectedly. It seems that keeping up with the Joneses is harder than anyone thought . . .

'Funny, sunny and wise. An absolute treat' Katie Fforde

'The new queen of the gripping, light-hearted page-turner'
Easy Living

Summer with my Sister

Polly has always been the high-flier of the family, with the glamorous city lifestyle to match.

Clare is a single mum with two children, struggling to make ends meet in a ramshackle cottage. The two sisters are poles apart and barely on speaking terms.

But then Polly's fortunes change unexpectedly and her world comes crashing down. Left penniless and with nowhere else to go, she's forced back to the village where she and Clare grew up, and the sisters find themselves living together for the first time in years. With an old flame reappearing for Polly, a blossoming new career for Clare and a long-buried family secret in the mix, sparks are sure to fly. Unless the two women have more in common than they first thought?

'A warm and witty read for sisters of all ages' *Candis*

'Seamless, engaging, believable, fun and heartfelt . . . a skilfully executed and charming tale that you'll want to pass on to all your friends' *Heat*

The Beach Café

A recipe for disaster? Or a recipe for love?

Evie Flynn has always been the black sheep of her family – a dreamer and a drifter, unlike her over-achieving elder sisters. She's tried making a name for herself as an actress, a photographer and a singer, but nothing has ever worked out. Now she's stuck in temp hell, with a sensible, pension-planning boyfriend. Somehow life seems to be passing her by.

Then her beloved aunt Jo dies suddenly in a car crash, leaving Evie an unusual legacy – her precious beach café in Cornwall. Determined to make a success of something for the first time in her life, Evie heads off to Cornwall to get the café and her life back on track – and gets more than she bargained for, both in work and in love . . .

'Romantic, dreamy and fun, this is perfect poolside reading'
Closer

'From witty to full of wisdom, sassy to sentimental . . . not to be missed'
Woman

Sweet Temptation

A story of love, friendship and cake . . .

Maddie's getting it from all sides. Her bitchy boss at the radio station humiliates her live on air about her figure, her glamour-puss mum keeps dropping not-so-subtle hints that Maddie should lose weight, and her kids are embarrassed to be seen with her after the disastrous mums' race at their school sports day. Something's got to change . . .

Maddie reluctantly joins the local weight-watching group where she finds two unlikely allies – Jess, who is desperate to fit into a size ten wedding dress for her Big Day, and Lauren, who, despite running a dating agency, has signed off romance for ever. Or so she thinks . . .

As they all count the calories, new friendships develop, and secrets are shared – but can they resist temptation?

'A healthy helping of friendship and love' *Press Association*

'Dealing with a lack of calories, fat days and man trouble is a lot easier when you have good friends by your side. Fab!'
Closer

The House of New Beginnings

One life-changing summer . . .

In an elegant Regency house near the Brighton seafront, three tenants have more in common than they know . . .

A shocking revelation has led Rosa to start over as a sous chef. The work is gruelling but it's a distraction . . . until she comes up against the stroppy teenager next door who challenges her lifestyle choices. What if Rosa's passion for food could lead her to more interesting places?

Having followed her childhood sweetheart down south, Georgie is busily carving out a new career in journalism. Throwing herself into the city's delights is fun, but before she knows it she's sliding headlong into all kinds of trouble . . .

Nursing a devastating loss, Charlotte just wants to keep her head down. But Margot, the glamorous older lady on the top floor, has other ideas. Like it or not, Charlotte must confront the outside world, and the possibilities it still holds.

As the women find each other, hope surfaces, friendships blossom and a whole new chapter unfolds for them all.

On a Beautiful Day

Treasure every moment. Life can change in a heartbeat.

It's a beautiful day in Manchester and four friends are meeting for a birthday lunch. But then they witness a shocking accident just metres away that acts as a catalyst for each of them.

For Laura, it's a wake-up call to heed the ticking of her biological clock. Sensible Jo finds herself throwing caution to the wind in a new relationship. Eve, who has been trying to ignore the worrying lump in her breast, feels helpless and out of control. And happy-go-lucky India is drawn to one of the victims of the accident, causing long-buried secrets to rise to the surface.

This is a novel about the startling and unexpected turns life can take. It's about luck – good and bad – and about finding bravery and resilience when your world is in turmoil. Above all, it's about friendship, togetherness and hope.

Praise for Lucy Diamond

'A hugely satisfying read' *Heat*

'An absolute treat' Katie Fforde,
bestselling author of *A Summer at Sea*

'Warm, witty and wise' *Daily Mail*